THE SHADLINE RISES

STARSIDE SAGA BOOK SIX

ERIC KENT EDSTROM

1

EVER VIGILANT!

No one had lived in the drafty and barren halls of Ceronhel for seven hundred years. The flat-face of her sheer battlements faced the winding approach up the mountainside. Arrow slits gazed like the black and soulless eyes of an under-realm Watcher.

Ever Vigilant! Ah, the sacred words of the lost lords of Ceronhel. They had died or fled long ago, subsumed beneath the tides of nosg-kin who had claimed the Haelshok Range north of Flyssn. No pennant flew atop the single remaining tower, where in the age of the now-forgotten, the Snow Hawk sigil had proudly waved.

The black stone of the fortress—quarried from the shoulder of the mountain upon which the fortress stood—rose in stern courses, unmarred by the wind and incessant mist and sleet that hung over Ceronhel like a gray shroud.

Beneath the foot of the wall spread the valley of the river Griln. Its ice-caked waters oozed in brown bends and stretches, offering little sustenance to the scraggle and scrub that grew where noble pines had once ruled. All was befouled by the nosg and their char-black forges, waste pits, and demaynic magics, the effluvium of which stained the meltwater of the surrounding peaks.

Those peaks towered on both sides of the valley, shoulders draped with the white vestments of the North, capes of snow that swept down to meet steel-blue glaciers as old as the world itself. And upon the ragged narrow road that held fast to Griln's muck-mounded banks, not a single footprint made of man sullied the brazen whiteness of winter's latest blessing of snow.

But other traces crossed it, of deer and wolf and hare. And the imprint of other feet, night-creatures upon two legs in hunt of meat. Nosg.

Within the echoey fastness of Ceronhel, deep in the Grand Hall where some lord of the First Race had established his home, there now burned a great fire. The hearth stretched a dozen paces and stood at least as many high.

The vaulted ceilings—borne up by columns of the same black stone as the outer wall—leaked much of the heat, for the slate shingles had fallen away in spots, leaving huge gashes to admit snow, wind, and bird alike.

The remaining heat was enough for the blind man huddled upon the cot near the fire. His wounds were still fresh, and the healing skills of his servant were none too good.

But the Hargothe lived.

His strength was returning. Now he could sit up and hold his tea cup, a crude bowl fashioned by hands too encumbered with gnarled knuckles and claws to do better.

Soon the Hargothe would be able to stand. Then walk. In time he would again be able to dymense, vanish in mercus green and instantly travel anywhere he wished. If he wished.

Winter was not the ideal time to retreat here. There were no fresh rushes to strew across the stone floor. Nor was there an excess of provisions for his supper. He did not relish the diet provided by his servant, a nosg-kin urchin who called itself Noi-Ick-Noi, the middle syllable more of a click in the throat than an intelligent utterance.

The Hargothe simply called it Noy, as close an approximation as he was willing to bother with. But where was that rascal? He called for him. "Noy!"

His voice was so weak it failed to lift above the hiss and howl of the wind. A flurry of snow-swirl fell through the gaping hole in the ceiling. It was followed by a few minutes of hard rain. And when that ceased, drips continued to fall and patter into the puddle occupying a third of the hall's floor.

The Hargothe finished his exceptionally bitter tea, a nosg brew of winter thistle cut with fermented coreberry. Vile. But he could not deny its restorative power. Tossing the cup aside, he fell back onto the cot. It was a rickety thing, assembled from fragments of ancient furniture left behind in this Til-forsaken place. Noy had been clever enough to securely lash the pieces into a sturdy enough structure. Unfortunately, the creature didn't understand the concept of padding.

But what could be expected of a nosg? The creatures were a half step above beasts, though they possessed a wolfish cunning when it came to the art of killing.

Annoyed by his servant's absence, the Hargothe felt for him through the bond. He could have lifted a finger and pointed in the direction where his sub-human servant was. But Noy was too far away for him to reach through the mental-speak the bond allowed. The fool had better be hunting. And preferably not for cower-rats. The Hargothe found their meat horrifically fishy.

He settled back and forced himself to sink into the subtle world of the mercusine. That was where his true power resided, and as it returned to him, so too would his bodily strength. A terrible thing, though, to have retreated from the mercusine. To fear it.

Something had happened recently, far to the southeast. A great uprising of the mercus that had flared and thrummed and thundered. The powers at play must have shaken the earth, like the exploding mountains of Iops.

Who might have caused such a display he could only guess. Her Enlightened was not so powerful, he didn't think. He didn't know, for she clouded herself upon the mercusine, hiding her capabilities from him.

The girl? The infernal Kila Sigh? She outshined everyone in power, but could she wield so much? Perhaps, if supplied with a heller.

But there had been a blackness in the power, too. A demaynic hatred that he'd felt even here. Every merculyn in the world must have felt it. Surely news would trickle into the world and reach the man he'd sent to Starside.

The Hargothe was patient. Soon more men would come, bringing all he needed to make Ceronhel the first holdfast of his realm. And from here, eventually, he would begin the march back to Starside. Not alone. Now that he had the bond to play with, he could control any number of servants. And the number would continue to grow.

He smiled to think of what he had in store for Starside.

Perhaps he need not march on that city, but would instead bring it down from within.

He let his senses roam across the many other force-bonds in his mind. One of his nosg-kin slaves was approaching. Still far off, but coming nearer. Which one was it?

He exhaled and sank deeper into his meditation. Ah. There it was. The nosg he had sent north was returning. He felt its state. Not exceptionally fearful to be returning.

Excellent.

That meant it had succeeded in its mission.

Most excellent.

2

FOR A SHADLINE

"And then she sent it back," Fallo said, holding up his precious rusty dagger. "Now it's mine."

The Cloak grunted and stoked the campfire with a stick, sending orange sparks floating skyward. He had told Fallo it would be their last open fire until they crossed the Sagmarsh, an insect- and snake-infested fenland west of the Honor Mountains.

"I know, I know," Fallo said, answering his mentor's grunt. "Nobody truly possesses a Shadline weapon. But surely even you can see this blade and I are a perfect match. It's ugly and flawed. But it's also unique . . . and deadly."

Lop slunk into the camp, wriggling vole clenched in her teeth.

"Like Lop!" Fallo said, pointing Ol' Rusty toward his cat.

Lop had struggled early on in this ridiculous adventure. Especially when she discovered they would not be having meals with the regularity to which she had become accustomed. Henley and Kila probably wouldn't recognize her now . . . if there were any other cats to confuse her with.

Cloak Einlin twisted off a hard bit of dried pork and chewed it. He was all in black, immaculately clean despite the travel and training he had subjected Fallo to. "The blade is deadly," he said in his usual low rasp. "You are dangerous— mostly to yourself. The animal has progressed much more quickly than you."

That was an accurate statement. Fallo could not fault it. Especially that last part. Lop had started the journey rather obese and utterly disinterested in hunting. Hunger had quickly awakened her wilder instincts, however. She now kept herself fed, the Cloak's rule. The exception was if they were moving too quickly to let her hunt. Now she was lean, maybe leaner than Huff. But still bushy-furred. And still less than cooperative.

Well done, Lop, he sent.

Your judgment is meaningless.

Fallo leaned back, stomach not quite satisfied with his repast of half-over apples, dried pork, and a few wild radishes the Cloak had scrounged up. But all in all, this camp was not bad. A shelter tucked against the foot of a nameless mountain where a great thrust of striated rock leaned overhead enough to keep snow away from its base. A second and third such rocks formed walls to either side, making it a sort of shallow cave. The ground sloped away, so there was good drainage.

Not a bad camp at all. A dry stretch of ground without too many pokey rocks to perforate his hide. A fire for warmth. And not least of all, the warm-hearted, engaging, compassionate Cloak for company.

"You have first watch," the Cloak said, drawing his namesake black garment snuggly around his body. He leaned against a log he'd dragged in, gray eyes mere slits. Slits of icy flame.

"I was going to suggest that," Fallo said wryly. The notion that he'd suggest *anything* to the Cloak was, of course, a joke. The Shadline master was as humorless as his grave-lord's clothing suggested. "But since you won't sleep during my watch, perhaps to pass time we discuss the objective you've been keeping from me."

Lop had not yet killed the vole. She released it in the corner and watched it move, ears up, eyes intent.

"I haven't kept it from you," the Cloak said.

"You haven't told me it."

"That's true."

Fallo waggled his single, forehead-spanning eyebrow, a black creature unto itself that had caused him no end of humiliation in his seventeen years of life. "Do you not see the contradiction there, Friend Cloak? You haven't told me, but you haven't kept it from me. How can those statements both be true?"

"Answer your own question, Shadline."

The man had a knack for *cutting* responses. And that wasn't merely a joke that Fallo used to keep himself entertained. Fallo *was* a Shadline, inasmuch as anyone who happened to possess a Shadline blade was also considered such. But he was no master. Not yet.

Lop snatched the vole up and tossed it. It didn't run. Bored, she bit down, gave a violent head shake and set to the task of devouring it. She liked the juicy insides the best.

Fallo looked away. "The only way to reconcile both statements as true is to posit that you, Cloak, do not know our objective. I have seen many strange things in my life, but the idea that you are traipsing all over the wilderness without knowing where are were going is absurd."

The Cloak's teeth showed. Not a smile. Not exactly. But it contained a rare flash of the man's wolfish humor. "It is indeed absurd."

Fallo flipped his blade through a series of flourishes the Cloak had taught him as he considered the puzzle. The man before him had a peculiar way of teaching. If the subject was fighting, he said nothing at all. He merely attacked, with fists, sticks, rocks, anything but his Shadline sword, Tosuin. But if the subject had to be conveyed verbally, he waited to be questioned and then answered in riddles.

Fallo sent his blade into the air, watching the shabby, rusty surface spin. Instead of catching it, he spread his legs and waited until the blade pierced the ground between his knees.

"Let me talk it through," he said, musing on the puzzle. He was helpless before little mysteries like this. Perhaps he had too fertile a mind. Perhaps he lacked trust in his master, or in the strange blade-cult to which he had rather impulsively sworn allegiance. "You don't know where we're going or what we're looking for. But the Shadline council who gave you your orders also directed you to drag me along." He plucked his blade from the dirt and tapped the tip on his thumbnail. "Hmmm. It must be *me* that is the objective. Which means that my training is the objective. No. That can't be it. You would know that one." He glanced at Lop, who was gobbling down half of the vole. "Wait! We're hunting."

"Hunting what?" the Cloak said. "I would like to know."

"So we *are* hunting." This was fun. "But you don't know what we're hunting . . . which seems unutterably stupid. Truly, that's Kil-kissin' ridiculous. It is like prospecting for gold without having any concept of what gold is."

Lop ate the second half of the vole. Except the tail, which she'd learned she would inevitably choke up along with a ball of fur the size of a dog. She moved nearer the fire and sat primly to begin a proper grooming.

Fallo scraped a bit of dirt from his blade with his filthy thumbnail. "I don't want you to mishear my meaning when I say what I'm about to say, Cloak sir. But given what I've now discovered about our mission, I'm beginning to think that Shadline council of yours is bunch of yolks out of their shells. You could have trained me to fight in Starside."

"But not to travel."

Now Fallo was getting irritated. "'Traveling' infers a destination. Which we don't have. This is a prolonged hiking excursion. An exploration. The kind of thing my father did twice a year to prove his manhood to himself. True travel, my dear Cloak, involves ships, carriages—I'll go so far as to say a mere wagon would serve. At minimum a sturdy horse, and lacking that, how about a *road!*"

They hadn't seen a road for days.

He hadn't bathed for a ten-day. If you could call fording an icy river a bath.

"I have my own guesses about our objective," the Cloak said. It was uncharacteristic of him to reward one of Fallo's tantrums with any words at all.

Fallo leaned forward. "Do tell."

"As you've guessed, we are hunting. Hunting for an objective. And this is the training for how to do that. We have no schedule. We have no particular destination. We are enjoying absolute freedom."

"Enjoying?" Fallo said. "Have you seen the blisters and bruises on my body?"

Many noises come from you, Lop sent. *I listen for noises when I hunt. But I remain silent.*

Normally Fallo would have ignored the comment. *Did you recognize the word 'hunting' when ol' blackblade and I were speaking?* Lop had always claimed not to understand words that were said aloud, but Fallo wondered if maybe some were beginning to penetrate the animal's fuzzy brain.

I merely observed how I behave differently from you. You might learn from the comparison. She resumed swiping her lick-dampened paw across her ears and face.

The Cloak had ignored Fallo's complaints about blisters and bruises. "Two more pieces of the puzzle." He held up a finger. "You are a new Shadline." He held up another. "Your blade was unknown to the Order until I discovered you with it."

"Unknown? It's been in tales for a thousand years." Fallo's blade was the legendary Telt, one of three blades supposedly forged from a dragon's tooth. A tooth shed from Qaj'sh, the dragon who supposedly killed Til's daughter Mayla just moments after she stepped from the giant clamshell from which she was born.

The Cloak dismissed Fallo's point. "What is not known is what your blade's power is. It clearly does not force anyone to carry it to its intended wielder, as some do. Nor does it perform an ecstatic bonding, as others do."

Lop finished her grooming and climbed onto Fallo's lap. He waited for her to nestle in and allow him to begin stroking her fur.

He knew of a blade that had both of the characteristics the

Cloak had mentioned. Black, Quinn's dagger. Telt had done nothing like that. It would still be in an old hermit's possession if Fallo hadn't stumbled on his cave. And as for bonding . . . he felt a fondness for the blade, but no deep attachment. "So this little sojourn is to help me find out what Ol' Rusty does?"

"In part. But we must consider that Kila Sigh is a factor. The force of destiny brought you together, both of you with previously undiscovered blades. She's a great merculyn and possibly a force for great destruction."

"Oh, you can't say truer than that. She is a walking fell-storm, that one. I quite like her." He stroked his beard—well, his whiskers. Even Fallo couldn't call it a beard without snickering. "You think the council wanted me separated from her?"

"They didn't say that." The Cloak tilted his head forward, a slow nod. "But yes, they wanted you two apart. And you from Quinn."

That was a sore spot with him. "Why? Is it because she kissed me? Kil's eyes! I'll never have such a beautiful girl kiss me again as long as I live."

Lop meowed, agitated from her snoozing by Fallo's rising voice.

"That is why," the Cloak said.

"Kil's tears in bucket. You should tell a man you're going to pull such tricks before he vows his life to your cult."

"It isn't a cult." If there was one thing the Cloak wouldn't tolerate, was anyone saying something against the Order of the Shadline. And he punished Fallo by closing his eyes and falling asleep.

Fallo fumed for several hours before the burning in his chest turned to a dull ache. He'd never really loved a girl before. He'd felt a whole lot of burning attraction all right, but he'd never allowed himself to entertain the possibility that it would be returned. But, inexplicably, Quinn had given him looks she did not shine on others. Not only did he enjoy looking at her, he liked talking to her, and just being with her.

How nice, then, that she was exactly a Kil-thousand miles away at Garden Island. He considered how long ago he'd seen her. The day of the kiss. Four ten-days? It felt like a year. And he didn't know if he'd ever see her again.

Quinn gave me treats, Lop sent.

The cat had definitely understood Fallo's spoken words. But he didn't care about that at the moment. *She did? When?*

When you were asleep.

Ah. When he'd gotten his leg injured. He rubbed the spot of the old wound, an itchy scar now. He rarely thought about it. But the news that Quinn had been slipping Lop treats was good. That meant she took care of Lop. Which meant she—he cut that line of thought off. It led nowhere good or happy.

The Cloak had once told him that Shadlines did not marry because: "For a Shadline, every kiss is goodbye."

A light snow started at the end of his watch. He didn't have to awaken the Cloak. The man had an uncanny ability to sleep exactly when he wanted and for exactly how long he wanted. He tilted his head sideways to indicate that Fallo should sleep.

He felt like he'd just closed his eyes when the Cloak nudged him awake. The fire was out, but the sun had not yet risen.

3

SWEET AS SEAWATER

In the pre-dawn of early morning, a low fire snapped and popped in Kila's strange new bedchamber. She had opened the window to allow the warm tropical breeze to soothe her to sleep, but in the wake of the fellstorm, the air held an icy chill. The winds had turned northerly, bringing a hint of winter to Garden Island, a land of tangled jungle and azure seas.

Kila could not believe the breeze was else but an omen. Black times to come.

She slept on Annisforl's strange bed, which folded down from the wall. She'd been perplexed at the absence of any bed in his tower-top room. But her mercus vision had shown her clever hinges concealed in a wall, which prompted the exploration that led to the discovery of a pull handle.

The featherbed was a delight to her. One of the few delights she'd experienced in the days since her battle with Dunne Yples. A battle that she had lost, yet survived. And now the madman was in her power. Which she supposed meant she'd been victorious.

The window was still open, the fresh chill balancing the warmth of the fire. She had hoped it would help her sleep, but it had not. For her mind was troubled.

She did not lie on the bed now, but instead folded her feet under her as she sat in one of the armchairs, eyes on the dancing flames, Nax asleep on her lap.

Her lock-picking kit lay open over the arm of the chair, the various picks and probes gleaming in the firelight. Each was nestled in a long, narrow pocket, the stitching certainly done by her father long ago. But one pocket was empty, for she held that tool in her hands.

The shaft was a connected series of ever smaller tubes. These pulled out from each other, forming an extensible rod. Mounted to the tip, a tiny mirror. It was for looking around corners, and if the angle was just right, it might be thrust under a door while a thief peeked through a keyhole, allowing her to study a bit of the room she was about to break into. Kila had never mastered that technique, but her bother, Wen, had said Father was very skilled at it.

She called upon her mercus vision again, bringing the glows of metal into view. The shaft of the mirror tool shone with a pleasant gray-blue. For perhaps the hundredth time, she brought the tiny mirror close to her nose and studied the gold script placed behind the silvering of the mirror, where only one with her particular mercus vision could see it.

It read: "Open for Kil's Daughter."

The phrase had unlocked both this chamber's door, and a strange destiny.

Kil's daughter.

The phrase sounded like a reasonably good curse. The kind of thing you'd exclaim after encountering an especially churlish woman in Cheapsgate: "Kil's daughter! That woman's got thorns for eyes!"

But when Kila uttered the phrase, the door to this room had unlocked.

The phrase was written where only she would find it. On a tool made by her father. Which meant he'd known of her ability long before she'd awakened to it. Just as he'd known her mother was the fabled water spirit Semūin.

How strange it was now to remember her mother, when all her life she had never thought of her. And when asked about her mother, she had been made sick with blinding headaches and nausea. All that was now past, thanks to Annisforl.

The strange wizard had been waiting for her here. He'd said he'd trained for years just to clear the occlusion that blinded her to her own memories.

Kil's daughter. And now, by virtue of wearing Annisforl's garnet ring, she had become Highest of Kil. If she weren't so perplexed, she would have fallen in to convulsions of snort-laughs at the notion.

As a life-long skeptic about the very existence of the gods, Kila found herself in an odd position. Highest of Kil. Or to put it in other terms: Highest of the Despised God, Highest of the Father of Hate, Highest of the King of the Under-Realms. It wasn't a post anyone with a lick of sense would *want.* Furthermore, she was the only member of the Way of Kil.

Nax stirred, stretching a trembling forelimb. Her tongue curled as she yawned and rolled onto her back.

Oly is here, Nax sent.

What? Kila scooped up Nax and stood. If Oly was there, so was Flaumishtak.

She didn't smell the demayne's usual odor of burning hair.

In the great hall, Nax said. No particular note of concern came through the bond. Nax had spent time with Flaumishtak after the demayne had taken her from the Hargothe. She liked the demayne.

Oly is annoyed. Flaumishtak is waiting for you. He warns that you are not to come down by the stairs.

Did Oly tell you all of that?

No. Flaumishtak speaks to me.

Can I trust him? Kila couldn't believe she was asking such a question. The beast was a demayne. It had killed Sens Goolsoy, a novitiate, and who knew how many others.

For cats the notion of trust was both essential and vague. They were loyal to their bonded humans and to their littermates. They could sense whether someone was an enemy or not. But the concept of trust was too abstract to have much meaning. Nax merely answered with: *I like him.*

Kila tucked her mirror into its sleeve and rolled up the canvas. She set it next to her few other possessions—a hand mirror, a banknote, Quinn's blade, Black, and another Shadline blade called Shinane. She grabbed Cayne and strapped the scabbard around her thigh.

With a mercus feat, she pulled heat from the flames, leaving only embers in the hearth. With another, she yanked the window closed and secured the latch.

Are you coming? she sent to Nax.

Of course.

Together they stepped from the room and entered the decaying interior of the tower of Kil's Keep. The door closed behind her and would only open for her. She'd had both Quinn and Henley speak the unlock phrase. It hadn't worked for them.

Birds rustled in the rafters above her, and a draft curled down from a hole in the roof. Morning had broken and a haze of light drifted in here and there.

A winding stair descended into darkness, curving around a long empty drop. Far at the bottom, the great hall was a gray circle. No sign of the demayne from here.

Kila closed her eyes and felt for Flaumishtak's mercus spark. Nothing.

There were other sparks in the tower. Henley was a few floors down. Sensual Sliy, emissary of Ori's Way, across from him. A newly arrived emissary, Spinster Moirina Fiolt, occupied a room a floor lower. Lower still was the former novitiate, Pennie. Ten years old and now blind from a blow to the back of her head during the Yples battle.

Flaumishtak is impatient, Nax said. The cat conveyed her intention to be carried, and Kila opened her arms to receive the slim gray bundle. *He says that since you mustn't take the stairs it should take no time at all to get down there.*

No stairs. That meant the beast wanted her to jump. Kila did not fear heights. Even now she stood with her bare toes jutting over the landing. The Way of Kil had not felt a need to install railings. But to simply jump would be idiotic. Despite her feat of hovering upon buffeting mercus winds when facing off against Yples, she did not have the first clue *how* she had done it.

Or maybe he wanted her to dymense. That made more sense to her. She'd done it once before. In a moment of desperation. Since then she'd tried it a number of times.

She knew the feat called for emotion—what Dunne Marlow had referred to as the "demaynic senses." Urgency was surely a component, and determination. Those were easy feelings to notice when one is feeling them, but hard to bring into mind and body by choice.

Hurry, Nax sent. *He's going to leave.*

There was the urgency, sent by Nax. Apparently, the cat was eager to see the demayne and didn't want to miss this chance.

As for the rest of the feat, Kila did what she always did: she let fly. Mercus power flowed through her, formed bolts, most of it incoherent.

A green fog formed around her feet. Nothing to get excited about. She'd gotten this far before. The haze had an eerie glow, and tendrils of it reached upward.

She wanted to be standing in the great hall, next to the hearth. She pictured the destination. She was determined.

Some of the haze went into her nose and she began to cough and sneeze, losing all grip on the bolts she'd formed. The fog dissipated and faded.

Nax let out three head-shaking cat sneezes then meowed an official complaint.

A rumbling laugh came next. Kila wiped her eyes and turned to find Flaumishtak standing a dozen steps down the stairs. "You truly have no idea what you're doing, do you?"

He carried Oly in his huge arms. The black velvet sleeves of his rich robes were littered with stray bits of Oly's long fur. Flaumishtak stroked Oly's head with a black-clawed forefinger. His fiery eyes narrowed slightly as he climbed the final steps on his ox-like hooves. Each step sent out a sharp report that echoed in the hollow of the tower.

His mane of bluish-black hair was swept back, the ends wisping away into smoke. Not quite animal, but certainly not human, he was frightfully large. But what put Kila off more than all that was his constant mien of self-satisfied amusement.

The beast reached the landing and raised one of his brow-ridges in a rather human way. "Perhaps we go in." He offered Nax a formal bow, which irritated Kila and pleased Nax to no end. Oly hissed at Kila and turned his head away.

Please have Huff wake Henley, she sent. *Tell him who's here.*

She had to hope Nax obeyed, for the cat was rubbing against Flaumishtak's shin. Strange creatures, all of them, Kila decided, turning to her door.

"Open for Kil's daughter."

The lock released and the door swung in.

The demayne let out a delighted booming laugh. "I had not foreseen this strange turn," he said, still chuckling. "Perhaps I should have paid more attention to the great strokes of luck that kept you from my grasp. Alas!"

Kila entered. *Get away from him,* she sent.

Nax ignored her.

"Would you believe I had never been here prior to your ascendance to Highest?" the beast said. "All these ages, and I never had occasion."

"Why are you here now?" she said.

"Why did you try to come to me in the manner I requested?"

Kila eyed Shinane, sitting on the sidetable with her other belongings. She wondered if its bone chill curse would freeze this odious creature.

"You don't answer because you do not want to admit the truth," he said. "You attempted to dymense because you remembered my words when we last met. You *want* my training."

"If your idea of training is to make me attempt things I don't know how to do, you are likely the worst teacher in all the realms of hell."

"If you knew how to do it, you would not need training. I merely sought a demonstration of your current abilities. What I felt when you were dancing with the madman, that was spectacular. I'm disappointed that something as trivial as dymensing has eluded you so long."

"It *all* eludes me!" she shouted. "If it's the five senses, I can do it. If it's the higher senses . . . I have to be terrified or angry before I can do anything at all."

The beast took hold of an armchair and pulled it close to the fire. He turned it so he could face her, then sat. There was no way his massive frame should have fit in it, but it did. For in the act of sitting, his stature decreased to accommodate the chair.

Kila discovered her mouth was quite dry. With her mercus touch, she lifted a goblet of water from a table and floated it to her hand. She never once took her eyes off Flaumishtak; even as she sipped, she eyed him over the golden brim.

Henley was coming. She felt his spark winding up the stairwell. Running.

"Begone, demayne," she said.

He looked taken aback. The smokey tendrils of his hair puffed a bit more vigorously. "I don't think you understand, Delicious One. You must be better prepared for what's to come. I feel a few sparks in this tower. By the time Dem-Kisk comes, you will need many more than that."

"Open for Kil's daughter," Kila said just as Henley reached

the landing. The door opened. He pushed through, breathless, face flushed red.

Huff squeezed past him and leapt joyfully into Flaumishtak's lap. Henley's orange tabby sniffed Oly's ear and allowed himself to get a chin scratch from a black demaynic claw. Henley's face turned a deeper shade of crimson, eyes bulging at his cat.

"Ah, the boy is here," Flaumishtak said, twisting slightly to see. His chair groaned under the movement. "We can begin."

The mercus haze that surrounded someone with the spark shone brightly around Henley. He had a bolt prepared should he discover Flaumishtak attacking Kila.

Kila motioned him to join her. He made a wide circuit to avoid getting close to the demayne. His ginger hair was flat on one side from his pillow, and his clothes had the disheveled look of having been thrown on. He had dispensed with the robes provided by the Way of Pol and had secured Garden Islander garb, loose pants that ended mid-calf and a light linen shirt with a deep scooped neck. He hadn't bothered with shoes in his haste.

Flaumishtak regarded them both solemnly. His eyes didn't have pupils so much as a darkening at the center of the fire that illuminated his strange orbs. "The Hargothe gathers strength. What his aims are, I can only guess. But I know something he does not. The force of destiny guides him toward Kil as surely as it does you."

"Where is he?" Henley demanded.

He and Kila had vowed to kill the old seer. But their plans had stopped there, for they didn't know where he'd fled after Kila had nearly killed him in Starside. The Hargothe had dymensed away at the last moment, a skill they surmised Flaumishtak had taught him.

"North. Far north. In the fastness of Ceronhel."

Kila blinked. "Ceronhel is a real place?" She'd always assumed it was a storybook fortress.

"It's in the Haelshock Range. North of the Rachtooths," Henley said. "Infested with nosg-kin. Why would he go there?"

"Safety. It was a delight to witness that altercation. You despise the old man, and it was glorious to behold. But you failed to kill him, and he retreated to where none can reach him save by dymensing. Or a long, long overland trek."

"Show me," Kila said. "Teach me nothing else, but let me dymense to Ceronhel."

"No."

Henley was staring at her, agog with disbelief. "You don't actually mean to train with this thing."

"Why won't you show me how?" she demanded.

Flaumishtak uncurled a claw. "Because you will kill yourself within minutes and a fate will be sealed. I'm not sure I *want* that fate yet."

"I dymensed once and survived. I brought three people with me."

"Truly?" Flaumishtak leaned forward, gently cupping both cats to keep them from spilling from his lap. "And had you previously been to the place to which you dymensed?"

"No."

"Miraculous. But let that be the first lesson in dymensing. You cannot safely dymense to a place you haven't placed your feet. Not with any expectation of surviving. But perhaps the ash-barrens don't count. You must have possessed a memory of it."

That wasn't far from true. Though Kila had never been to the ash-barrens, she had felt a strong sense of familiarity when she'd come here.

But Flaumishtak's revelation that dymensing was limited to where she'd been was a huge disappointment. She hadn't been anywhere except Starside, a ship called *Sea-Hound*, and Garden Island.

"You said you'd never been in this room, yet you dymensed here the other day."

He chuckled, a skin-tingling growl that made the cats' ears perk up and Henley take a step backward. "You misunderstand. The limitation I spoke of is for one of *your* kind, not mine. All realms are one for demayne. Think of this world as an island. A very dangerous island for one of my kind. I come here under certain rules, admitted by one you call a demayncor. But once permission is granted, I can move anywhere I wish, for I can see all places."

"If so," Henley said, "what is the Hargothe doing at this moment?"

"I said I can see all *places*, not all people. I see Ceronhel, empty. I see the Citadel, empty."

"But you knew I was here," Kila said.

"When one sparks so brightly upon the mercusine, it is impossible to miss. But enough of these quibbles. Shall we train?"

Kila looked to Henley, he looked back. He licked his lips and tilted his head. Finally he nodded. "Huff says we should listen to him."

Nax? Should I train with Flaumishtak?

How else will you learn?

Succinctly put. As far as Kila could discern, she had already surpassed every merculyn on Garden Island, the supposed center of the mercusine arts in the entire world.

She'd already been peppered with questions about mercus healing by the Way of Ori's best surviving healer, Sens Sliy. That Kila hadn't been able to answer *how* she did what she did was a source of frustration for both of them. Sliy thought Kila was lying and Kila thought Sliy was willfully thick-headed.

"Well, Hen. A thief shouldn't be too proud t' pluck a skillet from a genr'ous hand if it be offered."

Henley's Cheapsgate patois was stilted and painful, but he made an effort: "If this Kil-kissin' ox-head knows a trick'r two, I s'pose ya ought ta listen to 'im."

"Excellent," Flaumishtak said. "I'll see you both at the so-called Garden Tower at midnight. Kil's Fifth, of course."

And then he was gone, a cloud of mercus green dissipating to reveal Nax and Huff sitting on the chair he had just vacated.

"Burn my arse!" Henley said. "That demayne is right down"—he spluttered before finishing—"demaynic!"

Coming from Henley, this was quite a vicious insult. Kila burst into laughter. Even her anger at Flaumishtak and his games couldn't spoil the fun of seeing Henley turn red in frustration.

His hurt look sapped the humor from the moment. She bumped his shoulder with hers. "I'm sorry. But did you hear yourself?"

His jaw bulged as he clenched his teeth. "You called me 'Hen'. You know I don't like that."

Kila pulled back, lips parting in surprise. She knew that he hated it, but in the moment it had seemed appropriate.

Henley's grim look broke into a wicked smile. "Got ya, *Highest*."

They shared a laugh and eventually wound up in the chairs, facing the cooling embers of Kila's fire. In the quiet that followed, they petted their cats and fell into darker thoughts as the reality of their situation returned. Kila looked at her friend. A boy who had once knocked her down and threatened her with a dagger. But he hadn't been able to stab her. That was Henley.

"I'm glad you're here," she said. "I don't know what I would do without you and Quinn."

"I suspect you would wreak havoc one way or the other." A wry joke, with no smile. The calm sadness that he carried made him seem much older than he was.

"How old are you, Henley?"

"Almost sixteen. You?" He was looking at her, eyes suddenly intense.

"At least sixteen. But maybe older. I don't know when I was born exactly. Quinn is nineteen, I think."

"Gian was eighteen."

Kila had no response to that bit of information. She'd not known much about the boy who'd shared the Princes Ward at Ori's Home with them. He had been a blademaster. He had been her first kiss. And then he'd fled the island, horrified by what Kila was. She felt foolish to have become so attached so quickly.

Shaking her head to shed thoughts of him, she brought her attention to what was important. "The Ways on this island are pretending to take my title as Highest of Kil seriously. But that is only because they saw what I did with Dunne Yples. There is no Way of Kil, and I care nothing about it. The only thing I care about is finding the Hargothe and ending him."

"Ceronhel is thousands of miles away. First by sea, then by land, through lands and realms I know little about."

"So we start by sea. We'll board the first ship to come here. I have gold now. Over three thousand gold Ravens. Quinn is itchier than a mange-hided mongrel to get off this island."

"That's not why she's itchy," Henley said, casting an eye to the side table where Black rested. Quinn had surrendered her Shadline blade because she couldn't master its constant compulsion toward violence. "But I agree she'll go. She never wanted to come here in the first place. Or so she tells me several times every day."

"So, you're talking several times a day, eh?" Kila flashed her brows at him.

"It's not like that. Besides, her heart is elsewhere."

With Fallo. As strange as it was. A lovely Radiant's daughter had fallen for a villainous-looking, disinherited Terri-side merchant's son. "I wonder where Fallo is now," she said. "Probably in trouble."

"As true as that?" Henley said, there was a glimmer in his eyes. He truly missed his best friend.

"As true as that," she answered. "Then it's settled. We'll arrange passage off this island, and make our way north. The cats will tell us if Fallo is near enough to track down."

"I hadn't thought of that. It would be good to see him again. But I doubt the Shadline Cloak that Quinn told me about will be eager to let Fallo join us on a trek toward certain death."

Kila respected the Cloak, but she didn't fear him. Blades were crude weapons, even magical ones. She could immolate the man before he got his own flaming sword from its scabbard. Not that she wanted to.

"I think we should meet our smoke-haired friend tonight. Maybe he will teach us something useful."

Henley shrugged and sighed. "What do you think about his prophecy? That either you or the Hargothe will bring Kil into this world?"

"I think the words of demayne are as straight as knitted yarn. Have a care when we see him. Do not make anything that could be interpreted as an agreement with him."

Nax stood abruptly, claws digging into Kila's thighs.

What is it?

Huff was doing the same. Both cats were looking north and west.

It's Startle. He's . . . he's bonded someone.

Henley met her gaze, having heard the same from Huff.

Who did he bond? Kila sent. Startle was the fifth of Nax's surviving litter-mates. A near twin of Lop except for having white blotches on his fuzzy black fur. Kila had named the cat for the constantly surprised look the white markings around its eyes gave it.

I don't know, Nax sent.

And then both cats relaxed as if nothing had happened.

Henley stood, holding Huff. "I'll meet you later. I'm going to eat some breakfast before exploring the keep. I found a staircase leading to what appears to be a basement area. Want to join me?"

"The emissaries." She couldn't keep the glum dread from her voice. Even now she could feel the first one's approaching spark. "Maybe I'll catch up later. These women are as sticky as honey and sweet as seawater."

Henley made a sympathetic face, but he didn't offer to stay.

It was too late for Kila to mask her mercus and pretend she wasn't home. Since there was nothing else to be done without further alienating the other Ways, Kila steeled herself and prepared for battle.

4

____

ENGLEBERRY

The first emissary to arrive was Sensual Sliy. Twenty-two years old, handsomely plain, and serious as stone. She was determined to pry from Kila every one of her mercusine secrets. That Kila possessed very few such secrets was utterly irrelevant to the newly raised Sensual. She bore a tray of eggs and bacon, and miraculously, fresh baked engleberry muffins.

Kila appreciated the woman's effort, but saw through it. Bringing breakfast was meant to soften her, make her more amenable to incessant questioning about a subject she knew almost nothing.

Kila waved Sliy to set the tray on a side table, and went to the basin to splash her face. The mirror over the basin showed dark circles under her eyes, no surprise. Since Quinn had beaten the notion of grooming into her, Kila had taken a bit of pride in her appearance. What she saw in her reflection now was almost a stranger to her, what with her hair having been shorn off by Sensual Thine.

She turned away from her sad face, blotting her cheeks with a towel. The previous occupant of the room, Annisforl, had managed to survive without importing food or supplies of any kind. This had perplexed her until Sensual Sliy had pointed out he had likely had a demayne servant who could dymense into the office with whatever the man required.

Whether this was true or not, Kila had no way of knowing. But she did know that without Sliy's assistance, she would have eaten much less and her clothes might have fit much better.

"I have sent word to Voluptuary Minn," Emissary Sliy said. "I've asked for her to send a young novitiate to serve as a sort of lady's maid to you. Though I don't mind fetching your meals, such work is not customary for an official emissary of the Way of Ori."

And of course the Way of Ori would just love to have a girl hanging around Kila's room, listening to her conversations, reporting back all she heard. As much as Kila would like to have the help, she would not accept it.

"No need," Kila said. "I can see to myself. As I've told you a dozen times before, I've been taking care of myself for most of my life."

"Yes, as a . . . thief," the woman said. She tried to make her face flat to hide her skepticism. No one Kila had met on Garden Island had believed her tale of growing up in Cheapsgate and stealing for rent and chowder. She wondered why they preferred to think she had better breeding. To represent the Despised God, if he existed, a thief should serve just fine.

"Would it be more convincing if I told you I was a murderer?" Kila sat at her small round dining table and allowed herself to be served her breakfast. The food was hot, the tea was delicious, and the engleberry muffins nearly rivaled the sweetbake she had once pilfered from a Radiant's greathouse pantry several months ago.

But the Sensual was done with the topic of Kila's past in Starside. She dove immediately into her true business. "You have been most reticent to share your secrets about your power," Sliy said, pouring herself a cup of tea. She remained standing, and would do so until Kila invited her to sit.

The woman continued, "I have considered the matter from all angles. Withholding your healing techniques seems a terribly selfish act. Why would you reserve such knowledge for the Way of Kil if there be any merit to your assurances of your good intentions? By refusing to share, it sends quite the contrary message to all the other Ways."

Kila understood Sliy's point. If it were Kila's intent to keep her methods secret, all that would be true. "Emissary Sliy, what must I do to convince you that I do not *know* how I do it?"

Sliy gave her a flat look, as if to say, "Not this again."

Kila shoved an entire strip of bacon into her mouth, chewed angrily while shooting irritated glares at the woman across from her. "Sit down," she commanded around her mouthful.

The woman sat, primly, and sipped her tea. Kila didn't offer her any of the food.

Kila reached for the last engleberry muffin. But not with her hands. The more she'd practiced the mercus touch, the better and quicker she'd gotten. Sensing Sliy's tension at the sudden appearance of mercus bolts, Kila said, "Relax. I'm not going to hurt you."

The muffin was soft, still warm, and she felt these things

through her fingertips as if she were pressing them to the delicious treat. And then she lifted it. The muffin floated from the platter and drew toward her. The same way one would draw one's hand to one's mouth, not by focusing on the tension of the muscles or the looseness of the elbow, but merely by doing it. She brought the muffin to hover in the space between her and Sensual Sliy.

"Mercus touch," Kila said, putting on the tones of a lecturer. "Simple, really. Deciding to do it. Feeling it. Practicing it." Kila slowly lowered the muffin to the table. Changing her focus until she felt her palm on top of the treat, she squashed it flat. Releasing the mercus, she had to restrain herself from licking her palm. "That's all I know. Truly."

"Hefting muffins is not healing wounds."

"No. But the feat is the same. Intend to heal. Then heal. I think that all of the five mercus senses you've been trained to use are fundamental pieces, but the rest . . ." She held her hands up and shrugged. "Emotion. What you in the Way of Ori call the demaynic senses."

It was the first time Kila had truly tried to explain her mercus healing abilities and techniques.

Sensual Sliy immediately shed her skeptical and rather confrontational demeanor. Her flat expression had changed, her lips parting, her tongue probing inside of one cheek as she considered Kila's words. But there was also a stiff surprise, and she was pressing back into her chair as if there were a snake on the table.

Finally she said, "I saw you do incredible feats during the battle with Dunne Yples. I thought nothing could shock me again. But seeing you move that muffin . . ." She laughed humorlessly. "There is no one in the Ways of Ori, Pol, or Til who could do that without joining with a circle of source-taps."

"Highest Fley did it," Kila said. She scooped up the squashed muffin and shoved it into her mouth. She was glad Quinn hadn't joined them, for the young woman insisted Kila use knives and forks for eating.

"Highest Fley had several hellers," Sliy said. "And you and Dunne Yples were serving as force-taps at the time. But watching you do it here . . . I felt the power you used. I think any merculyn could do it."

That was true. Even when Kila flung Cayne with the mercus, or flew it back to her hand, she didn't require anything near the power she had used to dymense. Or lift herself from the ground.

Sensual Sliy said, "Thank you for sharing that insight. I think we are making progress. In that spirit, Voluptuary Minn invites you to the Tower to discuss your intentions going forward. She believes the force of destiny pushes us toward a culmination. It is essential that you have good counsel, which she is willing to provide."

Kila dabbed the remaining crumbs from the table with her forefinger and popped them in her mouth. "Emissary Moirina made the same offer. Apparently, the Coin has tossed her medallion and has news she wants to share with me. But she won't share it unless I'm there, face-to-face. And then there's the Way of Til, sending a new emissary today, apparently. And did you know that the governor of Docktown has sent a letter, asking my intentions and inquiring about"—she paused for a moment, still incredulous—"taxes."

"So your answer to Voluptuary Minn's invitation is no?"

"For now. As I have also told you time and again, my role

as Highest of Kil means nothing to me. I do not worship Kil. I'm not certain I believe Kil exists."

Sensual Sliy nodded and finished her cup of tea. She stood, gathered the dirty dishes, and started for the door. But before she left, she said: "One more thing, Highest. Voluptuary Minn anticipated your refusal. She told me to tell you that were the positions reversed, she would refuse as well. But she wants you to know the Way of Ori believes Dem-Kisk is at hand. The force of destiny has guided you to this point, but it has not yet reached its culmination. She heard what the demayne Flaumishtak said when he visited all of you here. She urges you to refuse his training. And furthermore, she says that his statement that you will bear Kil into this world is surely a lie."

Kila said the words to open the door, and the woman left.

Heaving out a frustrated sigh, she leaned back in her chair. But she did not have time to even think up a solid curse, let alone voice one, before Emissary Moirina from the Way of Pol strode in.

5

DECLARE AGAINST ME

Spinster Moirina was twice Sensual Sliy's age. Slim, serious, but with a bolder carriage. Like all Spinsters of Pol, she wore white. Unlike most others, her gown was sleeveless, her upper arms encircled by silver braces. Kila suspected these were hellers of some sort. The woman waited for the door to close behind her, hands held loosely at her sides. She was muscular, but not in the way a Starside housemother might be sturdy and strong, but instead like someone who had trained in the art of fighting. This carried through in the way she spoke, as if every conversation was on the verge of devolving into hand-to-hand combat.

"I trust that Novitiate Sliy wasn't able to buy you off with muffins this morning." There was a wryness to the statement, conveying contempt for Sliy, but also a hint of question. As if Kila were just simple enough to be swayed by food. Moirina was very skilled at this sort of statement. Kila had noticed how such words subtly planted opinions into Kila's mind that she had never considered. If she wasn't paying attention. Which she now was.

"It's *Sensual* Sliy now. Just raised yesterday," Kila corrected. Like any bully, Moirina needed a hard shove to check her behavior. "As a matter of fact, I'm considering meeting with Voluptuary Minn face-to-face. She extended a rather polite invitation just now."

If it irritated Moirina as much as Kila hoped, the woman didn't reveal it by her expression. She was always formal with Kila, but not as deferential. Nor was she as dedicated to shows of protocol as Sliy. Kila assumed this was because of the great difference in their ages, and the fact that Moirina had not witnessed Kila perform any of the mercus feats that Sliy had.

"Please sit, Emissary." The woman took her position in the chair Sliy had recently vacated. Kila sat quietly, sipping the last of her tea, waiting for the woman to begin whatever harangues she had planned for this morning.

Moirina reached to her medallion, which she wore like all Spinsters, on a gold chain around her neck. Kila knew that these medallions could be removed from their settings and tossed to perform a fortune-telling trick.

She had never seen it done, but Henley had told her the Spinsters gave these tosses—or "spins" as they prefer to call them—great consideration. He had witnessed rather extraordinary tosses, with improbable bounces and rolls.

"The Coin is most vexed at your reticence to declare Dem-Kisk," Moirina said to open the conversation. "Surely the great battle waged just outside this keep, and the four tellings of the seer Roya Reth, along with the Coin's own many spins on the subject, prove that the time of Dem-Kisk is upon us."

"So it's upon us." Kila lifted shoulder. "What difference does it make if I declare it?"

Nax stirred in her lap, kneaded her paws into Kila's thighs, then snuggled in to resume her snooze. Emissary Moirina notice this of course, betrayed by a slight flick at the edge of her mouth. Not a frown or a smile, but discomfort.

The Way of Til hated cats; the Way of Ori respected them. But the Way of Pol had been rather silent on the subject, and Kila wondered which side of the question they fell on.

But this wasn't the time to ask. This wasn't the time to even have this conversation. Kila said, "Can we skip all of the Gristenside sideways talk? Just state what you want and save us both some time. I have other things to do."

"Very well. The most that's known about Dem-Kisk is what's contained in the rather cryptic prophecy in the Theb. The late Roya Reth has added a few equally cryptic footnotes. What cannot be denied is that the force of destiny guides you with a much stronger hand than it does anyone else. I was not present to hear the words of the demayne Flaumishtak. But they resonated very deeply with the Coin. He asserted that the Despised God is waiting in his demaynic hall, waiting for you to bear him into the world. And he furthermore stated that either you will bear him forth or the seer from Starside will."

Kila nodded and made a hurry-up motion with her hands.

"The Coin—" Emissary Moirina stopped abruptly and swallowed. She cleared her throat and started again. "Though it goes against *all* the Coin has believed during her life in the Way of Pol, her counsel is that you *must* train with the demayne. She has tossed her medallion one hundred times on the question. In an unprecedented result Pol smiled seventy times." The woman leaned forward, eyes burning. "But you must not go alone. I must come with you. I must be there to chaperone, to hear the lies in his words that you in your youth might miss. And if you refuse me?" She leaned back, expression going stoney. "The way of Pol must consider you an enemy of mankind."

So there it was. The threat. The ultimatum. Quinn had warned Kila that this was coming. The Ways wanted to control her, and each would pursue that end in their particular way. Ori wanted to manipulate her and guide her. Pol intended to the boss her around. She had no idea what Til would propose, but knowing them, it would make her very angry.

Kila was prepared for this, thanks to Quinn. "If I met with this demayne, and I had only a representative from the Way of Pol as my chaperone, the Ways of Til and Ori would see that as favoritism. And it would most certainly force Ori to declare against me."

She couldn't believe she had just uttered the phrase "declare against me." It sounded like something from a sword and armor tale, like the one about the Seven Kingdoms and the battle for a throne of iron. Not much comfort there. All her favorite heroes had gotten killed in that tale.

She reminded herself that Moirina was an Emissary, which meant every conversation with her was a negotiation. And so she chose the path that Quinn had taught her: "I cannot make any guarantees at this point. I need to discuss it with my advisors."

Spin Moirina raised an eyebrow. "Advisors? You mean the Peline girl? The ginger-headed Mast boy? Perhaps you mean to consult with the blind child and the madman while you're at it."

This was good. The woman was provoked. And Kila knew

why. She saw Kila as a child, a wisp of the girl who would be beneath notice had she been a mere devotee of Pol. Furthermore, Moirina saw *herself* as Kila's advisor. The idea that Kila had now placed in open-air that Moirina was an adversary in these conversations brought home to the woman that she had absolutely no control over what Kila did or didn't do. Moirina didn't like not having control.

Kila waved a dismissive hand. "Tell the Coin that if she wishes to make threats against me, she should do so in person. But I don't understand the need for threats. I'm not an evil person. I have no love for Kil. I don't want to be the head of this ridiculous cult. But you asked me whether I'm prepared to declare that Dem-Kisk is upon us. Why, yes. Of course it is. But what does my declaration mean? You've been all over this Keep, I'm sure. Have you seen my army of merculyns? Have you seen my armsmen practicing with their swords and whipaxes? No. You've seen me and three friends. And a poor mad Donse Master wearing a *vaz'on* to keep him quelled."

The woman started to speak, started to protest, but Kila cut her off with a sharp chop of her hand. "I am not a devotee, Emissary. If you think you can lecture me into submitting to your will, you'll find yourself talking to an empty chair. I'm not a fool. You seek that which serves *your* interests, not mine."

"The Way of Pol serves the interest of mankind, not that of individuals."

Kila had heard this manner of speaking before. All the Ways boasted that they only intended the best for mankind. "Tell the Coin that she has my assurance that I do not seek power. I do *not* seek to bring Kil into this world, and the only goal of any import is to make sure that the Hargothe doesn't either. It seems rather obvious to me."

The woman stood, smoothed her gown, and gave Kila a formal bow before proceeding to the door. It must've been some manner of training for emissaries to offer one parting word at the door because Emissary Moirina did the same as Sliy had done. She stopped, as if something had just occurred to her, and turned. "The force of destiny is set on bringing Kil back to this world. I ask you this: do you think it better that he be brought back by you or the Hargothe? For my part, I'm not certain."

She turned to face the door, waiting for Kila to utter the phrase that would open it. Kila hesitated. The woman's question bored into her brain. It certainly was something she had asked herself in the moonlit hours of sleeplessness.

"Open for Kil's daughter," she said.

The door unlocked and swung in. Spin Moirina walked out. Kila heaved another huge sigh and closed her eyes. The sparks of mercus power in the keep came brightly to her, especially Moirina's as she descended the winding stair. And in the distance, approaching slowly, came another.

Kila assumed it was Til's Emissary. Gauging by his progress, he would be at the door within fifteen minutes. He would immediately proceed up the stairs to seek an audience with her. She debated trying to sneak down the stairs and find Henley.

On the other hand, it seemed she was going to have to contend with these emissaries and this ridiculous morass of politics for a good time to come. Or at least until she, Quinn, and Henley could get passage to leave the island.

She decided to start things off on a good footing. She

would be polite. She would listen. And she would make sure that the emissary found accommodations to his liking.

And then she would join Henley and explore.

But first, she had a job for Quinn. One she thought Quinn would quite enjoy.

6

FATE'S-PIECE

The Sagmarsh had no end as far as Fallo could tell. It was an infinite hell of soggy ground, sprouting shoulder-high stalks of thick green grass. Each was topped with a sausage-like seed pod that emanated a repulsive odor, like unwashed sailors on a very hot day. The variety of insects boggled Fallo's mind. Eventually he cared only about one particular flying menace, which he dubbed a blackdart. It was a narrow, long-snooted beastie with gossamer wings. So lovely in flight. Such a pain when those snoots stabbed one's flesh. The blackdarts rose in swarms and circled his head, coming closer and closer, then on some buggy signal known only to their kind, they all struck at once, poking their thorny noses into his scalp or neck or face. Or, should they squirm up a pant leg, even more sensitive regions.

And the welts! The itching and burning only worsened with scratching. And no matter how he resolved to resist the urge, he could not keep from scraping at his skin to ease the torture.

Only caking his exposed flesh with mud deterred them, but not much.

The leeches were another thing. Fallo did not like them. When the swampy stretches deepened—sometimes reaching his midriff—the opposite shore would find him fully unclothed and pulling the bloodsucking worms from rather inconvenient and painful places. He did discover by chance that the leeches liked blackdart welts and eased the itching quite nicely. All they asked in return was all of his blood.

Lop found the frogs delicious, the snakes terrifying. But the marsh was bad ground for a cat. She rode in Fallo's satchel now, occasionally poking her head out to inspect his progress, which she always declared to be insufficient.

The Cloak bore all these annoyances with his usual stoney equanimity, reserving his ire for Fallo's complaints. Making any sort of comfortable camp in the Sagmarsh required luck. The occasional hillock would rise from the marsh, often supporting a single gnarled tree. These formations were not land so much as a dirt-covered boulders. Other creatures liked these little rises, too. Especially snakes.

Five nights into this trek, Fallo demanded a fire. The Cloak merely shook his head. When Fallo demanded to know why not, the Cloak said. "Why do you think I do not allow a fire when such would provide relief from the insects, provide warmth for our bones, and offer the chance to cook a frog or hiccfish?"

"Because you want to torture me?"

"I endure all you do."

"I've not seen an insect or leech on you."

"A man who turns a jealous eye on others cannot see his

own fortune. But answer me. Why do I forbid the fire given the benefits of such?"

"Because it will attract something worse than it repels."

The Cloak showed his teeth. They glowed a strange orange in the hazelight that hung over the marsh as the sun started to set. The moon had already risen opposite the sun, a huge globe just peeping over the eastern horizon where the Honor Mountains made vague bumps in the distance.

Lop squirmed from the satchel and stalked off to inspect the hillock that would be their miserable home for the next few hours. Ten paces by ten and rising perhaps three from the squishy ground. It was mostly rock, covered over by a layer of lichen. A few lonely stalks grew from cracks. The tree that crowned it had a trunk that bent in a twist, spreading a flat spray of green needles. Nightcrone's parasol, the Cloak had called it.

"Was there a reason you led us into this bog?" Fallo asked for the hundredth time. The Cloak shook his head.

"If you didn't have a reason, then something other than reason compelled you to undertake this insane crossing. An instinct! You had a hazy feeling that this was the way to go."

"An instinct or hazy feeling would be a reason, no?"

Stumped, Fallo sat and leaned his back against the trunk of the nightcrone's parasol. He swept a family of ants from his sleeve. He kicked his shoes off to let his feet dry. He studied his sorry, waterlogged toes, all shriveled and pale as frog bellies.

Daylight surrendered to twilight, and the blue-gray oozed out of the sky, leaving thick darkness to mask all that surrounded them.

Despite the winter chill, there arose a chorus of insect

chatter and frog shouts. What a crop of hardy nasties, Fallo thought, to live here even in the midst of winter. But the Sagmarsh Wash stayed fluid all year, according to the Cloak, heated from below by fires deep underground.

Finally, having given the question of the Cloak's motives for coming here careful thought, Fallo said, "For you, sir Cloak, a reason is a fully formed notion. It is not vague. A bear chasing us, that would be a reason. As would be a specific type of suffering you wanted to me to endure. I think an instinct or feeling would not rise to your standard of reason."

The Cloak was a black shape against the darkness, punctuated by a set of eyes gleaming with reflected moonlight. Whether he agreed with Fallo's reasoning or not, there was no way to tell. Fallo intended to press him on it, but the hiss of the man's sword drawing from scabbard interrupted him. Fallo responded immediately. He drew his blade from its plain leather sheath.

Lop scurried into Fallo's satchel to hide.

Something snuffled in the gloom. A great fog had risen as night had fallen, but the moon was fully above the horizon now, casting a mercus-like light across the rising fingers of marsh mist.

"This is it," the Cloak said, raising Tosuin as he stood. Not the slightest breeze stirred the moon-glowing fog. Insects rioted in their countless hordes, buzzing and chirping soliloquies bemoaning their infinite insignificance.

Below that buzz and hum, a grunt, followed by the unmistakable wet sucking noise of an enormous foot pulling from the muck.

"This is what?" Fallo hissed.

"Our objective."

"How do you know."

"Instinct." The Cloak raised his sword higher. Red and orange flames burst forth along the blade. Whether he called upon this power or the blade decided, he'd never told Fallo. But the light from the flames made the fog glow red, and answering flickers glimmered from fetid puddles all around them.

The Cloak lifted his eyes, looking up and up. Fallo followed his gaze and saw new sparkles of reflected fire overhead. Great, glassy eyes ten spans up, set above an elongated snout. Curved fangs, each the length of Fallo's legs, protruded from the sides of the mouth, and wisps of feathery brows plumed from the ridges over its eyes.

Mind going blank with terror, it was up to Fallo's body to protect itself. He raised his dagger, a nine inch blade, pocked and rusted. To the beast looming over them, Ol' Rusty's bite would be of less consequence than a blackdart's was to Fallo.

The great orbs narrowed, and all the beast's attention turned to Fallo. It nosed closer, lowering its massive head on a long, scaly neck. Fallo retreated a step, but a sudden pressure on his back held him in firm. The arm-thick end of a serpentine tail pressed against him. Firmly, irresistibly.

"Forgive Ulagatin," came a woman's voice, clear and mundane in the eldritch mist. "He never appreciates how fearsome he looks to men."

The Cloak relaxed, just a hair. He raised his flaming sword in front of him, now serving as more of a torch than a weapon. "Zirhine?"

"Well met, Cloak Einlin. Do extinguish Tosuin."

Fallo held still, casting his eyes left and right, searching for the source of the voice. But his attention returned to the beast, which had to be a dragon. It now pressed so close its sulfury breath blew back his hair. The dragon appeared to be sniffing his dagger.

"Ulagatin told me a great blade had come to the Sagmarsh," the woman said. "I did not believe him. But now I see. Which is it?"

Fallo said nothing.

The Cloak lowered his blade and the flames went out. In the following dark, Fallo could see nothing but a great black mass looming before him, outlined in moonlight.

"Answer her, lad," the Cloak said. "She asks the name of your blade."

"You told me not to tell anyone."

"She has a dragon as an ally. Do you truly intend to refuse?"

"Telt! Its name is Telt."

The beast's head withdrew. It raised its snout to the sky and opened its great maw. On an ululating roar that rumbled in Fallo's chest, it released a bubble of blue flame into the mist. The fire rose up and up before finally losing shape and dissipating.

Before the light vanished, Fallo saw the woman, momentarily lit in dragon-blue. Just ten paces ahead, standing between the dragon's front legs.

Ulagatin retreated a step and brought his head low to rest on the boggy surface of the marsh. The woman stroked its brow.

"He pays respect to this blade, forged from the tooth of his ancient sister, Qaj'sh. And to the one who bears it."

"He does?" Fallo's voice cracked. He cleared his throat and tried again. "He does?"

The Cloak returned Tosuin to its scabbard and waited for the woman to approach. Fallo's eyes slowly adjusted to the moon-washed mist-light.

Zirhine was dark-haired, dark-eyed and of indeterminate age. He couldn't grasp any detail about her face in the moonlight. Boots to her knees, drab shirt cinched at the waist with a belt holding a knife. She carried a satchel, strap crossing her chest. It was her posture that told Fallo she was dangerous—even without her pet dragon.

"May I?" she held out a hand. Long fingers, but strong. Nails trimmed but dirty.

"It might burn you. It did that to one person."

She did not balk, but accepted the hilt. Holding it reverently, she pulled something from a pocket and put it in her mouth. Chewing and breathing heavily through her nose she hummed quietly.

She worked a bit of her mouthful to her lips and hooked it out with her forefinger. A blob of chewed leaf. With a throaty whisper, she said: *"Rahsh!"*

Her fingertip blob began to glow with a soft blue light. She swallowed the rest of the bolus and smiled, lips closed, eyes closed. There was a moment of reverence, then she brought her glowing finger close to the blade.

I'm coming out, Lop sent.

Stay.

For a wonder, the cat obeyed.

Turning Telt this way and that, Zirhine examined it minutely, spending long moments over each nick and notch while mouthing a silent narrative to herself. Her eyes were full of wonder.

"You're a ferneater," Fallo said, marveling at the light

she'd created. He'd heard of such folk all his life, but he'd never met one. Donse Masters said they cavorted with demayne, but Fallo figured the Way of Til was merely jealous of anyone wielding power they didn't control. The light was different from the mercus light Fallo was used to. It was dim, like a dozen firebugs in a bottle. The blue was beautiful, enthralling.

Zirhine had an interesting face, now clearly lit. Perhaps she was fifty. Skin lined from exposure to sun and wind. She had a strong jaw, square. Almost masculine. This was offset by her high brow, and delicate nose. A unique face. Her shoulders and arms were thick, speaking of power.

"So it's true," she said at last. She handed the blade back to Fallo, gently, as if it were a baby bird. He returned it to his scabbard and looked over his shoulder. The dragon's tail had retreated.

Zirhine went to the gnarled tree and dabbed her glowing weedball onto the tip of a bare limb. She whispered to it and the light brightened.

"We must talk," she said, folding herself onto the ground cross-legged. The Cloak joined her, laying his scabbarded blade across his knees. He dug in his own satchel and offered the woman a bit of derpvine. She cooed in delight and quickly set about skinning and slicing it. "You've been through the Honor Mountains," she said, chewing a piece of the sweet vine. "The only place you can find these."

"Wandering. The council in Starside wouldn't tell me anything."

"Neither did mine."

"But you said, 'so it's true'," Fallo pointed out. "You must have known something."

"I knew what Ulagatin said. Nothing more. Certainly nothing from the Shadlines I've spoken with the past moon."

"And what did they say?" the Cloak asked.

"That a powerful new merculyn has arisen in Starside. That spark spirits have been felt there, too." She eyed Fallo's bulging bag. "And a rumor that two previously unknown blades had surfaced."

"How could a rumor like that spread so quickly," Fallo asked. "Nobody knows about them."

"The Shadline council in Starside knows," the Cloak said. "A fast ship could put lips to ears as far south as Trine within two days. Why must we talk, Zirhine?"

"The Dirth has called an Armory. Every Shadline is expected."

"But not us," the Cloak said.

Fallo was still trying to figure out what a Dirth and an Armory meant. The Cloak's statement interrupted this musing. "Why not? This Armory thing sounds like something to do. A real objective."

"We likely have a more pressing assignment," Zirhine said. "Our meeting here is a fatehand."

The Cloak nodded but said nothing. Fallo had a hundred questions. What is a Dirth? What exactly is an Armory? Why is everyone expected except the three sitting in the swamp? What in Kil's name does "fatehand" mean? Instead of uttering any of these, he clamped his mouth shut when the Cloak gave him a warning glance.

Zirhine continued, "Here is the fate's-piece I possess." She unlimbered her satchel and pulled forth a small roll of paper, no longer than her thumb. She unfurled it and showed it to Fallo and the Cloak.

Scrawled in a shaky hand was an inverted V. A squared off notch had been cut from one side. To the right, the shape of a waning moon. On the left, a cluster of stars. The distinctive six-star shape of the Chalice.

"That looks like a mountain peak," Fallo said, intrigued by the sketch. "Where is it?"

Zirhine eyed him. "I said it was a fate's-piece."

"The boy doesn't know," the Cloak said.

So, here was another bit of Shadline business the Cloak hadn't told him. "Do you all carry little drawings that don't mean anything?"

"No," the Cloak said.

"Do you have a fate's-piece that isn't a little drawing?"

"Yes."

"What's yours?"

Zirhine shook her head and laughed. "They're funny when their just a few days into their vows, aren't they?"

"Funny is not the word I'd use," the Cloak said. He took the sketch and held it closer to Zirhine's blue light.

"Now, now," Fallo said amiably—though he was growing more irritated by the minute. "No reason to tease me. I am a Shadline, after all."

Zirhine laughed. A low barking noise.

And then Fallo got it. And he did not like it. "Oh. *I'm* your fate's-piece, aren't I?" He still didn't know what it meant.

The Cloak nodded, just the slightest dip of his chin.

"That doesn't sound good to me. In fact, it sounds mighty dire. I thought leaving Starside and keeping me from going with Quinn and Kila was supposed to be good for me."

"I never said that."

Zirhine seemed to take pity. She offered him a chunk of

derpvine from her blade. He munched on it and considered what a fate's-piece was. But before he could mount much speculation, Zirhine told him.

"Once a Shadline has reached a certain maturity, a council will entrust her with a fate's-piece—a bit of information, or an object, or perhaps an enigmatic rumor. This will be carried with the Shadline on her travels. Whenever she meets with another Shadline, both share their fate's-pieces. In this way, the Order circulates bits and clues that do not fit what is known. Or perhaps things that have not found a home, allowing the force of destiny to guide each piece to the ears or eyes or hands of the one who needs it."

She pointed her knife at the roll of paper in the Cloak's hand. "That could be important in the battles to come, or it could be a child's drawing, scrawled in a moment of boredom."

"Even such can be of great import," the Cloak said. "Without the child even knowing it. The same force that guides our blades can push a quill, could it not?"

"Surely," the woman said.

"What a tub o' fish lard!" Fallo said. "My father's numbers-master could solve your puzzles in half a day."

"Could he?" Zirhine asked. "For within the Order are many such men, and they have seen again and again the fate's-pieces find the right person at the right moment. To stave off illness, to disrupt greedy schemes, to win battles, to save towns from fires, and to uncover the deep secrets of the First Race."

"Will you travel with us, Zirhine?" the Cloak asked. It wasn't an invitation, just a question.

"I will. For a time. But Ulagatin will not. With Telt revealed, he must attend to tasks of his own."

"Tasks? He's a beast." Fallo looked glumly at his satchel. Poor Lop didn't dare come out or the dragon might make a nibble out—

The satchel had gone flat. Fallo felt the bond.

Where are you?

With Ulagatin. Where else?

But he might eat you.

No. I like him.

Zirhine said, "Much like your Beloved One speaks to you, Ulagatin speaks quite clearly to me. Perhaps one day he will to you. Right now he is too shy, for you bear a relic cherished by his kind."

"Sleep, lad," the Cloak said. "And do not think yourself large now. The dragon's admiration is for the blade and the bearer, not for you as a man."

Fallo thought that a hair-thin distinction, but leave it to the Cloak to slice a compliment to shreds. Fallo seized on the permission to sleep, for that meant he would not be expected to keep watch. And why would he? There were two Shadlines and a dragon to keep an eye on things.

"Zirhine?" he asked as he curled on his lichen bedding, cuddling his satchel close. "Is that knife on your belt a Shadline weapon?"

"No."

"Then how can you be a Shadline?"

She reached over a shoulder and withdrew another blade, one cleverly strapped to her back. It was curved in the manner of weapons from Jilin. It was hard to say for sure in the blue light, but it seemed to have a coppery shine to it. "Reft," she said. "Ecstatic binding." She threw the blade past his head. It made a whirling noise as it flew into the moonlit fog.

Moments later the sound increased, and the blade whipped by Fallo's other ear. The hilt slapped into her waiting hand.

"And if it strikes something during its flight?"

She raised an eyebrow. "It returns. A bit more slowly."

The moon rose, the fog thickened. Occasionally a thump and splash sounded nearby, Ulagatin's tail. Lop stayed with the dragon. The Cloak and Zirhine exchanged news, mostly about people Fallo had never heard of. It didn't take long for Fallo to succumb to sleep, and he was only vaguely aware that the insects had not bothered him since Zirhine had come.

7

THE STAFF OF NIHIL

The Hargothe stood at an uncovered window of his great hall. The icy mountain air stung his lips and cheeks, but he was hale enough now to master his body's natural reaction to the cold.

In fact, he reveled in the chill. He admired it. For cold was death, the drawing away of life's warmth.

A man could leave his home and venture into such air and only through continuous exertion keep his blood warm. Should he grow weary and rest, the ineluctable cold would embrace him, digging icy fingers into every pore until it gripped his very heart.

But the Hargothe could stand still in it. Now recovered from his near-destruction, he had new depths of mercusine to draw upon. He could stand atop the parapets of Ceronhel and spread his arms to receive the gentle caresses of the mountain wind, and his power could keep him safe and warm for a hundred years.

He had force-bonded seventeen nosg so far. He felt them

as extremities of his own body now. One of his "hands" had finally returned. It was coming to present to him his long-awaited prize.

Without eyes, there was no need to look at his servants. In fact, with the exception of Noy, they rarely came into his presence. Besides, he could command them from afar, just as he could move his fingers without seeing them.

Even as far away as Starside, he could feel the tendrils of his force-bonded hands. One such was a man, a lone trapper the nosg had captured on the northern slopes of the Rachtooth mountains. He had just recently arrived in Starside. Very distant, which gave the man too much independence. For now. The Hargothe very much wanted to know what transpired in Starside. Soon he would.

The newly-returned nosg opened the door and shuffled in. Its breath was heavy but not ragged. All nosg breathed through their mouths like idiots.

"You have my prize?" the Hargothe asked.

In answer there was a soft thunk as something solid struck the stone floor. The Hargothe reached out with his senses which returned to him through sound and subtle curls in the air currents to paint an image in his mind.

Yes. There it was.

It would not do to show too much eagerness. So he approached slowly, hungry to seize this thing which the nosg held.

"You have done well, Hanglit." He held out his hand. The nosg placed his prize into it.

The Staff of Nihil. A mercusine relic of legend. And now it was his. What a surprise it had been to discover its whereabouts within the memories of his force-bonded nosg. They *all* knew where it was because it was kept in their mountain halls far to the north, a prize of some forgotten war. As nosg did not possess the mercusine spark in the same way men did, they had never learned its power. It had been, as far as the Hargothe could tell, a trophy. A decoration.

"It cost me," Hanglit said in his gruff and tongue-troubled way. Nosg had a language of their own, mostly clicks and pops and a few long warbles. Manspeak strained their mouths nearly as much as it did their minds. They especially struggled with T's due to their protuberant upper snouts, and so Hanglit's words came out sounding like "Ih cos me."

"You must rest, dear Hanglit. Eat. Noy has killed a deer just this morning."

A feeling rumbled across the bond, sullen and bitter. Also, rage. The Hargothe plunged his mercusine probes into the creature's mind. The force-bond did not make a subject loyal. Sometimes he had to use a mental whip on these nosg-kin fools to keep them cowed. Their minds were dull as river rock, just as their squat bodies were strong as oak limbs. He therefore used the mercusine as a chisel and axe. A strong tap here and a stronger strike there and . . . Hanglit's heavy breaths turned to wheezes and finally moans as the Hargothe carved terror into its dull mind.

Whatever retrieving the staff had cost Hanglit, it was nothing compared to what the Hargothe could take from him. "You should count yourself lucky to be in my presence. Serve me loyally and those you despise will one day be your slaves."

"Yuh! Yuh!" Hanglit said with spirit. He backed from the room and left the Hargothe in peace.

The Staff of Nihil emanated warmth into the Hargothe's hand, for he was sensitive the subtlest yearnings of the mercusine. This relic would be of great service to him in the trials to come. He wished only that it were a general purpose heller— an artifact that concentrated and amplified mercusine feats.

But it was not. Like a queller, or any of a hundred other relics, it did one thing. But what it did . . . the Hargothe felt a grin lifting his mouth. It made his skin stretch most uncomfortably.

It required no concentration at all to use. And use it he did.

8

HOW IT SCALDED

Fog flooded Starside, shrouding the Street of Sorrows. Mercus lights glowed atop their poles, beacons that illuminated the gauzy air, yet did not reveal more than a hazy circle around themselves.

But fog was not all that hung heavily over the city. The few people Tym Hamlickten passed shot him nervous looks, and they traveled in pairs. They all wore blades on their hips, too, many of them old and rusted, attic castoffs from some grand-uncle's war days, now brought out for protection.

The reason these city folk went about armed was simple. There had been murders in Starside. Horrific murders.

The trapper walked uphill, following the switchbacks. He had not been to a city as large as Starside before. Over the past few ten-days he had seen more of cities and towns than he had ever desired. There was a reason he'd gone into the wilds of the Rachtooths, risking nosg-kin and bears, to live a life of solitude.

He had bought new clothing, as instructed. The wool was

fine, warm. But his bare cheeks and chin chilled him. Who knew that shearing one's hair short would shed so much heat? He pulled up the hood of his cloak. Sounds were strange here in this fog, with all these structures around. Not like the open air of the mountains.

This place felt closed in. The weight of the Divide pressed especially hard on his mind, even lost from view as it was. An atmosphere of dread permeated everything. The murders. A dozen of them. People in their homes, on the streets, men of the Watch, Cheapsgaters. Some rumors told of a band of murderers escaped from the Westbunk. Others said, no, it was a lone madman using mercusine power to rend off heads. No. It was Her Enlightened Majesty, full of wrath for her sinful subjects. No. It was the thinnies from the sewers, rising up to claim vengeance on the city. The speculations went on and on.

Horrific tales. But nothing he'd heard chilled him nearly as much as the old man had. The old man. The blind wizard of Ceronhel.

The trapper shivered against a cold welling up from deep inside in body. He did not like to think of the old man. Not that he had much choice. He was *there.* In his head. A constant pressure at the base of the skull, like a headache. But worse. So much worse.

Winter had come to Starside. The street was piled with snow at the edges. The center had been trampled under boot and atlen talon into a muddy slush. He was thankful he'd decided to keep his hunter's boots, knee high, and oiled against the damp. Perhaps they didn't match his newer frocks. He didn't care. Damp feet were death. Every man of the mountains knew it.

His destination was ahead. Heart thumping, he pushed on a broad door and stepped into quiet warmth.

The Yin Inn was a landmark in mid-Terriside, set right at a turn of the Street of Sorrows. Two turrets, shake shingles painted white. A huge wooden sign affixed to the front touted the clean rooms, fresh beer, fine trezz, and entertainments nightly. Inside it was like most inns he'd visited on his restless rush to this city. Trestle tables and benches in the common room, the surfaces polished to a dull shine by the scrapes of platters, buffs of elbows, and swipes of serving girls' rags. A double-sided fireplace stood center, the huge stone chimney dividing the room into roughly equal spaces. It smelled of hickory smoke.

Mid-morning. A few late risers. Several local men bent over tea with papers spread before them. Merchants, most likely.

The trapper went to the barman, a slender fellow called Chicky. Bald, with a huge mustache covering his lips. He was bent over a ledger, poking at it with his stylus and muttering figures under his breath. The trapper knew not to interrupt a man in the middle of his ciphering. He took a stool and shed his cloak. The common room was hot.

The trapper had been told what to do. What to say. He was glad of that. He had never been much of a talker.

When Chicky reached his total, he scribbled it on the page and sighed heavily. Setting aside his stylus, he capped his ink bottle and gave the trapper a look. "If it isn't trezz or beer, you'll have to wait. I've got a pot on for tea."

"Tea would be a blessing," the trapper said. He wanted to continue, get this over with, but though he was none too skilled at gauging a man's mind by his face, he knew he should wait to make his inquiry. Otherwise he would appear too eager. Too desperate. A good trap was subtle, invisible to its quarry.

He drank two cups of tea. "Hard black" the barman called it, waggling his mustache in amusement to discover the trapper had not heard of it. He declared it as strange as not having heard of Her Enlightened Majesty.

"Where're you from, sir?" Chicky asked, returning to his ledger.

"North. Flyssn." A vast region of the Rachtooths, with dozens of small villages nestled in valleys and alongside mountain lakes.

"Lockt?" Chicky asked. It was Flyssn's one true city. But Lockt was not as large as Starside.

"Near enough. My business takes me all over. My first visit to Starside."

"Business?" the barman said, speculatively. A gleam in his eye spoke to the growing interest the man had in his customer. "What sort?"

"Furs, mostly. Perhaps you might help me. I'm looking for a man named Tarek PiTorro. Said to be a caravanner."

The trapper had been advised that PiTorro owned a significant interest in the Yin Inn.

"Aye, I can help you." The gleam was still there, but hardened into expectation. The trapper understood bartering. He had traded furs for necessities for years. In this case, he did not have a fur or anything else of value from the mountains. Instead, he had a sack of coin. He opened it now.

The barman cleared his throat. "The tea is a copper plug."

The trapper had been told what to do. He plucked a coin from his purse and set it on the bar. It made a hard, heavy click. And then it rasped as he slid it over the lovingly sanded and polished surface.

A silver skillet.

Chicky eyed it and said nothing. His mustache drooped a little at the sides.

The trapper added another then cinched his purse tight and returned it to his belt.

The coins disappeared in a quick swipe of the barman's hand. "I'll introduce you to him. He comes in here every evening. Return after six bells."

It was ten bells, morning. A long wait. But trappers knew patience. He liked this establishment better than the one where he had taken a room. "Any rooms? I'm at the Cherry Bottom presently."

The barman made a face. "Might as well be sleeping in Cheapsgate. Go collect your things. I can put you up. A gold skillet per night."

The trapper did not use coin often, but he knew that was a ridiculous rate. He didn't argue. He wanted this fellow pleased and willing. "I am carrying all I brought to Starside."

"No pelts? I know Tarek PiTorro. He will not strike a deal with you if he cannot see samples of your goods."

This caught the trapper off guard a moment. He ran through the things he had been told to say. And then arose some things stuck into his mind without his knowledge. A response came to his tongue. "My samples are stored else-where. Would *you* trust valuables to the chambermaids of the Cherry Bottom Inn?"

The answer struck true. The man chuckled and shook his head. "That I would not, sir. That I would not. What name should I give PiTorro?"

"Tym Hamlickten."

"Tym. Welcome to the Yin Inn. I'll have Weese open a room and lay a fire. Weese! WEESIE!"

A beanpole of a girl entered, wiping red hands on her apron. She was twenty, Tym thought. She blew a stray hair from her face. Pale blue eyes, prominent and earnest. She gave Tym a good looking over. Once she determined he met her minimum standards, she told him to follow.

"Are you Chicky's wife?" he asked as they climbed a sturdy old stair.

"Daughter."

"Your sisters and brothers work here too?"

"I'm an only."

So this was the girl. The old man had not known the girl's appearance, for he was blind. He hadn't known her name, either. Just that she was a maid at the Yin Inn and the proprietor's daughter. There was something special about her. What it was, Tym didn't know.

She opened the door to a tidy, spacious room. Bed, table, whale-oil lantern, a box of complementary flashtapers. A few books were stacked on a shelf next to a small portrait of a dark-haired woman. Presumably Her Enlightened Majesty, based on the raven perched on her shoulder.

Weese set about preparing a fire in the tiny hearth. He watched her, wondering how the old man had known about her. He supposed he'd kept his eyeless sockets on all sorts of people, considering how he liked to use folk. Perhaps Weese had been kept in mind for some unknowable future contingency. Like this one.

The fire started, Weese straightened and again and wiped her hands on her apron. "Will you require anything else?"

He spoke the word he'd been taught: "*Aprhen.*"

The pressure at the back of his skull crushed forward, squeezing around his brain like a casing of ice. His vision retreated until Weese was just a tiny figure far away. Then *he* took command and spoke through Tym's mouth.

"Weese, daughter of Chicky. I have been watching you." The voice was Tym's, but stronger, bolder, and full of arrogance. It was the old man's manner of speaking.

"What?" the girl said. " What do you mean?"

He strode forward, boots thunking the floorboards. "I have felt your spark. Do not deny it."

Weese stuttered a string of objections. What was this all about? How dare he approach her so brazenly?

Tym no longer controlled his own body. But still he snatched her elbow to keep her from fleeing, then his palm pressed to her forehead. And it was his power—one that had lain dormant inside him his entire life— that thrust into the young woman's mind.

How it scalded Tym, a glowing firebrand to the mind. There was no retreating from it or letting it go. He would have screamed had he any control over his voice.

Weese gasped and went limp. Tym caught her before she fell. He helped her to the bed, sat her down. Slowly, she caught her breath and her focus returned to where she was.

"It's—it's beautiful."

"It is the mercusine, child. Your spark is faint. Perhaps it might never have awakened without my help. But it will suffice. Now go to the Baths of Ori and join their order."

He placed his hands on her temples and forced the remainder of his commands directly into her mind, deep, where they would not be known even to her until the time was right.

A high, keening cry came from her lips and then went silent as her eyes rolled up and she flopped back onto the bed.

The trapper's vision blurred and suddenly he was back in command, breathless and terrified. The old man had used his body, had spoken through his lips. But beyond the command to join the Way of Ori, Tym had no idea what else Weese had been instructed to do. And he was glad of it.

Blinking tears of pain from his own eyes he helped the girl up and told her she had grown woozy following lighting the fire. She shirked off his hands and stumbled to the door. "It is a bit warm in here," she muttered to herself.

And then she was gone.

Tym had hours and hours to while away before his meeting with PiTorro. He lunged onto the bed and gripped his skull. The fire of power had faded, but he felt scorched and blistered.

Mercus had flowed through him. Impossible. Unwanted. Excruciating.

His only solace would be sleep. If only he could escape the agony long enough to sleep. Weeping, he covered his face and suffered. After he'd done with PiTorro he'd be free. That was all the hope he had left.

9

VERY UNLADYLIKE

Kila found Quinn in her room, a dusty and drafty shell on the second tier of the tower. The raven-haired woman claimed being farther from Black made it easier for her to sleep.

Quinn was in the center of a room that held nothing but a pallet of ratty old blankets, a small round table, a single chair, and a washbasin with mirror. The windows were open, admitting fresh morning air.

The woman herself stood in the middle, barefoot on the tiles, moving through a series of lunges and spins. They reminded Kila of blade-fighting forms she had once seen Gian do. What Quinn lacked in fluidity and precision, she made up for with power and palpable anger.

The truth was Quinn didn't know any blade-fighting forms. A Shadline she might be, but she had not received more than one night's training from the mysterious Cloak Einlin.

She had answered Kila's knock with a stern "come in." But she'd forced Kila to wait until her made-up form was complete. When she finally turned to face her friend, Quinn's brow pearled with sweat.

Like Kila, she wore black. A loose blouse, tight-fitted trousers. A lovely pendant at her throat. Her hair was a tumble of black that in certain light held a blue tinge. At the moment it was tied back with a leather thong. Her face was pretty, arch, and flushed. A Radiant's daughter, she carried herself with a natural arrogance and refinement at total odds with her simmering ferocity.

"I need you to go to Docktown," Kila said. She handed Quinn her bankdraft. "Her Enlightened said that only a bank on Garden Island would honor this note. I want it all. In coin."

Quinn knew of the note. And she came from a rich family. Neither the note itself nor the amount it represented surprised her at all.

"That will be heavy. Even if I get some of it sheaves." When Kila said nothing, she drew a stray hair from her eyes and plopped onto her pallet. "There was a road once. I wonder how deep under the ash it is."

Kil's Keep stood on a coastal cliff, as far from the central Garden Tower as it could be and still remain on land. But some catastrophe had happened an age ago and the entire landscape was an ash-barrens.

"Get the coin, buy a wagon, a horse, hire a man, do what's needed. I trust your judgment."

Quinn looked away. "I don't."

"You're a Radiant's daughter. I doubt you will steal from me."

"That's not what I meant."

She was talking about Black. The blade that had bonded to

her, but which had a strong will of its own. It had made her take risks she wouldn't have usually done. It provoked her to anger, and she always found herself on the verge of combat with people who merely irritated her. So far, she had not succumbed to its bloodlust, but she had given the blade into Kila's safekeeping until she could master herself.

"And that's not all," Kila said, lowering her voice. She didn't feel one of the Emissaries lurking outside, but all of the Ways had their secret mercus relics. She wouldn't be surprised if one of the women had a queller. "We need a ship."

"We do?" Quinn's lips curled up at the corners. "We do! Where are we going?"

"Starside, to begin with."

"And then?"

"The Hargothe."

"I was hoping you'd say Trist, or someplace even farther away from here. And from Starside."

Maybe someday. But Kila wouldn't let herself think about it. There was a job of work to be done and no point wishing for roasts when the bowl's full of oats.

"Where is he?"

"Ceronhel. That's all I know."

Quinn whistled. A very unladylike thing to do, Kila had learned. From Quinn. Who had admonished her for doing just that whistle during their voyage to the island aboard *Sea-Hound.*

As Kila had hoped, this mission provided Quinn with a new source of energy. The young woman bounded to her feet and patted her hip. That's where Black should have been. She eyed Kila momentarily, speculative hope rising. Kila dashed it with a curt shake of the head.

Kila walked down with Quinn, through the great hall, and out the huge iron-bound entry door. Squinting against the sun, Kila bade her friend good fortune and warned her not to attack the emissary from Til who was even now approaching up the debris-strewn road that lead to the keep.

As Quinn's form diminished, Henley's presence grew. He appeared next to her a few moments later. "Kila, you need to see this."

He wasn't holding anything. He pointed over his shoulder, back into the Keep.

"You see that man approaching," Kila said. "That is the emissary of Til. I must greet him and get him settled before I can have any fun."

Frustration rose and fell within the span of a single breath. Henley nodded. He said, "Let me greet him here. You should receive him in your room. Show him how high above him your station is."

The thought of climbing all those steps again did not appeal to her. Not at all. But she trusted Henley's judgment on things like this. Like Quinn, he had grown up among wealthy people who played wealthy people's games.

She patted his shoulder and nodded a thank you.

"You'd better hurry. It would be awkward if he caught up to you on the stairs."

Nax, I'm going back upstairs.

I'm with Huff. You need to see this.

Show me.

Kila knew to brace herself for the catsight. When her vision switched to Nax's, she didn't even fall over. And the usual sick feeling in her stomach didn't bend her double.

She saw part of Huff, sitting on a stone-tiled floor, tail

wrapped daintily around his front feet. Beyond him an arched corridor ending in a tumble of debris.

I've seen that before.

No. Look.

Nax began to move. Kila had to steady herself against the wall. The more her body tried to resist, the quicker she'd lose her engleberry muffins.

The view approached the wreckage, the angle low to the ground. Kila saw a hole had opened up near the base. A bit of stone had been moved back. Henley's doing, certainly.

Don't go in there!

But telling a cat not to explore a hole was like telling a hound to balance a bit of bacon on its snout. Nax went in. Total darkness.

And then: *Listen!*

The catsight was not just vision. It encompassed all the senses. And Nax's hearing was sharper in some ways than Kila's. From the distance came a rumbling. It resounded all around, as if Nax stood in a vast cavern. The rumble she recognized deep within her body. A waterfall.

Come out, Kila commanded.

Nax was sending skittish feelings through the bond, so she didn't need much encouragement. For now. Soon curiosity would overcome her nervousness and she would probe deeper into the darkness beyond that wall of debris.

This must be what Henley had wanted to show her.

Stay there. I will be down soon.

Step by unwilling step, Kila ascended to the top of Kil's Keep.

10

IF ONE IS VIGILANT

"My father told me the Sagmarsh was impassable," Fallo said as his feet sank into shin-deep water then squished into a layer of mud beneath. "He was right."

Zirhine was scouting ahead, so Fallo was stuck with the Cloak for company. Lop slept in the satchel slung over Fallo's back. At least the cat gave off some heat. Huge snowflakes fell all around. Some had begun to accumulate atop the weird, stinky stalks of the marshlands.

He pulled his foot up, slowly this time. He never wanted to dig in the underwater muck for a boot again. The Cloak didn't seem to have this trouble. Either he had very tight footwear, or he knew some Shadline trick for traversing a marsh. Fallo would ask, but he didn't want another round of having questions thrown back in his face.

"Ol' Ulagatin would be a help right about now," Fallo said. "Fly us out. Or at least burn us a path with a blue belch."

"Ulagatin is not a horse to be used for our needs," the Cloak said.

It was the most the man had said in two hours, and a measure of his irritation with Fallo. Resolving to keep his mouth shut, Fallo trudged forward, cold, wet, and rather irritable with himself.

He should have asked to see a contract before he agreed to speak the Shadline oath. Now that he thought of it, he couldn't remember what he'd sworn to do. Ah well. Quinn had been there, looking at him all pretty and flashing her eyelashes. He'd been swept up in the moment.

They were heading north. Supposedly the shortest way out of the Sagmarsh. The stretches of open water grew larger this way and the mud deeper. Soon they'd need a—

Boat.

It lay among the reeds, fifteen feet long, tapered stern and bow. Two paddles. Beyond it, an ice-crusted expanse of water. Beyond that, barely visible through the thickening snowfall, a rocky bank. It was a river.

Zirhine stood next to the boat, hair dusted with snow. She pointed west. "The Sagmarsh Wash flows that way a hundred miles before turning south. It comes out into the Sorgeal Sea.

"Sorgeal?" Fallo said. "Are we going to Tordain?" That would be lovely. Warmer. Nice wines. Rich food. Olive-skinned women with dark lashes and flowy-clingy dresses.

The Cloak pulled his hood and looked at the boat, the river, the snow, the sky, the reeds, Fallo, Zirhine, his hands. He looked and looked, saying nothing until finally, "I don't feel anything."

"Neither do I," Zirhine said. Both looked troubled.

"I feel it," Fallo said. "It's cold, damp, and getting worse."

The Cloak glared then stomped off, probably to relieve himself. Zirhine bent over the boat and dug in her satchel. "Here."

It was a flask. Fallo uncorked it and gave it a sniff. Trezz. And nice quality. He hadn't had a nip for days. It went down hot and smooth and finished with a pleasant warmth in his belly. Zirhine took it and tipped back for a swallow.

"What we don't feel is the push or pull of destiny. Call it intuition. For a Shadline, such feelings show the way when the path is uncertain. But we have reached a point where such subtle impulses are not speaking to us, either through our inclinations, our instincts, or reason. All pathways are open."

Fallo had surmised much of this insane philosophy already, but hearing it spoken aloud made him laugh. He stifled it quickly. There was nothing to be gained by antagonizing his companions.

"Let's get in the boat and head south," he said.

"Why?"

"Because it's snowing here and it will be warmer in the south."

"Why is warmer desirable?"

"Because I'm freezing?"

"Discomfort is often a lie. Be mistrustful when it seeks to guide your decisions."

Her statement sounded rote. Like doctrine. Which it obviously was. If discomfort had factored into the Cloak's decisions they never would have left Starside.

"By that logic, we should forge directly into discomfort."

She seemed surprised by this. "Cloak Einlin!" she called. He was standing upstream, looking all around as if listening for a secret to be whispered to him on the wind. At her call, he returned.

She repeated Fallo's words. The Cloak, too, looked surprised. And then he did something that made Fallo's gut churn. He smiled.

"My fate's-piece speaks at last," he said. "And with shocking wisdom. North it is!"

Fallo had never seen the man so eager. He and Zirhine were already pushing the boat into the water.

"Get in, lad," the Cloak said, handing him a paddle. "This will warm you a great deal."

It took Fallo a mere second to see they had put the bow against the current. They were to paddle upstream. He set to the task, cursing with each stroke. "Why don't I learn to keep my mouth shut?"

The Cloak snorted. "A question I ask a thousand times a day."

It was Zirhine's boat. She was in charge of who paddled when. She made sure that Fallo had the longest shifts. But she said it was merely for his training and character. Would he like to be cold and lazy, or warm and helpful?

The only advantage of having the center bench was that he didn't have to look at the Cloak, a man he held in especially low regard at the moment.

A few hours into this chore, Zirhine decided to distract him with a lecture: "At the time of the Synod, when the Ways were forming the Triumvirate, a band of seven Donse Masters near Jallisea fled their abbey. Their sect was small, and the new Way of Til would not tolerate their independence, much less their unusual doctrine. As armsmen of the newly formed Triumvirate approached the abbey, the self-proclaimed

Knights of Til fled, taking with them every mercusine weapon from their reliquary vaults. It was the largest such collection in existence, the work of many generations to gather.

"Once the seven had reached safety, they divided the weapons among themselves and dispersed. They abandoned allegiance to the Way of Til, and instead turned their minds and hearts to listening to the subtle pulls and pushes of a greater force than that of the gods."

"The force of destiny," Fallo said. "Doesn't that describe the Way of Pol?"

Zirhine twisted to eye him. "In some ways yes. In others, no. The difference is that we do not ask for guidance by tossing coins. Nor do we involve ourselves in the intrigues of politics."

"Then what do you do? Besides wander the wilderness in search of discomfort?"

The snow had thickened. The air was so full of huge white flakes that Fallo could barely see a boat-length ahead. Soft piles of the stuff had begun to accumulate on the benches, the rails, and in the bottom of the boat.

"We listen," Zirhine said, answering his question. "As you have witnessed."

"That's it?"

"That's enough. Since the Dispersion of the Seven, the Shadline weapons they saved have found their way into the hands of men and women who would become the Shadline Order."

"So I can call myself a knight?"

"No. There are only seven Knights. Pray you learn to hold your tongue before you meet one of them. The question you should have asked is, how did those weapons find their way into these people's hands? The answer is simple. The Knights listened. Day by day—sometimes second by second—they listened and obeyed the subtlest pulls on their intuition.

"And now I feel the call to tell you the story of Erig, a Shadline Knight who was bonded to a massive maul called Shatter. Erig was a huge man, with boulders for shoulders and hams for thighs. It was impossible for him to move quietly, and if someone saw him, they could easily describe him to the Triumvirate armsmen who continued to hunt for the Seven.

"Despite his frightful appearance, due in large part to a ragged scar across his brow, he was a gentle man and supremely sensitive to the tugs and shoves of the force of destiny. For years he eluded notice by listening and obeying. And then one day he became trapped in a horse barn, seventy Triumvirates surrounding the building, all with flickbows and whipaxes and swords. To escape would require him to defeat all these men, a near impossibility even for a man of his strength and skill. But he listened and obeyed."

The Cloak nudged Fallo's back with his oar. Fallo had been so rapt by Zirhine's tale he'd stop paddling. He resumed, still leaning forward to better hear the woman's voice.

"Erig still had several Shadline weapons in his possession. Some had spoken their names to him, others had been more secretive. But as he sat in deep meditation upon the question of escape, one of them drew his attention. Trusting this pull, he retrieved it from his bundle. It spoke, whispering a name to him. Not its own name, but of the man it wanted to find. Royin."

Fallo knew that name. There were all sorts of tales about Royin, a master of the sword and bedroom alike.

"Erig listened and listened, even as the armsmen outside

rattled their blades and chanted their warnings. Even as they set fire to the barn and the horses shrieked and bucked in their stalls. And then certainty came to Erig. He flew to the door, shouting: 'Royin! Royin! A word!'

"Royin, it turned out, was the captain of the Triumvirate guard surrounding him. Seeing that Erig had laid aside his maul, the man trotted his horse forward. Erig simply presented the Shadline sword, hilt first. A universal gesture of surrender.

"The moment the man gripped the hilt, the blade bonded him. A change came over Royin, years of greedy righteousness falling away, as if his eyes had shed a veil and he saw the world anew. He now held Lightstorm, fearless blade.

"Erig smiled and said, 'You have been chosen, Shadline. You must take the oath.'

"The man with changed eyes leaned close to Erig. 'Surrender and I'll see you safely away from these men. And me with you. I know now that I must commit my life to justice for the weak.'

"And so it came to pass that Erig and Royin trotted away from the armsmen's encampment a few nights later, horses laden with supplies. Royin went on to become a Knight."

"A vigilante," Fallo said, approvingly.

"Yes. If one is vigilant, one hears more clearly."

The keel scraped over stones as it softly ran aground. "We must walk from here," the Cloak said. His voice was soft and tense.

Zirhine had gone quiet, too. She drew her curved blade.

"Do you feel that?" the Cloak asked Fallo.

Fallo listened. The river lapped against the shore. The

slightest breeze stirred the snow as it fell onto the scrub climbing the shallow slope. The air tasted of winter.

"Feel it," Zirhine commanded.

He didn't know what he was supposed to feel. The force of destiny had never spoken to him before that he knew of. He closed his eyes, feeling nothing but silliness. This whole journey felt like play-acting at being a Shadline. He'd expected a lot more sneaking in dark alleys, fighting murderers, and discovering whispered secrets. And cozying up to friendly ladies who were impressed by Ol' Rusty.

"Let's wait for him," the Cloak said.

"We may not have a choice," Zirhine answered.

"Feel it," the Cloak said. His voice was a low rumble.

All Fallo could feel was the cold. Drips of sweat from paddling ran down his face, leaving chill traces on his skin. No. There was something else. A pressure to his right, upstream. A presence. Man, beast, or tree, he hadn't the first idea.

Well . . . this is Kil-kissin' creepy, he decided.

He opened his eyes and peered in that direction. The snow was falling too thickly. "There's something that way." He pointed with his dagger, which he didn't remember drawing. This was strange, dreamlike.

The Cloak drew Tosuin, which gave an impressive metallic zing as it came forth. "Yes, Fallo. Zirhine?"

The woman started forward, stalking now. This was more like it. Fallo could sneak with the best of them. He just wished his heart wasn't trying to escape through his throat. Or that he knew what they were hunting.

Zirhine raised a fist. They stopped.

She was testing the air, like Lop would do if there was food to be had. Fallo couldn't smell anything. Not smoke or animal droppings. He closed his eyes again, letting that peculiar feeling of something ahead return. It was a presence. Nothing more. Like being aware of another person coming into a room without hearing them enter. Some people had a good sense of this presence, others didn't. That's why picking pockets worked better in crowds, where people expected that feeling and ignored it.

Zirhine and the Cloak were looking at him.

"Again?" he said. They wanted him to decide what to do next. He had no idea what to do. "Stay here." He crept past Zirhine, working his way over slippery stone, taking care not to step on anything that might give away his presence to whatever lay ahead.

Incredibly, they allowed him to proceed alone. He supposed their intuition was telling them to do that. What a strange pair of atlen-minded goons he'd gotten mixed up with. He wished he could share this adventure with Henley. At least then he'd have someone to laugh with.

The ground sloped up here, rocky and slick with snow. The presence now tugged at him, leading him away from the river. The smelly marshweed didn't grow here, thankfully. Instead, a ramble of last season's berry vines, dead brown stalks arching up and returning to the turf, made his progress just as slow. The thorns caught on his trousers and scraped his chilled skin. The sneaking he'd hoped to accomplish—and impress his Shadline companions with—became impractical. He took to slashing his way forward. His blade might look like junk, but it cut like a razor.

Why was he making this noise, though? If there was someone—or something—ahead, it would be smarter to approach quietly. Fallo realized an eagerness had arisen in him. Part curiosity, part need. Behind him, Zirhine and the Cloak followed, picking their way with much greater care.

The heavy snowfall of huge, fluffy flakes blinded him now. It might as well have been a fog. He could see only a pace ahead. So when the huge granite slab appeared, he had to jerk to a stop to keep from smacking into it. A sheer face of rock like this would be expected in the mountains, but the region north of the Sagmarsh had appeared flat from the other side of the Wash. A boulder this large should have been visible for miles.

He touched it, looking up into the white snowfall. It wasn't a boulder. It was a wall. He switched Ol' Rusty to his left hand and turned north, trailing his right hand along the barrier.

As a caravanner's son, he'd had plenty of opportunity to study fine quality maps. Alas, he had not availed himself of those opportunities. But his tutors had pounded some things into his head, and he thought he would have remembered a major fortification bordering the Sagmarsh. Especially one that could not be seen until you nearly walked into it.

The wall subtly curved as the ground began to slope downward. Here in the lee of the structure the snow fall lessened. The mass of the seamless granite joined to a stonework wall that continued east. Whoever had built it had used the natural thrust of rock as part of the structure, then built more around it.

A parapet marched along the top of the wall, thirty spans up.

"This shouldn't be here," the Cloak said, joining him. He was talking to Zirhine.

She shrugged uncomfortably. "It *isn't* here. I've gone up and down the Sagmarsh Wash dozens of times. I've seen every inch of the shoreline on blue-sky summer days. This could never have escaped my notice."

"There's someone inside," Fallo said. He didn't know how he knew, but he was sure of it.

No trepidation now. He skittered downslope to a flat spot clear of brush. The doors were twenty feet high, banded with iron. One stood slightly open, wide enough for a man to squeeze through. Fallo did so and found himself in a court-yard, paving stones covered in snow. A cold smithy stood to the right, unlit forge, frozen quench barrels, and rusty anvil under a wooden canopy. Opposite that, a stables. Empty.

Straight ahead, stairs to the inner fortification. A railed walkway ran along the inside of the wall. An old man leaned against it, dressed head to toe in armor. A great two-handed sword leaned against the railing next to him.

He beckoned Fallo forward.

The Cloak and Zirhine both cursed. It was the first time Fallo had ever heard such language from his mentor.

"Come, all of you," the man called down to them. "Can you hear it? A culmination approaches." He took hold of his sword and retreated through a door, which he left open behind him.

The trio shared glances, but the Cloak and Zirhine looked to Fallo for what to do next. Shrugging, he headed up. If nothing else, there would be shelter. And he thought he smelled smoke in the air. Fire. Perhaps some tea. And if lucky, warm food.

Food! Lop sent. She squeezed from Fallo's satchel and slipped up the stairs to disappear inside the fortification.

11

BLOODLESS DECAPITATIONS

The stink of Cheapsgate was unpleasant. The slush was unpleasant. The blood was unpleasant.

Odd how a snowfall could cover almost everything but leave the gore unspoiled.

The Shadline woman knelt in the alley, the tail of her fine cloak bundled over one arm to keep it from dragging in the blood. Not quite frozen. Not dry.

Not new.

Odd.

Jil Pokkti had followed the vaguest instincts to come to this place at this moment. And yet she had the distinct feeling she was too late. What she had been called upon to witness had already happened.

She stood and edged away from the blood. Boots had spoiled the mud here, obliterating useful tracks.

She closed her eyes and listened, not only with her ears but with all her instincts. Her hand went to the hilt of her sword, a short blade of unparalleled quality. Perhaps it was older than

Starside itself. She did not need to draw it to feel its power, but merely to grip the hilt.

She did so.

Yes. A merculyn had been here. The scent was faint. And it was off. Not in the way milk might go blinky, but in the way spiced wine tasted when one expected trezz. Unexpected. Momentarily alarming.

A faint, faint whiff of burning hair.

And then she knew.

Demayne.

And that did not fit at all. The other kills in the city had been committed by a demayne. Of that there could be no doubt. Bloodless decapitations were beyond the skill of ordinary men, or merculyns for that matter.

Not a minor demayne either, for they left plenty of blood spatter. No, most of the recent killings had the signature quality of a yoznithan demayne.

Jil climbed to the roof. It was time to return to her room at the Cherry Bottom and see about that bath the proprietor had promised. A bit too eagerly, she thought. But if he attempted to spy in on her nakedness, it would be the last delight his eyes ever beheld.

With a swish of her cloak she was off, running for the sewer outlet the thieves here used.

12

A CULMINATION COMING

K ila propped her door open. The less often she had to claim to be Kil's daughter the better. She put the Shadline weapons in the wardrobe to keep them out of view of the Til's-boy emissary. That lot were jealous of all mercusine relics and she didn't want to create more discord than already existed between her and them.

If she had been able to pick an emissary from Til, she would have asked for Dunne Marlow. He was the only Donse Master she respected, and that was mostly because he'd been expelled from the Way. He'd since been reinstated and brought onto Her Enlightened's small council. But Marlow was in Starside, and unless he learned to dymense, he would not be visiting her here anytime soon.

The approaching mercus spark had a familiar feel to it. She wasn't as good at discerning people by their spark as Pennie or Henley were, but she was certain she'd met this person before.

He appeared at her door, tall, thin, with lank brown hair.

He had a Gristensider's arrogance to him, though he smiled. He had a bulging leather satchel over one shoulder.

"Highest Quiv? I expected an emissary, not the captain of the ship." She didn't bother to stand. If he insisted she was Highest of Kil, then she was his equal. "Have a seat. I've asked Pennie to bring us tea."

"The blind girl?"

"She sees in her own way."

The greeting had not gone as he'd expected. He'd probably hoped to shock her by his presence. But it would take more than a pleasant-faced Donse Master to shock Kila.

He cleared his throat and composed himself before speaking. She liked that quality in a person. Too many people jumped into talking before they knew their own minds. On the other hand, Quiv was a sly fellow and he could speak sideways almost as well as a demayne.

"I have decided to remain here for a while," he said. "As emissary and counselor. To help you structure the Way of Kil and hopefully guide you toward a peaceful place within the Ways of Garden Island."

"Structure? What structure? This tower? It seems to be standing just fine. Maybe a few holes need patching."

"That's not what I meant. I speak of the administration of the Way. Rules, roles, treasury, recruitment."

"No rules. No roles. No treasury. No recruitment. There! All done."

He had the nerve to smile at her. And it wasn't the disdainful sort of smile she expected from a Til's-boy, but a bit of genuine amusement. "If only that were our lot," he said, rubbing his hands on his thighs and sighing. "But the more people who join you here, the less you will be able to tolerate such chaos. If you do not lead them, they will begin forming their own structure: houses or gangs, parties with incompatible views of what the Way of Kil stands for. Better for you to lay it all out first and enforce your policies."

"Did you come here aiming to bore me into the grave? Each thing you just said was duller than the last. I'm not going to do any of that. The only thing I want is to get out of this place and leave this ring on that table." She waggled her pinky to show the garnet ring of the Highest.

This provoked a look of horror. "You mustn't! You are our only hope."

When she looked at him blankly he leaned forward and tapped his finger onto the table. "The Synod of the New Pantheon was formed specifically to exclude the Way of Kil. It was thought at the time that the Ways had purged evil from the world. You and I have the benefit of a thousand years' perspective to see that wasn't the case. Corruption, power-madness, hate. These all persist regardless of the Ways. Because it persists in the people of all realms. My predecessor, Highest Fley, was consumed by a delusion that he could unite the Ways under a single god: Til. But did he pursue it for the good of the realms? No. In the end he sought only his own glorification."

Fley had made both Kila and Dunne Yples force-taps, sucking their power in order to destroy the Ways. Toward the end he viewed himself as a god. Until Kila had figured out how to sever the force-taps, leaving him vulnerable to the Coin. Who happily killed him.

Nax came into the room, surprising Kila.

I didn't expect you, Kila sent.

Huff went in the hole. I got bored waiting for him to come out.

The small gray was followed by Pennie, bearing a tray. The girl walked unerringly, relying on her mercus senses to guide her to the table. Without a word she served tea. Her face was so like a weary housemother's that Kila was both amused and saddened to see it. The girl had known suffering beyond what Kila had experienced at her age.

At her age, Kila had been . . . where? In between times. Born and not yet born, living a vergent's life with Mama Semūin.

Kila touched the girl lightly and thanked her. Pennie said nothing and departed. Nax hopped into Kila's lap. Quiv's eyes moved fractionally, taking note of the new arrival.

"Hate," Kila said to him, latching onto something he'd said. "Aren't hate and jealousy and anger all part of the Despised God's realm? Isn't that why he sent the dragon Qaj'sh to kill Mayla? How can building up the Way of Kil help defeat hate? You saw what Dunne Yples became, a black cloud of hate. *I* nearly became that, too."

Highest Quiv dug in his satchel and pulled out a slim book. It was old, leatherbound, plain. "My service to Highest Fley suited my abilities. It allowed me to spend most of my hours reading and writing in quiet solitude. I had no other duties, and my closeness to him provided certain privileges."

He opened the book, which appeared to be a diary. Pages were filled with neat handwriting in faded ink. The smell of oak gall traced lightly through Kila's awareness thanks to her heightened senses. If ancientness had an odor, this was it.

He gingerly pressed the pages flat. "It is in the language of Cigil-Tine. Are you familiar with it?"

Kila could read Ennish, but nothing else. She doubted Father had known the tongue of the First Race or he would have taught it to her and Wen.

"I found this in a library—" He jerked himself upright and shook his head. "I promised myself I'd be forthright with you. All else depends on trust between us. I found this in *your* library, in the Garden Tower. In Kil's Fifth."

"I told you to stay out of there," she snapped.

"This was long before you came to the island." He paused a moment, nose wrinkling. "I have never slept well, and I took to wandering the Tower, exploring the nooks and crevices, imagining the intrigues of the Synod. Did you know there are secret doorways, allowing access from one Fifth to another? But of course you wouldn't know. You've only just passed through the Tower. I found one such passage when Fley had the crypts dug out of the basement to construct the arena. I was able to conceal the passage before the workmen realized what it was. Just another old tomb, I told them. I waited two months before braving that darkness. And to my delight, I came out in a wondrous library. Many of the books and scrolls were duplicates of the ones in Til's library, but one section was all new. A paradise for me." He tapped the book. "And this was the most important treasure I've found. So far."

Kila liked books. The idea that there was an entire library for her to peruse took her breath away for a moment. But then she remembered she wasn't staying long on Garden Island and that she had to go off in search of the Hargothe. Maybe after that she would come back and pilfer some goodies from the library.

Quiv snapped his fingers, startling her. "Please listen, Highest of Kil. This was written by a First Race queen named

Illizshian. She ruled the city of Cigil-Tine for three hundred years." He pointed to a passage. While the letters were similar to Ennish, the order was different. And many letters sported extra hooks and dangles that Kila didn't recognize. But she could read four names as clear as day: "Ori, Pol, Til, Kil. What's that word after them," she asked, pointing to a long string of letters: *andiolesbrilia.*

Quiv licked his lips. "It translates to 'Who are they?' In this passage, Illizshian wonders to herself who the gods are. She goes on to say that these names cannot be *virinomi,* which translates to 'true names.' I surmise that she does not believe these names refer to individuals. They aren't distinct entities or separate godheads. They are collections of ideas, bundled into words that mortals assigned." He continued reading silently, lips moving as he enunciated the ancient tongue to himself.

Kila had heard the term "true name" before. Flaumishtak had attempted to rat out on his agreement to return Nax by refusing to acknowledge Nax's name. Marlow had said that although you could name a cat what you will, it wouldn't be its true name.

But then she *had* named Nax, that final time. Something more than mercusine had happened in that moment. The bond had returned. But so much had happened since that she'd never asked the cat about it.

Is Nax your true name? she sent.

Yes

Was that always your true name?

No.

What was it before?

I don't remember.

Why didn't you tell me? I would have honored your name and not made one up.

Would you tell me your true name?

You already know it. It's Kila.

No it isn't.

It isn't?

How can it be? It is a name your father gave you; it came from outside of you. That cannot be your true name.

But I named you.

Nax had no response for this other than to roll onto her back and let Kila rub her belly.

What did I do when I named you?

I don't know.

Did it hurt you?

No.

There was a connection between naming Nax and what Quiv had just read. It was as if there was a secondary, deeper realm of language to things. But knowing that didn't help Kila understand what Quiv was up to. "What do you make of it?" she asked.

"What I suspected for most of my life. The gods as we know them are made up. Kil is no more the god of hate and death than I am. There is this idea that Highest Fley was taken with. That the gods we know are four faces of one god. Perhaps the names had specific meanings long ago, but people have overlaid them with their own meanings. Because it is dark and painful and powerful, hate was pulled from love and given into the domain of a god. Kil."

"It's like the Divide," she said absently, stroking Nax's pale belly and marveling at the wickedness of the world. It was deep in a person's nature to assign blame, especially if one could put it from one's own shoulders and onto another's. "A great wall of separation that no one can pass through. One side shrouded in darkness, its people either all dead or permanently imprisoned. The other side is vibrant and alive, noisy and smelly. But free. Most of them, anyway. We see the Divide every day, but we rarely stop to think why it was built. What is over there the First Race so desperately sought to conceal? Or contain?"

The silence stretched a good long while before she became aware of Quiv staring at her. When she noticed, he said, "You claim to be from Cheapsgate. But I've rarely had such an insightful conversation, not even with scholars of the Way. You are not burdened by dogma. It is like a fresh breeze, carrying new air into my lungs."

"I don't trust you, Highest Quiv," she said, annoyed that she'd fallen under his spell. The nerve of this man, showing her something interesting. "And I have no reason to trust the scribbles of a long-dead queen of Cigil-Tine. You brought this to me for a reason. Out with it."

"The demayne who appeared before us that day. He said either you or the Hargothe would bring Kil back to the world. I had thought it a metaphor. But now I think otherwise. I believe the force of destiny wants Kil to rise. A true entity of power. The destruction of your Way a thousand years ago was a disaster. A mistake. Hatred, deceit, war, and all the other evils attributed to Kil did not vanish with his Way. That's because he is not those things. The demayne spoke of him as if he were a person, existing in a demaynic realm like an exiled king in a foreign court, scheming to return. I believe you must be the one that brings him—it—to the world of humankind."

"You just said there weren't separate gods."

"I think we cannot begin to know the nature of the gods. Who's to say one god cannot be several, the way a river can divide and rejoin? Perhaps, too, the essence of what a god is takes on the shape of its container, as does tea in a cup." He tapped his temple. "Perhaps we shape the bowl that holds our gods." He laughed. "Perhaps I'm as mad as Dunne Yples."

Kila followed the man's twisting reasoning rather easily, which surprised her. There was an odd sort of sense in it. And she liked that he admitted to not truly knowing. But it still struck her as odd that he—Highest of Til—desired her to prevail over the Hargothe in an effort to bring Kil into the world.

"The Hargothe is a seer in *your* Way," she said.

"I do not know the Hargothe. My informants have reported disturbing stories. Stories that even troubled Highest Fley. One such report claimed the Hargothe used to drain young merculyns of their power. That does not sound like the behavior of a true adherent to faith. You can call a bear a bunny, but that doesn't make him hop."

Kila laughed at the unexpected humor. "He used both me and Henley in that way. Did you know that?"

Quiv didn't seem surprised. "I am not a faithful man, Kila Sigh. The Way of Til was a path toward scholarship, to satisfy my curiosities about the world. Early on I discovered I was quite skilled in scheming. I found ways to play dangerous games while keeping myself well out of reach. But you have had an effect on me. I find myself quite unable to turn my considerable skills against you because I *see*. There is a culmination coming. I will not retain my post as Highest of Highests long if I attempt to guide you toward the glorification of Til to the exclusion of Kil or the other Ways. I believe the decision of what 'Kil' will mean in this world is at hand. It will be for you or the Hargothe to decide."

"I know you like to read and stay in your study. So this might come as a bit of a surprise to you. But the name 'Kil' is not well regarded in the world," Kila said, growing impatient with the man's speech. "The meaning of that name is as clear as the meaning of 'sword' or 'moon' or 'blood.' As you said. You can call him a bear . . ."

Quiv did not smile. Instead he grew more serious, his brows lowering, his posture squaring. "For anyone else, yes. But for you, no. You have not even begun to explore your true power. An age of ages has not seen a merculyn like you. Dunne Yples only defeated you because you were vulnerable to his influence, not because he outshone you upon the mercusine."

Someone was approaching, running up the winding stairs. Henley, she thought. Coming quickly.

It's Huff, Nax sent. *He has gone . . . far away.*

"You must train with the demayne," Quiv said. "It is clear he has more to show you about the mercus, and more to teach you about Kil. But I must be there, too."

So she had Ori giving her ultimatums on one side and Pol on the other. And here was Til siding with Pol, but demanding the same as Pol, which Emissary Moirina would not like one bit.

Henley burst through the door, stammering about Huff, but he stopped, gasping, when he spotted Highest Quiv.

Kila beckoned him forward. With a strong negation she enclosed him and herself in a space of quiet. "What is it?"

Henley easily sensed her mercus feat, so he let fly. "Huff went through the gap I found in the barrier."

"Nax showed me. She went through. But she came back."

Quiv stood and pressed his hand in the air as if he might feel the bubble of silence Kila had created. He shook his head in amazement.

"Huff went through against my wishes. He was poking around, showing me things through the catsight. Not much to see. Darkness and a bit of a gleam in the distance."

"The waterfall?"

"Perhaps. And then all at once he was far away. Very far way."

"Flaumishtak?"

Henley considered it but shook his head. "Huff would have told me if ol' Smokey-Hair had showed up."

"Would he? The cats love him. If Huff was dymensed, then you should know his direction."

Henley pointed at the floor. "Still below us, right where he should be. But *far* away."

And then Kila knew exactly where Huff was. She dropped the silencing. "Highest Til, you may choose your own quarters. The furnishings are likely not what you're accustomed to. Scavenge what you can from the other rooms. Thank you for your counsel."

And she meant it. As irritating as it was, Quiv had made the most sense of the three emissaries.

"Is something amiss?"

"No. But as you know, the work of a Highest is never done."

The man slipped his book into his satchel and stood. He wanted to ask more questions, and he clearly wanted to know what had upset Henley. Pursing his lips speculatively, he nodded and left the chamber.

"Where is Huff?" Henley said.

"I'm certain that beneath this tower, Huff has discovered a Derslin Wheel."

"A what?"

Kila grinned. "I'll explain on the way."

13

———

LISTEN AND OBEY

The armored old man was waiting for the Shadline trio inside the fortress's main hall. The vaulted ceiling was crossed by thick beams. Below, the chamber held a dozen benches and tables, all save one bare. Stone walls were bare, too, except for oil lanterns. The man stood by a roaring fire. "Welcome to Rethnian."

Lop was at his feet, devouring a roasted chicken leg.

Careful, you'll choke yourself, Fallo sent.

Impossible!

Zirhine and the Cloak came in behind Fallo. There was a moment of silence, then both of them were on one knee, heads bowed, one fist to the floor.

"I'm not your king," the old man said. "Rise and let us enjoy a small repast." He motioned to a table, already set for four. Two roast chickens (one minus a leg) sat on platters, billows of steam rising from them. Bowls of potatoes and some sort of creamed green sat amidst baskets piled over with warm bread.

The smell brought a tear to Fallo's eye. His stomach rumbled. But he didn't need intuition to tell him not to tear into the meal. "So this is a Shadline Knight, then," he said, knowing it was true.

"Indeed," the old man said, smiling. His grin was absent several teeth. And not from rot. He'd lost them from good old fashioned fighting. He eyed Fallo's dagger. "Interesting."

The Cloak didn't seem to have any words to express his emotion. To Fallo, he looked like a man about to sick up his dinner. His face had been pale to begin with; now it was white.

It was Zirhine who found words first. She spoke with reverence. "I have seen depictions of you in the Shadline texts. That armor, the great battle sword, Whelm. It has long been thought lost at sea. You are Linas, First of the Seven."

"And last. They chose me for this duty. Made me and this stronghold a fate's-piece against the day of culmination." He had placed Whelm in a wooden stand. The blade gleamed in the firelight, a garnet in the pommel glowing with its own light. "The Shadline marry their weapons. Isn't that the saying? It does not make for a life of warm nights, nor of much conversation." He chuckled and began to unbuckle his armor. Piece by piece it went onto a stand next to the sword. He was frail, lean, and knobby of knee and elbow underneath.

"You expected us, Shad Linas," the Cloak said.

"Dispense with the title, son. Linas will do. And surely there is a new Seven. No. I am retired from that duty. And soon I shall be from this one."

He shrugged into a thick, blue robe and slippers and went to the table. "Please. Enjoy."

They did. Fallo's companions seemed content to eat in

silence, staring at the legendary Shadline Knight with child-like awe. Fallo shared out bits of his meal to Lop, who sent impatient demands the very second each morsel went down her gullet.

"So you are a thousand years old?" Fallo asked amiably.

If glares alone could strip one's bones, he'd have been a skeleton after receiving such looks from Zirhine and the Cloak. Fallo didn't see why it was impolite to ask. It was obvious. If he was among the original Shadline Knights, he had lived a thousand years.

"One stops thinking in terms of years after a while, lad," Linas said. He didn't eat much, but enjoyed a goblet of wine. "By your reckoning I suppose it has been that long. For me, the rising and falling of the sun moves quickly. This stronghold sits astride the realm of man and demayne, I suppose. I am no merculyn, so I cannot speak to the how of it. My purpose is only to speak to the why of it."

"Good. Why are you still alive and why is this place unsee-able to anyone even though it sticks up like an atlen in a henhouse?" Fallo asked.

More glares. Fallo didn't care. He liked the old man and didn't see the need to treat him like a god.

"From one fate's-piece to another," Linas said, "all I can say is that people did not see Rethnian because it *wasn't* here for quite a while. As I said, I'm no merculyn. But those who concealed this place were great ones. It was heavy work for them, requiring a hundred source-taps, many of whom knew they were going to go dry in the aftermath. We had among us one great seer, a man from Wantin. He saw three futures: one black, one dun, and one bright. The clearest to him was black, and he shivered with seizures from fright of that possible world to come. The other two futures were vague, he claimed. Still possible, but unlikely. The force of destiny seeks its own ends. But which end was it if the black was so clear? Toward the end of his great vision, the man became lucid and calm. Our healers said he was dying and no mercus feat could prevent it. As we stood vigil for him, he looked at me and spoke: 'Three will come. Three and a Beloved One. Outriders of Dem-Kisk-tide. Wait for them here. Speak only to them.'"

"That's us," Fallo said. The false cheer in his voice rang hollow in the chamber. "And what were you to say to us?"

"I don't know. The seer died."

"And so upon those words you and your merculyn friends decided to mask this place from the world and step you outside of time?"

"Yes."

"Our coming here is a fatehand," Zirhine said, awestruck. "Guided moment to moment across the age so that we would come here at the needed time." Eagerly she dug out her roll of paper. "This is my fate's-piece, Linas."

He unrolled it and held it at arm's length, squinting down his nose. "My vision is not so clear these days. But I see this well enough."

"Does it mean anything to you?"

"No."

Fallo barked a laugh and immediately felt bad for it when Zirhine's face collapsed in disappointment. This encounter meant something to her. And to the Cloak. He understood it, but he didn't feel it. He'd never heard Linas's name prior to arriving here.

"What was the purpose of this stronghold?" he asked. "To fight off Triumvirate armsmen?"

"No, no. Rethnian existed long before all that. Part of it is a First Race structure. Nobody knew what purpose it served for them. The realm of the grasslords encompassed this area after the old ones fled. They added this part of the hold. Good, solid masonry. I believe it was a post from which to send patrols into the northern grasslands. They were always watching for nosg migrating out of the Rachtooths. There were likely docks in the Sagmarsh Wash to send fast messengers to Tordain and beyond should they be overwhelmed here. But that is all conjecture. It is a more extensive fortification than you would believe. Most of it is underground."

Fallo continued to eat, digesting the wonderful food along with Linas's information. By and by, even Lop grew too stuffed to eat more. She retreated to the hearth to sleep, so full she lay on her back, legs splayed to make room for her bulging belly.

"Who made this food?" the Cloak asked.

A simple question. An obvious one. Fallo wished he'd thought to ask it prior to eating an army's-worth of the meal. Clearly, Linas, First of the Seven, had not been toiling in the kitchen in anticipation of their arrival.

"There are men and women like you serving here, brought here by the force of destiny. They have kept themselves below-stairs. I believe a man is preparing rooms for you, though I do not expect you'll stay. He tapped the rolled up picture Zirhine had given him. "I have a fate's-piece that may illuminate this. I didn't realize it until just this moment." He picked up a small crystal bell and gave it a shake.

One of Lop's ears turned to listen, but the cat didn't wake up.

Moments later a man bustled in, carrying a tray of sweetbake. "Already, Linas? I had thought you would prefer to digest a while before the next course."

"It's very well, Wez. Serve the sweetbake and then do please fetch the candle."

"Ah. Yes. I will bring it directly."

The sweetbake was a brown, bready cake with a layer of creamy brown frosting atop it. Fallo sneered inwardly. It looked none too appetizing. Out of politeness he tried a small bite. It was delicious. He finished it in less than a minute. "Needs milk," he said, mouth working the last of it down.

Wez departed and returned, this time bearing a candle upon his tray. Linas took it and shooed the man away. He had not touched his sweetbake and Fallo was tempted to ask him if he planned to eat it.

"This is a farlinbright," Linas said, pushing his plates and utensils aside to make room for the candle. The wax was white, flecked with gold. It stood upon a glass dish. The wick was black, and two dried blobs of wax had congealed down the side. "Vergent-craft." He tore a flashtaper and lit the wick. It sputtered and threw tiny sparks before catching. The flame was low and green. Linas's face took on a strange hue in its light.

He watched it a moment, tongue caught in his lips. "I wonder . . ." He unrolled Zirhine's fate's-piece and held it close to the flame. He hummed and mumbled under his breath, turning the paper this way and that.

Zirhine went to look over his shoulder. Curiosity got Fallo onto his feet as well. The Cloak remained where he was, unblinking gaze locked onto the flame.

The slip of paper showed the mountain peak with the notch on the right side. A cluster of stars on the left was clearly the constellation known as the Chalice. On the right, a sliver of moon, the horns facing left. The farlinbright-green shone through the crescent, and caught in dimmer dots all around the empty sky in which it sat. Those would never have been visible without the vergent candle.

The old man pursed his lips a moment as he studied the image. "Given the shape of the moon, it is a waxing crescent. Perhaps a ten-day past new."

"Two tens from full," Zirhine said. "But what do you make of all these little stars around it?"

"Lumne traverses the sky, does she not? These stars must have been just so the day the sketch was made."

Fallo didn't recognize any constellation in them, but he wasn't much of a sky-watcher.

"It shows a place and a time," the Cloak said. "That was obvious from the first moment. But unless someone recognizes the mountain, we are no closer to finding it."

"Patience, son," Linas said. "The farlinbright works slowly. Let's wait until the full picture is revealed."

Fallo scanned the sheet, pressing close over the man's shoulder. This earned him a sharp look, forcing him to back off a bit. The mountain shape, the inverted V, was beginning to glow now, too. Not solidly like the moon, but with traces of lines.

The Chalice constellation also took on a glow, but no new stars or lines showed there. Along the bottom of the sketch, a shape began to appear. A jagged curve. It spread and looped into a letter. It was joined by another, and another. A message wrote itself in a sharp, angular, and inelegant hand.

Mati il waun Kil. Entir il umak.

Zirhine interpreted the tongue of Cigil-Tine, the words of the First Race: "Birthplace of Kil. Tomb of man."

"The farlinbright . . ." Linas paused, obviously astonished at what the flame had revealed. "I had forgotten I had it until just a ten-day ago. I discovered it at the bottom of an old chest. Oh, I've been pulled into more than my share of fatehands, but this . . . this is remarkable!"

There was that word again. Fatehand. Fallo thought he understood it now. More of the Shadline yimmer-yammer. If all these coincidences were fatehands, then he'd surely experienced his share. Surviving his father's scheme to have him murdered, for one. Meeting Jikki and receiving Ol' Rusty. Meeting Kila Sigh. The list went on. The more he thought about it, the less he liked participating in fatehands and— what was the word Zirhine and Linas had used?— culminations.

No. He preferred the ideal presented in a popular trezz round:

A jolly life and a hardy wife
A pack of kids and a hound;
A Tilsday roast with a hearty toast:
"To Til! And save the Crown!"

Funny . . . The phrase on the sketch and the last phrase of the song reminded him of the notecard Her Enlightened Majesty had sent to him. He hadn't looked at it recently. Mostly because he didn't *want* to know if she'd written something there.

Now he was burning to look. But of all his meager possessions, he was careful to keep it secret. Not even the Cloak knew he had it. Kila and Henley knew, but only Kila knew what it was.

Zirhine and Linas were debating the significance of the dire words about Kil's birthplace and men's tombs. Fallo knew enough to know that nothing good could come of such teasing clues. Whoever had made the sketch was as evasive as the Voluptuary in Starside, always talking big and mysterious instead of coming out and talking plain.

He excused himself, citing the demands of his bladder, and left the chamber. Linas had pointed him to the hallway, where Wez stood watch. The man guided Fallo to a needs-closet. Inside Fallo attended to such, then removed the now-battered notecard. The insignia of the Raven-in-Flight was embossed into the thick paper. The gold leaf had flaked away in spots. The corners were blunted from riding in his pocket, the edges marred with black smear from Fallo's hands.

It had shown him two messages so far. Once telling him to find Henley. Once to tell Kila go see Her Enlightened. It was blank now. He was tempted to throw it in the needs-pit, but he couldn't bring himself to do it. In a way he felt indebted to Her Enlightened. He couldn't say why, though. Maybe because she'd let him keep Ol' Rusty.

Had she known what the blade was? How could she have? He returned the card to his pocket and rejoined the so-so-serious silence of three Shadlines gazing into their own thoughts.

Lop was sleeping contentedly, sending a vague sense of warmth and cat-dreams through the bond. Fallo sat next to the animal and stroked her fur.

"It's obviously a map," he said. "The Chalice to the left, the waxing moon to the right. The stars and Lumne move to their own pace, so this exact configuration can only happen occasionally. Maybe once a year. Perhaps once a ten-year. I don't know what the nonsense about Kil and tombs means, but if I accept that this is a fate's-piece and our little meeting a fate-hand, then it's clear we are meant to go to that mountain at that particular time." He scratched his nose and shrugged. "I don't want to go. So there's another sign we must." He laughed humorlessly. "I thought being a Shadline would be all jolly adventure and warm women. So far it's been only long walks and cold nights."

Linas burst out laughing, his face going red. Zirhine joined him, eyes tearing. The Cloak just looked at Fallo. Then he stood and came to sit next to Fallo on the hearth next to Lop. He extended his hand.

Fallo looked at it, confused for a moment. But then he understood. They gripped forearms, the Cloak's hand firm and strong. He kept his gaze pinned to Fallo's. Slowly, the man's lips spread to reveal his wolfish grin.

Linas wiped his eyes, growing serious. "Listen and obey."

"Listen and obey," Zirhine echoed.

The Cloak and Fallo held to each other. One seeing, the other seeking. "Listen and obey," they said together. Fallo felt a warmth spread in his chest, and determination sealed itself there.

"So who can guide us to that place?" he asked Linas.

The old man again held the paper to the farlinbright.

"I have no idea."

14

KILA BLOODY SIGH

The blocked corridor lay deep below Kil's Keep. Old storage rooms and suspiciously grizzly-looking cells lined the hallway. Henley said they were locked. That bothered Kila, but she dreaded unlocking them to discover what—or who—had been mouldering in them for a thousand years.

"It looks intentional," Henley said, kicking at one of the larger rocks blocking the way.

He was right. What at first looked like a collapsed ceiling was an intentional barrier. Each piece had been fitted to minimize gaps.

Nax nosed into the hole Henley had made. Kila snatched her by the scruff. *What is wrong with you?*

Nax had no answer.

Kila put the cat on the floor behind her. "How did you move that stone?"

"It wasn't easy, but I'm getting better at grasping. That one felt loose." He shrugged.

Grasping. A good word. She realized this was the first time she'd ever talked about a mercus feat with him. But he was right; to move an object, one relied on mercus touch—at first.

She relaxed her vision and let her senses come to her, unimpeded by names or concepts. She turned her focus to the barrier and felt the stone. Rough, cold, slightly damp.

With a shove, she pressed on the barrier, pushing it inward.

It didn't budge.

She knew she could blast it down, but in a confined space like this she feared she'd truly collapse the ceiling by mistake. "Can you pull on that one while I push on these others?" She pointed to a rock at the base of the stack.

Henley's bolt formed immediately, resonating with a faint pressure. He didn't need to say anything. She felt when he began to pull.

She pushed.

A great scraping noise tore through the hall. The rocks began to move, and then all at once the wall collapsed forward as Henley's stone jerked toward them. He released his hold on it, but momentum carried it rolling down the hall into the blackness behind them.

Kila laughed in delight and Henley joined her.

I nearly got crushed! Nax sent.

The cat was ahead of her. She hadn't been paying attention during her feat and Nax had slipped through the hole to explore ahead.

Serves you right, fuzz brain. Why couldn't you wait?

Huff's in there seeing things. I want to see it too.

Kila loved Nax, but the cat was worse than she was about unexplored spaces.

Henley had provided the mercus light so far. He now sent the glowing orb ahead of them. "It's a dead end."

Twenty paces on, the corridor ended in a wall. No door.

Kila said, "Follow me."

She marched ahead and walked directly through the wall. A chill passed over her skin as if doused with icy water. Once through she brought her own mercus light into existence. She was exactly where she thought she'd be. In a vast, black chamber.

She waited for Henley. It wasn't long. He sent his sphere of mercus light ahead. His hand poked through, fingers wiggling. Kila grabbed his wrist and yanked.

He stumbled through, gasping.

"The Derslin Wheel in Starside did not have a waterfall," she said once he'd gotten hold of his panic. "But this has exactly the same feel."

Henley was staring in astonishment at the wall he'd just walked through. "How does *that* work?"

Kila didn't know, as usual. "Is Huff close now or not?"

"Yes. He's over there. He pointed deeper into the darkness. The waterfall might be in that direction, too, but the way sound resounded in the chamber, there was no way to be sure. "You've been in one of these Derslins before, huh? Strange."

"You said Huff saw a glimmering. But I don't see anything. Put that light out."

They both extinguished their lights. Henley's vanished in a shower of blue sparks. Completely unnecessary.

"Clever," she said. "Someday you can do skyshows with that trick. You'll be rich."

"I do miss having coin," he admitted. "So now what? Do we just walk around?"

"Yes. You can't get lost. Just walk for fifteen minutes and it arrives. I want to keep the light down until we know nobody else is in here."

They started moving, very slowly. Absolute darkness did not inspire confidence in taking forward steps. Henley cursed quietly, his voice coming from a ways to her left.

"You're already drifting," Kila said. "Come back."

"Maybe you're the one drifting."

Fair enough. But the darkness had her skin thrilling with trepidation. She reached for Henley, found his shoulder. Reassuring. She kept it there as they continued.

"Where's Huff?"

"Ahead. He says there's light where he is."

They continued on, growing a bit more comfortable in their blindness. Kila remembered how she had traversed a Derslin Wheel and had "seen" with her senses. She didn't know exactly how that had worked. Experimenting with it now didn't do much but bring the smell of water to her nose. Very faint. The rumble of the falls didn't seem to get louder as they walked.

"Huff says there is nobody there."

"Where?"

"Wherever he is. He drank some water. I guess he's near the falls."

"Why can't cats ever just speak clearly?"

"They're cats. They think they *are* speaking clearly. They just assume we're too feather-headed to understand them."

Nax was creeping alongside Kila. Nearly getting smushed by the rock wall had made her nervous. Good. The little gray hadn't learned much from past close calls.

A faint glow appeared in the distance. It could be a

hundred paces or a hundred miles away. No way to tell. Kila dropped her hand from Henley's shoulder when she realized she could see a hint of him now, a white ghost hovering close by her side.

Nax darted ahead.

"Huff doesn't smell anyone. I don't think there's anyone here."

"Fine. Do you want to light it up or . . . ?"

Henley formed the bolts and sent a shining ball of light high overhead. Kila noticed interesting nuances in the mercus bolts: the careful negation of heat and how he moved it with nudges of touch.

"If you can sustain that without much effort you can easily learn to mask," she said.

The light cast a huge circle onto the floor, which was plain tile. The light did not reach any walls or ceiling. A vague scent of wet stone came to her, and the slightest touch of an air current.

Nax stalked ahead now, Henley's light casting a crisp shadow beneath her. The glow Kila had seen before lay beyond the range of Henley's light. She nudged him. "Higher. Brighter."

He lent more power to the globe and shot it upward. If they were still beneath Kil's Keep, it would have been level with Kila's room atop the tower. But the Derslin Wheel chambers existed beyond the usual world. Perhaps it occupied a niche within a demaynic realm. But it did not have a ceiling or sky.

Henley stopped walking, brow furrowed as he attempted to force more light into the chamber. The effect was strange as it made the tile beneath their feet more stark, and their shadows blacker.

"That's it," he said, breathing hard. "I can't do more."

Kila considered forming her own light, but she didn't want to outshine Henley. Instead she formed a thread, like she'd seen source-taps providing other merculyns, and again touched Henley's shoulder.

He looked at her, uncertain. "Truly?"

"Go on and use it. It's better than having it swiped from my head like everyone else has done."

With a tilt of his head he smiled and accepted her as source-tap. His face went slack and he nearly fell over. Kila caught him and steadied him. Swallowing hard he bent to the task.

"Til's teeth in a basket!" he said on an out breath. "*So much!*"

The light tripled in brightness, forming a white sun high overhead. The circle of light expanded to encompass the glow ahead. And now the range of the light had no end; it didn't touch anything but the floor. No walls. No ceiling. An infinite expanse.

With a groan he released Kila's power, shoulders sagging. His weight pressed against Kila. He straightened and shook out his hands. "That was . . . terrifying. You have that all the time? How can you endure it?"

Kila didn't know how to answer that. The mercus was like her hands or feet. A part of her that *felt* like part of her. "I'm sorry. I thought it would help."

"No no. Don't apologize. I'm actually rather flattered that you'd let me . . . you know. It's a personal thing."

It was personal. But Henley was her friend. Offering her

power to him hadn't felt like a violation. It had been like offering to help carry a heavy barrel of trezz you may or may not have appropriated from the back of a wagon.

She scoffed and bumped his shoulder with her own. "I s'pose we know each other rather well now. 'Specially after that joining thing." The Cheaps came out in her voice as she tried to add humor to what was suddenly a discomfiting conversation.

His face reddened, freckles disappearing as the flush made his skin match his hair. "That was a desperate moment."

"I'm not angry about it. You saved my life. I'm just saying I trust you." Her words shocked her. She knew she trusted him, but saying it out loud made it more real. More significant. "I don't think I thanked you for that."

She saw she was torturing him. He looked away and rubbed his hair and coughed. "You are welcome, thief girl. Shall we stand in this weird place forever or go see what trouble the cats have found?"

He brought his light down to hover above and ahead of them, the light bright enough to show a twenty-span circle. "Did you know acolytes usually have to train for months to offer themselves as source-tap? You just . . . did it."

"Yes. I tend to do that from time to time."

The circle of pillars came into view rather faster than expected. It was just like the arrangement in Starside, even with the strange patterned tile that made Kila queasy to look upon. Each column had a flat spot inset at eye-level, each with a symbol carved into it.

There was a difference, though. A narrow canal cut through the center of the circle. Nax and Huff crouched at the edge, drinking with dainty laps.

Stop that. It could be poison.

It isn't.

How do you know?

It tastes good and I'm not dead.

Apparently, Henley was having the same conversation with Huff. Neither cat stopped drinking. Kila squatted and let the water filter through her fingers. It was cold and smelled vaguely metallic. Like the good well water near the Yin Inn.

She was thirsty. Shrugging, she cupped a bit of water and sipped it. Cold, refreshing. Perfect. "It think it's safe."

"You know what I think?" Henley said. "I think the force of destiny would shove us onto our backsides if this was going to kill us. It's got too much suffering planned for us to let us die here." He shook his head and bent to drink. "I'm starting to think we're not much wiser than the cats."

"As true as that?"

He froze, just for a second. Meeting her gaze he grinned. "As true as that."

They drank their fill and then inspected the circle of columns. Kila knew from what Dunne Marlow had told her that the symbols on the columns did not stay put. She passed one with a triangle and dot symbol four times. And when she doubled back, none were in the same place as before. It was just the nature of the Wheel.

She stopped before one with three angled strokes. "This is the one I opened in Starside."

On the way down from her chambers she'd explained how the column had opened a mercusine doorway to somewhere else. This one had opened on a sunny beach. A dragon had swooped down and nearly swallowed her.

"What bolts did you use?" he asked, tracing a circle bisected with two lines on another column.

"Why do you even ask questions like that?" she said, laughing. "I don't know. I think I brought it into my mercus vision, like when I see metals. I added to the color or the light somehow."

Henley bit his lower lip and scrunched his brows. "My father had a balladeer come to perform in our greathouse once. Foolin Foolin, he called himself. He mostly sang trezzhall bawdies and good ol' ear-burners. Mother was still alive back then. She tried to send me out of the hall to protect my innocent mind. Father forbade me to leave, saying I was going to hear these things whether or not she liked it. But as the evening wore on, Foolin Foolin grew somber and played all manner of songs on his nickelharpa. Some I had never heard before nor have I heard since, but I can still recall bits of melody. The next morning at breakfast, Father treated him to a table meal with just the family. I asked how he learned all those wondrous songs. And do you know what he said?"

"Ten years of diligent study and practice?"

"Practice, yes. But not study. He said he heard the songs and his fingers always knew what to do. He was a virtuoso. I think you are like Foolin Foolin."

For a moment she thought he was teasing. But when she saw he was serious, she considered it. Maybe that was it. Maybe it was just something she was born to, the way Henley had been born to his ginger hair.

"It does make a sort of sense, considering who my mother is."

"Yes. But do you ever think about what it means to have such talents?"

"What it means? It means everyone thinks I'm Dem-Kisk and I get to be Highest of Kil for some reason."

"Not that. Obviously, the force of destiny moves you. Perhaps it created you. But what I mean is—" He squared off and faced her. "Please look at me."

She hadn't realized she'd turned her eyes away. She met his gaze, astonished by how green his eyes were. How intense. Gone was the terrified street rat who had stolen a sack of cats out from under her.

"What I'm talking about is what your talent is *for*. We agreed to find and kill the Hargothe. And we both have good reason to hate him. But that's not why we must do it. We have to do it to keep him from hurting many more people. I just wonder if you understand that."

"Of course I understand that."

"Do you?" He stepped closer. "Dunne Yples found your weakness. You were lucky that Fley and the others pulled you down. Even more lucky that I was there. But what if we hadn't been? You would still be whatever it was you were becoming. A mercus giant of hatred. And what would have happened to Garden Island? To Gian and Pennie and Quinn? And when you were done with the island, what would you have destroyed next?"

Eyes burning, Kila fought to keep her lips from trembling. How had the fun they'd been having turned into this lecture? This was like something Wen would say. Henley didn't have the right to say any of this.

"I know you, thief girl. You can be kind. You can be generous. You are loyal. I'll never forget how you came to rescue me from the Hargothe. But you are selfish. I feel it in you. You want to escape your responsibility. The responsibility that comes with your extraordinary talents."

"I asked for none of it!" she shouted. The cats twisted their heads to look at her, ears straight up and alert.

Henley did not back from her anger. Instead he stepped closer, until their noses were just inches apart. "Neither did I. I tried to escape, but I got pulled right back in."

"Escape what? Starside?"

"No. You!" The words should have been full of anger, but his brow had softened. "You are a dangerous person to be around, in case you haven't noticed. And it's not just because you are the most powerful merculyn in ages. Ragin and Gian saw it. The Voluptuary forced Ragin to come with me, to separate him from you. He loves you, Kila, absolutely. I tried to stop Gian from leaving. Do you know what he said? 'I can't be so outshined.' But I made a choice to stop fighting your pull, whatever cruel power it is that keeps drawing me into your swirl of chaos."

Kila lost her battle to hold in tears. "Gian said that? He said I outshined him?"

Henley's eyes glistened. "You outshine the sun, Kila Sigh. I think Gian was heartsore to leave. But he's an heir to a realm, and I'm sure he saw his duty could not allow him to be bound to . . . what you are. You were *flying!*" He tried to laugh, but his voice hitched.

Kila did not know Gian was an heir to a realm. She did not know why her power should so frighten him, either. He was a master bladesman who moved with the fluidity of a dancer. Even now she could feel his arms around her. His lips on hers. "We never had a chance. Why couldn't he just *talk* to me?"

"I think that's what he feared most. If he talked to you, or let himself be near you too long, he knew he would forsake his duty. How could he return to Losstra without you? Or with you? You are Highest of Kil. You are either Dem-Kisk or a large part of it. You are not going to Losstra to be subservient to the future king. Nor to any man. Not now. Not ever. This is what I'm saying. You have a great purpose. You are supposed to do something. It's on your shoulders."

She turned away. "What? What am I supposed to do?"

He came to stand next to her, shoulder touching hers. But not presuming to hold her or comfort her with anything but his presence. "I don't know. I—I believe you need to decide that. Maybe it ends with killing the Hargothe, but I don't think so. What will you be afterward? Powerful, intimidating, Highest of Kil, daughter of Semūin. History will not fold you into last year's field rows to be forgotten like an old cornstalk. You're the history-maker of this age."

Kila slumped to the tile. Nax was in her lap instantly, purring and nuzzling her face against Kila's. *Why do you ache?*

I don't ache. I am *ache, Naxie. I hurt all the way through. And I hurt everyone I love.*

You don't hurt me. I hurt with you.

And then Huff was in her lap, too, and her arms were filled with warm softness. Henley sat next to her. And this time he did put an arm around her shoulders.

"All will be well, thief girl."

"How? I don't even know what I'm supposed to do. How can it be well?"

"I don't know. I don't need to. Because I know *you.* Once you decide upon an objective, it is only a question of how crazy the path will be. That's why I urge you to *decide* who and what you are and what your power is for. If you fix that in your mind . . . why, the force of destiny be damned. You're Kila bloody *Sigh*."

A weak giggle escaped her throat, but it wasn't long lived, and she succumbed to another bout of sobs. She leaned into Henley's comforting embrace and cried for a good long while.

And he held her, saying nothing more.

15

PUPPY IN THE PANTRY

The common room of the Yin Inn was beginning to fill when Tym went down to meet Tarek PiTorro. The fire had been allowed to burn down to embers. There were enough people providing their own heat to pull sweat from his brow. He was a man used to the outdoors, the cold. This place felt like a Flyssn hotshed already.

The barkeep Chicky saw him and waved him round the fireplace, the opposite section being reserved for workmen, and a few outsiders. The real business transpired on the other side, where merchantmen with doughy faces imbibed too much beer and argued over contracts. Or so Tym supposed.

He was taken to a large table far from the fire, in a quieter section partially walled off by the entrance to the kitchen. Three serious men sat there, gripping their mugs and wearing the faces of men who made enormous decisions and wanted everyone to know it.

Introductions were made and the barkeep retreated to see to the rest of the evening's custom. Tarek was the oldest of the men, narrow of face and with thatch of black hair that looked like it didn't attach to his scalp underneath. If a strong gust came through, Tym guessed the man's head-pelt would go flying off like a bat from a cave.

"Chicky told me you have a business proposition for me." PiTorro's voice was arrogant but not impolite.

The other men regarded Tym with red-rimmed eyes looking down sallow noses, bored and already certain this intruder would offer no diversion at all. "I have come on behalf of a man you don't know, but have certainly heard of." He had been instructed not to mention the Hargothe in front of anyone other than PiTorro. The alternate name come to his lips: "A man called Tenn. He has close connections to Highest Binel."

PiTorro's companions laughed. One, a fat man wearing a handful of rings on each finger, lifted his mug. "To the man *without* a connection to Highest Binel! If such a creature exists."

His mate barked a laugh and met the toast with a clink of his cup. They downed their liquor. Trezz by the smell of it. But PiTorro didn't join them. Where he had been obviously skeptical of Tym before, he now grew grave. "Excuse us, friends, but this man is expected. I don't believe our discussion will be lengthy. Go stir up trouble at Keel's table for a while."

The effect of his words were instant and dramatic. The men stopped laughing, stood, and swept off as if they'd rather be anywhere else. Apparently when PiTorro was polite, one knew he was on the verge of violence. How Tym knew *that,* he couldn't say. The old man had put all manner of knowledge into his mind. But even so, he didn't fear the man in front of him. Life in the wilderness had taught him what true fear was.

Little burbles of tension like this barely registered. "May I?" he asked, motioning the vacated bench.

PiTorro nodded. Tym took a seat to the man's right and checked all round to make sure nobody was eavesdropping. Satisfied, he started: "The Hargothe lives."

"I never doubted it."

What else could a man in his position say? Tym didn't care if the man was ingenuous or not. "The Hargothe has moved his center of power to the ruins of Ceronhel. The state of the fasthold is deplorable, but not beyond repair. He requires supplies."

"Why not go through the Abbey, or make an appeal to Highest of the Garden?" PiTorro was speaking cautiously, trying not to commit to something he didn't understand. Wise, considering the Hargothe was the other side of the deal. PiTorro continued: "I'd be happy to train the needful things there. I would need time to assemble the caravan and armsmen."

A man couldn't form a caravan without wagons. The Hargothe was not a stupid man. But neither was he patient. And then Tym spoke words he didn't know and his vision receded. The old man took command of his body and mouth. "You always angle for advantage, PiTorro. I think had circumstances been different, we would have been great rivals."

The man stiffened. "I don't know what you think—"

"Be still! You no longer speak to the man Tym. You speak to *me* now."

"Seer Hargothe?" PiTorro's face slackened with sickly fear. He made a slight bow, eyes darting to see if any in the common room saw. It was a difficult position for him. He didn't often offer obeisance to people, let alone in public. "How can you speak through this man?"

"The subtle realm of the mercusine makes many things possible that one without the spark could never understand. But let us put aside the shock of this manner of speaking. I require you to assemble your caravan and begin the trek to Ceronhel within a fortnight. Do you understand?"

"Y—yes, Seer." He licked his lips, desperate to inquire about his favorite topic but clearly fearful of broaching the subject. "There is the matter of cost . . ."

"You will be well remunerated for your efforts. This man will provide to you a catalog of the items, materials, and men I require."

Tym suddenly stood, not of his own volition. "I will return here tomorrow with the list. You will be here at dawn to receive it."

PiTorro stood, coughing in his discomfort. "Yes, Seer."

"Any attempt to harm or waylay my man will be seen as an attack on me. Understood?"

"Understood."

Tym turned from the table and wove through the common room to the stairs. Many eyes followed him. He ascended the stairs until he was out of view. "You will continue to your room and bolt the door," the old man said to Tym through Tym's lips.

So, he couldn't speak directly into Tym's mind when doing this trick. Interesting. Control returned to Tym as he staggered to his room. Once inside the Hargothe said, "Lie down."

He did.

"I cannot continue this for much longer, so attend carefully."

Unable to respond, Tym simply waited.

"You have done well, trapper. I am pleased. You will hire a scribe named Flekk on Sanlin Street. Have Flekk write out the list for PiTorro. When that task is completed . . . you know what needs to be done. Then deliver the papers to PiTorro tomorrow morning. Next, you will explore the taverns in lower Terriside and begin asking after a man named Marlow. He was until recently a regular among the vulgar throngs in that area. Some lowly villain or other will introduce you. Pay what is needed. When you come face to face with Marlow, speak the word and I will attend to the matter."

Without a farewell, the Hargothe released his hold on Tym. He worked his jaw side-to-side and put his hands over his face. "How much longer must I serve you?"

No answer came. Tym knew none would be coming. Besides, he knew the answer. The Hargothe would control him for the rest of his life. The scribe, Flekk, would have to die, he knew. Slamming his fist onto the straw-stuffed bed, he cursed his life.

Suddenly determined, he shot from the bed and stormed down the steps. He burst from the Yin Inn into a day still misty and cold.

The mercus lights atop the Starside Wall were faint glows to the south. The Divide was lost entirely in the gloom. Tym trudged downslope to the Cheaps, then cut south staying close to the ringwall. At the point it met with the Starside wall there was a public stair leading to a whaler-wives' lookout. Anyone could come here and see the entirety of Brinsto Bay spreading out from Starside.

He climbed to the platform, a large paved circle bordered with stone parapets. To his right, a gate. That lead to a tower at the end of the Starside Wall. A man of the Watch stood guard, a whipaxe and sword resting on a stand next to him. He held a flickbow.

Tym went to the water side of the circle and looked down. The fog was total. He could see nothing below him. The reek of Cheapsgate reached him, nearly made him gag. The sound of falling water rose to the right. A canal ran between the Starside Wall and the Divide. At this point it plunged to drop a hundred feet into the Brinsto Bay. Beyond it, the Divide continued into the water and far out to sea. None of this was visible.

Good. Tym pushed himself onto the parapet, cloak fluttering behind him in a soft breeze.

"Hold, sir!" the guard shouted.

Tym glanced back at the man, who was pointing his flickbow at him. Tym laughed. He desperately wanted to say, "Shoot me. Please." But he couldn't.

The guard marched toward him, armor rattling and clanking. "Get down. You'll fall on someone."

"That is exactly what I—I—I—" Tym drew in a final breath and—

Froze. His legs would not move. Heart hammering, he swung his arms forward, desperate to fling himself from the height and bring an end to his misery.

"I said get down."

Tears welled in Tym's eyes. His lip quivered. The Hargothe had foreseen this. Somehow he had planted a refusal into Tym's mind, preventing him from taking his own life. Cruel, vile man!

Tym found he could easily climb down. The guard lowered his flickbow. "Ya don't look too good, man. What's yer name?"

"Tym." He wiped his eyes and forced the sobs down. "I apologize for troubling you."

"You want t' end it, there're simpler ways. An' more polite to those what haffta clean up yer carcass after." He motioned with this flickbow. "Get goin'. If I see ya up here again, I'll double yer misry an there won't be death at th' end of it."

Tym returned to the streets, now wandering aimlessly. The blade on his belt felt heavy, weighted by the blood it had spilled since he'd fallen under the Hargothe's sway. Killing animals did not trouble him. They gave him sustenance and warmth. He tried to make their ends quick. But when the Hargothe used him to kill men and women, he was not always quick.

The slightest resemblance in a passing stranger would change their faces in Tym's mind to that of one of his victims. If a child laughed, Tym saw fear and agony. If a man nodded politely, Tym saw his throat split open and blood pouring out. He never knew why the Hargothe demanded this of him. Did he draw a perverse pleasure from it? Or did he merely enjoy the risk, that Tym might one day be caught for the murders? Another possibility had come to him. At some future day, the Hargothe would come forward to point an accusatory finger at Tym and say, "This man is a murderer," and give name and place for each of his crimes.

He needed to end it. He needed to end himself. But if he could not do it himself, how?

The Hargothe's commands pressed on him, as powerful as the instinct of hunger. Tym found himself navigating his way to Sanlin Street. He asked a few passersby for directions until he found himself at the door of the scribe, Flekk.

A kindly-faced old woman opened the door. She was

plump, smooth skinned. She smiled pleasantly. "How may I help you?"

"I have a list needs scribing. Is Flekk in?"

She brightened. "Oh, I'm Flekk. It's a nickname my husband gave me long ago. Come in."

Tym followed the woman to her study, where a wide scribe-slant stood against one wall. Ink pots lined a shelf above it, and an array of quills lay in little wooden stands next to them. The smell of cooking pervaded the rooms. Soup, Tym thought.

He heard the stomp of small feet and matching voices overhead.

"My grandchildren. Their father is in the city Watch. They know not to disturb me in here. Do you have something you need copied?"

"No. I will tell you what to write. It is a list of items for a caravanner. It is long."

"Proceed."

He began to speak the names of items as diverse as shovels and pick axes to smithy tools and horses. The words tumbled from his lips as easily as the lyrics to "Puppy in the Pantry." Flekk kept up, writing in neat columns, stopping only to dip her quill or to take a knife to sharpen the tip.

Tym paid the list no mind. He could speak and think at the same time. And all his thoughts were on the children upstairs. *Please don't come down. Please don't come down.*

It took an hour, and the woman filled seven pages with the list. Tym paid her two gold skillets, which she refused. She returned one and a silver skillet from her pocket. "If you need anything else scribed, do come."

So now it came to it. "What does your husband do?" he asked as they walked down the short hall to her front door.

"He's dead. It's just me and the girls now. My son comes on Tilsdays to see them."

"What about their mother?"

Flekk paled and sighed. "The sickness, I'm afraid. Two years ago."

Inside, Tym screamed curses at the old man. He would not kill this woman. He would not do that to her or to the—

Two faces peered from the kitchen. Blond heads, bright eyes. Four and five years old, he guessed.

Tears in his eyes, he drew his blade.

None of them would live to see another nameday. Tym only hoped he would soon join them in Lumne's wakeless dream.

16

THIS BEAST'S TUTELAGE

Flaumishtak had not specified the exact time of the training. Kila supposed he would simply arrive when he chose to. Given that she had to trek through the ash-barrens to get here, it was full dark by the time she finally trudged through the gate to Kil's Tower.

Henley followed her in, trailed by all three of her emissaries. A thousand years had left the air inside Kila's Fifth of Garden Tower quiet and cold. Gray light filtered through dust-blocked windows. Green stains tracked down the walls, evidence of leaks in the panes.

Like Kil's Keep along the cliffs at the seaside, the entrance to the main hall was guarded by two huge statues. Kil, naked and brandishing a spear, faced off against a serpent, fangs arcing down from its upper jaw like Losstran sabers.

Water dripped somewhere deeper in the hall. The floor was coated with bird droppings. She eyed the start of another winding stairway. "I suppose I have an apartment at the top. It would make more sense for the lowest ranks to have the highest rooms so I wouldn't have to climb so many Kil-damned stairs."

Emissary Moirina smirked and shook her head, apparently disgusted by Kila's ignorance. Or maybe her cursing. Emissary Sliy's face was drawn, severe. She had accepted Kila's invitation and agreed that Voluptuary Minn need not declare against her if her meeting with the demayne was supervised by representatives of the other Ways.

Emissary Quiv had been eager to attend and confided that he was glad the other two emissaries had come along. Whether he was lying in order to ingratiate himself with Kila, or if he merely wanted to keep an eye on his counterparts, Kila couldn't say. Perhaps it was both.

Nax and Huff were nosing around, sniffing at unseeable things on the floor and creeping between the legs of ancient trestle tables. Both had been impatient to get here. They did not want to miss seeing their demaynic friend.

Kila unlimbered her backpack, which was stuffed with provisions. She began setting out a little dinner for herself. Henley joined her. The Emissaries observed, uncertainly. According to his title as Highest, Quiv had a reasonable expectation to join her. But in his capacity as emissary, his footing was less certain.

Kila waved them all to join her. Soon they were all munching on cold meats, bread, oranges, and tea.

After wiping his lips, Quiv folded his cloth napkin embroidered with the Father God's Hand. "While we are all here, there is a matter of concern to the Way of Til that I would like to discuss. It involves Pol and a number of mercusine relics that have recently come into their possession."

Spin Moirina raised an eyebrow. "You refer to the ones Highest Fley bore with him when he came to murder us?"

Quiv dipped his head. "Yes. Exactly those. I require that they be returned to the Way of Til at the soonest possible moment."

"No. They are small recompense for the lives your order cost us."

"You have no leverage, Quiv," Kila said. "What's the point?"

Moirina laughed despite herself. "Exactly what I was thinking."

Sens Sliy watched the exchange with keen interest. She was like a cat for cheese when it came to anything mercusine.

Quiv pressed: "Considering the devastating losses Til has suffered, the return of our relics would be seen as a gesture of goodwill. A way to assure comity between our orders. I would think Ori would agree. Emissary Sliy, don't you find it concerning that Pol hoards relics in this way?"

Sliy was much younger than the other two, and in Kila's estimation, much less experienced than even herself. But the Voluptuary hadn't had much choice in who to name as emissary. Her own Way had suffered nearly as badly as Til's. Most of the Sensuals and Novitiates had been at Ori's Home when Dunne Yples's had gone on his rampage. Only a handful of them had survived.

"Yes. I do find it concerning," she said. And nothing more.

"I'll leave you three to debate this," Kila said. "I want to have a look around. Henley, come with me."

The emissaries went quiet as Kila and Henley, accompanied by their cats, started up the winding stair. Kila felt a calm weariness in her bones. It had settled on her after she and Henley had left the Derslin Wheel. She had cried herself to numbness. In a way it felt good, clean, like having had a bath. But also sad, like having said goodbye to a friend you knew you wouldn't see in a long time. In this case, the friend was her future.

"Why are we climbing?" Henley asked.

"To get away from those headless atlens down there. Quiv could have demanded those relics back at any time on the walk here. But he waited for that moment. He knew he had no leverage and he knew he had no right to them. He's a clever man, so why did he make that demand?"

"Perhaps he has more leverage than we know."

Kila considered it. Possible.

"Perhaps he wanted to remind you of the relics in Pol's possession."

That was more likely. She sighed. People could talk sideways even when they weren't talking directly to her.

The stairs did not make a circle the way those in Kil's Keep did. These went straight, turned at a landing, then up another flight. Like those in the Keep, they were dusty but sturdy. She guessed they were infused with mercus qualities.

The cats got bored walking up steps, so they jumped onto their people to be carried. Kila and Henley continued up and up, noticing the dark corridors leading into darkness at each landing. They all held the sad silence of once-busy halls gone still.

"What do you think the Way of Kil did?" Kila asked. "Blood sacrifice? Who would join such an order?"

"I was wondering the same thing. What we know of Kil has come through the Triumvirate, mostly from Til. They have no incentive to tell the truth. Maybe the Way of Kil was just like them."

Kila told Henley what she'd seen in the book Quiv had taken from the library here. The four gods' names, written by the First Race queen Illizshian. "They are not our gods at all," she said.

"Foxes and snakes aren't ours either," Henley said. "They just are. Same with the gods, I suppose."

They found the Highest's apartment at the top of the stairs. It looked well-kept, and only slightly dusty. The furnishings were of rich woods, stained dark and polished. A canopied bed, long enough for Annisforl, occupied most of one room. A separate dining area enjoyed magnificent views through a row of glass windows.

"There's another staircase," Henley called. He stood by a door near the entrance. They went up and found themselves on the roof of the Tower. It was pie shaped, bounded by walls demarcating the beginning of other Fifths.

Flaumishtak was waiting for them, Oly in his arms. A fog of mercus haze glowed green around his cloven hooves.

Why didn't you tell me he was up here? she sent to Nax.

You were going the right direction. I thought you knew.

"Greetings, Delicious One," the beast said, making a mocking bow. "Greetings, Champion of Pol."

Kila glanced at Henley. The boy didn't seem surprised by the title. "Truly?" she asked.

"It means as much to me as your title does to you."

Flaumishtak laughed and bent to set Oly gently on the tiles of the rooftop. Nax and Huff crowded forward to receive chin scratches and bits of some disgusting meat he produced from thin air. He straightened. "Kil's Tower! How high you've risen, my dear. Does this vantage make you feel powerful?"

"Not particularly. I'm not supposed to meet you without my chaperones."

"The fools downstairs, eh?" His slash of a mouth twisted into a frown of condolence. "Saddled already with counselors and leeches, are you? Ah, but that is the nature of power. It attracts the vain and the self-righteous like flies to dung."

Henley elbowed her. "I think he just called you dung."

Flaumishtak held up a long, monstrous finger, the black claw glimmering in the moonlight. "Shall we begin?"

He flourished his hand and brought into existence a mercus sphere of blue. Kila recognized it immediately. Dunne Yples had hurled the same sort of formation at her. One had nearly killed Gian.

"You've seen this before?" Flaumishtak asked. He seemed a bit disappointed. "Light and muscle spasms wove through with righteous anger." He hurled it over the ash-barrens and a great blue gout shot up where it impacted. "Now you."

He had told Kila a recipe. The bolts to form the blue sphere. Light was easy. She flared a ball of light into the palm of her hand. Righteous anger was trickier. But why not any old sort of anger? She had plenty to spare. Just picturing her emissaries brought some into her heart. Muscle spasms gave her pause. The higher senses were all emotion, she'd thought. She'd never thought of manifesting bodily sensations. And she'd never had a muscle spasm as far as she remembered.

Henley already had his sphere of anger formed. He hurled his into the ash-barrens where a similar blue gout shot up.

Flaumishtak laughed and patted Henley's back, making the boy stumble forward. "Well done. Well done!" He turned to Kila. "You see? If you have not felt a feeling, how can you recall that feeling? Allow me to help you." His fiery eye narrowed as he pointed a claw at Kila.

Her body erupted with spasms, muscles twitching and convulsing, making her skin crawl with the sensation of a million insects burrowing through her flesh. The feeling stopped. "Now. Try again."

Glaring at the beast she said, "Warn me next time."

She felt the sparks of her emissaries approaching, making the long, arduous climb to the roof. She'd forgotten about them. And now they would all suspect that she'd come up here to meet with Flaumishtak without them.

Bringing the bolts together, she formed a blue mercus sphere over her hands. There was something different in it than what Flaumishtak and Henley had done. She threw it over the ash-barrens.

"Oh no," Henley said, covering his ears.

Flaumishtak laughed.

The sphere struck. But instead of sending up a gout of blue light, an explosion of ash and mud and blue flame shot up. A concussion rumbled through the air moments later.

"You got ahead of your lesson," Flaumishtak said approvingly.

"What did I do?" she said. "It was the same as yours. For the most part."

"No it wasn't," Henley said. "You added something else. I didn't see what it was, but the amount of power you put in . . . I thought this was training, not an ash-barrens excavation."

"What did I put in?"

Instead of answering directly, Flaumishtak asked, "What were you thinking about before you did it?"

"The emissaries." Who were half way up the stairs now.

"What emotion was going through you?"

"Irritation. But it took righteous anger to form the sphere. Why would irritation magnify it so much?"

"It didn't magnify it. It changed it. Perhaps it was more than irritation?"

She turned to face the doorway onto the rooftop. The emissaries would be bursting through in a minute. She didn't want to face their outrage, their manipulations. She didn't want to do any of this. It came back to what she'd felt in the Derslin Wheel with Henley.

"Trapped," she said softly. "I feel trapped."

Flaumishtak chuckled softly. "Ah, fear. Fear has many flavors, some almost sweet, some very bitter. Put it in a corner and it grows into panic."

Kila smirked at him. "I'm not afraid of these people. I'm just sick of them."

"Nevertheless. It was fear you wove into that feat. And if you learn nothing else today, learn this: fear magnifies everything."

Henley came to stand close to Kila. "You want me to stop them from coming out here?"

"No."

The moon was bright, and a luxurious breeze blew over her, caressing her face and head. The cats had moved into a slant of moonshade along the wall bordering the way of Ori's Fifth. Their eyes were sparkling gems as they watched their people work magic.

"You could always fly away," Flaumishtak teased.

She gave a half-hearted laugh. "If only I knew how." Something Flaumishtak had said was worming through her mind. A seemingly unrelated memory popped up. Of her teaching Pennie how to use her anger to start a fire. "If fear is such a mercus magnifier, why don't all merculyns use it? We all use anger instead."

She wasn't looking at Flaumishtak now, her eyes fixed on the silvery horizon out to sea. His hoofs clopped on the rooftop as he paced. "Astute. Very astute. For most of your kind, fear is difficult to form into mercusine bolts. Why? Because one must feel it and wield it at the same time. But fear is the mercus-killer." He jabbed a claw toward the emissaries now emerging from the doorway, their faces drawn with different degrees of upset. "I doubt any of them could manifest a bolt of fear. But you do it without thinking. You could command them with it. They would fall to their knees and tremble if you chose to use your full power."

Spin Moirina reached Kila first, forcing her way between girl and beast. "I told you not to meet with this vile devil alone! Stay back, beast!" She formed a mercusine ward, moving her hands through a series of unnecessary shapes. Kila noted the ward would be effective against a rabbit.

Sens Sliy held back, five paces away, obviously fearful of the demayne. She looked more afraid than angry. Highest Quiv kept his face calm, but he slowed to a stop well out of the demayne's reach. As if the extent of the beast's arms mattered at all should Flaumishtak decide to attack.

"He was waiting here on the roof when Henley and I got here," Kila said, angry at having to defend herself. "Spin Moirina, if you use that tone with me again, I'll send you back to the Coin by way of the ledge over there. You do not tell me what to do. Ever."

Flaumishtak's suggestion squirmed in her heart. She felt

the fear now, understanding intuitively just how to meld sweet smells and sounds into bolts of allure that these people would not likely resist. And if leavened with fear just so . . . "Do you understand me?" she whispered.

All four humans—Henley included—stepped back, hands raised to deflect a blow. Their faces sagged, lips whitening.

Flaumishtak laughed, nodding so vigorously the smokey tendrils of his hair made spirals in the air. "Excellent. Even I felt a bit of that. Next time give it a little more effort and they'll prostrate themselves and beg forgiveness."

Horrified, Kila dropped her bolt. "Henley. I'm sorry. I didn't mean—"

He glared and strode off to join the cats. His hands trembled. Putting his back to the wall, he slid down to sit. Huff immediately climbed into his lap to comfort him.

Quiv and Moirina licked their lips and shared nervous glances. But Sens Sliy held a hand to her heart and gasped as if she couldn't catch her breath. Quiv went to her, steadying her. "Stop, Kila," he said.

"I—I did."

Moirina stiffened, still struggling to master her fear. Her hand was raised and a rise of mercus swarmed around her as she prepared a feat. But for defense or attack?

Sliy's knees gave and Quiv lowered her down. Her face had gone white and she strained to draw in a breath.

"Stop it!" Quiv shouted at Kila. "You've made your point."

"I'm not doing anything!" Kila rushed to the fallen woman. "Why can't she breathe?"

Hooves sent sharp reports into the air. "I believe her heart has failed. You scared her to death."

Death? No. Not death. Kila gathered her mercus and

plunged, searching the young woman's chest. Her mercus vision showed the iron in Sliy's blood. It did not flow. Grasping the woman's heart she sought the flaw, the broken thing that needed fixing. But this wasn't like a wound.

She recalled how she'd saved Nax, by coaxing her to breathe through the bond. Kila slapped a force-bond onto Sliy. Behind her Flaumishtak made approving coos. The others cried out in shock.

Sliy! she sent. *You must live. You must!*

Closing her eyes, Kila sank into the bond, trying to remember just how she had melded her breathing with Nax's.

But it wasn't there. She couldn't find it.

This had worked with Gian. After he'd taken one of Dunne Yples's blue spheres, she'd brought him from the shallows of Lumne's depthless sea.

And then the force-bond unraveled all by itself, a string turning to smoke.

"She's merely meat now," Flaumishtak said. "There is no one there to save."

"NO!" Kila screamed. "I won't allow it!"

But her mercus probes found no mind at all in the girl.

"I *urged* you not to meet with this beast alone!" emissary Moirina hissed. "This was his plan. To have you kill us. All of us."

"You flatter yourself, sweetling," Flaumishtak said to her. "Whether you live or die is of no concern to me. You should consider yourself honored to be among Highest Sigh's first grovelers. And one of only two who survived!"

"Go away, Flaumishtak," Kila said, sickened and horrified by what she'd done. "I didn't mean to hurt her. I didn't mean any of it."

Quiv was putting on a brave face, but even in the brash moonlight his features were awfully pale. He knew it could just as easily have been him lying there lifeless. He looked at Kila with grave respect, but also fear, as if seeing a deadly snake behind glass.

But there *was* no glass. His life depended on her control, her character. The same held true for Henley, and Quinn, and Pennie.

She had turned on them once already, in the depths of her battle with Dunne Yples. She had been so infected with his hate, she had spurned even Nax temporarily.

Giving voice to her thoughts, Moirina said, "Dismiss me if you will, but I will speak plainly. You are a danger to this world. Powerful but weak. Throughout history, that's been worst combination of qualities. A wild thing grown on dangerous streets, you are. What does a thief wearing a crown wish to steal? Nations? Realms? More crowns? Kil's blood runs rich in your veins, girl. Is there any quality of goodness in you? Any at all?"

"Stop it!" Henley shouted. Kila hadn't seen him rise and return to the small group crowding around the dead emissary. "Kila is good. She erred. That's all."

"And how many must die or be shriven with fear by her errors? If she will not accept wise counsel, how will she learn?"

"And what is *your* counsel?" Highest Quiv asked.

The woman stiffened and looked down her nose at him. "That she continue to train under this beast's tutelage, but only while I am present to guide her and protect her from his twisted words."

Henley laughed, an icy sound Kila had never heard from him before. "Had you been here earlier, nothing would be different now. Except that you would have failed at your self-assigned task."

Spin Moirina was winding herself up for a big how-dare-you, but Henley shoved past her and guided Kila away from the body. "I know you didn't mean to do that, but you have to promise me you won't use that power again."

"I promise. I didn't mean to. I—" Kila covered her face. She did not recall ever feeling such shame before. Henley had said she was good, but was she? Did her intentions matter when her mistakes had such terrible effects?

Henley put his hands on her shoulders. Without thinking, she stepped forward and made it an embrace. He held her gently, patting her back. "Remember the Hargothe, Kila. If you ever doubt who you are, remember that you are not him. Not even close. These people are terrified of you. They don't know how to control you. Don't let Moirina's tantrum get into your heart. She seeks to manipulate you as surely as does Flaumishtak."

The boy speaks truth, Flaumishtak sent. His voice was soft in her mind, even soothing. *Except for that last bit. I do not need to manipulate you. The force of destiny will take you to the culmination it needs. My only desire is that you arrive at that moment prepared, so that the Hargothe does not prevail.*

Kila stiffened. She had forgotten that he'd first spoke to her this way. Just as the Hargothe had done. Mistaking her change in posture as an effort to break contact, Henley released her and stepped back. Even with the warm breeze, she felt cold now. But she wasn't about to pull him back to her.

I'll return to you tomorrow, Flaumishtak sent. *Think on what you have learned. And remember to practice.* Oly ran to him and leapt into his arms. He raised a fist and dymensed, leaving a swirl of mercus green to drift away in the wind.

"Excuse me, Emissaries," Kila said stiffly. "I must take Sensual Sliy's body to Ori's Fifth." With a scoop of mercus power, she lifted the young woman's body, taking care to cradle her head so that it would not droop. Kila went to the stairs and carried the woman down. Henley and the cats followed, the other two emissaries trailing after.

17

GOTTEN THE BELT

The procession was quiet save for their footfalls. At the bottom, Kila wound her way to the main courtyard of the Tower and guided the floating woman into Ori's Fifth. There were few remaining here, since most had been killed by Dunne Yples. A young novitiate was posted at the entrance, more greeter than guard.

The girl shrieked at the sight of Sliy's lifeless form drifting unsupported a pace above the ground.

"Take me to Voluptuary Minn," Kila said.

The girl scurried ahead. She made a brave effort to hide her shock, but her shoulders shook with the effort. Sliy had been well-known in the order, and well-respected.

The girl ran ahead and went through a door. In Ori's Fifth the Voluptuary's apartments were sensibly located on the ground floor. Henley caught up to Kila. "What are you going to say?"

"The truth."

The door opened and Voluptuary Harrisan Minn stepped

out. She was about Kila's height, erect, square-framed. Graying hair was bundled into a tidy bun. She did not wear the jeweled headpiece that the Voluptuary in Starside did. Not that she needed it. Though recently raised to her post, her bearing was forceful, her blue eyes demanding respect and attention.

She wrung her hands as her strong face crumpled with sorrow. "Ah me. Dear Lea."

Kila hadn't known Sliy's first name. Seeing the Voluptuary's sadness stoked the shame in her breast.

The Voluptuary stroked Sliy's short, fawn colored hair and folded the limp arms across her chest. "What happened? An accident? I see no injuries."

Kila started to speak and found her throat tight and dry. She tried again. "I killed her. Henley and the other emissaries witnessed it."

The woman spoke a word to the young novitiate who had fetched her. The girl darted away.

"I will hear of it. I invite both emissaries to my study, if they are willing to offer their testimonies."

"I am," Spinster Moirina said.

"As am I," Highest Quiv said. "But perhaps the Coin ought to be summoned."

Strange. Of all those who sought to control her, Quiv was the most reasonable. The most . . . what was the word her father used? Politic. In normal circumstances, Kila would have called it 'sideways talk,' but given the delicate situation she realized Quiv's wisdom. He saw that leaving the Coin out of the conversation when three of the Highests of the Ways were present could be seen as a provocation. Especially when Moirina reported back to her.

Voluptuary Minn nodded curtly, sadly. "Spin Moirina,

would you extend the invitation? I assume the Coin is in the Tower?"

"She is. I will go to her at once provided you agree to hold the conversation until she or I return."

"It is agreed."

Moirina departed. The novitiate girl returned, leading two Sensuals. A fit man of thirty and an elderly woman leaning on a cane. Both already had tears on their cheeks.

The Voluptuary instructed the man to take Sliy away. Kila released the dead woman into his arms and let her mercus go. The elderly woman was already chanting a prayer for the dead, commending Sliy to Ori. The two strode slowly away, the woman's voice lingering as faint echoes in the sorrowful corridor.

"Come," the Voluptuary said. She turned to lead them into her apartment.

Kila hesitated. She recalled an occasion when her Father had done the same, led her to a room she did not want to enter. It was a faint memory with all the color faded from it. An upstairs room Father rented in lower Terriside. Kila had been no more than ten, just recently come to Starside from Semūin's Vale. She had picked a pocket without his permission, without his supervision. It hadn't gone well. She'd been caught. Somehow Father had gotten her back from the Watch. The room was dim, lit by candles. Wen wasn't sick yet.

Father led her to his bedroom. The door shut. A sharp click. As a locksmith, Father's latches were always well-maintained.

She'd gotten the belt. Three sharp cracks on her bottom.

When he was done, Father's eyes glimmered and his lip quivered. The only times he'd ever came close to crying in front of her. Kila's bottom burned. Her vision, blurry with tears she struggled to hold back, made him waver before her eyes.

There were no words. His disappointment and disapproval were spears to her heart. She went out and nothing more was said.

"Kila?" Henley put a soft hand on her back. Highest Quiv was looking at her. Nax and Huff stood at her feet.

Wiping a sleeve across her nose, she blinked wetness from her eyes. She went into Voluptuary Minn's apartment, knowing that there would be no belt. But she wished for it. Wished for a way to atone. Wished she could believe Henley's assurance that she was good.

18

MERELY BY SPILLING IT

It was a fine little house on a well-kept street in mid-Terriside. The mercusine trail had led here. Jil knew the merculyn she tracked was weak. Likely not even awakened to his or her spark.

Before going in she knew she'd find blood. She could smell it from here.

Blood did not disgust her the way it did some men, making them bend over and sick up their meals. While she did not relish the sights and smells of murder, what left her feeling filthy was her ability to imagine the violence. The very thing she both loved and despised.

It was the paradox of the Shadline way. Seek justice to reduce violence. Do violence to deliver justice.

She longed to be done with her task in this city and begin the journey to the Armory. Perhaps she would join Critt Sanglo and go by sea. The massive tavern-keep had not been pleased when she'd told him about the Armory. She doubted he'd hefted his Shadline maul in a ten-year.

Listen and obey.

She went in. The door was not locked. She knew it wouldn't be, for the pull of her instincts had been so hard, so obvious, it was clear she was meant to witness the horror within.

Murder. She could feel murder in her fingertips before she'd come to Sanlin Street.

The story of struggle was obvious from the blood. She picked her way as best she could past the body of Flekk. The first child was on the stairs. The second had made it to her room, had hidden under the bed, which was now overturned.

The killer had covered the children with blankets, but the blood had wicked into the weave and made the covers sag and cling to their small forms.

Appalling.

Jil had killed many bad men and women. She wished she could kill this one. The merculyn who did not know he was a merculyn.

He? Till now that had been an open question. And she could have sworn the blood she'd found in the Cheapsgate alley had spoken of feminine rage.

Not the same killer? No. It wasn't. Interesting.

This was not the work of a demayne. Not related at all to the demayne's killings. But there was still that mercusine connection. She gripped the hilt of her sword. She couldn't be rid of the feeling that this murderer had fed here. Not by consuming the blood, but merely by spilling it.

She'd seen this before. Once. Merculyns far south of Iops in the Shudderlins used a demaynic magic involving sacrifice. Practitioners received power from the killing.

Demayne did too, but only when they consumed the blood. That was the difference.

Jil discovered she was sucking air through her teeth. The small forms of children reminded her of her little brother and sister.

Listen and obey, she reminded herself.

Right now, that instinct was ordering her to leave the house. She did so by a rear door and was over a fence and down a parallel street within a minute.

19

A SIGNIFICANCE

Winter struck a heavy blow, blanketing Linas's hidden Shadline Keep of Rethnian in fluffy white. Fallo marveled at the glistening drifts that hugged the south walls of the courtyard. Starside got snow, but it usually turned to slush by day's end. Occasional storms left more, but nothing like this. Lop insisted on being carried after disappearing into the sea of white, leaving only a furrow trace along the surface to mark her struggles.

There was much less room in Fallo's pack for the cat. Linas had given them all a hefty load of provisions for the ridiculous bit of wandering ahead. Also added to Fallo's burden, warm weather gear. This was very welcome indeed.

Zirhine had not needed it, but the Cloak now had a fur-lined coat under his cloak. They all enjoyed fresh woolen socks and fur caps. Linas had offered a sewn sleeping sack, down-stuffed and lined with summer wool. He claimed it would keep them warm through the chillest night under the stars.

The Cloak had refused them, saying they were already too

weighted down. Fallo expected they would regret that decision. At least he had Lop to snuggle with. He wondered if the Cloak had ever snuggled with anything or anyone in his life. For all he knew the man had been born wearing a black cloak and a permanent scowl.

Linas stood on his balcony, waving down at his departing guests. Zirhine and Fallo waved back. The Cloak was heading for the gate.

The snow came to their knees. The Cloak stopped and looked to Fallo. "Well?"

"Kil be a merry maiden! You want *me* to lead this trezz-ramble?"

"Listen and obey."

But Fallo didn't need to listen. He'd realized that the map sketch held another detail that would be somewhat helpful. But not much more than that.

The Chalice was only upright when it stood over the eastern horizon. As it approached the western horizon, it appeared to be upside down. The sketch showed it to the left of the mountain peak, upright.

The horns of the moon faced the mountain peak. Fallo knew that would narrow the time somewhat. He didn't know if it would help locate the mountain.

But he did know who to ask. "How far are we from Tearling?"

Neither of his companions showed shock or doubt at this question. The Cloak looked into the middle distance, considering. But Zirhine answered first. "A ten day if the weather is with us. We would take my boat down the Sagmarsh Wash to the Sorgeal Sea. Hug the coast south to Tearling."

"Boating through the fen and then open seas in a tippy

bark-raft," Fallo said with false cheer. "Sounds terrible. What more sign do we need?"

Instead of finding humor in his sarcasm, the Cloak merely nodded. Fallo patted the hilt of Ol' Rusty. He had a mind to march into Her Enlightened's bedchamber and demand to know what in Kil's name she meant by saddling him with a Shadline dagger. If it could make him silent like Black, or if the blade would burst into impressive flames like Tosuin, then perhaps he'd overlook some of this discomfort. But Telt hadn't done anything except wrangle him into a cult that prized discomfort above all things.

Zirhine led the way to where they'd pulled her boat ashore. It was mounded over with snow and Fallo was tasked with clearing it. Lop peeped from Fallo's pack and watched him work through squinted eyes.

We're going to sea, Fallo sent.

Fish!

How are you going to catch them?

Lop had no answer for that, but Fallo's stomach rumbled from a strong hunger sending. The Cloak would have to allow Fallo to feed the cat in these conditions, but Lop would surely become accustomed to it and when they got to Tearling, it would be another rude adjustment.

When are we going home? Lop sent.

An unusual question, and an unusual sentiment from the cat.

I don't know. A long time from now. If ever. Survival in the long term seemed doubtful. *Why?*

Startle bonded someone. I'm curious to find out what Startle's name is.

And likely see if Startle's human companion had any bits of food to offer.

"Why are you standing there, Shadline?" the Cloak barked.

Fallo bent to work, scooping heaps of fluffy snow from the boat and thankful for the warm gloves Linas had given him. He hadn't thought of Startle since leaving Starside. The unbonded cat had only occasionally visited the Warren.

Listen and obey. The creed popped into his mind, reminding him to pay attention.

He stopped his work again and turned to look east, toward Starside. He closed his eyes and dropped his thoughts. The air was cold and tasted of steel. The wind numbed his cheeks.

The feeling was like a tingle on the nape of his neck. A hunch. It was like that earlier feeling. Of knowing that something lay ahead of him in the midst of the snow storm. But at the same time it was different.

"Fallo—" the Cloak cut off at a hiss from Zirhine.

"He's listening."

"I see."

Fallo felt them pausing in their tasks, watching him.

Startle had bonded someone. Why now?

One thing was clear to Fallo. Having a bonded cat was rare. Perhaps limited to those of Lop's litter. Kila Sigh was more than a fate's-piece. That was obvious to him. Henley, too. His young friend now a merculyn and studying at the Garden.

So who was this mysterious new person being brought into their circle?

Can you feel anything else about Startle's person?

No. The bonding was loud. But now Startle is quiet.

Fallo continued to listen. The hunch he'd felt was still

there. He thought about Tearling. Yes. There it was. The pull to Tearling was much stronger. The Starside feeling was not a command to come.

"Interesting," he said quietly, opening his eyes and looking to his companions. "Lop just told me something. Her litter-mate has bonded a human in Starside. And it feels . . ."

"Significant," Zirhine said, nodding and coming to pat his arm. "You learn quickly. Think of a Significance as a fate's-piece, but merely as a bit of knowledge. When you meet another Shadline, share it just as you would any other fate's-piece."

"Not everyone is tolerant of cats." There was no way Fallo would divulge Startle's existence to someone who might harm him.

"No Shadline would harm a cat," the Cloak said. "There's no special love there, but it is only the Way of Til who revile cats as doctrine. Now get back to work."

Fallo again bent to his task, but hardly saw the snow before him, his thoughts drifting again to the fuzzy black and white cat in Starside.

Would Kila and Henley have felt it? he asked Lop.

Yes. I felt when Huff left Henley and then came back.

What? Why didn't you tell me about that?

You were asleep and you said never to wake you again unless your shirt was on fire.

Why did Huff part with Henley?

I don't know. But they are again bonded.

Good.

They got the boat into the water. The surface of the Sagmarsh Wash was skimmed with ice from the overnight chill. The boat's narrow prow broke through it easily.

The current was with them, but the Cloak made them paddle anyway. It was easy work compared to going the other way. It occurred to Fallo that neither of his companions had asked why they needed to go to Tearling.

"We must go to the observatory there."

Zirhine turned and nodded.

The Cloak said nothing.

20

THE WAY OF KIL

Nighttime enjoyed a slow death over Garden Island, surrendering in a flaming violet sunrise that painted the interior of Kila's Tower-top apartment. The Highest of Kil enjoyed even larger accommodations here at the Garden Tower than at Kil's Keep. Several rooms had no obvious purpose, but Henley suggested they were likely offices for scribes. That made sense.

A stiff, warm breeze had arisen, bringing the scent of salt air to freshen the staleness inside the ancient chamber. Kila welcomed both the burgeoning daylight and the cleansing air.

The audience with Voluptuary Minn had been brief. It ended with a warning that if Kila chose to meet with the demayne again, she would declare against her. "I will do all in my power to stop you."

The Coin had come, too, tall and boney and serious, wearing one of the mercus relics Highest Quiv had demanded be returned. She scolded the Voluptuary for her closed-mindedness and told of numerous medallion spins landing in support of Kila learning from the demayne.

When Kila had left, Highest Quiv had been reasoning with both women that a culmination was coming regardless of their opinions. Would it not be better to have Kila as an ally than to push her toward darkness through alienation?

And that word now resounded in her mind, like a balladeer's tune one could not shed for a ten-day.

Alienation.

There'd been precious little sleep after that. Just a long period of quietude, she and Henley staring at the fire, the window, their hands. He did what he could to comfort her, providing her tea, and once forcing her to swallow a bit of muffin. She was grateful for his quiet strength.

She had hurt him, she knew. After his kindness in the Derslin Wheel, she had turned her power against him, however unintentionally. He seemed to have forgiven her. She could not.

Henley and Huff sat on the rug before the hearth now. Kila enjoyed having a fire, even though the breaking dawn was warm. She'd created a bolt of heat negation to keep things comfortable.

Nobody was speaking. That suited Kila just fine. Even with her friends near, she felt alone. Nax had only been confused by the situation. *Emissary Sliy died of fright. That means she was weak, no? Rabbits die of fright.*

When have you ever seen a rabbit?

"Someone comes," Henley said softly.

Kila felt for it, but nobody with the spark approached.

Quinn strode in, weary-looking, boots mud-stained, and hair wild from the wind. But she had a satisfied look on her face, and a heavy sack in both hands. She thumped it onto Kila's small dining table. It clanked and chimed with the sound of many, many coins.

"That was interesting," Quinn said of her sojourn to Docktown. "Didn't expect to find you two here. Rather relieved, actually. I could use some sleep."

When Kila didn't immediately tear into the sack, Quinn blew a stray hair from her face and put her hands on her hips. "What happened? Did somebody die?"

Henley groaned and made stop-talking motion with his hands. Kila found herself laughing, slow and sharp convulsions on her abdomen that produced sad little laugh-sniffs through her nose. She felt no humor, only the sting of irony of Quinn's unintentional jab.

"I killed Sensual Sliy. It was an accident." Kila hefted herself to her feet and unfastened the tie on the thick leather coinsack. It was filled with gold. With the money inside, she could set up in Gristenside, have a staff of servants, an atlen barn, carriage, and driver. She would never have to get out of bed, but merely have food brought to her at mealtimes. She could even hire a maid to spoon it into her mouth. "I skipped right over it," she said to herself, thinking of her lifelong goal to become a recovery agent. "Father's dream. Wen's. Mine."

"What are you talking about?" Quinn demanded. "What happened to Sliy?"

Quinn had mistrusted the emissaries from the start, but she had liked Sliy as a person. Or so she'd claimed.

Her hand was on her belt, fingers vaguely forming to grasp a hilt that wasn't there. Catching herself, she dropped her hand to her side.

Henley explained the murder—though he didn't name it

such— while Kila cinched the sack shut and set in on a side-table, unable to be interested in her own riches.

She had killed before. Ashing the thinnies. She'd stabbed an acolyte at the Cathedral of Til. And now Sliy.

Quinn sat and rubbed her palms together between her knees. "I see that diplomacy isn't going to come easy to you."

She was trying to lighten the mood. Kila understood that and was grateful for it. But she couldn't bring herself to smile.

"How do I resign?" she asked. "I can't be Highest of Kil. I don't want to be Highest. Why can't we all just pack up and leave. The Keep will be empty. I won't recruit any acolytes or novitiates or whatever they're called in this cult. We'll just board a ship and never talk about it again."

"The news of your ascension is already spreading," Quinn said. "I spoke to the Governor of Docktown today. It was remarkable how he showed up at the bank just as I was leaving. He requested back-taxes for the past one thousand years. He's lucky I wasn't carrying Black."

"Just because the Docktowners know I'm here doesn't mean the rest of the world has to know."

"Two ships have come and gone already. Both carry the news." Quinn leaned to the side and jabbed fingers into a narrow pocket sewn onto the left hip of her trousers. She pulled out a mangled roll of paper. She handed it to Kila.

It was an etching print. Of Kila. Except this version of Kila was dressed in a long fur-lined cloak. A crown sat atop her head, the tines shaped like spear points. Across the bottom in fancy script it read: BEHOLD! HIGHEST OF KIL! KILA SIGH! THE MERCULYN WHO FLIES!

Peeping from behind Kila's great draping cloak, a small cat's face. It looked nothing like Nax. In fact, it looked more foxlike than catlike. Kila handed the sketch to Henley, who took it near the fire to study.

Kila dismissed it. "A blotchy print on a slip of paper. And not even a good likeness." They had scribbled far too much hair on her head.

"A thousand such have been inked so far. Still more are being prepared as we speak. The governor commissioned it. Your name, face, and title will soon be known in every far-flung realm. Councils and senates, barroom bargainers and harried housemothers, trezz-fiends and harlots—they will all gather and chatter about you. 'Is it war?' 'But with who?' 'Surely the Ways will rally to slay her!' 'I hear she cannot be slain! She flies!'"

Kila leveled a disbelieving stare at her friend. But Quinn pressed on. "And then the ships will begin to arrive at Docktown, spilling forth strange-hearted folk who have risked all to come find you. To throw themselves at your feet and swear allegiance to the Way of Kil. Leave the Keep an empty shell if you wish, but you will return to find it a teeming hive of cast-offs and villains."

"If I don't return, how is it my problem?"

"You are Highest whether you wear the ring, sit in this apartment, or sleep under a pine tree in the Rachtooth foothills. What is done here, whether by your will or despite it, will be done in your name. Like it or not, there is now be a Way of Kil. And you are its Highest."

"I thought you wanted to leave."

"I do. I even found us a ship. It left yesterday." Her sideways smile carried so much irony Kila couldn't help but chuckle.

"You can't leave the place unattended anyway," Henley said. "Who will care for Dunne Yples?"

Who indeed. Kila had kept the man at the Keep to shield him and his power from the other Ways. He was made safe through the *vaz'on*, a mercusine crown that quelled his power and calmed his madness. Kila could not turn him over to one of the Ways without upsetting the other two.

"How fares our hateful friend?" she asked.

Henley had spent the most time with him, aside from Pennie. He had reported him lucid and rather sad.

"He doesn't eat much. He sleeps a lot. He found a flagon of wine the other day and consumed nothing else."

Kila had stayed away from the man since her very existence drove him to such hate-filled rage.

"He will miss Sens Sliy," Henley said. "She was very compassionate, trying to soothe him. A rather impressive thing, considering what he did to . . ." He trailed off. "Oh, I'm sorry, Kila. I didn't mean to—"

She waved his concern away. "So my choice is to stay and rule the riff-raff or go hunt the Hargothe."

"You know my opinion," Henley said. "There is only one thing that matters. I say turn Yples over to the Voluptuary and let Quiv and Coin splutter themselves out."

Hunt the Hargothe. That task felt necessary, even without Flaumishtak's warnings. But she couldn't leave Garden Island unprepared for a flood of Kil followers.

She doubted there'd be anything but chaos if she stayed. Disciplining the alley-urchins who flocked here would be as easy as bringing order to Cheapsgate. What would she have them do? What would she teach them? There was no doctrine for the Way of Kil . . .

She sneered and scratched her head. There had to have been a doctrine before the Way had been demolished.

She remembered the diary of Illizshian that Quiv had showed her.

"The library," she said, standing. "Who wants to find the library?"

21

THE CONSEQUENCE WAS CORPSES

The nosg labor crews were beginning to return, bringing with them timbers and cartloads of stone. They set about making improvements to Ceronhel as best they could. They were not engineers, nor did they possess the wit to even mortar the stacks of stone they called walls.

But with the Hargothe's inducements, they had patched the leaking roof. Fires now burned in several of the hearths. The great puddle in the center of his hall had been sopped up, making the space almost comfortable now.

Save for the smell of the despicable creatures themselves, for whom bathing was thought to make one vulnerable to vergents' spells. The Hargothe had long ago formed bolts to soften their stench. A simple negation. The Staff of Nihil gave him strength to maintain it without effort.

But now he had a problem, and it was not a simple one to solve. Dead nosg. The staff derived enormous reserves of mercus by draining the life from the living. But the consequence was corpses. He thought he could go another ten-day without draining another of the creatures. But their friends were not best pleased by their comrades' involuntary sacrifice.

He could kill any who raised so much as a fore-finger claw toward him, but more killing would make more resentment and on and on. Not even dim candles like these nosg would tolerate his abuses forever. He had more important things to attend to than putting down a nosg-kin insurrection.

Standing by the fire, he leaned on his staff. He felt nearly as strong as the day Kila Sigh had performed her demaynic healing on him.

But he was a bit bored. Speaking to Tarek PiTorro through his force-bonded trapper had been rather enjoyable. And now that the tavern-tart Weese was bound for the Baths, he was impatient to do the same with her. But she would have to speak the word first, else he would waste an enormous amount of the staff's stored power for nothing. And then there would be more bodies to dispose of.

He had been fortunate in discovering that trapper. The man had had the smallest mercus spark. It would never have awakened on its own, but it made all the difference now. Proof that the force of destiny wanted him to proceed.

Noy called into the hall: "Visitor." The servant nosg scraped in, his left leg now quite sore from a recent punishment.

"Show it in." The Hargothe suspected he knew who this nosg was. Knew what it would demand.

He felt it enter. By its shape he thought it wore thick furs and perhaps a headpiece. Yes. Antlers. A clank of metal told of weapons, perhaps scraps of armor. This must be one of the many clan-heads. He hadn't the slightest idea what they called themselves. To him all nosg were vermin.

"Speak," he said.

The voice that drifted to him surprised him. Female. And human. He dropped all numbing of his senses. The stench of nosg was always pervasive in his grand hall. But the new smell was human. Or was it? There was a smokey quality to this person. Not unpleasant.

"I've been looking for you, Seer," she said. Sharp clicks resonated from the stone floor as she approached. An air of aggression wafted to him.

The Hargothe feared nothing. One swipe of his power and she would be prostrate before him. He drew in a breath, sank into the mercusine web. She possessed no spark. Or was she quelled?

"Three days ago, I caught a nosg," she said. "The story the poor creature told was incredible. It spoke of a lone invalid man being nursed to health by a nosg. Here, in haunted Ceronhel. I had to see it with mine own eyes." Her voice was clipped, the consonants harsh. "The Staff of Nihil. I've seen drawings. The library in Lockt is not particularly impressive, but it has its treasures. Especially texts concerning the north."

The Hargothe didn't like her tone. Not at all. If she knew who he was she should be more servile. He sent a bolt toward her mind, determined to rip from her what he wished to know. His attack was deflected by an absolute barrier.

"Now, now, Tenn. That's what you were called on the plantation, was it not? Only a fool would come here unprotected. Do you think I passed so many nosg because they felt kindly toward me?"

He'd been wondering why his guard had been so lax as to

let her pass freely. "Quelled. Which makes you an enemy of the Way of Til, for all such relics are to be remanded to our—"

She touched him. Lightly. On the chest. "I suppose you were handsome once. But you never felt the sensual pull, did you? The mercus is your mistress."

He shoved her away, bringing a bolt of fire to bear. It shot forth and Noy cried out and scurried backward. The woman accepted the flame, let it wash over her like water. It had no effect on her whatsoever.

"Who are you?" he snarled, cutting off his attack.

He felt the shape of her. Stocky. But perhaps that was due to her layer of furs. Tall, perhaps his own height. He sensed her warmth, so close to him. Not much movement in her body. Not tensed to attack with a blade. Not that such would matter; he'd restored his mercusine protections against such a strike long ago.

Her immunity to mercus fire told him little. She might have a relic that provided such protections.

"My name is Yiothizandra. You may call me Yioth when I'm in this form."

The Hargothe drew in a rasping breath and stumbled backward. "Not possible. NOT!"

She laughed. "And yet I am here. I have information for you. From the Garden, where Kila Sigh has recently been raised as Highest of Kil."

"What?" He stammered for another few moments before biting his tongue.

"I believe our interests align. Kila Sigh held a council of the Ways in Kil's Keep. They all accept her and her title. Remarkable girl. The meeting was disrupted by Yoznithan

Flaumishtak, who promised to help her bear Kil into this world."

"The words of that demayne mean nothing. Flaumishtak lusts to consume the girl." And if he did, the Hargothe would harrow the beast with such agony it would surrender its eternities of life to be free of it. "He means to trick her somehow."

"Flaumishtak also said that if Sigh refused, *you* would bear Kil into this world."

"Absurd. I'm a seer in the Way of Til, the Father God. I am the most righteous of the righteous. Kil was defeated and driven from this world and the hearts of men a thousand years ago. Highest Fley would never sit in council with one claiming to be a follower of Kil."

"Fley is dead. Taken by a madness of some sort. He attacked the Coin, who immediately slew him in retribution. A man named Quiv has been named Highest of Highests."

"Who?"

"Your isolation here leaves you vulnerable in a swiftly shifting world. I know you plan to bring a horde of nosg south to capture Starside. You may prevail. But Kil grows restless in his exile. He awaits one with enough power to pull him here. If it were you, perhaps you might sit upon the Raven Throne for ten-thousand years, your reach long enough—your grip firm enough—to grasp the rest of the world and bring every mortal soul to righteousness." Yiothizandra let out a guttural, bawdy guffaw. She patted his arm. Her hand was fiery hot even through his thick robes.

"A culmination comes," she said. "Would you rather Sigh bring Kil into this world and reap his rewards?"

"What difference does it make to you and your . . . kin?"

"Because Kil's nature will be decided by who births him

here. Just as one of my kind's first flight—beneath the sun or the stars—dips a wing toward comity or animosity with man."

"By that reasoning Kil might be good? Nonsense. And what of the Father God? He would never allow such treason against his rule."

"You may not have noticed, holed away as you are in your crypts and haunted ruins, but Til is as feeble as a doddering oldster on his deathbed. The force of destiny moves against him, pulling the Way of Til with it."

Blasphemy. Unbridled blasphemy.

And it tingled the Hargothe's spine with the resonance of truth. "Would you have me change allegiance?"

"Why would that be necessary?" With false shock she went on: "Oh! You don't *truly* believe Til is man-shaped godling bethroned among the stars, do you? Surely you are not so simple-minded."

He knew when he was overmastered by a being with more experience and knowledge than he. Debating theology with Yioth would win him nothing.

Her hands return to his body, this time slithering around his waist. She pressed close to him, nose hovering inches from his cheek. Her breath was hot, scalding. "If you desired to summon Kil, do you know the rites? Do you know the place? Do you know all what's needed?"

"I know nothing of such vile rituals. I'm a man of absolute morality." A heat he'd rarely felt arose in his abdomen, spreading downward.

"Absolute morality? Oh yes. Except for your constant lying and unrepentant killing," she said. She placed her lips on his skin. Searing pain caused him to inhale sharply, but he didn't pull away. "Except for sucking the mercus-marrow from younglings. Except for conspiring with nosg-kin to overthrow my little cousin in her fortress Citadel. You weary me, Tenn." She pulled him closer, hips moving against him. "You are a man. Morality is unnatural to your kind. Til would laugh at your Theb and your doctrine—if he had mind enough to comprehend it."

Stirred by her lascivious tone and the painful heat of her body, the Hargothe struggled to form words. Part of him knew Yioth's allure was unnatural, but not mercusine. It was a magic he could not understand, unique to her kind. He tried to force an image of what she really was into his mind, seeking to douse his arousal. Even before he'd put out his eyes, he'd rarely felt the slightest attraction to women.

"I will show you the way to Kil," she whispered, her breath torching his ear.

He retained the presence of mind to ask, if weakly: "Why do you need me, Yiothizandra?"

"I cannot move freely in this world. Certain things are forbidden to me."

Her mouth pressed to his. Glorious and excruciating fire consumed him.

Outside Ceronhel, in the valley below the stern face of the fortress walls, a deer tracked through the snow, trailed by her yearling fawns. They stamped and scraped their fore-hooves in the snow, seeking bits of green underneath.

A shriek, inhuman and dire, pealed from the old ruin. A second later came a man's cry, of the agony of a long pent desire releasing.

The deer started, then bounded into the trees.

Nosg beneath the sun and those in their deep cavern hives lifted their heads. The sound rang out again and again. A shaman called Poc rattled his skull scepter. In his lurkmire tongue, he pronounced a rare word. Few among his people knew its meaning.

In Ennish it was a ten-skillet word. One Kila's father might have used.

Consummation.

The lurkmire word did not have that word's exact connotations, but it was as close as Ennish could get. But nosg had their seers and oracles and knucklebone readers. They had their oral tradition, passed from generation to generation since the hated First Race had subjugated them and driven them from their crops and lakes.

Men were even worse. But men were powerful. The blind man was the most powerful they'd ever known. And now he'd found his *aggalamas-alamas*.

Mother would soon give birth to Mother.

The age of the nosg was upon them.

Poc stood and rattled his skull. He chanted his chant. *"Aggalamas-alamas! Aggalamas-alamas!"*

Those around him soon joined. From chamber to hall to chamber the chant rose. Runners burst from caves to cross snowbound passes to spread the chant. In a ten-day twenty million nosg would have uttered the chant. Shamans threw knuckles. Grotto-crones spread fern-paste over obsidian and drank wolf blood and mushroom slurry. Visions overtook them and they, too, chanted their insights.

The age of the nosg had returned.

In barren Ceronhel, the Hargothe had shed what remained of his robes. The Donse Master brown lay in shredded scraps. He lay upon the bare stone of the floor, immune to the drafts and damp of the winter-locked north.

Yioth had gone still next to him, her inferno flesh still searing him.

He wished for eyes. To see the glorious abomination to whom he had joined himself. He was no fool. He knew she did not offer him the way to Kil for his benefit. She sought something else. He would discover what it was in time. Til was the Father god. Of that, the Hargothe had no doubt.

But if Kil was to be brought into this world, why should it not be into a prison of the Hargothe's creation? Why settle for the rewards of a god, when godhood itself lay upon the table for the taking?

22

YOU CAN'T MAKE ME

Kil's library lay deep beneath Kil's Fifth of Garden Tower, beyond a stretch of black crypts. The air was musty and silent, and the barrel-vaulted ceilings created weird echoes that doubled their footsteps, making Kila's hackles rise.

"I swear we're being followed," Quinn said. Her final word whispering back twice from the corridor behind them.

Nax had found the needed staircase. Kila had unlocked the great double doors using her father's lockpick kit and a bit of mercus vision. The air inside the library was stale but dry. Their feet kicked up clouds of dust that swirled in Henley's mercus light.

Though the long chamber was dug deep beneath ground level, there was a light present. Kila crept forward, Henley and Quinn trailing. Kila wondered if Quiv had decided to come rummaging through her books despite her demands.

But he wasn't there.

A single candle burned on a reading table, the surface of

which was covered with a thick layer of dust. Quiv hadn't mentioned a candle. But that didn't mean much; he had been absorbed in his theories about the gods at the time.

Perhaps the candle was mercusine. In fact, Kila was certain it was. But why not use mercus lights? She remembered long ago—or so it seemed—sitting in Finta Sahng's tidy kitchen, a strange candle between them.

She bent to inspect the wax. Black as night. The smoke smelled familiar, too. "It's a mercus-black," she said. "Finta had one. It clouds the mercus so those who can feel the spark will not find us here. She said the smoke offered some protection, too. If inhaled."

Tendrils of it began to climb from the wick and wove with eerie intelligence toward Kila and Henley. Henley tried to wave it away, but his motions had no effect.

The smoke burned a bit. Kila felt her mercus fading. Alarmed she backed away from the candle. "Put that thing out!"

Though dulled, she still sensed her power. She reached for it, formed the bolts to make her own light. It wasn't as easy as it should be.

"Can a candle burn for a thousand years?" Quinn asked, blowing it out. The wick sizzled and Kila thought she heard a whispered cry as the last reddish glow faded to ash.

"Can a man live at the top of an abandoned tower for ages, waiting for me to arrive?" Kila countered.

"So many books," Henley said. There were dozens of shelves, each laden down with thick tomes. Along one wall, an enormous rack of narrow cubbies, each holding a scroll.

Kila pulled a tall volume from the nearest shelf. There were hundreds just like it. "Ledgers. Boring." Kila moved on.

Henley called: "The Tavernkeep's Book of Bawdies!"

"Keep that one out!" Quinn said.

The tomes were leatherbound for the most part. Some were attached to their spots by chains, each with a delicate lock. A few had embossed titles on the spines, but most did not. There were no markings on the shelves to indicate why they were placed where they were placed.

Kila moved to another shelf and pulled *Silin-Tine: City of Spice*. Inside, maps. Each a detailed section of a city. The streets and wells were labeled in tidy letters. At the back a fold out sheet showed the entire city and surrounding land. Kila had never heard of Silin-Tine and nothing on the map gave her the first idea where in might have been. Perhaps the name had changed and it was now Jallisea or Tearling.

She put it back and pulled out the one next to it. *A Soul in Search of Satisfaction*. She cracked it open, observed a page full of rather disturbing drawings, then immediately slammed it shut. "Wasn't expecting it to be *that* sort of satisfaction," she murmured.

The book immediately to the right of that one was so heavy Kila needed both hands to drag it free. Hugging it to her chest, she hefted it to a standing table at the end of the aisle. The book thumped down, sending a cloud of dust swirling up. The particulates choked her and she was overtaken by a coughing fit so bad both her friends came running to see if she was dying.

"I'm fine," she croaked, waving a hand at the cloud of dust. "This place needs a hardy scrubbing."

"What'd you find?" Henley asked, peering at the enormous book.

"Who knows? There's no order to any of this."

He opened the book. Kila saw gold and rich reds and blues.

"Beautiful," Quinn said, awed. "Illuminated by monks."

The frontispiece showed a woman with scarlet hair standing in profile. A huge cloak, covered with black feathers hung from her shoulders. There was a sharpness in the depiction, ears, nose, shoulders coming to unnatural points. Kila didn't think it was meant to be an accurate depiction, but a stylized one. It was art, she supposed.

Along the bottom, huge gold leafed letters gave her a name. Kila's skin flashed cold to read it here, so soon after Highest Quiv had mentioned her.

Illizshian. Whose diary Kila had so recently seen. The First Race queen of Cigil-Tine.

Inside, page after illuminated page of Ennish writing. A history.

"That's a keeper, but it's not what I'm looking for," Kila said. She scratched her scalp. The new growth there itched, and the layer of dust that had now settled on her skin made it worse. "I want a book of Kil's doctrine. You would think such would be displayed prominently. Many copies, too."

"One would think," Quinn said, making her posh Gristensider tongue trip over the words to mock Kila's accent.

Kila had been trying to speak more uppity as of late. As much as she'd like to use Cheaps-talk all day, it never seemed to have the effect she desired. Which usually was to irritate someone. "I don't make fun of your sailor-mouth cursing, *Lady* Peline."

"Yes you do. You do that all the time." Quinn wandered to the next aisle, tipping volumes out and scanning them before returning them. Kila knew she was trying to help find the doctrine, but her true aim was to find more Shadline lore.

Henley went to the scroll cubbies. "These are very crumbly. I don't think we should unroll these until we get a Reader to advise us."

"A what?" Kila called. She had picked up where she'd left off. Why wander when every book was Pol's choice?

"A Reader. It's a type of Donse Master who curates libraries. Before I escaped Til's Tower I thought of pursuing that path."

"You'd trust a Donse Master in here? Wouldn't he declare it all Wrong and confiscate it?"

"Not if Highest Quiv tells him not to."

The next book Kila selected was a slim volume, and not very tall. Its cover was wrinkled and stained. It looked like it had been rescued from a flood. The pages had a crinkly quality, though they had been mashed to flatness by virtue of being squeezed among the other books around it.

The frontispiece was blank. The second page was blank. The third page was blank. Every page was blank.

She was about to return it to the shelf when she changed her mind and placed it on top of the one about Illizshian. Maybe she would start a diary.

"Did any Readers survive the collapse of Til's Tower?" she asked.

Nobody knew.

"This could take a handful of ten-days," Kila said. "I want to be to in Starside by then."

"You going to swim?" Quinn asked. The Docktowners weren't expecting another ship for three or four days. Maybe longer.

Frustration was making Kila's nose and scalp itch worse. And something else. A different sort of itch. There was a mercus feat growing above her. Far above. She quieted her mind and felt the mercus sparks in the tower. There were many, mostly concentrated in Pol's Fifth. But the most powerful were at the top of the tower. Together.

"What sort of knot are they weaving?" she said under her breath.

"It's the Voluptuary and Coin," Henley said, looking at the ceiling as if he could see through it. "And I believe Highest Quiv, too."

"Well, since they're all together . . . I'm going back upstairs. I think I know how to arrange things so we can leave."

She scooped up her books and marched out. Nax trailed after her, leaving tiny prints in the dust next to the larger scuffs from the humans' feet. The cat sneezed and snorted then demanded to be carried.

Her companions followed her out, each carrying a few selections of their own.

"How are you going to arrange things?" Quinn said. When Kila didn't answer, she grew imperious. "Kila? Answer me. How are you going to—Kil's teeth! You sure can be stubborn."

Henley's snickers were abruptly silenced. Kila wasn't looking, so she could only guess that Quinn had rewarded him with one of her icy glares. Nobody could freeze someone with their eyes as well as the Lady Peline. Kila had made a study of the technique. It required no mercusine, but merely a trick of the muscles around the eyes. She'd never quite gotten it, probably because she wasn't beautiful like her raven-haired friend. Beauty could be the coldest quality.

Kila could almost feel that very chill striking her back as she climbed toward her apartments. But she was not about to share her plan with Quinn because Quinn would try to talk her out of it.

Once in her apartment, she stuffed her books into her backpack which lay next to the coin bag.

The strong mercus sparks were concentrated close by. Closing her eyes, she sank into the mercusine, allowing her senses to sharpen. She had remembered Highest Quiv's story of a secret passage from the basement of Til's Fifth into Kil's Fifth. He'd also said there were other such passage between the Fifths.

The Tower was round, which meant that all the Fifths shared a central core. But what was in that core? Surely not solid stone.

Kila didn't know how a secret door worked, but she knew it would have hinges. And so with her mercus vision showing her all the metal in her vicinity, she scanned the narrowing where her apartment met with the central core of the Tower.

What she sought could not have shined brighter or been more obvious. Hidden hinges. She went to the section of wall. Stone block. Or so it appeared. But opposite the hinges was a latch, hidden behind the wall. There was no handle, which meant it required mercusine efforts to move. It moved easily at her command. A section of the wall rasped and swung inward. It stopped when the slightest gap had been revealed. Just wide enough for a person to slip through.

Her companions shouted warnings.

Kila squeezed through and shoved the door closed, slamming the latch back into place. Her mercus light was already ablaze.

She was in a perfectly circular room. And it was occupied.

"I thought I sensed some sneaky sparks in here," she said to Highest Quiv, Voluptuary Minn, and Coin Inlina. They were all too composed to betray any caught-pinching-bread dismay, though the feat they'd been cooking up dissolved.

"I told you she'd sniff us out," Highest Quiv said. He plucked a fat disc from the table and held it out to Kila. "This is yours."

Still shamed by Sliy's death, Kila couldn't sustain much snooty disapproval about them meeting behind her back. Voluptuary Minn had her hands folded in her lap, the picture of equanimity. But Kila felt mistrust and dislike as she approached to take the disc.

Each of them had a similar disc, the size of a saucer and thick as a Theb. Heavy, too. It glowed in Kila's mercus vision, reddish with iron.

"Loadstone," she said. A sheathing of gold alloy encased it, one side embossed with a crown, the tines shaped like spear points. Just like the crown she wore in the Docktown etching prints. "The symbol of the Way of Kil?"

Quiv nodded and held his so she could see the insignia. The Father God's Hand. A hand, palm out, with a crown above the center finger. The Voluptuary made no effort to show hers to Kila, but it was face up on the table. The circle atop a staff. Just like atop the belltower of the Baths in Starside. The Coin's showed the two profiles of Pol, smiling and frowning, joined at the back of the head.

"The key to opening this room from your chambers," Quiv

said. "The loadstone is just strong enough to release the latch through the wall."

"And you had mine?"

"It was thought wise to wait until we had time to assess what sort of Highest you would become."

"And how often do you meet here?"

"Rarely," the Coin said. "Highest Fley had nothing but disdain for us. I occasionally met with the previous Voluptuaries."

Kila weighed the loadstone key in her hand. "Any of you could move the latch without this. You have sufficient mercus power. Especially you, Coin Inlina. With all those hellers."

"But not the skill," Quiv said. "You have revealed that our studies have hampered our progress."

Voluptuary Minn said, "She's revealed the dangers of using the demaynic senses."

"I'm not the first who has manifested feelings into mercus bolts," Kila said. Feeling a bit more confident, she went to the empty space at the round table. There was no chair there. Hadn't been one there for a thousand years. She clunked her loadstone key onto the table, claiming her spot. "But such isn't required to move the latch. That feat uses nothing but touch. Why can't you do it?"

It was Quiv she locked onto now. He cleared his throat. "I have made every effort to move objects, since I awakened to the spark when I was just five. I have moved a gold Raven coin twice. Barely."

"Highest Fley accomplished a much greater feat on his way to kill me," the Coin said. "A boulder through the wall separating our Fifths. But he had both you and Yples as force-taps, along with several hellers."

"Brute force," Quiv said, nodding.

They were spending a lot of time on the topic. They were humoring her. Kila realized that *she* had diverted attention from their scheming.

"I'll teach you, the best I can," she said. "But first I have an offer to make to you three."

They said nothing, merely waiting for her to speak.

"Highest Quiv, I request the services of a Reader. One you trust, to catalog and organize my library." Before the other two could object: "The Coin and Voluptuary can assign representatives to observe and assist these efforts, to make sure no volumes go wandering."

"Why?" Quiv said, though his eyes shone with eagerness.

"I wish to find books regarding the true doctrine of the Way of Kil. All we know is what *your* Ways have said."

"So you doubt that the Despised God stood for violence, hatred, and greed?" Voluptuary Minn asked.

"I do. Even the name 'Despised God' has the stink of a brand-burn. A cow doesn't choose its brand does it? No, the cattleman burns its hide to suit his own needs. I knew a boy in Cheapsgate who gave everyone nasty nicknames. Some of them stuck. Stinky Symin. Cryin' Jojo. They became Stinky and Cryin' forever after."

"What did he call you?" the Coin asked. There was a slight smile on her lips. Kila suspected she knew what Kila said was true.

"He called me Chickenlegs. I bent his little finger back until it snapped. After that he called me Kila."

"Is that what you mean to do us? Break our fingers?" Voluptuary Minn seemed set on being obtuse.

"I only wish to understand the truth of Kil. If it can even

be known. Somewhere in that library there must be texts about the doctrine of Kil. I'd settle for learning what the acolytes or devotees were called."

"I can answer that," Quiv said. "They were called votaries. The analog to Donse Master was Spear. I've seen depictions in my studies. They carried spears as staves."

"Lady Quinn Peline believes the Garden will soon be overrun with folk seeking to join the Way of Kil. I wish to be prepared for these votaries. I need doctrine—true doctrine—structure, rules, and activities to keep them from hurting anyone."

Quiv raised an eyebrow. He'd warned her she'd need all those things.

The Coin leered at her. It was a smile, but cold and strange in that woman's hard face. "I told them there was wisdom in that pretty bald skull of hers."

"We were just discussing that very thing," Highest Quiv said. "Weren't we, Voluptuary Minn?"

The woman gave a grudging lift of her shoulder, unwilling to concede anything.

"My next request is to you, Voluptuary. I cannot look after Dunne Yples properly. But since the *vaz'on* would give any merculyn access to his power, I can't imagine Pol and Til would tolerate you having sole stewardship over him." Kila wiped a bit of sweat from her forehead. She was hearing herself talk, but couldn't believe how snobbishly Gristensider she sounded. *Stewardship?* she sent to Nax. *What's happening to me?*

Nax was sitting in the shadows, grooming her feet. *You worry about exceptionally boring things.*

There was no denying the truth of that.

"I propose you three work out a way to keep Yples safe

from each other. Voluptuary Minn has placed wards on the *vaz'on* to prevent anyone but her from accessing its power. But I doubt they are impenetrable."

The head of Ori's way frowned, but she didn't object.

"Yples is like a dead man. He no longer rages, but has slipped into wine-soaked hopelessness."

"He must stand trial for his crimes," the Coin said. "I'm surprised my counterparts have not already demanded it."

Minn sighed. "'Vengeance is not justice is not healing.'" Probably a quote from the Theb.

"I would tend to agree with the Coin," Quiv said. "But . . . I had opportunity to study the man while he was quelled in the Tower. I also saw what he manifested upon the ashbarrens. Dunne Yples wasn't acting as a clear-minded man."

Again, Quiv seemed to agree with something Kila had intuitively understood. How strange to find herself allied with the Way of Til. She needed to be even more wary of the man. He was as sneaky as a demayne. But he raised a recurring thought in Kila's mind. Something had happened to Yples before she ashed the thinnies. Something had gotten into his mind before that. The ashing was like the release lever on a flickbow. Not the cause of his madness, but merely the event that allowed it to overtake him.

She needed to find out what the man had been doing before he'd been assigned to help the thinnies with their mysterious sickness.

"This is all very impressive, Highest Sigh," the Coin said. "But why do I feel like this is all prologue to your true aim?"

"Because it is. I'm leaving the Garden."

Quiv smiled. "I told you. I told you and you didn't believe me."

"Abandoning your role will not relieve you of it," the Coin said. The Voluptuary said nothing. Her bright blue eyes were locked on the middle distance. She had picked up her load-stone disc and was absently spinning it on edge before her.

"And who will rein in these new arrivals? Who will you post to oversee their activities?" The Coin was full of questions. But she knew full-well what Kila was going to say.

"You, of course," Kila said. "With representatives from the two other Ways to assist."

"You expect us to teach your vile doctrine?" the Voluptuary asked. "And where will you be?"

"You don't know if my doctrine is vile or not. I don't expect you to teach them anything but discipline. I also expect you will do all in your power to lure the best candidates to your own Ways. I welcome that, in fact. You have the perfect person for it such a task in Spin Moirina."

Quiv sucked in a sharp breath and nodded. His eyes showed the light of respect. Probably a put-on to trick her.

She went on: "I will learn what Flaumishtak teaches. But I do not expect to stay on Garden Island a moment longer than I must. The first ship that can take me north will have me on it."

"To where?" the Voluptuary asked.

"Starside. Then onward to Ceronhel." She hadn't meant to tell them that much. But proving she had a plan—as much of one as she could ever have—seemed important. "I am going to find the Hargothe."

It was the Voluptuary who laughed now. A sad and ironic little laugh through her nose. "I must admit, Highest Quiv, you have better insight into her mind than I do." She turned her bright eyes to Kila finally. There was sadness there. And a searing intensity. "You should face a tribunal of the Ways for the murder of Sensual Sliy."

A tribunal. To be judged for her actions. "What punishment would they dole out?"

Highest Quiv leaned toward the Voluptuary. "I was there. I suffered the same assault. As terrible as it was, it was not intentional. Is a punishment warranted? Yes. But you said yourself that vengeance isn't justice isn't healing."

"I don't seek anything but the last bit. Healing. If found guilty, her penance would be to refrain from using her power for anything *but* healing. For the rest of her life."

"Unenforceable," the Coin said dismissively.

If only it were possible. Kila said, "When I return. I'll allow the tribunal."

Quiv made slow-down motions with his hands and shook his head.

The Voluptuary nodded, not with appreciation, but with solemn acceptance of Kila's promise. "Will you promise-bind your vow? That would give me the assurance I need."

Beware, Nax said.

Of what?

I don't know. Be wary.

A flutter of nervousness came across the bond. Cats could be skittish, sometimes for no obvious reason. Kila trusted Nax's instincts. *Is it this promise-binding nonsense? I'll keep my promise anyway.*

Nax's response was a mix of emotional grousing and nervousness. She thought this was a trap. Maybe the whole meeting was an elaborate trick to get her to agree to the promise-binding.

I think you're right, Naxie.

She was a Cheapsgate girl. She'd seen every con there was. These people had their own aims. Controlling her through some mercus-locked vow would serve them more than it would Kila.

They were all looking at her, waiting for her answer. Kila gave it: "Nax thinks you're trying to trick me into the promise-binding. Her instincts are sharp. So the answer is no. I won't submit to whatever mercus manacles such a vow would place on me. You'll have to accept my word."

"I do not accept it," the Voluptuary said.

Kila reconsidered the Voluptuary. When they'd first met, she'd felt Minn would be the most cooperative. The most reasonable. The opposite had turned out to be true. But why? It wasn't just Sliy's death. Sensual Sliy had come just that morning to make ultimatums about Kila and Flaumishtak.

It had to be Kila's use of the so-called "demaynic senses." Emotion and interior feelings. Perhaps the woman knew much more about such practices than she let on. Perhaps she had seen hints of the power Kila had not yet tapped.

"The girl must go," the Coin pronounced. "I have spun on it. Highest Quiv agrees. Even *she* saw to the heart of what must be done. Relinquish your personal grudge, Voluptuary."

Quiv spoke next. "Think of your own view, Voluptuary, if you were in her place. Would you allow yourself to be commanded?"

The Voluptuary didn't answer. But in the silence was an admission that Quiv was correct. She was a strong person, not accustomed to obeying others.

"How does this council work?" Kila asked. "Do we need to be unanimous? Does it matter? I'm going regardless."

The Coin sneered at her. "You place burdens on us to

curate your library, be nursemaid to your madman, and orga-nize your Way while you are absent. Show a modicum of patience."

Kila backed from the table and joined Nax. She sat on the floor and took the cat into her lap. The three at the table conferred in whispers, but Kila heard nothing. Apparently Highest Quiv had learned her bubble of silence trick.

The Voluptuary became very animated, jabbing her fingers first at the Coin, then Quiv, then herself. She thumped the table with her fist and cut off the Coin when she tried to inter-rupt. Highest Quiv nodded vigorously, agreeing that the woman's view was valid but also showing that he thought it beside the point.

The Coin removed her medallion and offered it to the Voluptuary who refused to take it. Highest Quiv rubbed his temples.

Kila watched this silent drama unfold with equal parts impatience and amusement. Did they truly think they had a decision to make? She *was* leaving, even if she had to take Yples with her.

Be wary, Nax sent.

I'm not going to let them promise-bind me.

She felt a flare of mercus from behind the door leading to her apartments. Henley. The latch moved, ever so slowly. The door swung open. Henley's shadowy shape peered in. Quinn pressed close behind him. Huff burst in.

We must go! Nax sent.

Why? What's—

"Kila, hurry!" Henley said, waving to her.

The trio at the table noticed. The silence bubble dropped.

"Wait, Kila Sigh!" Highest Quiv called.

The Voluptuary smiled with grim satisfaction. The Coin grinned at the Voluptuary.

Hurry! Nax sent, pushing so much urgency through the bond that Kila leapt to her feet and began stumbling toward her friends.

Quinn had turned. She had Black in her hand, dug from Kila's backpack. Her mouth moved, but no sound came out.

An enormous mercus feat was forming beyond them. The only merculyn on Garden Island with that much power was Dunne Yples.

Kila squeezed through the opening.

"Kila! Don't go that way!" Quiv called.

The cats darted through and Henley pulled the door closed. "You ready to fight?"

"Is it Yples?"

"Yes and no. I can feel his flavor here, but his power is being controlled by someone else."

The *vaz'on*. She should never have left the man alone with Pennie at Kil's Keep. But with the *vaz'on* warded by the Voluptuary she hadn't feared anyone would—

The Voluptuary.

She'd know Kila was here in Garden Tower. She must have sent someone east to the Keep with instructions for disabling the ward, giving them access to Yples's power. Her act in the secret chamber had only one purpose: to stall Kila until Yples's power could be brought to bear.

Henley cursed. "There are several source-tap circles forming. I think all the surviving Sensuals and Novitiates. They've blocked the stairwell down from here."

Trapped. Unless she wanted to fight. She sank into the mercusine, feeling for the threat. Three merculyns approached, all aflame with power. They would be no match for her. But she didn't want to hurt anyone.

"Quinn, put that blade down."

Her friend's head jerked around in surprised. She began to mouth an objection.

"I did not return it to you. Put it down. Right now." Kila was tempted to enforce her words with mercusine commands, but she would never resort to that again. Not against a friend.

Quinn held the sheath in her left hand. She looked at, swallowing hard. Slowly she thrust the blade home and dropped it.

Kila pulled it to her with mercus bolts.

"What do we do?" Henley asked.

The secret door swung open behind them. Highest Quiv stuck his head in. "This way. Through Pol's Fifth!"

The merculyns were nearly to the top floor. Kila's door here was not protected by her pass phrase. With the power they were wielding, the door would blow off its hinges.

Nax's warning returned to her. *Next time be more specific,* she sent to her little gray friend.

"Follow me," she said. With quick mercusine feats she reached for her backpack, the flap lay open from Quinn's theft of Black. Cayne was already on her thigh. Bone Chill was tucked in the pack. She slipped Black in. The sack of coin flew to her next. She caught it and stumbled backward into Highest Quiv. The thing was heavy! It went into her pack next to her books, and the pack went onto her shoulders.

She squeezed into the secret chamber. The Coin and the Voluptuary were staring at each other, both surrounded by mercus power. Only Highest Quiv had restrained himself from grasping it.

Quiv pointed across the circular chamber. Kila's mercus vision flared, showing her the latch that would open the door to the Coin's chambers.

"There are merculyns there," Henley warned.

Kila stopped, realizing the trap. Three more source-tap circles had formed in Pol's Fifth. The Coin had thrown in with the Voluptuary to secure the trap.

Henley got it a second later. A strange ward popped over him. Kila couldn't spare the attention to see what he'd done.

Tendrils of mercus lashed toward them both, from all sides. The Coin accepted source-taps from her quarters. The Voluptuary accepted the combined power of her people, save the one controlling Dunne Yples's mercus.

Mind probing fingers struck at Kila's mind. She sliced them away. Highest Quiv shouted for the women to stop. Was he true or was he play-acting?

It was the same strategy that had brought Kila down over the ash-barrens. She could deflect any one of the intrusions easily, but when there were five, ten, thirty, they began to take hold, worming their way toward the center of her power, seeking to quell her.

"Submit!" the Voluptuary shouted. "Submit, child!"

The answer to Kila's problem was simple. Cayne came free of the sheath on mercusine wings. It would take two slashes and the Coin and Voluptuary would die. Their power would dissipate and the backlash would render their source-taps dazed and confused for an hour.

And Kila would be the Highest of Kil who slew her counterparts. And how many more would she have to slay? All of them?

"No," she said, sheathing Cayne. "I won't kill you. You can't make me."

Five hooks had caught in her mind, sapping her focus. One of them was a strong allure mixed with emotion. The same thing she'd done to Sens Sliy. A strong component of fear. Kila noted that came from Voluptuary Minn.

"Submit!" the woman cried. "Be promise-bound and you may live."

"No."

Henley held onto Kila. She realized she was trembling and would have fallen if not for his support. Quinn stared from one person to the next, oblivious to the mercus battle going on all around her.

A merculyn came through Kila's door. A Sensual Kila had never met. He was lean with a long nose. His teeth were gritted and his neck corded with his efforts to maintain control over Yples's flows. He held a glowing orange gem in one hand. Kila recognized it as a Sink Gem, the same that Highest Fley had used to drain excess mercusine and protect himself from total annihilation.

He struck with waves of chill and heat. Then the air was gone and every breath Kila drew did nothing to fill her lungs. Black spots appeared in her vision. The room began to tilt.

"Submit! Submit!" the Voluptuary cried.

Desperation took hold.

Nax, come! Tell Huff to climb Henley.

Henley's orange tabby scaled the boy like a tree trunk and Nax did the same to Kila. Gasping for air that wasn't there, Kila reached for Quinn, gripped her forearm.

Quinn's eyes went wide with understanding. Then they shut and she breathed a silent prayer.

Kila swung a scythe of mercus to sever tendrils worming into her mind and sapping her will. And then new bolts formed purely from her need. A blend of emotion and sensation took form.

The mercus green lifted from the floor. Kila lifted her free hand and released it. Ice water poured over her skin and a hollow reverberating scream followed her and her friends into dymension.

23

BEST NOT TESTED

Jil kept her hood up as she strode downslope. Her hand rested on her hilt. The mercus in the city was rank. A thin trail led toward the wall separating Terriside from Cheapsgate. It was this tendril that pulled her forward. It was like a string of spittle dangling from a cow's muzzle, repulsive but deceptively strong.

She followed it up a set of stairs and onto the wall. A public observation area. The lone Watch man eyed her with the appropriate level of suspicion and coldness. A terrible post on a day like today.

She approached him, removing her hand from her hilt and pulling back her hood so he could see her face.

She had been told many times of her loveliness. Such comments usually began at about eight bells in the evening when she was in a tavern common room. The later the hour, the more frequent the compliments. She supposed that to a sober man, she would be considered "reasonably beddable."

That's the term her father had used to describe her the day she had driven her newly found Shadline sword into his fat gut.

Feminine charms were not her usual weapon, but when they could save her time, she wielded them with vicious efficiency.

"I'm afraid I'm lost," she said. A flash of eyelash, chin down, looking up at him to create a sultry look. Not too difficult. Her lovers had sometimes complained that she was too aggressive, had too much lust and hunger in her eyes. Sometimes. Most of them had discovered they rather liked her strength. And her appetite.

This man had no chance. He could have been a Tilsday altar boy and she would have him panting to help her in any way he could.

"Miss, it's a chill day to be out. Where're ya tryin' to get?"

"Not a place, exactly. I was to meet a man here."

His expression went cold for a moment before warming under her gaze. "Ah, well. As I say, it's chill. Not many comin' up to look into the mist."

"Nobody came here? I'm quite late, you see."

"There was a man earlier." He leaned down, eyes going soft with concern. "I hate to be the one what tells ya, but I reckon he was 'bout to jump off yon wall."

She almost failed to show the necessary shock and concern. Almost. But the man had looked to the wall in question. She was able to bring a bit of dewiness to her eyes and quiver to her lips.

"Now don't be afeard, lass."

Lass. Thirty years old and still a lass to some men. It shouldn't irritate her, but it did. She let him continue.

"I stopped him. An' I told him to think of those who would have to clean up his carcass after—"

"What did he look like? I can't believe that would be my—my—" She put her hands over her face and managed a sob-like noise in her throat. Jil hadn't shed a true tear in seven years. And those last had been over a beloved hound who had traveled with her those first years as a Shadline.

"It might not have been your, er, friend. He was lean, tall. Hard eyes. Looked mighty mis'rable, if y'ask me. But a strong man. I noticed his hands were hard. Working hands."

Another warbling sob came out of her. She winced at how ridiculous it sounded, but the Watch man didn't seem to note anything but a woman's distress. He hazarded a pat on her shoulder. Had his mitt lingered a second longer, he would have lost it. But he pulled back. A nice man, she decided.

"I'm sorry to have taken up your time, sir," she said.

"I'm no sir, lass. It's my duty to help citizens in need."

She rewarded him with a squeeze of her hand on his wrist and a red lipped smile, very sad, but appreciative. The look vanished the instant she turned away.

A murderer who considered suicide, but who had been talked out of it? A man so wracked by guilt that—

She turned back. "When was he here?"

"I reckon at 3 bells. My watch ends in a quarter hour. I could see ya home, if—"

"Thank you, but no. My father is expecting me."

Jil faded into the misty afternoon.

It would be a long carriage ride to the Citadel from down here. A discussion with Ell was in order, but it would have to wait. An incompleteness in Jil's gut insisted she was close to what she was looking for.

If only she knew what it was. She thought it was the murderer. It *had* to be him. And yet . . . that did not address the demayne, or the Cheapsgate murder she'd been pulled here to witness.

As she walked, she listened. And soon her footsteps led her to a tavern. The Grunting Hog.

Jil loved taverns. Jil hated them.

A man at the door tried to collect a coin. He got a steady look as she pulled back her cloak to reveal the hilt of her sword. Most people didn't know exactly what they were seeing, but the gesture alone seemed to communicate that she was a threat best not tested.

The common room was busy, but not full. She paid the barkeep a gold skillet and told him to keep water coming and that she should absolutely not be disturbed by the help unless she beckoned to them.

She sat in a shadowy spot that seemed meant for her. It felt good to be out of the cold. It also felt right.

She closed her eyes and listened. To the rampant speculation about murder, to the concern about inland crops, to theories about a recently burned merchant greathouse, and the same merchant's ship burned at the docks, and about thieves running the roofways. And thinnies burned in their tunnels beneath the city.

She listened also to her instincts. And for the moment, they told her to stay right where she was.

24

___

LEAVE A SCAR

They lay sprawled on the floor of Kila's great hall in Kil's Keep, far east of Garden Tower. A haze of mercus green still hung over the dazed companions. The raging mercus of Yples's power throbbed like head-crushing pulses nearby.

The *vaz'on!*

Kila picked herself from the floor, groaning at the headache that threatened to burst her skull in twain. Nax's fur stood out, and she hissed at nothing and everything. Huff was more composed, but his tail flicked in irritation.

Someone was screaming. Quinn. Kila turned and instantly began echoing her friend's cries. The horrific scene made her mouth drop even as her heart went cold.

Quinn's right hand was embedded in the stone of the floor. Agony contorted the young woman's face. Her body writhed as she struggled to free herself. Kila rushed to her, barely noting that Highest Quiv was on one knee, searching for strength enough to stand. He must have grabbed onto Quinn at the last moment.

Henley met Kila at Quinn's side. "Kil's eyes!" He held his hands out to comfort Quinn but pulled them back as if fearful that his touch might wound her more.

Kila plunged her mercus senses into her friend's arm, seeking the hand and the stone that encompassed it.

"No. Oh no," she said, eyes now blurring with horrified tears. "Oh Quinn. I'm so sorry."

There was no distinction between stone and flesh. They were intermingled and inseparable as the copper and zinc that formed the alloy of brass. Kila listened for the pain, negated it. Quinn collapsed, breath heaving and tears of relief streaking her beautiful cheeks.

"I'm so sorry," Kila said again. "Ah me."

"Don't be sorry. Get my hand out of this Kil-damned floor!"

When Kila didn't immediately obey, Quinn went still. She tried to sit up, gave her arm a few more futile tugs. Highest Quiv squatted to inspect the situation. He sucked air through his teeth and offered Kila a furtive and sympathetic look. "Come Henley," he said softly.

Something about his tone and Kila's curt nod in response got through to Henley. He moved back and clicked his tongue at Huff to follow. But instead, Huff went closer to Quinn, wove his way beneath her and pressed to her stomach and legs, offering comfort.

The two had grown close when Henley and Huff had been separated. Seeing Huff's compassion broke Kila's heart. Nax nuzzled into Kila's embrace.

"Quinn. Listen to me."

Quinn was blinking very fast. It looked like she was fighting off the realization that was dawning on her. "No. No, Kila. No. I'm a Shadline."

When Kila didn't deny the truth, Quinn screamed. "But I'm a SHADLINE!"

Pennie came down the steps, hand trailing the wall for guidance. Her eyes were unfocussed, staring off to some unseeable place of darkness. She found Quinn and put her arms around her. And then Kila joined the huddle, dripping tears into her friends black hair. "I can free you. But I can't keep you whole."

Sobs shook Quinn's body. Pennie murmured quiet assurances. Then: "You'll be surprised how quickly you adapt. Strong girls like you and me, we don't need so many hands or eyes as everyone else."

Highest Quiv cleared his throat. "They are coming. It will be an hour, perhaps less. But they are coming."

Quinn calmed and wiped her nose on her free sleeve. "Do it. Just do it."

"Henley," Kila said. "You're better with the mind. Can you . . . ?"

He formed the bolts and struck just as Quinn began to object. Kila caught her friend's weight as she went unconscious under Henley's mental intrusion. Settling her gently onto the stone, Kila began.

HIGHEST QUIV MOVED close to watch, holding his stomach. Dymensing had left him queasy to begin with. Seeing the Peline girl's horrific entrapment merely added to his nausea.

The mercus feats Henley and Kila performed dazzled him. He noted with great interest that they did not use much power. Henley's touch was very slight. Quiv himself possessed sufficient power to achieve these feats. He only lacked the understanding to perform them. Ah, what beautiful and subtle bolts!

Kila's performance—he could only equate her practice of the mercus to a master of dance or music—once again took his breath away. That such feats were even possible was a miracle. That she accomplished them without understanding them, frightening.

He had suspected the Voluptuary's snare, but the Coin's involvement had surprised him. He'd had little to go on since all of Fley's spies among the Way of Ori were dead. But he knew Voluptuary Minn was a savvy woman, and she desperately wanted to yoke Kila with the promise-binding.

A burning smell curled toward him. Flesh cauterizing.

Kila used Cayne, not sawing back and forth through Quinn's wrist, but merely pressing. It oozed through flesh and bone slowly, like a knife through frozen butter. Wisps of smoke curled away.

And then it was over. The dark-haired woman's arm came free, red stump cauterized. Kila was already diving into the wound with her power, stirring up a mercus red in one cupped hand. The light took on an almost liquid form, which she poured over her friend's stump.

Highest Quiv gasped to see the redness and swelling fade. Skin drew over the exposed bone and sealed.

"Leave a scar," Henley said softly. "She's earned it."

Kila stopped her healing when the knitting crossing the center of the stump had turned pale. A scar—a white line, looking ten years healed—remained. Quiv bent forward and nodded in appreciation. A smaller scar crossed it, giving the impression of a cross-guard. Kila had marked her friend with a dagger symbol, in remembrance of what the missing hand would never again grasp.

Henley released his efforts and blew out a long breath. Huff nestled next to Quinn's unconscious form, purring softly.

"I hate to push you along, Highest of Kil," Quiv said. "But they are coming. And quickly. I believe someone has appropriated an atlen drawn wagon. The ash-barrens will slow them some, but it has not rained since the fellstorm. The mud has hardened. The route will be quite direct.

Kila rubbed the fuzz of regrowing hair on the top of her head. Quiv thought her rather striking in her elfin, bright-eyed intelligence. Had he any interest in women she might have struck his fancy. Though, she was at least a ten-year too young for him. Her eyes were red, cheeks tear-stained.

"They cannot win," Henley said. "They have to know that. Even with their source-tap circles and Dunne Yples, they cannot win against Kila. And we can sever the tap on Yples long before they arrive."

Highest Quiv cleared his throat. A habit he'd picked up serving under Highest Fley. His predecessor was a keen-minded man, but often lacked perspective. He had certainly lacked an appreciation of nuance. "They do not *need* to prevail. I believe Highest Sigh understands. If she had fought them in the Tower, killed some of them, they would immediately spread word of her attack. They could honestly report that she had declined to devote her power to healing."

"Politics!" Kila spat. "Father warned me never to dabble in it. And now here I am up to my ears in it."

Quiv smiled warmly, pleased that she understood what

Fley never had. There might be an objective truth. But it mattered little. What mattered was the perceived truth. The truth that people believed.

He said, "You wish to define what the Way of Kil stands for. If you kill them, it will stand for murder. Regardless of the facts. Regardless that they tried to spring a trap on you."

"You dymensed us out of there," Henley said. "You know how to do it. Take us to Starside."

Kila blinked at Henley. She stroked Nax's head, absently, but clearly drawing comfort from the contact. "I have no idea how I did it."

"Perhaps address the more pressing issue," Quiv said. "Dunne Yples. Can you interrupt the flow through the *vaz'on?*"

"I think so. First let's move Quinn to the table by the hearth. Pennie, fetch water. Food. Healing will have exhausted her. She'll be hungry when she wakes. Henley?"

"I don't know anything about the *vaz'on,*" he said.

"I've had some experience with it." Her face was grim as she began to ascend the stairs to where the madman was kept. Highest Quiv followed, nervous about the fast approaching merculyns, but satisfied. He was Highest of Til, if in name only. Highest of what? Thirty-three surviving acolytes and Donse Masters. He could stay and administrate and oversee the rebuilding of Til's Tower. But that was not his purpose.

Kila Sigh was carried upon winds of destiny. The fate of millions of lives—perhaps their very souls—depended on her. His duty was to guide her, counsel her.

And if it came to it. Kill her.

25

WINTER SICKNESS

She still wore her apron as she climbed the broad, low steps to enter the Baths of Ori. Her shoes were soaked from the long, slushy trek up from Terriside. Her nose, chilled.

But her heart blazed with eagerness and pride.

"My name is Weese, daughter of Chicky," she said to the Sensual sitting at the receiving desk just inside the great Dome of the Gentle Goddess. She didn't add that until very recently, she had been the housemaid, common room mistress, and do-all for her father at the Yin Inn.

That had been her old life. It would have been her *whole* life if not for that strange, wonderful man who taken hold of her. She'd forgotten his name. But she'd never forget his face. And if she ever saw him again, she vowed to give him the biggest, wettest, deepest kiss he'd ever gotten.

"I have awakened to the mercus," she announce proudly.

Sensual Beth was a stout woman with a rather intimidating bosom. The bangs of her bowl-cut hair were just long enough to cover her eyebrows. It gave her a helmet-like aspect. But her eyes were keen and kindly.

"I feel it in you, child. You are welcome here." She rang a bell and a novitiate came forward to attend to desk-duty. "Come with me, Weese."

The woman led slowly, winding around the three huge pools glistening beneath the dome. A few elderly Gristensiders were bathing in the smallest one. They wore long dark robes for modesty while their hair remained perfectly coifed in the ridiculous manner of the Radiant class.

On most days Weese had no use for their kind. But today she loved them. All the world was glorious, because she was going to be a Sensual and that meant she no longer had to slave away for her father, rising with the sun and collapsing into bed at midnight, spending the days toiling with brooms, carrying wood, shoveling ash, peeling potatoes, fending off grabby hands, and staring down those who discovered their purse was just a coin or two short for their bill.

As a Sensual she would be respected. She would be important!

"I believe Voluptuary Sinlop is in her quarters," Sens Beth was saying. "She likes to greet all new novitiates, merculyns or not."

This was getting better with every passing moment, Weese thought. Her palms grew a bit sweaty at the idea of meeting the Voluptuary. And her head was a bit achy. Just there, behind her eyes. Too much excitement and too little food.

Sens Beth eyed her as they walked. "A bit old for an awakening. Not too powerful. But if you study hard and practice, you'll do well."

They'd just see who was powerful and who was not. If

mere hard work was needed, Weese doubted they'd ever seen a novitiate who knew the meaning of work more deeply than she.

They wound through halls and down a stairwell before coming to a rather plain door. Inside they found a well-appointed apartment, but none of that gilded nonsense Gristensiders went in for. Weese had overheard stories in the Yin Inn of how Donse Masters lived in opulence to rival Her Enlightened Majesty. In truth, Weese had been negligent with her tithing to the Way of Til. She didn't go in for all those incense censors and Tilsday haranguing about filthy human urges and about how Til could see her innermost thoughts and kept a record of them against the day she croaked off and her soul was weighed on his great banker's balance in the sky.

She harrumphed, drawing a raised eyebrow from Beth. The expression folded up the woman's bangs a little, like an armsman tipping up his helmet. What an odd bird she was, Weese thought. A bit overfed and perhaps underworked. Weese hadn't had padding on her bottom since she could carry a chamber pot.

The Voluptuary was at a desk, reviewing a parchment in one hand and holding a plain white teacup in the other. She didn't look up as her guests entered. She said, "A merculyn has awakened. And here she is. Curious, isn't it, Sens Beth?"

"Unusual. Make no mistake."

"What's unusual about it?" Weese demanded. "I woke up to the, uh, mercus and here I am. Didya think I'd go stalking off to the Spinsters so I could *gamble* away my life on coin tosses?"

This drew the Voluptuary's attention enough that her blazing blue eyes shifted to take in her new novitiate. Weese shuddered. Not because the stare was cold or mean. But because she felt it penetrated right into her skull (like Til!) and riffled through her memories.

The ache behind her eyes intensified. Her knees were starting to come unhinged. "Kil's eyes, I think I'm goin' to faint."

Sens Beth caught her and eased her into an armchair. "Poor thing is overwrought."

"Poor thing is a dim spark," the Voluptuary said. "I've never heard of such awakening happening spontaneously. Not at her age. How old do you think?"

"Eight and twenty. Mayhap thirty."

Weese pressed her fists to her eyes. She was sure her eyes were going to pop right out of her head if she didn't hold them in. "Twenty-four, ma'ams. Just last month."

"Still rather old." The Voluptuary came round to take Weese's cheeks in her firm, warm hands. "Fetch Sens Renna. I think this girl is ill."

Sens Beth hustled off in a rustle of robes.

"I'm not ill. Just a case of the cold-feebles. My feet are soaked through. I'll be pert as a pollysprig once I—"

Weese convulsed, bending forward and gagging. Her headache brought up a grating ring in her ears, like metal scraping metal. All full of hisses and rasps. And then consonants emerged from the noise.

A word.

A word she was supposed to say.

And then it came to her. Her lips moved to form the strange syllables. *"Aprhen."*

"What did you say?" the Voluptuary said.

But Weese was already receding, the Hargothe filling her mind.

THE CALL HAD COME UNEXPECTEDLY. The Hargothe had not yet pulled his robes back on. Yiothizandra stood by the open window, winter air flowing around her nakedness. He knew her state of undress because he could feel the shape of her garments and armor still in a pile where she'd tossed them.

He required the Staff of Nihil to steady himself as he stood and accepted entry into Weese's weak mind. Her mercus was as dim as the fading glow of a blown-out candle wick. He took hold of it, wishing he could flow his own power—and that of the staff—through her.

But he didn't require much for this effort. Skill counted for more than raw power in most things.

"What did you say?" the Voluptuary demanded. She stood before the Hargothe, staring down imperiously. How he wished to drive a blade into the woman's papery throat. Just there, where her pulse moved the flesh in shallow flutters.

Alas. Weese had no weapon on her. Just as well, for his goal was not to kill Voluptuary Sinlop. Perhaps later he would have her paraded along the Street of Sorrows wearing nothing but her ridiculous jeweled tiara. Like the harlot she was.

His disgust twisted Weese's face and the transformation must have been frightening to behold. The Voluptuary stepped back. "What is wrong with you? Are you going to faint again?"

"I am quite well, I assure you. But we have never met, have we? All those years together in Starside, appearing to one another as flames upon the mercusine."

She still didn't understand. But how could she? She who claimed to the public such righteous virtue while engaging in her Way's vile rituals during full moons and Winternight freaks.

"The Hargothe," she said finally. She sneered at him. "Indulging again in your demaynic tricks, are you? I know all about your so-called awakening to prophecy. Did you think you could keep your years in Ittiti secret?"

He would kill her for that. But not now. She was trying to provoke him.

It felt strange to occupy a woman's body. For one thing, Weese was short. For another, weak. But there as a litheness to her limbs he discovered he quite liked. He stood, eyes drawing even with the Voluptuary's.

He raised his hands to beckon to her. "Get him out of me!" He pitched his voice high to imitate a weak woman's plea, forgetting he already had a weak woman's voice. The result was a high-pitched squeak. Utterly pathetic. And it turned out rather convincing.

Thinking Weese was fighting the Hargothe's possession, the Voluptuary came forward and took Weese's arms. As expected she brought her own mercus to bear, prepared to plunge the girl's mind and sever the Hargothe's connection there. She would have to search long and hard to find it. The force-bond was subtle, very subtle. And now he'd learned to spread it from merculyn to merculyn. Just as the winter sickness spread to every member of a household.

He grasped the woman's face and brought his own feat to bear. So quick. Like slipping a dirk into an abdomen. This mercus blade penetrated the Voluptuary's mind almost without notice. Until it was too late.

He caught her on the way down, lest she crack her head. The effort helped somewhat, but Weese was already losing consciousness. Her vision faded from his eyes as she died. Even that little mercus feat had been too much.

Perfect. He doubted the Voluptuary would remember what had happened. She would come to, discover the new novitiate dead, and assume it was from a chill.

And when the time came, without knowing what she was doing, the Voluptuary would call to him. And then his plan would accelerate.

It had been interesting to see through Weese's eyes. A shorter perspective than the trapper and a body of quite strange proportion. Not unpleasant, but strange.

During his brief occupation of the girl, Yiothizandra had returned to him. She now embraced him from behind. Snaked her arms around his waist, pressing her body to his. Again she scalded him with her impossible heat.

"Kil awaits, Tenn. You must do your duty."

26

A FLOW OF POTENTIAL

Kila tried to force thoughts of Quinn from her head. She had not dymensed the woman's hand into the stone floor on purpose. But her heart could not accept anything but guilt over her friend's loss.

Her *friend*. She did not have any of those to spare these days.

Sensual Sliy hadn't been her friend. But neither had she been an enemy. Not truly. It seemed nobody was safe if they were close to her.

Watch your tail, Naxie, I might stomp it before I know what I'm doing.

Nax meowed and hopped onto Dunne Yples's lap.

The Donse Master hadn't moved since Kila had entered his room. It was a mess, with dirty food trays and a scattering of empty wine bottles on the floor. His bed was in disarray, the blankets twisted and matted from his night-time tossings and turnings. At Kila's entrance he looked up, "Go away" on his lips. The words died before escaping his mouth.

He wore a loose tunic, the ties unlaced at the throat. His plain, charcoal pants had smudges of ash, mud, and dried egg on them. His white hair had been smoothed back over his skull, and his beard trimmed to respectability. But despite the weary lucidity in his eyes now, Kila could not help but recall his insane straining when she'd battled him at Ori's Home. And then his hell-spawn form, a gigantic oily black demon, towering over the ash-barrens.

Now he looked like a man, dignified, except for the exhaustion that pulled the skin beneath his eyes into black half-moons.

The *vaz'on* gave him a regal, almost kingly aspect. Unless one knew that the gems that circled the gold band concealed bolts that threaded through his scalp and into his skull. Sensual Thine and her foul protege, Hannah, had installed the hateful relic on Kila's head. She knew its effects well.

Before, Yples had always looked at Kila with abject hatred. Now it was suspicion. "I saw you in the thinnie cavern," he said.

She was well aware of this fact. "I saw you, too. I was distracted by the rat queen's ritual. She tried to drown my Beloved One." She continued weakly: "I might have said hello otherwise."

Yples had not made the slightest effort to dislodge Nax from his lap. Why the cat had jumped there was beyond Kila.

You do remember that he tried to kill me many times, don't you? she sent.

I can tell he won't hurt me.

"Huff has spent time with him," Henley said, explaining what Nax would not.

The thinnies. Sliy. Quinn. All victims of Kila's anger, or her fear. But not Yples. The only thing she'd ever done was defend herself against him. And she'd not done that very well.

She searched his face even as he did the same to her. She sought echoes of that implacable hatred she'd seen before. What did he seek? Perhaps evidence that she was worthy of such animosity. Or maybe he wondered how such an unlikely person had been cursed with so much power.

"Don't worry, girl," he said at last. "I won't hurt you."

"Highest . . ." Quiv said, urging Kila to get on with severing the approaching Sensual from Yples's power.

The mercus was alive to Kila, moving through space like cables of sensation. She saw them as light. She could just as easily have heard them or felt them with her fingers. An even bolder way to study them would be to bring their tastes and smells to her senses. The power flowing from Yples had not been manifested into bolts of the senses yet. It was all of them and none of them. A flow of potential.

But a flow nonetheless. That was the trick with source-taps, the power pushed toward the merculyn attempting to wield it. Someone strong, like Kila, could hold it at the ready. Someone relatively weak, like Highest Fley, had to use the excess or dump it. Otherwise they'd be burnt out by it. Which was why the Sensual coming for her had Fley's Sink Gem.

Yples's power had not diminished since being crowned with the *vaz'on*. The tap gems were at his temples. Emeralds. Each worth a Terriside rowhouse.

A purple gem—Kila thought it was amethyst—was positioned between the eyebrows where the golden band dipped to a point. Had it not been a mercusine prison, the *vaz'on* might have been an impressive crown indeed.

Over the ears were rubies the size of nightskirl eggs. Kila

knew the one over his left ear shone brightly when the wearer told a lie. It also punished lies with spikes of agony through the brain. The one over the right ear allowed for willshift. She didn't know what the ones at the back of the skull did. Those were sapphire.

Only one of the emeralds was tapped. Henley stood next to the Donse Master, leaning close to the activated gem.

"You broke my nose," Dunne Yples said to him.

"I did. You were trying to kill my—my friend."

"But later you kept me alive. Made me stronger when my Way quelled and chained me like a bat-bit hound."

"I did."

Yples lifted a hand. It seemed to take an extraordinary amount of effort. He took hold of Henley's hand. "Curse you for that. Curse you, you Kil-damned bastard!"

Henley drew back. Huff mewled in irritation. The orange cat had been rubbing against Yples's shins.

"He saved your life," Kila said.

"That's why I curse him. True compassion would have had him slide a blade across my throat."

"What? And have Highest Fley kill him for it?" Kila said.

Yples had no answer for this. But what tortured man could look back with forgiveness for those who prolonged their pain, no matter their intention or situation.

"You might sever that flow of mercus any time now," Quiv said. "They *must* have atlens pulling their wagon. That Sensual is coming, and fast."

Kila felt it. The ever-growing spark at the end of the cord of power streaming from Yples. The truth was she was tired of severing things. "If I cut it. If I *could* cut it. What happens to the Sensual?"

"Like a rope under strain," Henley said. "I spent a year before the mast on one of my father's ships. When a line breaks, it whips back. Strikes like a snake. I saw a sailor lose an eye from such a break. Same thing with severed taps."

Kila nodded. That made sense to her. "But who does it strike? The Sensual or Yples?"

"*Dunne* Yples," the tired Donse Master said. "I may be your captive, but I will not tolerate disrespect."

"Highest, please," Quiv urged Kila. "The Sensual comes to promise-bind you or force you to attack him. The others follow close on his heels." He had moved to a window, a narrow flickbow slit covered by a blanket for a curtain. He pulled it aside. "There. I see the wagon. There are other merculyns aboard. Cut him off and perhaps he'll give it up as a lost cause."

"It is a lost cause," Yples said. "None but me can stand against her. She will scorch them from existence as surely as Father Til burns the damned."

"These gems are mercusine relics," Kila said, doing her best to ignore both men. "I think each of them is independent of the others. These green ones are force-taps, allowing any merculyn without the skill to perform a force-tap directly to access the power."

"So we unbolt it?" Henley asked.

"I think so."

"I've tried," Yples said. "You're all daft as beggars."

"I was a beggar for a while," Henley said. "Until I was a thief." He lightly slapped Kila's hand away from the gem. "I'll do it. If something bad happens, I don't want you getting hurt."

She wasn't sure if she should be offended or flattered. Both feelings warred in her, muting her objections. Henley threaded a bit of mercus and began to twist the active tap gem. Yples grimaced. Kila well knew how weird and painful the removal was.

The turns of the screw made grinding sounds inside Yples's head as the threads of the bolts turned in his skull.

"They're to the crumbled arch," Quiv said. "The road is strewn with debris. They'll have to—"

Mercus feats flared. Quiv gasped.

"No. He knows how to fling the fallen columns aside."

"There it is," Henley said softly. The bolt pulled from Yples's skull and the flow of mercusine ceased instantly. Yples winced and squeezed his eyes shut.

"The Sensual collapsed!" Quiv cried. He let out an indecorous whoop then cleared his throat and gripped the collar of his Donse Master's robes, looking embarrassed. "The wagon has stopped. The other merculyns are coming on foot."

"They will force me into combat, won't they?"

"As long as you are within reach. Voluptuary Minn has made a cold calculation. If you kill her Sensuals, the truth of your evil will be proved. If you submit to the promise-binding, you will be hers to control."

"But doesn't she care about the truth?"

Yples laughed at that. He fingered the loose gem. "Perhaps loosen the others, lad?" he asked Henley.

"No," Kila said. "We've got to go."

"Where?" Highest Quiv asked. "If you dymense us across the island, they will still come. Or do you think we can outrun them all?"

"She can fly, what cares she about you?" Yples said. Then in a mocking tone added: "*Highest* Quiv."

But Henley caught what Kila meant to do. There would be no flying. No running. But plenty of hiding. "Can you walk, Dunne Yples?"

"No."

"We must not leave him here," Quiv said. "He's too powerful a resource."

"I see the Way of Til has completely forsaken me," Yples mourned. "When they should be rescuing me."

Quiv bent close to the Donse Master's face. "I was there when you became that hell-spawn. I *felt* your hatred. Do not lecture me. It is you who have forsaken the Way."

That got Yples to his feet. And from the satisfied smirk on Quiv's face, the provocation had served its purpose. "Where are we going?" Quiv asked.

"The basement," Kila said. "To the Derslin Wheel."

27

APRHEN!

Sens Beth reeled back as the Voluptuary released her head. She felt faint, slightly ill. Confused.

"Pardon, Voluptuary, I think I must sit."

For her part the Voluptuary didn't look much better, her wide handsome face was pale, lips pulled back as if she'd bitten into a sourberry.

They were in her office. Why had she come? It was about the girl, yes, the dead girl. "Poor Weese never had a chance. I suppose her death has made me a bit overwrought."

Beth staggered to one of the supple armchairs in the Voluptuary's office. Red satin embroidered in thread-of-gold with the staff and circle of Ori.

The room swayed before her eyes and she pressed a hand to her stomach. Across the room the Voluptuary was doing the same. The older woman went to her desk and plopped into her chair. "I fear I did not sleep too well last night."

"I should go discuss funeral arrangements with Sens Renna," Beth said, trying to stand. But the room tilted again and she was forced to sit. The curtains covered a pair of tall windows, the gray light of winter seemed terribly bright through the slender gap between the thick velvet folds.

Beth forced herself to her feet. She decided she would not be remembered as the Sensual who had despoiled the Voluptuary's Iopsi rug with sickup.

Stumbling and holding a stout palm to her clammy forehead, she made it to the door and into the hallway beyond. A pair of novitiates came by at that moment. Darya and a boy whose name Beth could not remember.

"Come here, Darya," she said. Why she said it, she wasn't sure. Darya, a lovely blond girl with luminous blue eyes. Not quite twenty, and the image of what some folk thought the Way of Ori was all about, sensuality.

Some impulse was on Sens Beth, perhaps an instinct to see if anyone else at the Starside Baths was as ill as she felt. She cupped the girl's fair cheeks with her hands. Abruptly a word rose to her lips, as sudden and revolting as an unbidden burp. *"Aprhen!"*

Beth's mercus formed a bolt she did not know, using sense combinations as foreign tasting and smelling as Jallisean stew.

And then it was over. The novitiate stumbled backward and would have fallen but that her companion caught her.

"Come, boy," Beth commanded. Novitiates could no more refuse such an order coming from a Sensual than a man of the Watch could refuse Commander LiTishke. He stepped into Beth's hands.

Again the strange word came forth and the mercus feat formed. Darya was not recovered enough to catch her friend, who fell onto his backside when Beth released him.

"Don't dally about, novitiates, run along and see to your . . ." She didn't know what they should see to.

The Voluptuary's door closed behind her. The Voluptuary had stepped out. She gave the novitiates one of her cold stares, which sent them fleeing. She nodded to Beth and proceeded in the other direction.

Sens Beth wound down the stairs to the Novitiate Ward, seeking Sens Renna, the woman who looked after the novitiates.

She stopped in every room, looking for Renna. If she found a novitiate, she felt them for fever. Always the word formed and the mercus feat happened. But she thought nothing of it. A need moved her.

At last she did find Renna, sitting quietly in her own room, smiling faintly as she rested in meditative stillness. If she heard Beth coming, she did not react. It was nothing to feel her cheeks and speak the word.

When Sensual Renna recovered she felt a sudden need to check on Sens Taht. And so she and Beth went up to the Baths where they knew the woman—and many other Sensuals—could be found.

AN HOUR LATER, the Voluptuary stepped from her carriage and approached the entry to Pol's Well, a squat tower surrounded by plain and serviceable living quarters. The Coin occupied an office adjacent to the well.

The Voluptuary rapped her knuckles on the thick, iron-bound door. A peer-port slid open.

"I have come to speak with her."

The Voluptuary's headpiece alone told the person within who had come. But it was several minutes before the door swung open. The Voluptuary stepped into the chill interior. The Way of Pol in Starside was quite ascetic. No expense would go to firewood, and the decision whether to use mercusine efforts to provide heat was left to an annual medallion toss. The Voluptuary's informants said the toss had come up frowns ten years in a row. Unfortunate for the Spinsters and Devotees on a chill day like today.

The Voluptuary was admitted to the Coin's office, a spare space with a simple wood desk and three ladder back chairs. The woman herself was standing, her fingers toying with the great medallion at her throat.

The Voluptuary was a political creature. She admitted that to herself. But all in the service of Ori's doctrine of healing, compassion, and love.

She greeted the Coin, a skinny elderly lady with bluish white skin and popping gray eyes. The woman did not return her smile.

The mercus was strong in her. And noting that, the Voluptuary moved toward her. The Coin was spry, but taken by surprise.

"Aprhen!"

And then the Voluptuary's hands were on the old woman's papery cheeks.

28

DELICIOUS RUMOR

Rumor swirled about Starside like chimney smoke. It arose from housemothers and merchants and bookkeepers and smiths. Market cartmen, their wagons loaded with vegetables, listened with deep interest as the tendrils of rumor tickled their ears. Gossip was like produce, the market-men knew. A bundle of carrots came with a word or two. False or true, no matter. Rumor had no cost, but high value.

The Terriside greathouse chef, hustled home with his market bounty, eager to share all he'd learned on his errands. The under-chefs and scullery boys and ladies' maids all gathered, listening with rapt attention to the latest word gleaned from the market.

And what was that word?

Why it was their favorite word of all: Murder.

The chef fastened his kerchief around his head to keep his wispy hairs out of his master's soup. And as he tied the knot, he eyed his audience. "The body was headless as a chicken and not a drop of blood on the stones."

"Another?" asked a maid, silver tray in her hands. It was time for tea and her mistress was an impatient, frowsy old maid of seven and twenty. She could wait. She'd complain regardless. "That makes twelve dead by my count."

"Thirteen," said a footman. "They found an atlen keeper in pieces in the blasted quarter."

A scullery girl said: "What about them kids an' their nana over to Sanlin Street?"

"That's right. Ol' Flekk gut stuck and 'er grand-babes slit open."

"Blood all over, I heard."

"It's the thinnies killin' 'em," said the stable-hand. By rights—and by the state of his boots—he should not have been in the kitchens at all. But he was.

The chef plucked up his knife and set to coining his carrots. He listened to the simmer he'd started, pleased by the fear, pleased by the eagerness of it.

An under-chef said: "That makes thirteen as of today. How many more on the morrow? Blasted quarter tells me it's the thinnies."

"But what of the blood? Where does it go?"

"They drinks it!" cried the stable-hand.

"Them children an' their mama bled. Like pigs is what I heard. Just blood everywhere."

This idea was met with horror-gasps from some of the women, grunts of consideration from some of the men, and laughs from a few of the rowdy boys who would much rather hear about murder than fetch water or carry firewood.

"Mayhap the thinnies do drink it," the chef said, salting

his voice with grave doubts. This was his domain. King of the kitchen. It was well to allow a possibility you didn't believe in to be voiced now and then. It made the little people feel valued. "But there're direr whispers than that. Donse Masters are fearful something blacker than murder made these headless, bloodless corpses. The bloody ones, too. The Watch's on alert, rounding up rascals and listening to every accusation. Believe me, the Watch knows more'n they're saying."

"What's direr than murder?" the tray maid called. She had edged to the door, but still leaned an ear back to catch the slightest extra crumb of news before heading upstairs with the tea.

The chef completed his final carrot chop, flipped his knife, and caught it by the handle. Waving it like a mercusine wand, he prepared the eager ears before him for the most delicious bit of rumor. "Some are saying a word best not spoken aloud. So listen close and keep it close. No rumors spread in this greathouse. Understood?"

"Understood," rose the chorus of greedy ears. Hearts pounded with glee to be among the few to know this dark news.

The chef leaned close and cast his eyes to and fro to make sure that no uninvited listeners would hear this last morsel. The maid with the tray had returned. She stood on tippy toes and bent forward, pressing the edge of her tray into a footman's back.

The chef waited, letting their appetites mature.

"The Donse Masters are saying it must be a demayne."

There arose such cries and gasps and prayers that the kitchen bubbled over with the ruckus. The chef slammed a meat hammer onto his bench and scolded them all to silence.

"If I hear a peep o' this from someone who wasn't here. Why I'll know I can't trust any of you lot with fresh meat."

They dispersed, like a school of fish disturbed by a boy's tossed stone. They carried with them their chore burdens. But their steps were livelier for they bore something much heavier, too. A shoulder-load of rumor. Delicious rumor.

Solemn vows of silence were forgotten and their tongues wagged unrestrained.

The murders in Starside were done by demayne!

29

MERCIFUL TO ANIMALS

Tarek PiTorro took the sheaves of paper from Tym. He sat in his usual spot in the Yin Inn common room, but his sallow-faced friends were absent. His face was drawn. "Quite the catalog you've provided." He paused. "I recognize this scribe's hand." His eyes flicked up. "Did you hear?"

"Hear what?"

"Flekk was murdered. Along with her two grand-children. In her home."

"I had not heard. That is terrible. Who would do such a thing?" Tym wanted to shout that he'd done it, but the impulse was squashed by the same prohibitions that kept him from jumping to his death.

"Who indeed?" PiTorro dropped the papers on the table and rubbed his eyes. He had the haggard look of a man who had not slept. "I'll have the caravan assembled beyond the Moriterren Pass in a ten-day. There is a marshaling yard where the valley opens into the Neer Pass. I have a seasonal encampment there, but it will take a few days to prepare it. It is winter, and an unusually wet one. Surely, *he* understands practical constraints like that."

"I assure you, he does not. He will expect your train to arrive in forty days." Tym turned to go.

"And if I'm late? I cannot control the weather."

"Your client is not a forgiving man, PiTorro." And that was all Tym could say. What difference could a day or ten make? But he did not have permission to say such things. The Hargothe was not a negotiator. Perhaps he would be lenient with PiTorro, for he would likely need more trains of supplies delivered. But perhaps he would make him an example. Most likely, he would force-bond the man. If the man had the slightest spark, Tym would have been used to do it already. But apparently, if one did not have the spark, the Hargothe needed to lay hands on him directly.

Tym left the Yin Inn without another word to the caravanner. It was dark now. And cold, the day's slush hardening into lumpy ice. The walking was treacherous, but Tym had a light step. He preferred the outdoors, the chill, the crisp cleanliness of the air. Common rooms were aptly named. Common.

Lower Terriside was neither better nor worse than the wealthier middle and upper sections. People were of all sorts no matter where one went. Good, bad, wicked, vile. But the fewer comforts to go around, the more clever folk became in getting their share. He thought many of these folks would make excellent trappers. For they were cold-eyed, alert, and willing to sweat for their supper.

The Grunting Pig held a position of power at the final switchback of the Street of Sorrows. Positioned on the inside curve, it had three entrances. The proprietor hired men to stand in the doorways and occasionally kick them open. Tym supposed this served two purposes. First to show passersby the scantily clad serving ladies, and second to allow cool air to slip in and ease the boiling atmosphere. A thin man with a missing eye and immense mustache nodded to Tym as he entered.

"No sittin' unless yer sippin', mind?"

"Mind," Tym answered. "Know a man named Marlow?"

"I don't know anybody."

Tym went in. He wasn't particularly thirsty. No place to sit and sip. This time of the evening, folk had flocked here for the warmth, the companionship. And especially for the gossip.

"Hey, where ya live?" the man called, his one eye narrowing.

"Lockt. I'm a trapper."

"Good with a blade, eh? Ya like skinnin' animals, do ya?"

"It's honest work."

More suspicious eyes followed him as he left the doorman behind. Any stranger could be a murderer no matter what the times were like. But now, here, where so many had died so brutally, Tym was marked from the start.

He shouldered to the bar. Made a mug handle motion to the barkeep and turned his back to the oak plank so as to better eyeball the common room.

A vast hall, plank floors worn smooth by feet and darkened by a hundred years' worth of spilled beer. Heavy rafters hung with banners of The Grunting Pig wearing an armsman's helm and holding a mug of foaming beer in one hoof.

The hall was full of mismatched benches and tables. Workmen in their laborers' clothes—their *only* garb, most likely—were bent over tankards, heads and tongues heavy with speculation about murder. The nervous delight hummed in the room, setting Tym's teeth on edge. He caught snatches of conversation.

"A pair of Kil-touched convicts, I heard."

" . . . in the Blasted Quarter. Not a drop o' blood."

" . . . was over to the PiTorro greathouse. A guard said it was demayne what murdered those children."

"Binni Keel murdered . . ."

"Burned down the Mast greathouse. Set fire to Highest Binel's rooms at the Abbey . . ."

". . . they were whispering about Dem-Kisk!"

"I say it be vergent-kin, mark me. Sally's loaf were flat from th' oven and her shoes turned out from under th' bed."

" . . . I did so! 'Twas a cat or I'm an atlen's egg! Saw it creepin' along the roofs."

Tym's hearing had sharpened of late. As had his senses of smell and taste. Wrinkling his nose, he slid a coin across the bar. A silver skillet. Enough to last a while. The barkeep made it disappear.

A man next to Tym eyed him a moment. But he was five cups deep and not thinking too many thoughts. Awash in misery, by the looks of it. The woman beyond him laughed at a bawdy joke and slipped her arm around the drunken man. She pressed her lips to his cheek and whispered something lewd as her hand continued to explore into his pocket.

Tym let her steal the man's coin purse. Tym was not a man of the Watch and he was not to draw that sort of attention to himself. Nobody would thank a hero here, anyway. Not an outsider. Not tonight.

He settled in, absorbing the moods that washed through the room, carried on cooler air when a doorman thought to bang one open, or lifting on heated fumes as the conversations boiled. The rank smell of sweat and unwashed armpits mingled with the charred meat prepared in the kitchen.

Tym didn't know who he was looking for. Just the name, Marlow. He trusted his instincts, the way he knew just the spot to set a rabbit snare, or where to place the jaw-trap for a marten or fox.

By and by his attention alighted on a woman wearing trousers and cloak. A shine of perspiration covered her forehead. The room was too hot to keep on a woolen overcloak like that. She concealed a weapon most likely.

Others wore weapons openly. That was the purpose for most of the knives. To be seen. To forestall a fight before it began. But she kept hers concealed. That interested him.

She sat alone in a dark corner, nursing a tankard. It had not been refilled in a quarter hour. No serving maids had gone near her.

Tym approached.

"May I?" he motioned to the empty chair across from her. The only one in the whole place.

"No." She had short-cropped hair. Not haphazardly cut. Rather well-kept. Her fingernails were short, too. Not bitten off. Not dirty. Her clothes were fine. A tan tunic with a white laced undershirt in view at the collar. Ruffles spilled out. Rather jaunty. Boots were excellent work, if plain. Mud on the soles.

She sat with ease, legs stretched out and crossed at the ankles. Why would someone like her be here? Not talking to anyone. Waiting for someone? No. Observing? Yes. Just like Tym.

"I'm looking for a man named Marlow," Tym said.

"I'm looking for Her Enlightened Majesty," she said.

He allowed a smile. "She frequents this place, does she?"

"You'd be shocked where she ventures." Her eyes held no challenge, but they certainly weren't inviting. She wasn't pleased that he'd approached.

"There are no chairs open. Would you mind? We don't have to talk."

She didn't answer except to uncross her ankles and give the chair opposite her a little shove. It created space between the chair and the table. Not quite an invitation. Just permission.

He lowered his weight onto the chair, feeling more exhausted than he had in years. And he was used to walking twenty miles in a day, checking and baiting traps. Sometimes more.

"Who in here would know the man Marlow? I'm told he used to come to places like this often and then was lifted to snootier circles."

"I know the man."

Of course she did. His instincts had latched onto something he only now realized. A woman in fine clothes in a low tavern. Just as this Marlow had risen from low to high. Surely their paths had crossed.

"How can I find him?" he asked.

She lifted a shoulder and sipped her drink. Tym noted it was clear. Water.

"I have a small bit of coin. I could spare a skillet or two for a point in the right direction." He reached for his coin purse, but she tapped his shin with her toe. "I don't need your coin."

Her speech was crisp, not colored with low-quarter slang or lilt. He decided she was either an outsider, like him, or a Gristensider come downhill for a taste of the common life. Not too personable, though.

Sighing, she leaned her weight forward, put an elbow on the table. The other hand casually flipped her cloak aside. Briefly. Just a flash to show her weapon. A short sword. Scabbard black. Hilt black, a flat topped onyx embedded in the pommel. Ancient and expensive.

"Shadline," he said respectfully, offering a head bow.

She smirked. "Trapper."

So she knew him. Or of him. Perhaps like the doorman she suspected him of the numerous murders in Starside. Perhaps she had followed him here. He couldn't remember if she'd been there when he arrived or not. Perhaps the tankard she had before her had been left behind by a previous patron.

"I took a room at the Cherry Bottom Inn," she said. "The proprietor was complaining that you never returned to your room. Never paid."

"I didn't use the room."

"He held it for you."

"Are you going to drag me down there? I will happily pay the idiot."

"I would rather you throw your skillets down a rain gutter and let the thinnies collect them. That man's establishment is deplorable. But when I heard of you I knew instantly that we must meet. That we would meet. Listen and obey."

"I'm no Shadline, miss . . ."

"Jil. I know you're not a Shadline. I know you went to Flekk for scribing. I know she's dead."

Tym looked at her. He felt no fear. If she drove her magic weapon through his throat, so much the better. Her eyes were flat, gray, seeing everything. He'd met two other Shadlines in his life. None killed if they could avoid it.

"Marlow?" he said, not answering the question implicit in

the facts she'd rattled off. No point in answering it. She must have suspected something.

"The Citadel. He never leaves. Sits on Her Enlightened's small council. You have awakened to the mercus, trapper. But so faintly . . . Unusual. You know what else is unusual?"

He didn't answer.

"You moved from the Cherry Bottom Inn to the Yin Inn. And then what happened? The very hour of your arrival, Chicky's daughter awakens to the mercus and goes to the Baths of Ori to join their way. But that is not the most unusual thing."

"No? Then what is?" Inside he pleaded for her to attack. She was a Shadline, she could kill him easily.

"She died there. Right in the Voluptuary's office."

"How do you know all these things?"

"I listen. You'd be surprised how swiftly rumor drifts downslope."

An image of plain young Weese arose. His hands on her face, the light of mercus rising in her eyes. The vision dissolved, replaced by the hard woman across from him. Perhaps a ten-year younger than he. Weese's age. Maybe a little older. Appealing in her strength and hard openness. The sort of woman he might have left the mountaineering life for.

"I don't know Weese," he said. "I'm sorry to hear of her death. Was it a sudden sickness?" His voice sounded wooden to his own ears. He was half-listening, making an attempt to offer the correct words for the conversation. But his mind was roiling with the thought of the girl's death. Not another soul on his shoulders. Though he hadn't slipped his dagger into her throat, he had surely doomed her.

He hadn't thought anything could add to his hatred of the accursed Hargothe. But this news did.

The stuffiness of the room was getting to him. His clothes felt too tight, the air empty of nourishment for his lungs. Was this what Tym's prey had felt all those years? Trapped, but alive to feel and suffer each moment?

"I don't know how she died," Jil said. "I know you weren't there when it happened." She gripped the top of her tankard in slim, strong fingers. She spun it, absently, in a full circle. "Were you in the Blasted Quarter recently? How about Gristenside? The Gilok greathouse? A girl was murdered there a while back."

Tym wondered if the Hargothe had other force-bonded fools in the city. Perhaps the rash of murders was the hateful old man's way of sowing discord before his swarms of nosg came through to take over.

"I've heard rumors of murders," he said. "I have not committed them."

"Not one. Perhaps three?"

"No. None." The lie slipped out before he could stop it.

Her head tilted to one side. She ran her tongue under the lower lip as she considered him. "I was drawn here for a purpose. I just haven't discovered it yet. But you're caught up in it. I hear it in your voice. I smell it on you. A Shadline's instinct."

"Perhaps your mercusine powers have given you the sight," he said.

"I'm no merculyn. But I can feel it in others. A special skill I've developed during long years of hunting them."

The words slipped right into his mind. So easy, so soft. It was a moment before he comprehended them. "Hunting?"

"Aye."

"So you mean to kill me?" Hope leapt in his heart. *Please! Now. Do it right now. Here.* He attempted to spread his arms, to give her a clear stab. But the Hargothe's tricks kept him from doing it.

"Do you ever free your quarry?" she asked.

"Sometimes. If the year's not too lean. A mother about to bring forth a litter will find me merciful. A pup or kit will go free if not too sorely injured."

She smiled, broadly. Her femininity showed through the hardness, and he suddenly pictured her gowned and primped for a Gristenside ball. "Merciful to animals but not to children. I find that curious."

There was nothing Tym could say to that. The urge to confess to the Flekk murders made him cough. But the words could rise no farther than his throat.

"I can take you to the Citadel. To Marlow."

"Surely you mean to turn me over to the Watch for the crimes you think I've committed. Perhaps collect the reward. I hear Her Enlightened is offering a five hundred gold skillet bounty to anyone who leads to the killer."

"Interesting thing about murders," she said. "They happen every day in Starside. The number has declined, believe it or not, since the new rash of bodies began turning up. I think the usual villains are afraid to wander about at night. But you aren't a usual villain, are you? A usual villain would have a reason to have killed Flekk and those children. I want to understand why you did it. The Watch didn't report a single item stolen, and there was an obvious coinbox in Flekk's desk, with a rather flimsy lock. She had no enemies. A kindly woman, well-loved by her neighbors. The children? Their father is a man of the Watch. Do we think they were killed to wound him? If you'd met the father you'd know that's not likely. Captain LiTishke says he's a poor armsman and too soft on the riff-raff. I take that to mean he is a fair-minded and even-handed. Qualities Captain LiTishke sees as weakness. So why did you kill them?"

How strange. She declared that he had killed Flekk and the children, then skipped on past it to his motive. She didn't seem angry, or even disturbed to be sitting across from such a reprehensible person. He could hardly stomach being in his own skin; how could she refrain from sending him straight into Kil's gaping maw?

She blew out her cheeks and stood. "Shall we? Marlow will be in his offices at the Citadel. He works tirelessly."

"You knew I'd be here. How?"

"I didn't know you'd be here. I'm a Shadline, trapper. I listen and obey. Did you know Flekk's neighbors saw a man fitting your description go into her house? Did you know a Sensual at the Baths is a hopeless gossip? Rumor floats like smoke across this city. It is a testament to Captain LiTishke's incompetence that you are not already locked away in the Westbunk. But that is not where I'm taking you."

"Why not?"

She shrugged. "Were you a Shadline, you would understand. Since you are not, you must trust me. If you want to see Marlow."

He stood and waited for her to lead the way from the common room.

Tym was grateful for the cold, fresh air outside of The Grunting Pig. The fog had lifted. The sky was clean, and diamond stars stood proud against the blackness. This far south, the constellations were higher than he was used to, the northern ones hidden entirely. Mercus lights atop the Starside Wall marched inland. The black expanse of the Divide blocked part of the sky here. Tym shivered, as if the starshadow it cast stole heat from his body.

Jil started up the Street of Sorrows. "It's a long walk, but we'll be warmed by the effort."

Tym couldn't ask questions about her certainty that he was a murderer. Doing so would be akin to admitting it. So he asked the other question nagging at him. "Who are you that you can simply walk up to the Citadel and demand to see this Marlow fellow?"

"A Shadline can gain access to many places simply by asking. Not true in all the realms, but Her Enlightened holds to the old customs."

Jil would offer no more explanations during their long trek upslope. Tym knew he was walking into a trap. But since he was already in a trap, perhaps this next one would mercifully put him out of his misery.

30

UTTERLY RUTHLESS

They were a rag-tag band, Kila thought. A mad Donse Master wearing a *vaz'on,* a blind ten-year-old girl who had learned to see with her mercus senses, a lad of nearly sixteen with fiery hair and sad eyes, the Highest of Highests in the Way of Til, two cats, a Radiant's daughter missing her right hand, and one Cheapsgate waif recently turned Highest of a Way with no followers.

Was it so strange, then, that they had entered the unnatural no-world chamber of a Derslin Wheel?

Her companions were not so disinterested. Highest Quiv murmured with delighted wonder, while Dunne Yples cursed it as a demaynic hell. Quinn, still dazed and heartbroken over the loss of her blade-hand, even looked up and around to take in the odd blankness of the dark cavern.

Kila completed her work of blocking the corridor behind them. She would leave a secondary barrier in case her pursuers persisted.

With Yples removed from the gameboard, she thought it

would hold them for a while. The source-tap circles provided sufficient power, but the merculyn receiving it could not rely on brute force. They still had to know how to move objects, and most didn't. Only with the massive power coming from Yples would the main Sensual have blown through.

"We must hurry," Quiv said.

Kila didn't bother correcting him. The man was battling his own fear and at the same time trying to absorb the wonder of where he was.

"They feel distant to me," Dunne Yples said. Kila had forgotten that though he was unable to access the mercus, he could still feel it. Could reach for it, only to run into the *vaz'on's* glass-like wall that kept it just out of reach.

"They *are* distant," Kila said. "But also not." It was oddly satisfying to be the one with superior experience for once. Given time, she'd master the sideways talk of the Voluptuary of Starside. Odd how much she missed that woman.

She walked alongside Quinn, wanting to offer comfort, but also fearful that her raven-haired friend would lash out at her if she showed anything that could be construed as pity. Henley went ahead of the group, a mercus sphere shedding light around them.

Dunne Yples shuffled along, a man who didn't care where he was going and who was in no hurry to get there. Highest Quiv seemed to go two speeds at once. Alternately lurching ahead to escape pursuit then slowing to gawp at his surroundings.

Quinn held her stump wrist close to her belly, hand clamped around it. To hide it from herself? To squeeze off phantom pains, perhaps? Kila kept close watch on the disfigurement, making sure it didn't pain her friend. Quinn's posture seemed simply an animal instinct to draw inward when injured. Perhaps it was all those things.

"Don't you dare apologize, Sigh," Quinn said suddenly.

"I—" But Kila didn't know how to finish. What could be said? When Father had died, many had come forward to offer their sympathy. Father had been well-liked in lower Terriside. He'd had friends in Cheapsgate as well.

But consolations were not for the one who received them. They were for the one who offered. People comforted themselves by offering sympathy. A salve for injuries they imagined themselves to have received. Their words had been salt in Kila's wounded heart. And in the days following, how many had stepped forward to help Wen and her?

The only comforting words Kila thought of for Quinn were: *You'll learn to wield a blade left-handed.* But they were only words, and that meant they were salt. If she was going to hurt her friend more—even if it was for her own good—she might as well do it in a more direct fashion.

Shrugging off her backpack, she dug through it as they walked. Her hands found Bone Chill first. *Shinane!* it hissed to her. Releasing it, she scrounged until her fingers clamped around Black's scabbard.

She pulled it free and shoved it at Quinn. "Take it."

Quinn recoiled from her blade. "I—I can't."

Kila pressed the scabbarded blade flat against her friend's chest. "Take it."

When Quinn refused, Kila shrugged and dropped Black onto the floor. The hilt clanked on the stone. Kila kept walking.

Quinn stopped, face darkening with fury, nostrils flaring. Kila had heard many women teased in Cheapsgate taverns, told by beady-eyed men how anger made them beautiful. Invariably, women fell for the taunt and either fled in tears or grew even more irate, drawing laughter from the men gathered to watch.

But it was surely true of Quinn. Her fierceness made her straighten, drop her arms to her sides, one clenched in a fist. Arched brows flattened over dark eyes that caught the white-fire of Henley's mercus light.

Kila met this with iron. "We don't have time for your self-pity. Get your blade and come with us, or leave it for those who follow." Inside Kila wept. To treat her friend so harshly went against her heart. But she *knew*—knew deep in her gut —what Quinn needed now was anger. Kila would take it. She deserved it anyway. Maybe there would be day far in the future when they could discuss what had happened here. Maybe then Kila could apologize. For everything.

She felt Quinn finally give in and gather up her blade. One-handed she would struggle to buckle it to her belt. And Kila would have to let her struggle. Perhaps Quinn would find the strength to ask for help, but Kila doubted it.

"This cavern cannot be this large," Quiv said. "By my esti-mation, we should have reached the cliff overlooking the sea by now."

"A Derslin Wheel exists in its own bubble," Kila said. "Or so Dunne Marlow told me."

"Marlow!" Quiv and Yples cried at the same time. They looked at each other aghast and momentarily allied in outrage.

"What business did you have with the Hargothe's disgraced brother?" Quiv demanded.

"Of course you'd be friends with a wicked man like Marlow," Yples said. "A demayncor and a lover of Spinsters."

Both of those accusations were true. Marlow had once told Kila of his excommunication from the Way of Til, brought on by his love for a Spinster named Hetta.

"Marlow is not all one thing. He's just a man," she said, not really listening to herself. "He helped me. He has no love for his brother."

"And a murderer who gives to the orphanage is excused for his crimes?" Yples asked.

"How many did you kill on the ash-barrens, Dunne Yples?" Pennie said softly. She had been walking next to the man, silently observing all.

"Impertinent little hog-squirt! How *dare* you speak to me in that—"

"Silence your filthy maw, fool!" Pennie snapped in a guttural whisper.

Even furious Quinn was startled into open-mouthed shock by the girl's growled command. Kila heard an imitation of hateful old Sensual Thine in the girl's voice. She had even pinched her mouth into a tight inward pucker.

Pennie's eyes also flared in the mercus light. "If you have nothing to offer but hatred, then offer nothing. You receive mercy and return it with malice. I would pity you if I were not so overfilled with contempt."

She stalked forward to join Henley, whose eyebrows had climbed his forehead. The cats returned to Henley's circle of light, their eyes aglow, curious to discover why mild Pennie had suddenly exploded.

Highest Quiv blew out a breath and motioned for Henley to keep walking.

Yples stood still for a while, cheeks maroon with rage. A

hint of his former madness showed in this mask. Kila had a bolt prepared should he attempt to harm Pennie.

But it wasn't necessary. The man abruptly turned and headed the other direction, disappearing into darkness.

"What an obnoxious prat he is," Quinn said, forgetting her own problems for a moment. "Does he truly mean to join our enemies?"

"They're not our enemies," Kila said firmly. "They are just . . . mistaken. And I can't even blame them for that, considering what they've seen of me."

Her whole life had been about doing wrong things out of necessity. And it was time to do so again. Reaching with her mercus senses she found the jewels of the *vaz'on*, intuition guiding her to the one over Yples right ear. It shone bright red the second she attached her power to it. She felt Yples entire body. Just as she suspected. A willshift gem. She turned the man around and brought him back into the light.

"I'll keep the reins on you for now, Dunne Yples. I hate having to do it. But you can't be allowed to join them. They will use your power against us."

"Ruthless," Quinn whispered. "Utterly ruthless. I approve."

Kila spun on her. "Do you? Do you truly?"

Not wanting any eyes on her, Kila marched forward and briskly bypassed Henley to join the cats in the darkness. Moments later, the far fringe of the light caught the columns of the Derslin Wheel.

Behind, a mercus feat flared. A Sensual or Spinster attempting to unblock the corridor leading to the chamber. It was a sad moment. Kila could not allow them to ever find the Derslin Wheel.

She had weakened the ceiling beyond the barrier already. With sadness in her heart, she released the bolts that held it up.

The rumble vibrated the floor, but so faintly only the merculyns among them would have noticed. That excluded only Quinn. But she looked backward anyway.

Kila continued to the circle of columns. They had time now. But unless she figured out how the Derslin Wheel worked, she had committed them all to rather long, slow death by starvation.

31

COWER AND CRY

Hateful woman, the Hargothe thought as he extricated his trembling arm from under her blazing, naked body. Yioth slept now, her breath rising and falling in long, slow cycles, each exhale furnace-hot.

Noy had fetched a pile of rags and hides to offer some padding. Yioth had not required them, but despite his restored strength, the Hargothe was not a young man. His body ached from this creature's insatiable demands.

He wondered—not for the first time—if this was a strange sort of trap. Did she truly wish to bring Kil into the world through him? Or did she instead wish to corrupt him, lead him away from righteousness, and so defeat Til's conquest over the world? For that is what he sought. *Til's* conquest.

But if Kil lived, who was to say he could not be harnessed to Til's chariot? Could Pol or Ori or any other such striver challenge such a pairing, Kil pulling and Til with the whip hand?

No. The rest of forever would be decided. The father god

of disciplined righteousness, purity, and good would realize the total victory denied him by the sin of the Triumvirate.

So yes, let Kil arise and sit at Til's feet, a servile puppy. And what of Kil's supposed domain—of hatred and lust and murder and sickness? Were those necessarily qualities of evil? No. Their weight upon the moral balance depended on the intention behind them. Til could rightfully use a plague to punish a city, he could reward a king with a bevy of nubile and compliant lovers, he could bless Eyes of Til to peer into the hearts of men and pull forth their sins into His light. If grievous enough, then surely Til's men could rightfully execute those of corrupt heart.

The mistake Ori made was assuming what goodness meant. The so-called gentle goddess. Bah! Goodness was not compassion, which was another word for weakness. Goodness was not to be found in the concept of love, which was another word for weakness. It was not generosity, which was another word for weakness. Goodness was righteousness, and right-eousness was obedience to Til's will. Nothing less, nothing more.

Humankind was as adaptable as a chained hound. If born to its chain, it thought nothing of it. Freedom endangered it, for it would follow its base instinct to track and hunt and fornicate. But chained, it could serve its master at the master's need.

And the few who were chosen to interpret that need had the greatest burden of all. Until Til came to reign over his dominion directly, it was up to men like the Hargothe to translate Til's will into law.

Order. Compliance.

A single, world-encompassing Empire of Righteousness.

In service to that goal, all was permitted. All was required.

"Noy!" he called. His voice boomed in the barren hall.

The nosg hustled in, offering nods and bows the whole way. These registered to the Hargothe as swirls of air currents. "Yes, Your Greatness?"

"Don't call me that. Highness, if you must." A noble title was necessary now that he ruled over Ceronhel. It meant nothing to him, but the nosg only respected power.

"Yes, Great Highness."

He gritted his teeth. Punishing the nosg with more mercus lashes or mind probes would merely increase its desperation, resulting in ever more ridiculous appellations.

"I require tea. And bread." He had faint hopes that the loaf would be edible. If he didn't know better he would have sworn the nosg-wench who baked it cut it with saw dust.

"Deer meat?" Noy suggested.

"Ah, yes. That would be well."

Noy scurried away.

"Cooked! Not burned!" the Hargothe called after his servant. He longed for men to come to Ceronhel and serve him. Even incompetent ones would do better than these dimwitted urchins.

"I like my meat charred," Yioth said, stretching and purring as she turned to face him.

The Hargothe listened to her sounds, felt the air stir, built a picture of her in his mind.

She propped her head on a hand. How brazen she was in her nakedness, displaying all that should remain hidden save for a husband's eyes and caresses. "I quite like deer," she said.

She did not waste words, he knew. Perhaps she was truly

hungry. But she was also telling him that she could devour him, literally, if she chose.

"Tell me of the constraints upon your freedom in this world," he said, returning to lie next to her. He could do nothing else. Her unique power was to stir his lust. No man could deny such a pull, any more than that dog could release itself from its chain.

"Constraints?"

"You said your kind is not free to do what you will in this realm. You are a demayne, are you not? Then whoever brought you here must have bargained to keep you from overrunning every realm and ruling them yourself."

"You mistake the nature of my kind, Tenn. We are not concerned with lands and mines and gold and cities and thrones."

"Then what concerns you?"

"Freedom."

"Ah, to be unharnessed. To wreak havoc on us all."

"No. To leave this world altogether. Kil will set us free. He will return us to *our* demaynic realm."

A burst of power arose far, far away. It shook the subtle world of the mercusine like a fly striking a spider's web. "Another one?" he said. How could still another powerful merculyn awaken. A culmination was coming, no doubt. He felt Yioth slither close, fingers seeking the edges of his robes. This time he resisted. And in truth he had nothing left to offer on that front. Not until he'd eaten, washed, slept, and meditated upon the mercusine.

"Go feed," he said. "I must rest."

The woman-thing rose. He saw with mercusine senses how

she gathered her garments and flowed into them. Such dangerous grace.

"It is well," she said coolly. "I need to stretch my wings. And you keep it too hot in here."

Her armor clanked softly as she departed. He took hold of a force-bonded nosg, made it trail after her. She went to the very top of the remaining Ceronhel tower. His nosg struggled to keep up. She was aware of it, of course. Her senses were likely as sharp as the Hargothe's, though for different reasons. She did not use the mercus as did Yoznithan Flaumishtak.

The Hargothe took over the nosg's body, saw through its eyes. Nosg did not see color very well, but they could see in the dark, needing no light at all. Yioth appeared to him as a glowing figure, almost white with inner heat. She stepped onto the parapet and jumped off.

She immediately plummeted from view, only to rise again in the distance, a woman aloft on dragon's wings. She circled, gliding on the chill air currents of the mountains. One flap, two flaps and she gained altitude, turning back to the tower. The Hargothe watched, rapt to see the magnificent creature in flight. Dragnithan Yiothizandra!

Magnificent was too mild a term. Glorious did not serve either. Yioth did not take on dragon form as it was depicted in pictures he'd studied in his youth. No, unlike the dragnithor demayne, she was a dragnithan, retaining her woman-form, but with reddish wings sprouting from her back and shoulders. Her armor and clothing had accommodated these new appendages somehow. Like a vengeful minion of Til, she flew toward him, her sword now drawn.

Faster and faster she came. And in the final instant, her

mouth gaped wide and fire burst forth to crisp the nosg just before she hewed its head from its shoulders.

The Hargothe had withdrawn just in time to avoid feeling the agony of the slaughter. Awed and tingling with his newly awakened appetite for bodily pleasures, he went to a basin and splashed his face with cold water.

"Imagine her at the head of my army," he said to himself. "Imagine the *fear* she will strike into men's feeble hearts. They will cower and cry out and weep for their mothers."

He was no fool. She would not serve him that way. Not without enormous recompense. But what did such a dragon-kin desire that she was not already taking?

No. There would be no bargain as such. She would need to be ensnared. Had she not already lamented her lack of freedom? All he need do was constrain it further. His bargain, an eventual release from bondage.

Of course, he would never allow that.

But how could he collar her? She who had so much power over him?

He fetched his staff and walked to his curtained window. She was out there now. Hunting. Feeding.

He was at a disadvantage because he did not know much about her kind. But he knew one who did. And was not Til truly great? For the Hargothe would soon speak to that individual. Ah, the glorious force of destiny carried him forward, even when he did not see all ends.

His staff would need more souls after this. But if he was subtle he could take a dozen more nosg without fomenting rebellion among his servants.

He didn't hear Noy return with tea and bread. Both would be cold by the time he was done in Starside.

"Where are you, trapper?" he mumbled. Searching the force-bond and tracing it across the long miles south and east, he slipped into the man's mind. Not to take control this time, but merely to observe. The Hargothe was blind, what need did he have to see through the trapper's eyes? None. But he could tap some of what the man heard, smelled, tasted, felt. Yes. And he could nudge.

If needed, he could do much more than that.

32

FEEBLER STILL

Kila let Henley explain the Derslin Wheel to Highest Quiv. She immediately began walking the circle, searching for one particular column.

Dunne Yples stood like a statue in the center of the Wheel. Right where she'd left him. Maintaining the willshift took no effort at all with the *vaz'on*. It still made her skin crawl to think of what she was doing to the man.

Pennie had joined the cats who were sipping from the channel of clear water running through the circle.

"What are you looking for?" Quinn asked. She'd remembered Kila's transgression with Black and had grown sullen again.

"A symbol. Three slashes from upper left to lower right."

"Why those?" Highest Quiv asked. He had his nose pressed to a column, finger tracing a circle bisected by two vertical lines. "This feels like metal."

"It is." The symbols all glowed a brilliant white that turned to blue at the fringes in Kila's mercus vision. She had never seen this particular alloy anywhere else.

"Three slashes," Quinn said, voice tired and irritated. "There!" She pointed.

"Excellent."

"Will you tell us what you mean to do?" Highest Quiv asked.

"Yes. I mean to open a portal to a beach."

"Portal? Like a door?" Pennie said. "Why not dymense us?"

Kila flashed a glance at Quinn, who blanched at the mere mention of dymensing. "I can't do it yet. I don't know how."

"But you can open a portal to a beach here?"

"These columns are mercus relics. Each one leads to a different place. I think."

"Your confidence is inspiring," Quinn said.

"Quinn," Henley said softly. Kila didn't see what he did, but Quinn went to join him. She didn't bother listening to their whispered conversation. Her focus was on the three slashes as she tried to remember just what she'd done to open the portal before.

It had been similar to heating the iron in the thinnies' blood. But instead of heat, she had added to the glow of the metal in her mercus vision. It had failed once before, had thrown her onto her backside. She was glad Marlow hadn't been around to see that.

But he had been there to see her fall backward through the portal. And he'd seen her nearly eaten by a dragon.

Quiv was saying something. Warning her of something. She wasn't listening. The man was always nervous. He'd told her he liked to stay out of the reach of danger when playing dangerous games. Leave it to a woman, then, to get them out of this place.

She continued to add to the glow of the three slashes, paying special attention to the smells. At the edge of her ability to detect it came the scent of moist sand. Salt air ruffled through the fuzz of hair on her scalp. "That's it," she mumbled, seeking to enhance the smells. "Now open yer vergent ring window, ya overgrown post."

The column responded to her request in wondrous fashion. The white and blue glow intensified as it spread vertically. When it was two spans high, it puckered at the center. With a slow, ragged tear, the portal opened. Like a hole burned through the center of paper. Except this did not char the air so much as to rip it. An uneven hole, tall enough for an atlen, wide enough for three, stood in the air before her where the column had been.

A number of curses arose behind her. Quiv added an especially delicious one that Kila vowed to remember for later use. In the space beyond the hole, a beach. Blue sky met a turquoise sea in a sharp horizon line. Waves curled into the shore, foaming white before they tipped forward to crash and wash upon the sand. The surf rush toward them, thinned, slowed, and finally spilled a bucket's worth of seawater onto the floor at Kila's feet.

"Kil's babe in a bonnet!" Quinn said. "Where—? Where is that?"

Kila waggled her pursed lips back and forth a few times. "Let's find out." She stepped through, eyes immediately going to the sky. After the darkness of the Derslin Wheel, she was forced to squint. The sand blazed under the sun and glared from the ocean.

"It's like Garden Island," Henley said. "The air has the same feel."

"Not those trees, though," Quiv said. He pointed at a stand of scraggly ones, trunks twisted and gnarled. They stood in thick ranks along the top of the beach, just out of reach of the tides. The leaves were heavy and flat, bright green. Blue fruit hung from low branches.

Kila brought Yples through. Pennie followed, then Quinn.

"Watch for dragons," Kila said, scanning the sky.

"What was that?" Quiv asked absently. "Dragons, did you say?"

"Yes. I was nearly swallowed by one when I came through the last time."

That got Quiv's attention. He no longer looked around in wonder so much as in fear. "Why in Til's bloody name did you bring us here?"

She lifted a shoulder. "It's the one I knew I could open. I wanted to try it on something I knew worked before I just—"

"We should go back," Henley said.

"What? Why?"

"Huff says Startle is that way." He pointed. East. Out to sea.

"But if this is the eastern shore . . ." Quinn turned to orient herself to the blazing sun, which stood low to the east, as if just risen. "Then we'd have to be far, far west of Starside here. With the entire western realm, Losstra, the Destig Desert, the Neer Plain, and the Honor Mountains between us."

Henley whistled. "Back to the Derslin?" he eyed Kila.

Quiv was already stepping through, calling for Quinn and Pennie to follow.

They returned to the dark cavern, now cold and dry by comparison. Though it had no discernible ceiling, Kila felt the gloom press on her now. She brought Yples back through and stationed him in the center of the ring of columns. "At least there's one way out," she said as she released her power. The burning fringes of the portal collapsed and then vanished, leaving the column as it had been.

"Which one next?" she asked. "How 'bout this one?" She went to the one Quiv had been tracing earlier. The symbol was a circle bisected by vertical lines. Already the glow was growing.

"No! Wait!" Highest Quiv called.

"Why? We won't find a good one unless I keep opening them."

"Patience. Please. If you wouldn't mind releasing Dunne Yples. I think perhaps he might be able to help here." He scratched his chin and bent close to a different column. "These runes look familiar to me."

Kila let the willshift gem go. Yples sagged, shoulder drooping, head dipping. Kila realized she'd kept too tight a hold on the man. Next time she'd go easier.

Next time? Had she embraced the necessity already? She rubbed her elbows, suddenly chilled by the cavern. "Get what you can out of him," she said to Highest Quiv.

The frazzled Donse Master allowed himself to be guided to a column. Highest Quiv spoke with hushed enthusiasm, a note of speculation in his voice. At first Yples didn't respond, his shoulders rising and falling as he sought to catch his breath.

But then Quiv had out the diary he'd shown to Kila. He flipped through the pages excitedly, no longer showing the gentle reverence he'd demonstrated before. He jabbed a finger onto a page.

Yples was looking now. Keenly. Highest Quiv had ignited a dormant scholarly interest in the man. But Yples was shaking his head. "No. No. The Cigil-Tine form was lateral. And see here—" he moved to two columns along. "This has the ascender angled. They did not use this arm."

Quiv clucked his tongue and squinted to and from his book. "But the resemblance is there, no?"

Yples was unwilling to concede anything, but his mind had been captured by the notion Quiv had raised. "Misen-Tine reputedly had its own glyph style in the Half Age. It would have been derived from Cigil-Tinian. Not as fussy as all that." He waved his hand at Quiv's book.

"Misen-Tine? How would you know that?"

Yples got cagey all of sudden. "There are a handful of Wrong volumes in the Library of Dunne Francis LiMillar. I spent many a happy hour there—researching, mind you."

"Of course. Researching." Quiv flashed a meaningful look at Kila. She didn't catch the meaning, unfortunately.

"I learned to speak the language of the First Race," Henley said. "A little. But it was transliterated into Ennish. My tutor didn't have any texts to teach me the glyphs."

"Same for me," Quinn said. They had gathered around the two Donse Masters. "But if these runes are First Race glyphs then they should refer to place names, no?"

Quiv returned his book to his satchel. "That's what I thought, but another notion is coming to me. One I don't like."

"Simple identifiers," Yples said, nodding. "Which means

there was a catalog. And without it, we're back to the girl's guesswork."

"One of you better speak plain or I'm going to straighten your tongues,' Kila said.

It was Quiv who deigned to answer. Yples was wandering among the columns now, tracing glyphs and muttering to himself.

"What Dunne Yples is saying is there would have been a catalog list. It would show each of these glyphs and next to it, the name of the destination to which its portal leads."

"So the glyphs themselves might not have any significance?" Henley said.

"That doesn't make any sense," Kila said. "Nobody wants to bother with looking something up in a list."

"What do you suggest, then?" Quiv asked archly.

"I don't know. Perhaps they're like banner flags. You know, like in the throne of iron stories. All the armsmen marched under their lord's banner flag. Like the Raven-in-Flight for Starside."

"But these are glyphs," Quiv said with exaggerated patience. "Not symbols of heraldry."

"She is not wrong," Yples said. "Not entirely." Now he was rubbing his chin, scratching stubby finger through his beard. "The First Race's glyphs were derived from an older form of picto-glyphs. Very few remain for reference." He pointed at the symbol before him, three parallel squiggles. "River. Or perhaps running water."

Kila could see it. "But which river?"

"I need paper. Ink," he said abruptly. "I cannot think without scribbling."

Now Highest Quiv was nodding vigorously. "I have a goose stylus in my case. A pot of ink. But no paper."

"I do," Kila said, digging out the blank book she'd brought from the library.

"Rather small," Yples groused. "But I have cramped writing." Within a minute he was sitting crosslegged, ink at one knee, quill in hand, and Kila's book on his lap. "Bring your lightball down closer, boy," he snapped at Henley. "My eyes are old."

Henley complied.

Yples narrated as he sketched an oblong shape across a two-page spread. "This is the First Race realm of Helossin. It stretched from Starside to Alirya and subjugated all the nations in between." He dotted in Garden Island and Ansso next to it. A narrow loop to the south described Iops. "This is dreadful," he murmured, sketching in squiggles for rivers, jagged lines for mountain ranges, and dark dots for cities. "Truly, my skills are deplorable. But the orientation is all that matters, no?" He was speaking to himself now, drawing a map from memory.

Finally he made a little star on the coast. "What we call Starside," he said. "Or Stermūin, as the First Race called it. Star. Moon."

Kila's skin thrilled. "That last part is like Semūin."

Quiv shook his head and eyed Yples. The man didn't know anything of Kila's mother, she realized. And probably best to keep it that way, considering his already poor opinion of her. But Yples merely nodded. "*Se* could mean water, but also daughter. So, daughter of the moon. Daughter of the Water. But in relation to the fabled spirit, I'd say both were inferred by the name. Perhaps more strongly toward moon. Lumne is

Semūin's mother after all. Moonlight and water are kindred qualities in vergent lore." He bent to his map, now humming softly as he dotted in more cities and strongholds.

Kila straightened and looked at Nax. The cat was huddled next to Huff at the edge of the water channel.

I'm Lumne's grand-daughter, she sent.

Nax blinked, keeping her eyes closed for a long time before opening them to slits. *Who?*

Lumne. As in Lumne's wakeless dream. The mistress of sleep and death. The warming arms who receive those who perish?

Nax didn't answer except to close her eyes. Henley's hand on her shoulder startled Kila.

"Sorry," he said. "Huff said Nax is concerned because you were babbling."

If Nax was truly concerned she would have come over and nuzzled Kila's shin. No. Nax was just disinterested.

"Did you hear Yples? I'm Lumne's grand-daughter. The mistress of the wakeless dead is my nana? No wonder Gian bolted. I would."

"I heard. I'm still here."

She flattened her lips. "You're here because you're stuck with me in this place."

Yples cried with delight. "I've got it!" Now he had his tongue clamped between his teeth as he scrawled tiny symbols over dots. "So simple! So obvious!"

Highest Quiv was sitting next to him on the floor. They looked like two boys playing a game. "*Exle,* yes. *Walz.* Yes. I see that. But here"—he pointed to the oasis city of Trist in middle of the Destig Desert—"Surely not *Quoa.* That's better suited for something wet, tropical."

"YES!" Dunne Yples roared. "Like Garden Island!" He

scratched out the Destig glyph and scribbled it over Garden Island.

Kila understood the notations, if not the glyphs themselves. At the moment she only cared about one thing. "What about Starside? What's the symbol for Stermūin?"

Yples sucked in his breath and flipped to a blank sheet. Now he was making shapes. First a star. Then a circle. Then a waxing moon and a waning moon.

"Bisected, surely," Quiv suggested. "The Divide."

"Yes. Yes. Yes!" Yples crossed out his previous attempts and carefully formed a new one, mumbling to himself. "The southern moon, the northern star. Divided city. Mountains backing." He laughed softly. "Well it's obvious isn't, Highest Quiv? *Lorle.*"

Highest Quiv slapped his forehead. "There it is. Staring at us right in the face. Well done, sir. Well done." He scrambled to his feet and rushed to the columns.

The others joined him each searching for the glyph Dunne Yples had formed. The one Quiv had called a *Lorle*. A vertical line, half circle on the left, the right half of a pentagram on the right.

"I saw that one before," Henley said. "I'm sure of it."

"Rather a literal glyph, isn't it?" Quinn said, poking from one column to the next.

"If you're seeking the whole city," Highest Quiv said. "But we think of Starside as the whole city. It is not. The First Race surely would not have, or they wouldn't have called it Stermūin."

There was no point proceeding in a methodical manner. The symbols didn't stay put. Kila passed the three angled lines to the beach four times in a row before encountering a dome-topped square. A quick check with Yples told her he had not assigned that one, but he noted it down.

"Many will have no spot on my map, I fear," he said mournfully. "The lost realms of the First Race are many compared to the feeble civilizations of man."

"And what of woman?" Quinn called.

"Feebler still, girl! A Shadline you may be, but I'll show you a hundred-thousand daft housemothers to every one like yourself."

Quinn muttered several imprecations at Yples, his Way, and men in general. But it was Pennie who offered the most cutting rejoinder: "Who is dafter, the simple woman or the studied man who laughs at her?" She was tracing column symbols with her fingers. "I found it."

She had.

"This will open to Starside," Kila said with more hope than confidence. "But where? The last one didn't open to another Derslin Wheel."

"Yes. That's curious," Highest Quiv said. "Most curious. Something to ponder, indeed."

"Marlow will curse himself blue when he learns what we've discovered," Kila said, already adding to the glow of the *Lorle* glyph. "Pack your ink and quill, Dunne Yples. You can continue your scribbling once we're settled in our rooms."

"Rooms?" Quinn said. "What rooms?"

"Surely the Lady Peline can spare a few in her greathouse."

And then the portal burned open. Spread before them was blackness. Henley's mercus light probed ahead before Kila could step through. Columns lit up.

Her suspicion had proven true. It was another Derslin Wheel.

"That makes more sense," Highest Quiv said. But he didn't make any move to step through.

Kila did, and she saw at once it *was* the Wheel she knew. For it held many of the supplies Marlow had brought in when he'd been hiding here from the Hargothe.

"We're home," she said, and stepped through.

33

THE DARKNESS IS THICK

The Sorgeal Sea was angry when Fallo and his fellow Shadlines reached it. His mood wasn't much better. Three days into their downstream trip, they'd come to a sprawling delta of fingery streams and swamps that led nowhere. Zirhine said the way through changed from week to week. Sometimes hour to hour. She relied on her Shadline instincts to guide them, which only had them backtrack a dozen times, and portage the entire craft twice.

But now the sea opened before them, the Kovi-Mest coast to the west, the Sorgan Spit to the east. The Sorgeal was narrow here. Thirty miles wide. Fallo had hoped that meant for calm seas; he was quite disappointed. The waves were choppy and irregular, first striking the bow, then athwart the small craft's beam, threatening to tip them, cat and all, into the deep. Zirhine assured him that cats could swim.

At one point Fallo was tempted to test it out. Lop had grown surly during the trip, returning to her old ways of demanding food before responding to the simplest request.

"I think that animal is part pig," the Cloak said. "She's gained half a stone in six days."

That was an exaggeration. A quarter stone at most.

They put ashore early that day because Fallo told them he felt a pull to the land there on the Kovi-Mest side of the sea. They found a rocky beach, black stone polished by the surf. The rocks tinkled under their boots. Fallo had lied. He had only wanted to get out of the boat and stretch his legs. More than anything, he wanted a fire and a bit of cooked fish to chew on.

Fish! Lop sent.

How did you know I was thinking of fish?

Perhaps ask yourself why *you were thinking of fish.* Lop squirmed free of Fallo's pack and tender-footed across the stone, stopping to sniff empty clam shells and pools of salt water. *It's too wet here.*

Fallo helped drag the boat ashore. The Cloak was already ranging ahead, hand on his hilt in case he had to suddenly immolate a sea-shrub or a gull with his magic sword.

Zirhine was placid as ever. But even she seemed relieved to get off the water. He'd seen her slip a lip-full of some weed or other from one of her pouches. She'd looked a bit green prior, but soon she'd been hale as a Radiant's hound. Fallo had never had the seasickness. He liked knowing Zirhine had at least one frailty. He was still seeking one in Cloak Einlin. So far humorlessness was all he'd come with.

"I feel strongly that food and fire are required by the force of destiny," Fallo said.

"You think you are joking," Zirhine said, laughing lightly. "You do not understand 'Listen and Obey' at all. But you will learn. You will learn."

Well that took all the fun out of his deceit. And now she had him wondering if his lie was actually the Shadline instinct manifesting in a different way. "Do I have any say in my future at all?"

"Surely. You make decisions all the time. Each can lead to triumph or disaster, most are not so momentous. You are truly tired, cold, and hungry, no?"

"Uh, I have been since I met the Cloak."

She laughed again. A nice laugh with all sorts of very white teeth in it. "He loves the discomfort. That is his favorite tune, as we say."

"And what is yours?"

"The wind. The clouds. The pattern of wet leaves at the bottom of my teacup. They hold portents. For you the voice will be loud or soft, but you will always hear it once you know what to listen for. You must think us fools if you thought we did not know you sought respite from discomfort."

"But I thought—"

"Pain marks the path. But signposts themselves are not the path. You cannot serve the good of humankind if you are dead. For Cloak Einlin, resting discomfits his urgent mind. It took him many years to learn the wisdom in rest."

"So you're saying my pain has been his pleasure?" As if he hadn't known that already.

Again the white smile. "And the opposite is true, no? When you enjoy rest is when he struggles most. Life is full of perverse humor. But perhaps you think on these things too deeply. The Cloak is reticent to explain things to you for a simple reason. The more you hang words on things, the less you know the things themselves. A hunter knows the deer does not think of itself as a deer. So the hunter seeks to know it as it knows itself. So it is with your choices and the urgings of destiny. It is not one or the other. It is both, pushing, pulling, flowing in and out of each other. It is weather. Is the portent in the cloud or is it in my understanding of the cloud? I neither know nor care, for it works. Listen and obey."

With that she patted his arm amiably and left him to stew in the meaningless brew of words she'd just dumped into his head.

To Fallo's surprise, the Cloak discovered shelter and chose to use it. This made Fallo suspicious. During their first few ten-days wandering the wilderness, the Cloak had refused to use shelter, preferring to sleep in the open, without so much as a pine tree overhead to keep rain or snow off them.

The shelter here was a sea-side cottage, long abandoned. The roof was sound and there was no evidence that large wildlife had made it a den.

It was damp inside, the rough plank floorboards mushy and mossy. An iron stove crouched dejectedly in one corner. But being iron it was up to the task of holding and burning scavenged drift wood. The flue had a few rust holes. These the Cloak had Fallo plug with pieces of sticks mortared in place with mud.

Once it was fired and burning, the stove filled the cottage with a delightful warmth. Soon they began to dry out.

Fallo shed his cloak and shirt, hanging them on a wall peg near the stove. The Cloak did the same.

Zirhine's clothes soon hung from the single cross beam spanning the ceiling. Fallo's cheeks burned as he fought to keep his eyes from goggling her startling nakedness. She saved him from this struggle by retrieving a dry tunic from her pack.

Still, it barely fell to mid-thigh. There might be bit o' the gray in her hair, but curves were curves.

Lop was in particularly good spirits, taking up a position of honor near the stove and settling in for a good grooming. There'd be some moaning and vomiting from her later. Zirhine collected Lop's furballs. She said they were useful and rare.

Lop held Zirhine in high regard. *Finally, someone who recognizes my magnificence.*

The only furniture remaining was a table for two and two battered chairs, mostly rotten. The weary companions would have to make do with the floor for a bed. But first, food.

"I'm going to collect some dinner," Fallo said. "If we had a pot we could have a right good clam bake."

"They are good enough raw," the Cloak said.

Lop did not deign to join Fallo on the beach. Fallo was sure the cat would be in for an unpleasant surprise when the Cloak forbade her any of their dinner. On land she was to fend for herself.

Taking pity on his furry friend, Fallo sent, *You need to hunt.*

Later. I just got dry.

Only your paws were wet. You've been sleeping in my pack for ages.

Only a day or two, surely.

Cats had no sense of time. *You won't get any of my food from me. You know the rules.*

No answer except a discontented grudge coming through the bond. Fine, he thought. She'd been told. What she did with that information was her own responsibility.

Now *that* was a lesson hard earned. The Shadline blade Fallo carried came with a huge responsibility, according to the

Cloak. Fallo hadn't believed it at first because he didn't feel it. Only once he'd learned what the blade was had any sense of that responsibility awakened. But it was still very abstract.

Now here he was on a lonely stretch of the Kovi-Mest, gathering clams for his supper. Rather, *not* gathering clams. The shore was too rocky. He settled for the fat crabs sneaking among the rocks. Ol' Rusty did for them easily enough and soon he had half a dozen good ones.

He was returning to the cottage, his bounty bundled in his arms and jabbing his chilled bare chest, when the feeling came over him. It was different than when Startle had been bonded or when he'd felt the presence of Linas's hidden fortress.

He stopped walking. A gray mist had washed over the land here, though the skies were blue out to sea. Listen and obey was needed here. Something was calling to him.

He closed his eyes and let out a long breath. It took him a moment to find the sensation. A strange perception, like a soft brush of a feather over his bare shoulders. A snatch of song came to him. He sang in a quavery voice:

"On the foam-washed shore,
The salt-white fingers crawl,
The hand of poor Gin Wile
Tears apart his seaweed caul."

But this was not the ghost fingers of a lost sailor he felt. He turned in a circle, eyes still closed, letting himself feel whatever it was he felt. The breeze, the droplets freezing his flesh, the salt and seaweed and rotting fish smell of the sea, the rush and hush of the surf, like slumber breaths. The black stone tinkled under his boots, chime-like but discordant.

The tickle on his shoulders remained. The claws of dead crabs pressed into his skin. It was all discomfort, but behind that, another feeling. Trepidation, a hint of fear. A resistance. As if an inner voice called softly to him, *Do not go that way.*

The way in question was behind the cottage. Inland, where the land rose into a verdant, rock strewn heath. There was nothing there. But this sensation said there was.

He returned to the cottage and began dressing. "We must go up a ways."

Rather than ask him why, his companions simply dressed and girded themselves for whatever the day might bring. Lop squinted at him. She eyed the crabs he piled onto the moldering table.

You will never get into them, he sent.

What are those? Spiders? They can be tasty.

Spiders. Armored spiders. You will not get to the flesh.

A distinct we'll-see-about-that feeling came over the bond.

Out of irritation, Fallo sent, *Stay here.*

As if the cat had any intention of leaving the comfort and warmth of the cottage. Lop meowed and curled her fluffy tail around her feet.

The Cloak nodded to Fallo. Zirhine merely arched an eyebrow, as if to say, "Lead on."

And so he did.

Fallo was no tracker, but a different sort of thick grass had taken root in a narrow band that wound upward. It was bordered by the heather and gorse that blanketed the rest of the countryside. This overgrown path ascended a shallow incline to the top of a rise.

But that wasn't where the feeling told Fallo not to go.

"This is silly," he muttered. "I feel that we must not go this way."

"They why did you fetch us?" Zirhine asked. The Cloak merely drew Tosuin.

"I don't know. But I know we must." His heart began to pound.

"You are learning."

It irritated Fallo that her words warmed him. He waved a hand, shooing the distraction away. He didn't know if he was learning or if greater forces were simply using him as a hand-tool.

He broke from the overgrown track to go north. The feathery feeling still tingled his shoulders. Stronger now, more demanding that he turn and run away. His breathing and heartbeat responded accordingly. "Kil be a merry maiden," he said, drawing Ol' Rusty from its scabbard. "There's nothing ahead. It should be right—"

His foot caught something hard hidden under the heather, pitching him forward. He came down awkwardly, flinging his blade hand out to keep from stabbing himself. A shock zinged through his elbow and his cheek mashed vegetation flat.

The pain of the fall barely registered, for the trepidation he'd felt now coursed down his spine. He scrabbled to his feet and backed away from where he'd fallen. He bumped into Zirhine.

"Steady," she said. "It is merely a slab of stone." She held her curved blade, Reft, in her hand. She set about hacking the grasses clear.

The stone beneath had been eroded to smoothness by ages of rain and wind. But the form quickly became clear. The Cloak joined in, pulling up clumps with his hands. He never chopped things with Tosuin because the blade sometimes set them ablaze in a fit of pique.

Fallo forced himself to stay put, but he couldn't bring himself to help with the mowing. The slab was carved all across its rectangular expanse. The lines had likely been chiseled deeply into the gray and green flecked stone, but they had been smoothed away over the ages, the remaining depth filled with soil.

"It's a man," he said, studying the carving of an armored figure holding a sword on his chest.

"It is a tomb," the Cloak said. "This is a Lumne's Lay."

Fallo noted with rising alarm that his mentor had not sheathed his weapon. In fact he looked more ready for battle than before.

Zirhine ran her blade around the edge of the stone, revealing a thick edge. It was a slab resting atop a flat-hewn stone beneath. "Older than that, Cloak Einlin," she said. She traced a series of ruins along a simply carved border pattern. "vergent wards."

"This is a *vergent* tomb?" Fallo said, skeptically.

"No. It is a man's tomb. Whoever put it here, likely the fellow depicted, feared the vergent would come for his bones."

"First off, vergent-kin don't truly exist. Second, they are small. No way they could move that slab."

"Third," said Zirhine, holding up three fingers. "Some can pass through doors without opening them. These wards were placed to prevent that." And now she sounded skeptical.

"And why would vergent-kin want someone's bones?" he asked.

"Why else but to entrap their soul?" the Cloak said. "Do we go in, Shadline?"

The question caught Fallo off guard. He rubbed his bruised elbow and plucked greenery from his thick eyebrow. "In?"

The Cloak didn't dignify his question but simply waited, sword in hand, body tense. Why was he tense if this was a tomb?

The fear pushing Fallo back had a smell now. Not a true smell, but a remembered smell. A piquant quality of bitter but satisfying cheese or wine. Repulsively attractive. Kind of like Fallo himself.

"In. But I don't think the three of us can heft that lid. It's a ton at least. Maybe if we get Lop in harness . . ."

The joke struck unamusable ears and thudded into the gorse.

"A lever will have to serve," the Cloak said. He walked the perimeter of the stone, studying the edges. Lips pursed, he considered an angle. "Seems to slope a bit that way." With no more explanation, he lowered Tosuin close to the grown and began waggling the tip between the slab and the rock beneath.

The steel on stone grinding made Fallo's teeth shudder. Even Zirhine's lips pulled back in response to the horrific sound.

"That cannot be proper Shadline sword, uh, husbandry." He didn't know what the word was for caring for one's blade. But he'd known a couple blacksmiths who would have beat a man's head against an anvil if he attempted this trick with one of their swords.

The Cloak got the sword wedged an inch or two in, then to Fallo's horror, picked up a stone and commenced hammering it on the pommel. Clank. Clank. Clank. Scrape. Clank.

"The poor fellow below is trying to be dead," Fallo said. "Not even Lumne can hold his spirit beneath the surface with that ramming going on right overhead."

The slab lifted as the thickness of the blade drove in. "Get your blades in there and help," the Cloak ordered.

Zirhine shrugged and added Reft to pry bar duty. Fallo looked at Ol' Rusty. "Noble Rusty, forgive this indignity."

There was plenty of room for Rusty. But it wasn't that long of a blade, so he didn't think it would offer much leverage. The Cloak counted and they heaved together.

The slab tilted up, an inch. Abruptly the other side loosened its grip enough to slide. The slab slammed down, revealing a black gap six inches wide.

"Did you ask Lop to come?" Zirhine said, laughing.

Fallo wanted to laugh. He did. But opening the tomb even this much had tripled the scurrying tingles crossing his shoulders. A rank smell rose through the gap. "Ugh. It smells like the Sourwater."

"Heave!" the Cloak shouted on a grunt.

Fallo heaved. Zirhine groaned.

The slab slid a bit more, guided by Tosuin's steel. The black gap opened beneath it, revealing the first step of narrow stone stairway.

"Hewn from the bedrock," the Cloak said. Had that been a note of surprise? Perhaps even grudging respect for the poor blokes who'd toiled away to make this hell-tomb in the middle of Kil's own scrabble-land?

"I thought it would be just a hole," Fallo said, peering into the blackness. "Does it seem to you the daylight doesn't quite reach as far in as it should?"

Lop, get up here. I have a job for you.

Zirhine returned Reft to her the scabbard on her back. "What say you, Shadline? In we go?"

He swallowed and rubbed one elbow. His instincts told him not to go, not even if a dragon were swooping down to flame him to matchsticks. But another part of his mind insisted he go in.

Lop? Wake up!

He felt the cat stir. *I'm too hungry to walk that far.*

I thought you were going to eat all the crabs.

I couldn't get in.

Come here. I need you to go in a hole.

Why didn't you say so?

The cat began to move.

"I'm going to have Lop nose in there a bit. She'll be able to smell if anything, uh, dangerous is in there."

"The dangers won't be alive," the Cloak said.

Horrors thrilled over Fallo's skin. "You mean the dead are shuffling around down there?"

The Cloak turned away. Zirhine put a hand on Fallo's arm. She leaned close. "I believe he was referring to traps."

"Oh. Well. Of course. Ha ha. Just makin' a bit of humor, you know?"

Where are you? he sent to Lop.

The cat arrived five minutes later, ambling along as if she had all day and nothing to do. *Where's this hole?*

Fallo pointed. Lop stopped at the edge, feet daintily together as she peered into the unnatural gloom. Suddenly, she slunk down the steps until her inky fur blended into the shadows and she was gone.

Not so fast, Fallo sent. *There could be—*

The clank of iron against stone resounded from the narrow stairwell. Like a battle axe striking a hunk of granite.

"Lop!" Fallo shouted.

What do traps look like? Lop sent.

Zirhine covered her mouth. Even the Cloak tensed.

Fallo still felt Lop through the bond. "She is well. I thought—"

Zirhine gasped with relief. The Cloak did not relax. He merely watched Fallo and waited. And Fallo waited, too, though he didn't know for what. *What made that noise?* he sent.

A thing swung down and hit the wall over my head. Too loud! I can't see anything. The darkness is thick. The idea of thick was accompanied with a feeling of honey on her feet.

"She says the darkness is thick. It doesn't look natural to me. Mercus?"

The Cloak bent and sniffed the air rising from the tomb. "Perhaps to keep pillagers from going deeper. Zirhine?"

She dipped into one of her pouches and chewed some dried plants into a glommy paste. She took hold of Fallo's blade arm and lifted. With delicate care, she jabbed her gooey blob onto the tip of Fallo's dagger. "It won't be bright, but it will penetrate." She uttered a command under her breath and the glob glowed blue.

Fallo regarded this with great skepticism. "What if I need to jab something?"

"It's a tomb, Fallo. What are you going to jab?"

Lop, you still alive?

I'm starving.

What's in there.

No food. And darkness.

Besides that?

It goes on and on. Rot. Funny echoes.

And then Lop was fading, quickly. Fallo lurched down the steps, heels slipping and making him judder down in tooth-shaking bounces. He came to a stop where a heavy whipaxe had sprung a vicious trap. The shaft was mounted into the ceiling. It must have been held under tension somehow. When Lop came by, it released.

Fallo didn't see a tripwire.

Lop? What's happening? Who has you?

No answer. Not because Lop was ornery, but because she was very far away. Miles. But that was impossible.

His companions descended behind him. More elegantly than he, having used the steps for stepping rather than falling. Fallo's blade tip gave off a soft blue glow. It illuminated the walls of the narrow passage ahead. It was hewn rock, seamless. Dry and dusty. It showed small imperfections from the tools used to work it, but it was remarkably straight and even.

Fallo clambered to his feet. If Lop wasn't so far ahead, he was sure he'd turn tail and go back to the boat and start paddling for Jallisea that very moment.

Instead he went forward, Zirhine's blob of spit goo lighting the way.

34

GOLD RAVEN WINE

As a man, Dunne Marlow enjoyed his service to Her Enlightened Majesty, for she was beautiful. But his attraction to her was not the common, lustful sort. Though, should she summon him to her bedchamber, he would not refuse. But that was not the basis of his growing affection.

In his years as a Donse Master—interrupted by a lengthy excommunication—he had dealt with many scholarly men, many rich men, and many, many aspiring men. In them he had seen a range of appetites: for knowledge, status, pleasure, power. But only rarely had he seen in them any yearning to be of service to others.

That experience wasn't just with men. Women covered the range of good and bad, generous and greedy, too. But it was his beloved Spin Hetta who had shown him how self-interest might align with the greater good, that satisfaction could be derived from lifting others up, rather than defeating them.

His love for Hetta notwithstanding, such thinking did not come naturally to Marlow, and since her death he had reverted to his usual, baser ways.

But then Kila Sigh had come into his life. Soon after, he'd finagled a post on Her Enlightened Majesty's small council. Both women evoked desires in him. Higher desires. It was true, he felt a fatherly affection for the Sigh girl. He felt protective of Her Enlightened, as well.

Though neither of them needed his protection, these thoughts and feelings had taken control. And now, as he was preparing for a meeting with Her Enlightened, he again marveled at how a powerful leader could surface a man's good or bad qualities simply through the strength of his presence.

The door to the monarch's Citadel-top residence opened, signaling that he was allowed to enter. To his surprise she was not present. But someone else was.

"Who are you?" he demanded. "Where is Her Enlightened Majesty?

The man stood at the window. At *her* window, where Marlow usually found her peering out at Starside, thinking whatever wise things she thought.

This man was dressed in fine but slightly rumpled clothing. A woolen cloak was draped over a chair. His boots had dried with a cake of street-filth on the toes.

"I'm Tym Hamlickten, Dunne Marlow," the man said. "I'm sorry to intrude into your office like this. I was brought here to meet with you. By a Shadline named Jil."

Marlow covered his confusion with a casual, "Ah. I see."

Her Enlightened had never mentioned knowing a Shadline. He had never heard of Jil. "Where did she go?"

Tym looked at the rear door. "She said she would return momentarily. We only just arrived. It is a long ascent to your offices."

The man was trying to be polite. Marlow sensed he was putting on a style of talking that was not his usual. It reminded him somewhat of Kila Sigh trying to talk like a Gristensider. Stilted. "These are not my offices."

A fire burned in the hearth. Marlow moved to stand close to it. The Citadel was cold in the passageways and the stairwell at this time of year. As usual, the window was open, admitting a wintery bite. Tym Hamlickten seemed to prefer it.

"What did Jil wish you to tell me?"

"It is not Jil's wish, Dunne Marlow." The man approached. His jaw was square, firm. Keen hawk's gaze. His hands were thick, fingers blunt. Working hands. The skin weathered. A man used to being outdoors. A purposeful stride, well-balanced. Strong.

This looked like an intimidation ploy, to approach in this manner. To gain advantage in the conversation to come. Something was afoot.

They were now a pace apart and Marlow's hackles rose. Abruptly the man's eyes fell to Marlow's hand. Tym suddenly relaxed his stance and a weak smiled came to his lips. "I must apologize. I've heard . . . tales about you."

Marlow supposed that made sense. "I've earned them. I'd offer you a seat, but protocol demands we remain standing until she asks us to sit."

"Who asks us? Jil?" And a glimmer of confusion passed across his features.

Marlow didn't bother to answer. For she had come.

Marlow bowed low. "Your Majesty."

Caught wrong-footed, Tym gaped and dipped his head. "Majesty," he muttered. His cheeks flushed even as his lips went white. "I—I had no idea I was . . ."

Apparently he also had no words, for he trailed off in a string of nonsense apologies and fumble-tongued insistences that he had not meant to intrude.

Her Enlightened was followed in by a woman with short hair and long lashes. She wore a sword under her cloak. The Shadline was taller than the monarch, larger framed, but by no means masculine. She wore a wry smile, where the monarch wore a placid look that was neither smile nor frown.

Her Enlightened stopped mid-room and extended her hand. This was an unusual privilege, usually allowed to Radiants, high members of the Ways, and visiting dignitaries.

Tym didn't know what to do, so he took her hand and gave it a shake.

"Kiss the ring, fool," Marlow hissed.

The man dropped to a knee and planted his lips on the only ring she wore. A slender band of silver set with a small sapphire bordered by diamonds.

"Stand, Tym Hamlickten of Flyssn." She motioned for the two men to sit. They did, though Tym appeared loath to do so.

Marlow had developed a respectful, if relaxed, relationship with his monarch over the past few ten-days. Though sometimes warm, she remained mostly aloof. As was meet for one of her station.

Marlow ducked his head to Jil. "Shadline."

"Donse Master." Her tone was curt, cold, ironic. Eyes hard despite the smirk. She didn't like Donse Masters.

"Where did you find him?" Her Enlightened asked Jil, tilting her head at Tym.

"The Grunting Pig."

At this the monarch smiled. "Their winter ale is very good," she said. "I would dearly enjoy spending an evening there. Perhaps Maeda can go out for a binge. What do you say, Jil?"

The Shadline closed her eyes and let out a humorless laugh. "I learned my lesson last time. I have never sicked up so much in my life."

Tym's discomfiture amused Marlow almost as much as did his mistress's penchant for wandering the trezz halls and rowdy taverns of the lower slopes. But she had put aside her persona as the low-quarter thief Maeda long ago. She had never explained why.

"But enough of that," Her Enlightened said. "Tym wished to see Marlow. What is it you wished to say to my advisor?"

The man made a few attempts to speak, each time clamping his mouth shut. Marlow leaned forward. "Go on, man. I'm sure Shadline Jil would not have brought you to me if she didn't think it important."

"But I never told her," he said. "I—" He grunted and froze in place.

"Marlow, remove that queller," Her Enlightened said.

Puzzled he twisted off the queller ring. He instantly felt the tiny spark of mercus in the man. But outshining it by a million times was Her Enlightened's mercus potential. She usually kept herself masked, so this naked show of power alarmed him. Especially since she had wrapped Tym in mercusine bindings that kept all but his head immobile.

"You didn't recognize him," she said to Marlow. "That was

my first question. I wondered if he was one of your 'little mice.' Or perhaps you'd plotted with him an attack on my person."

Her mistrust struck Marlow like a blow. The rapport they'd established had been an act on her part. This wounded him more than he would have guessed. Masking this emotion came naturally. Being a Donse Master was a daily exercise in masking emotions. "I fully understand your suspicion, but I don't know who he is. You think his supposed message for me was simply to gain entry to the Citadel? A rather desperate and naive ploy, don't you think?"

"He is a trapper from the Rachtooths," Jil said. "He also murdered scribe Flekk and her two grandchildren."

The man's face went purple. Not with denial, but like a man straining against chains. Lips twitching he make a few guttural noises. "K-K-Kill—"

Like a black cloud covering the sun, his face *changed*. The lips pulled back into a sneer, brows furrowing over his eyes. The transformation was shocking enough, but Marlow *recognized* the expression. "Tenn?" He backed away in horror. He had come so close.

He slipped his queller back on. The queller. That was what had stopped the man before. He had intended to use the mercus against Marlow. Some mind-probing technique Tenn had mastered, most likely.

"Welcome back to the Citadel, Seer Hargothe," Her Enlightened Majesty said. She took Marlow's chair and leaned forward to study the trapper's face.

Jil moved to stand behind him, blade drawn. Totally unnecessary given Her Enlightened's power.

"Hateful witch!" he spat. He continued to struggle against

his invisible bonds, but all he could do was jerk his crimson face side to side and glare. "Enjoy this pitiful victory while you can." Tym's face began to slacken.

"No. No," Her Enlightened said. "I have not dismissed you."

Being quelled, Marlow didn't feel what power she used, but she clamped both hands to Tym's head and closed her eyes. Tym's bulged, and his tongue protruded. Foam bubbled from his lips.

The man's mouth twisted up into an insane grin, but his eyes held abject fear. "Harlot!" With that final cry, his body went slack. But Her Enlightened did not release him.

She stooped over him, now pressing her forehead to his. She murmured under her breath, knuckles going white as she strained with her mercusine feats.

Not knowing what to do, Marlow pulled his queller off, if merely to witness her skills. He was rewarded with an astonishing chorus of sensations. She used sustained tones of harpstring purity, rumbles of heavy carts over cobblestones, the smell of chicken stock, baking bread, caresses across the forehead, the sharp sting of a switch against the palm, bitter grass on the tongue, and lemon juice. But those were periphery senses. For she drew upon the demaynic realm, weaving longing, anticipation, the weariness of a long hike, the heartache of a sailor's wife watching the horizon for the five-hundredth straight day, and more. All with such dexterity and ease that Marlow could compare her to none but Kila Sigh herself. But most notable was that she did not use much power to accomplish these mesmerizing feats. She used just enough.

And then she released them. Tym's head drooped.

"He lives," she said, breathing hard and restoring her mercus mask. So, her exertions had not been as effortless as they'd appeared. Marlow found that reassuring for some reason. "But not for long. He yearns for death. The Hargothe has developed a new technique. Subtle, powerful. An intricate knot upon the man's will. There will be more in Starside so infected. I believe he intended to latch this knot onto your mind, Marlow. And then from you to me, perhaps."

"Pol smiles," Marlow said. "You detected the wrongness before he could do harm."

"Tell that to Flekk's son, who lost both children and mother in the same day." An iciness came over her. "At least he will have justice. Starside will have justice. I will have this man executed in Dunne Medow Plaza tomorrow. Declare it, Marlow, and have callers spread word throughout the city."

"But surely it was the Hargothe who killed them," Marlow said. "This poor fellow had no choice in the matter."

"Killed by your brother's command, yes. Gauging by the compulsion placed on this man, there was no choice at all. But Tym must live with hands that killed children. A heavy burden indeed. He wishes for death, the city wishes for justice. Both can be satisfied."

Marlow understood the calculation. A cold balancing of needs. "But he is not guilty."

"But he is awash with guilt nonetheless. Could it be remedied? Perhaps. In time. But the city simmers. The demayne plays with us, leaving his victims here and there, adding logs to the fire beneath a bubbling cauldron of fear."

"But those that Flaumishtak has killed—Captain LiTishke has been hunting them for ages. Incompetently, I might add."

The fool who commanded the Watch did not seem to possess the slightest skill for capturing known criminals. It was surely Dox Viller's corruption at work. The crime lord of Cheapsgate had strings tied to puppets throughout the government.

Marlow realized his tone was verging on the impertinent. But he could not understand how someone as good and powerful as the monarch allowed these things to continue. As for the Flaumishtak, he suspected her capable of subduing even him. But she did not.

The outer door opened and two of her Fell Guardsmen entered. They had left their immense spears behind. Hands on their hilts, they barged forward and bowed. They had steel eyes, stares so blank, so full of potential violence that Marlow shrank back. Each stood well over six feet tall. And he knew that beneath their burnished armor and rich red cloaks they were pure muscle. They were her personal guard, and they would die for her. And they would annihilate anyone who threatened her.

"Remove this man to the Westbunk," she ordered. "He is the confessed murderer of scribe Flekk and her grandchildren. See that he is kept safe. Instruct Captain LiTishke to prepare an execution on the morrow. If he dies prior, I'll personally secure LiTishke to the post in his place."

The men took hold of Tym's arms and lifted him. His feet made no move to support him, so they dragged him.

"Guardsmen," she said, as they reached the door. "Tell LiTishke that I wish the City's Justice upon the man. Flekk's son, Rathman, shall strike the first and final wounds. I will be present."

The Fell Guardsmen nodded their plumed helms in acknowledgement and took the man out.

She turned to Marlow, saw the judgment in his eyes. "I do not have the luxury of pity. Nor even of compassion." She moved a stray hair from her face and tucked it behind her ear. Her hand trembled. The other went to a pocket in her gown and withdrew a small jade fish figurine. A worry stone.

Jil had sheathed her blade. Her face was impassive.

"What do you know of the Shadline, Marlow?" Her Enlightened asked.

The change in subject caught him off guard. "I know the weapons are mercusine. Some blades have minds of their own. The order itself is secretive. Cultish. Given to delusions of magnificence. No offense, Jil. My understanding is that they wander the world in search of injustices to set right. Vigilantes, most of them."

"All of what you said is correct and yet wrong. Have you heard of the doctrine called Listen and Obey?"

"No. It sounds like what any monarch would expect of her subjects."

"Ah. But it is not intended to work in that direction. It is a rule for those with power. It is the basis of Shadline doctrine. All who swear the oath learn to listen and obey their subtle instincts, the pushes or pulls that nudge them through their days. I have trusted that call my entire reign, even as I have lamented the state of my city because of it."

"If you are dissatisfied with the state of your city, then surely you must dispense with this practice. You mus—"

He clamped his mouth shut before he went too far. One did not say "you must" to Her Enlightened. Not if one wanted to remain in one's post.

"It *is* a foul stew I've stirred, isn't it?" she said, moving to her favorite window. "Listen and Obey. That is all any monarch can do. Even the so-called mistakes of Duri LiMin-luit were the result of that doctrine."

Duri LiMinluit was a previous Enlightened, and rather infamous. Her nickname became the namesake for the Harridan Gate. "Her policies were greedy," Marlow said. "The rebellion was justified."

"And after she was deposed, Cheapsgate came into existence. Had her plans succeeded perhaps everyone would be better off. The Radiancies surely would have dissolved by now."

This was not at all consistent with what Marlow had been taught about the woman referred to in official doctrine as "The Harridan." But he'd been schooled by the Way of Til, the very power that had brought the woman down.

"So you are saying you are helpless to change things? You, with all your power? Rather than risk being deposed, you allow the corruption in every quarter to fester."

Jil tossed her head, apparently irritated by Marlow's thick-headed ignorance.

Her Enlightened merely gazed out the window, taking in her sad city. "I listen and obey. The trapper's execution is another of those decisions. Faintly suggested. Just there on the edge of my awareness. I listen. I obey. In this way I avert disaster."

"Forgive me, but it appears you listen and do nothing."

Marlow had never cared much for politics when younger. His goal to be posted to the small council had been for the status of it. Mostly. But he knew every corner of Starside, understood that each stratum of wealth was merely a layer of grime. Those at the bottom were not the lowest because of their innate character, but because they had the misfortune to be smushed beneath the upper layers of corruption.

Her Enlightened said: "Patience, my dear Marlow, is the strong hand of power." She was growing irritated with him now. Or perhaps it was with herself. "Do you think it doesn't rankle, sitting here while my subjects suffer? While Radiant Gilok tosses back gold raven wine like water and enjoys inherited incomes from his farms and mines and fisheries? I allow it because I must. The force of destiny whispers faintly. It pushes hard. All leads to a culmination I cannot see past."

When he didn't say anything she clasped her hands against her belly. "I hope that girl is worth the sacrifice. Cheapsgate exists—in large part—to foster her, I think. To prepare her. Same for Dox Viller and even that vile little fool, Parlo Odok. Starside is the cradle that nurtured Highest Binel, Radiant Peline, and her willful daughter. Some of this was shown to me. But when the PiTorro boy's rusty dagger showed up on a platter . . . it all moves quickly now. Would you have me tie strings to the very pieces that must be allowed to move freely? Even the demayne plays his part."

Marlow scoffed. "The unrest in the city is *because* of Flaumishtak. Surely that was my brother's plan when he granted him these murders. To sow discord."

"I doubt the Hargothe restricted the demayne's killings to criminals. No, Flaumishtak plays his own game. And perhaps that is an opportunity for me."

To his astonishment, she smiled as she turned away from the window. Then with motherly tenderness, she grasped his head and kissed his forehead. "Now. See that the execution is arranged properly. I have my own preparations to make."

She walked out. Jil stayed, lost in her own thoughts.

Marlow sat by the fire a while longer, though it wasn't exactly proper for him to linger. He'd not known of the monarch's devotion to the Shadline ways. And while he respected the Shadlines he'd met, he had not seen much evidence that they'd improved the world.

Jil took the monarch's seat and thrust her legs out, crossed at the ankles. She hitched her belt around a bit so her sword wouldn't get in the way of her relaxation.

Her eyes glimmered in the firelight.

"Who are you, Jil?" he asked. "Why are you here?"

"I listen and obey. Right now, I'm supposed to be here. Maybe to keep an eye on you. Maybe to kill you. I don't know. I don't care."

He left the Shadline there and began his long descent to his own apartments and office.

Her Enlightened's revelation about her 'Listen and Obey' philosophy bothered him. He wondered if that was why she had sold him dragon scales a few years back. He huffed out a curse. She had been disguised as a roguish loot-seeker at the time. Maeda. They had developed a sort of friendship then, before he'd known she was the Enlightened.

"Enlightened," he said, grunting skeptically. "And yet . . ."

She must have known he was using the scales he bought from her to pay off Flaumishtak. Which meant she had played a part in bringing Flaumishtak into this world.

Pinpricks marched up his back and over his scalp. Could she truly have seen so far ahead? Had she known that the demayne would eventually be unleashed to kill in the city? He doubted it.

Enlightened. Maybe the title wasn't ceremonial after all. Maybe it wasn't mere grandiosity. Perhaps her counsel to Kila

Sigh, sending her off to Garden Island had fulfilled some foresight she hadn't shared with Marlow.

That was a lot of trust to put in the force of destiny. Marlow was not convinced it had mankind's best interests in mind. Or that it had a mind at all.

Sighing heartily, he dismissed his dark thoughts. He had an execution to announce.

35

THE MADDENING CUP

The weather in Starside was atrocious. Damp and cold. The streets were thick with slowly melting slush of a recent dump of snow. There were few people about as Kila and her companions stepped into the Street of Sorrows.

"Something is wrong here," she said, mostly to herself. It wasn't her mercus senses telling her anything—she was masked —but merely her thiefly instincts. She had run the roofs for years, knew every alley, knew the city's moods. The misty fog hanging over the street felt like a manifestation of pervasive fear.

"The sun is different than on that beach," Pennie said, face to the sky. Her unseeing eyes were closed as she listened to other senses. The sun was hidden behind clouds.

"It is earlier here," Dunne Yples said. His poor mood had returned. He gripped his precious map book under one arm. The project had given him energy, but he was still a prisoner, still burdened with the *vaz'on*.

It had been Henley who had suggested covering the crown with a hood. "The *vaz'on* isn't the sort of thing a man wears around Terriside. Or anywhere else, for that matter."

They were a weird enough band of rogues as it was. A Shadline missing a hand, a very well-dressed (if not for this climate) Donse Master, a blind girl with rampant curls, two cats, a red-headed lad who might easily be recognized as the long-thought-dead Henley Mast, and finally the bald girl in the very find black jacket and trousers, which made her as exotic-looking as anyone seen on the Street of Sorrows in a ten-year.

"The Yin Inn is just down that way," she said. "Maybe we can rustle up an atlen driver to take us uphill."

"I'll go," Quinn said. "The whole idea is to keep you out of view, right? Go back inside until I return."

They knew none of the sketches of "Highest of Kil! Kila Sigh! The Merculyn who Flies!" had reached Starside yet. The sail from Garden Island to Starside was two months at best. But there were those Coin-talkers Henley had told her about. They could communicate through a coin-code by flipping their medallions from frown to smile in certain sequences. The Coin at the Garden would certainly be spreading the word far and wide.

Quinn donned her black cloak and proceeded with her hood up, right arm tucked beneath the folds to conceal her loss.

The rest of them waited just inside the jewelry shop, their breath frosting in the still air.

Kila was masked already. She had explained the principle to Pennie and Henley. Both were working on the skill but had not mastered it. Their efforts were muting their spark such that a passing merculyn not specifically looking for it would overlook it. Highest Quiv didn't have to mask, for he was a Donse Master. Nobody would challenge him.

While they waited, Kila decided to find out where they were going next. "Dunne Yples, do you have Ceronhel on your map?"

The man started, eyes flaring momentarily with his old mad rage. It faded as her question registered. He flopped his book onto a sheet-covered counter, sending up a cloud of dust. After a fit of sneezing he wiped his eyes and made little measurements and estimations with his fingers. "There!" he said, stabbing the countertop four inches above the top edge of the page. "Ceronhel, Ever Vigilant. A fastness in the Haelshock Range well north of the Rachtooths." He pointed to the mountains surrounding Lockt in the northern realm of Flyssn. "Passage to Ceronhel from Lockt requires traversing several hundred miles of shoulder roads."

"Shoulder roads?"

"Hewn into the side of the mountain, winding along treacherous climbs and descents. They were built to avoid the passes, which are all infested with nosg—or worse." He came back to himself, eyes narrowing. They gleamed darkly, like *vaz'on* gems. "Why are you asking about this First Race fortress?"

She saw no point in lying. "The Hargothe is there."

Dunne Yples closed his book, pressing his worn hands to the rotting cover. "The Hargothe," he said on a whisper. "A worm of a man, he is. Probing and crawling through the mercusine, burrowing and seeking and sniffing and gorging. A verminous slug. Never satisfied with power. 'Righteousness', he said to me last I saw him. 'I will establish a world-realm of righteousness and Til will hold it with an unrelinquishing grip.' Bah! The old snake seeks godhood for himself, make no mistake. Oh, he *seethes* with greed. And you—" He jabbed a finger at Kila, face now contorting with a rise of his old madness. "You he sought like a trezz-fiend seeks a sip from the maddening cup. Lusted, he did. How it consumed him. And he had the Abbey humming like a hive to search you out. Poor Highest Chilow never stood a chance. Where is Chilow now? Dead. And Binel? *Highest* Binel? Ha! What a mummer's farce the Hargothe makes of the Way of Til. Binel is a puppet of little mind and no spine, chosen to dance upon the Hargothe's twitching strings. And the Thebkine Table? Fools! No wonder Til fades and Kil rises." As his voice rose, tears formed and fell into his beard.

He stared into nothingness, no longer present in the cold jewelry shop, unaware of those who listened and witnessed his mad and angry grief. "Dem-Kisk," he whispered, more tears falling, lips quivering. "Ah me! I've seen the firesky. They call him Seer, girl. But *I* have seen more than he ever has. 'Hargothe' was a title for prophets, you know. The last true Hargothe was a kindly man, a scholar. He kept a diary, noting his visions and annotating them with analyses. He saw weather, crops, sicknesses, deaths. He was clear about what he knew and what he guessed. He did not merely declare his wishes to be prophecy as does the current man of the title. 'Hargothe,' Highest Quiv. A First Race term. Do you know the Cigil-Tinian translation?"

"*Haril gothzin,* I believe," Quiv said softly. "It means 'many ways'."

"Indeed. *Many* ways, not one way. Not the only way. Many. I have seen more than the Hargothe ever will. I saw it plainly, in the face of Til speaking to me. And here I am. A failure. The girl who will bring Dem-Kisk to doom us has crowned me king of fools." He was weeping again, face in his hands, shoulders wracked with sobs. "Ah me! I hate you, Kila Sigh, for all you appear to be kind. How can I but hate you? You who will pull Kil into this world?"

Kila wanted to put a hand on the man's shoulder. Offer comfort. But he wouldn't thank her for compassion. Likely he would see it as a great insult.

Pennie went to him. Leaned against his arm and murmured sympathetic words. Kila thought it strange, since the girl had been so vocal in denouncing him earlier. Even Huff jumped onto the counter and padded across the pages of the open map book to nudge the weeping man with is head.

"I asked about Ceronhel because I must go there," Kila said. "I mean to kill the Hargothe before *he* brings Kil into this world."

Yples froze in mid sob. "What? Him? Why would he? *How* could he?"

"I don't know. But the demayne Flaumishtak said either he or I would do it."

"And you wish it to be you, of course."

"No!"

The man was being deliberately iron-brained. No one could be that dense without intending to be. "I wish for it *not* to happen at all. If the Hargothe is dead, then it is up to me. I will refuse. That should put an end to it. Why would I be compelled to do something I don't want to do?"

Yples's tears turned to weeps of laughter. He shook his head, tears streaming even as sad giggles bubbled forth. "In this you and I are alike, girl. We do *only* what we do not wish."

The front door of the little shop opened. Quinn beckoned. "Come on, then. The carriage is waiting. I had to drag the driver from his cups by his collar."

Heads down they piled into the waiting carriage and crowded into the seats. With a knock on the roof, Quinn signaled the driver to go.

Nobody said anything on the long winding ride up the slopes to Gristenside. Kila sat wedged between Henley and Quinn, glowering at Dunne Yples sitting across from her. The man had given up his tears and now hugged his map book to his chest.

His last words haunted her. *"We do* only *what we do not wish."* Those words haunted not because they were true—they obviously were—but because he had sounded so resigned to the coming doom of mankind.

36

VERGENT BLOOD

Fallo's voice returned in odd echoes as he whispered a few appropriate lines of "Heartscrane Hill," one of his favorite tales. Until now.

"No sound escapes his prayerful lips
As skulls' eyes peer from nook-pocked crypts.
But still his fear disturbs the Deep
To roust the Dead-Guard from their sleep."

Whoever had penned that chill-tale had likely been in this place. The sense of dread and pressure to flee grew with every step. He began to wonder if having Zirhine's glowing spitwad on his dagger helped at all. The eldritch blue light did penetrate the blackness, but only enough to prove the darkness wholly unnatural.

And the air had grown colder, so much colder, though Fallo conceded his shivering was more from fear than chill.

Lop? he sent again. But his cat was too far away to

respond. Strange. So strange. Lop was ahead—and down. He could point to her. But she felt miles and miles distant.

"A rather deep tomb," Zirhine said. She had a low, calm voice. Probably a good singer. But in the closeness of this narrow, ever descending passage, it startled Fallo into a rather un-Shadline squawk.

"The slab was a misdirection," the Cloak said. "Clearly."

"Clearly," Zirhine echoed.

Fallo wanted to cut their tongues out. Why speak so loudly? There could be ghouls or some such ahead. Hadn't they heard "Heartscrane Hill?"

Since they were all going to blab at the top of their lungs he stopped and pointed Ol' Rusty back at Zirhine. "Can you blow a kiss on this and make it brighter?"

She forcefully pushed the dagger aside. "Never point your weapon at someone you do not mean to kill. And if I brighten it, the light will fade more quickly. Would you rather we return to absolute darkness?"

He would not rather that. No indeed. He continued, leading. Now he wondered if he was leading or if they were content to see him trip the traps the builders of this place had probably set. He'd avoided two so far. Both of the whipaxe variety. It disconcerted him that the axe heads seemed set to take a man in the groin. "Give me a neck-whack," he murmured. "I'd rather sink than be dismasted and left afloat."

"Stop your babbling," the Cloak said in a strong echoey voice.

Kil's eyes in a teacup! But Fallo kept his mouth shut.

He kept his dagger low, since that's where the trap triggers had been so far. This posture bent him awkwardly and soon his back began to ache.

Idiot cat!

Bah. Who was he trying to fool blaming this on Lop? The Cloak would've made him come down here regardless. Lop might be a fuzzy trial of a beast, but she was *his* fuzzy trial. No crypt wight was going to abscond with her while Fallo had breath in his body.

Images of storybook wights came to mind, bony fingers and fang-maws spread wide. This was not helpful in the least.

"Listen," Zirhine said.

"And obey. I understand."

"No. With your ears."

Fallo paused and tilted his head, concentrating on sounds other than his thumping heart. Ahead there came a low whooshing noise, like wind through a cavern.

The passage widened into a circular chamber with a domed ceiling. A sarcophagus stood in the center, the carved effigy of an armored man lying in repose on the lid. Around the room, set in tall narrow niches, more statues. They were all Ori, Fallo thought, raising his glowing spitwad. One version was weeping, hands in her hair. Another had clenched fists, brows furious. Another wore a high-slitted gown, hands to her throat as her face betrayed lustful yearning. At the feet of each statue rested an urn, gilded with delicate depictions of hunting, battle, or forest-pond lovers embracing.

In the blue light the statuary looked eerily lifelike. Like frozen flesh.

Lop was not there. Lop was straight ahead and down. There had to be a door here somewhere.

"There's writing carved on this," Zirhine said. She had her own glowblob on a finger now and was tracing graven letters that lined the edge of the sarcophagus lid. "More wards against vergents. The lid has been disturbed."

"Disturbed?" Fallo said, spinning away from the lusty Ori. "How?"

"The stone is chipped. Here and here."

"Pry bars might make those marks," the Cloak said. His hand rested on Tosuin's hilt.

The feeling that Fallo must immediately leave this place, run across the heath, get into Zirhine's boat, and paddle across the Sorgeal Sea came upon him especially hard at the Cloak's words. He was moving toward the door when he caught himself.

"This repulsion . . . It's coming from that coffin. I feel it pushing me away."

"The wards?" Zirhine mused. She was looking at the Cloak, not Fallo. The man raised an eyebrow and studied Fallo.

"What? Don't you feel it?" Fallo asked. A new thrill of fear crept across his skin.

"I feel only the grave chill," Zirhine said. "Somber coldness. Not fear."

"Nor I," the Cloak said. "I thought you merely cowardly. But perhaps you have vergent blood in you." He had to say it out loud, had to blurt out the niggling little idea Fallo wanted to quash.

Lop? Where are you?

No answer. Zirhine's words at the entry to the tomb returned to him. "Those wards. You said they prevented vergents from passing through the stone."

Zirhine's dark eyes collected the blue light, pools of

sapphire that regarded him with expectation. She waited for him to come to his conclusion.

He backed away from her until he bumped into lusty Ori, his heel catching the urn and knocking it over. The lid rolled in an arc across the floor and black ash spilled out. "I can't have vergent blood. For one thing, they don't exist. For another, they're wee little rascals who could not possibly mate with human folk."

"You think of storybook tales, Fallo. There may be some truth in them, but not all of the truth. Vergents are as diverse as we are. More so. Now Listen and Obey."

If there had ever been a contrary command it was that one. If he listened, he would be fleeing. Only Lop had kept him moving toward the ever-growing horror of this place. At first he had feared walking skeletons or haze-spirits. But now he confronted something worse. "I don't hear anything but 'run!'"

"Not so," the Cloak said. His boots made no sound as he rounded the sarcophagus to stand next to Fallo. "You came to the tomb before the cat went in. Remember?"

That was true. Something had compelled him forward even as the wards had tried to repel him. He closed his eyes and tried to swallow the tightness in this throat.

"The subtlest impulse can guide you," Zirhine coaxed. "A breath of breeze. An inclination to shift your weight. A glancing thought of a person or memory. Notice it all. As you unthinkingly scratch an itch, now let the force of destiny guide you. Your vergent blood is a great blessing. What it detests can be a beacon to your Shadline instincts."

He found himself lulled by her words, which drifted softly on her alto voice. Ol' Rusty was firm in his grip. The worn leather wrapping on the hilt warm and secure even as his palm sweated.

And it was the blade that now drew his attention. Opening his eyes, he drew the nicked and pocked edge close to his face. The blue blob shone weirdly along the surface, making sharp shadowed craters in the steel.

Telt! it whispered to him now. The first time he'd ever heard it speak its true name. He squished the spitblob of glowing weed between his fingers and plucked it from the tip. A faint residue remained, glowing faintly. Absently, Fallo passed the light source to the Cloak, who took it in his palm.

"Every Shadline weapon is a fate's-piece," he heard himself say. "A great puzzle, pieces scattered to the wind."

Taken by the strange spell of Zirhine's words he lowered the tip of his blade to one of the chipped notches in the lid of the sarcophagus. "Again," he said.

The Cloak needed no further explanation. Tosuin chimed as it threaded from its scabbard. Together they pressed their noble blades into the work of pry bars.

This time they slipped in easily. Eagerly, perhaps. No leverage was needed. The lid sighed as something thunked below and air burst out from the lip of the stone. A rattle of chain echoed from great depths as counter weight dropped to lift the stone on heavy black hinges.

A ladder led down.

And now Ol' Rusty began to glow with its own light. Not blue like Zirhine's ferneater magic. But a white gold. A noble light. It cut through the vergent-warded gloom that obscured the pit. The hilt grew warm and Fallo felt it draw the heat from him, not chillingly, but as if he were a conduit for it, from some other, unknowable force.

His fear dissipated. He climbed the sarcophagus and slid down the ladder. The moment his boots struck the stone floor, Lop's presence flooded back into his mind.

Where have you been? Lop complained.

Having a snack of pig and yams, Fallo said. *I've been looking for you, sweetie.*

I've been here waiting.

In this case, "here" was a domed, circular chamber much like the fake burial chamber above. Only this was much, much larger.

"I think we've found something," Fallo said as his companions reached the bottom of the ladder.

Though never a particularly attentive student, Fallo had a bit of the First Race language pounded into his skull. A tiny bit. In this case it wouldn't have been needed, though the lettering in the fresco on the far wall made it clear enough.

A single arched passage exited the chamber.

"A vergent pass," Zirhine said, awed. "The first I've ever seen."

Beyond the arch, impossibly, was a valley, open to the sky. The ruins of a city lay before them, a white veil of waterfall tumbling from a hewn arch in a mountainside to pool and wind away in silver curves.

Domed rooftops, some crumbled, some whole, were covered over with vines and moss. Broken columns marked where great palaces once stood. But towering above all was a colossus maiden, spear in one hand, scepter in the other. She looked beyond the city, down the valley, face illuminated in all its alabaster severity by the orange of the evening sun.

"Cigil-Tine," Fallo said slowly. "The lost city of the First Race."

Even the Cloak seemed awed. Zirhine allowed tears to stream down her cheeks. They picked up the warm sunlight and sparkled like droplets of light.

"How far from the Kovi-Mest are we?" Fallo asked.

"Far," the Cloak said. "It was midday on the Kovi-Mest. Nearly sunset here."

Lop sat in the arch, a silhouette of black, licking her paws. She looked back at them and meowed irritably.

"The wards were to keep vergents from coming here," Zirhine said. "From using this pass."

"Why?" Fallo asked.

She didn't offer an answer.

The arch leading to the lost city was carved with life-like vines. Baskets of fruit and vegetables stood at the foot of the columns framing the opening. These too were carved.

"Shall we go through?" Fallo asked. But it was a silly question. Of course they were going to go through. This was what had pulled him past the wards, past the burial chamber.

How did you come down here, he sent to Lop.

A hole behind one of the women's legs. Fresh air. The cat tested the slight breeze that passed through the arch. It was redolent with floral and pine scents.

Telt's golden glow seemed drawn from the dawn. Fallo stepped forward, through the vergent pass and into a realm forgotten.

37

PELICAN AT DAWN

Startle is gone, Nax sent as the carriage approached the Harridan Gate.

He left the city?

No. Gone.

The cat's luminous eyes looked up at Kila. She thought she could see worry on the cat's face. She certainly felt it through the bond. Henley had learned the same from Huff. His face was pale in the ghostly dim of the carriage. This was a hack for hire. No mercus light here except for what bled through the grimy window.

Dead? she sent.

Nax wasn't willing to commit to that much. And she didn't feel like explaining more. She squinted and rested her chin on Kila's knee.

The driver slowed and called down to them. Quinn's face was full of fury at the delay, but whatever imprecations she meant to hurl at him died on her lips. She was peering out the window. "Kil's blood! Stop this thing, driver. I said stop!" She was out the door before the wheels stopped turning. Kila piled out after her, fearful they were under attack.

Dunne Medow Plaza spread out before her. The great fountain shooting spews of water into the crisp air. The fountain statuary of Kil, Aslana, and young Ori were caked with ice. Mercus lights around the perimeter cast rough shadows across the paving stones and lent the fountain mist a white glow.

Beyond the fountain stood the Cathedral of Til, the abbey stretching to either side.

Kila hated this place.

A wooden platform, three spans above the plaza floor, had been erected on the west side of the plaza. At the front was mounted a thick pole, made from the stripped trunk of a thick pine. Stairs climbed both sides.

"An execution," Henley said. "Driver?"

The man was just a lump under an oilcloak, his hood leaving nothing but the tip of his nose exposed to the chill. "Aye. The man that killed Flekk and her grandbabes. It'll be the City's Justice on him. Her Enlightened'll be here. I 'spect the whole city'll try t'squeeze in. Not me. I seen enough blood fer two lifetimes." He shrugged deeper into his cloak.

The City's Justice. The idea horrified Kila. Death by hundreds, perhaps thousands of small wounds.

"The blood-draw'll be at dawn. I hope t' be sound asleep by then." That last was a hint. The man was cold, tired, and his evening trezz had been rudely interrupted by Quinn.

They returned to the carriage and the driver took them through the Trialti Arch to Gristenside. The baths passed to the left. Kila was tempted to drop her mask, to feel the Voluptuary and others there. But that was sentimental foolishness.

The carriage rolled over gravel as it turned into the greathouse drive. And then stopped. "Radiant Peline retired hours ago," said a weary armsman. "She'll not be receiving guests." He had a put-on accent that betrayed his lower-slope upbringing.

Quinn stepped out. "Don't wake her, Furly. It's just me and some guests. Including Highest Quiv of Garden Island."

Kila heard a choking sound and a rattle of armor as the man dashed away. Soon the house came to life as footmen in hastily donned livery burst from the house.

The butler was roused, the housekeeper, too. Quinn received a hundred "Yes, Lady" and "At once, Lady" as rooms were opened, beds prepared. The mistress of kitchens clanged pots and pans to make tea and "a few small sweet-welcomes as is only meet for a Gristenside greathouse."

Before long, Kila was in a room of her own, marveling at the speed with which servants rushed to attend to her one-handed friend. That disfigurement—as Quinn called it—was kept hidden under her cloak.

Dunne Yples had a room across from Kila's, between Henley's and Pennie's. Highest Quiv took the grand guest room, which every greathouse boasted. Reserved for visitors of the highest rank.

Kila would have been content to share with Quinn and Pennie, but in truth she was exhausted and the privacy was most welcome.

The cats had slipped into the house hidden under cloaks, irritable at having to keep out of sight after such a prolonged time of going wherever they pleased. Fortunately, Quinn had thought to have the kitchen send cream and a bit of cold chicken. The bleary-eyed maid who delivered it clearly wanted to ask questions about such a novel request, but she managed to keep her mouth shut.

Nax found the food to her standards then retired to sleep on a pillow Kila had stuffed under the bed.

Another chamber maid bustled around Kila's room, fluffing, and straightening, and asking a million questions and never pausing to listen to an answer. Finally Kila sent her running, with instructions to leave her undisturbed unless called for.

She enjoyed less than a minute of solitude before Highest Quiv and Dunne Yples came to her door. The madman kept his eyes to the floor. He clutched the journal in which he'd sketched his map in. Quiv was outwardly calm, but his nostrils flared as if prepared for battle.

"Dunne Yples pointed out to me that tomorrow's execution provides an uncommon opportunity for us."

She waited.

He licked his lips. "We will go to the Abbey in the morning. To the Library of Dunne Francis LiMillar. I'm telling you so that you don't discover us missing and assume we went there to betray you."

At this Dunne Yples chuckled, an echo of his old madness breaking through. "Dem-Kisk," he whispered. "Ah me."

"Why?" she asked.

"Books, obviously. Dunne Yples seeks a particular atlas, declared Wrong due to the inclusion of certain heretical notions. But it may be of great use to us. To you."

She allowed that idea to roll through her mind. It hadn't been that many days ago that she'd been battling Yples above the ash barrens on Garden Island. "Why help me if I'm Dem-Kisk?"

Dunne Yples finally lifted his head, but kept his eyes on Kila's chin. "I have considered our conversation in the jewelry shop. I do not doubt my vision. I know you to be the bringer of doom. And yet . . ." He met her gaze. There was such sorrow there. Such desperation. "What if the culmination requires a cataclysm? Dem-Kisk is prophecy I sought to prevent." A muscle twitched under his eye and his lips seemed to fight between a smile and a snarl. "The *vaz'on* protects me. Allows me to think more clearly. I no longer believe the prophecy can be circumvented. So I shall help you to defeat the Hargothe, a man I know to be thoroughly evil. The firesky will come. But in the aftermath there is hope that a flower might sprout from the ash. If the Hargothe wins, the world will remain a vast, unrelieved graveyard for all eternity."

"You are not known here, Highest Quiv," she said. "Will they recognize your authority?"

He waggled a pinky, flashing the begemmed ring of his station. It was similar to Kila's, but with a green stone.

She could stop them. But to do so would require her to use powers in a way she hated. Besides, this atlas sounded like it could be helpful, especially if could guide to Ceronhel.

"Thank you for informing me," she said.

Yples backed out of the room. Quiv nodded. Almost a bow, but not quite. How strange. And then he was gone.

Despite the racket of their arrival, the Radiant Peline managed to sleep through it. Kila did not relish the confrontation ahead. If Quinn was willful, her mother was doubly so.

And of course she was. The Radiant was the younger sister of Dunne Marlow and the Hargothe. What an odd path the force of destiny had blazed for that family. Kila could scarcely imagine what the Hargothe had been like as a boy. Or that he'd ever *been* a boy.

She was not close to sleep as she lay comfortably in the dark, when someone knocked softly.

Quinn slipped through the door. She'd changed into fresh trousers and blouse. She held her scabbarded blade in her hand, the belt drooping like a dead snake. "I can't get this on one-handed." It was an explanation for why she carried it, but it didn't seem to be the reason she'd come.

"Can't sleep?" Kila said.

"No. The execution tomorrow has kept the whole downstairs awake. There have been loads of murders in Starside. Heads torn from bodies. Bloodless corpses."

Kila sat up. "That sounds like the work of someone I know."

"Flaumishtak. The Hargothe granted him a number of kills at the summoning with my mother. Apparently he has confined his victims to thugs and murderers. But everyone thinks the execution tomorrow will put an end to it."

"Flaumishtak must be laughing heartily about that."

"The Watch are looking for another murderer now. Binni Keel."

"Ragin's sister?" Kila had met the girl once, under extraordinarily bad circumstances. Binni had been mistaken for Kila several years ago, in fact, and taken to Dox Viller's Cheaspgate lair for torture. Wen had saved Binni's life and returned her home only slightly scathed. Kila said, "That seems unlikely. She's just a soft merchant's daughter."

Quinn gave Kila an arch look, reminding her that station of birth said little about what a person was capable of. "They saw her standing over a dead man called Targle. One of Viller's Killers. She had gutted him with his own blade."

"So it'll be two executions tomorrow?"

"I said they're looking for her. She got away."

"A Terriside girl eluding the Watch? Where did this happen?" Nax stirred next to Kila and unconsciously jabbed a set of claws into her thigh.

"Cheapsgate. Near Critt Sanglo's. She's about your size. Presumably untrained. The man, Targle, was strong, a skilled fighter. Ruthless."

Kila searched her friend's face. There was something hidden there. Something she was hesitating to say. Something she had to say.

"Binni Keel was last seen with a cat."

"Bloody Kil! Startle?"

"Who else?" Quinn had never seen Startle, but since he was the only other cat in Starside, it was easy enough to deduce.

Binni Keel had bonded to Startle. How strange.

Wake up, Nax.

No. The cat squirmed to snuggle deeper under the covers. How she could breathe at all under there was a mystery to Kila.

Startle bonded Ragin's sister.

And?

Kila jerked the covers down to expose the little gray to open air. "And?" she said. "What do you mean, 'and?' Don't you think it's significant?"

You are making a lot of noises at me.

You know what I said. Don't pretend you didn't. But why would Startle bond her *of all people? She's a Keel!*

Nax had no answer to this except to cover her face with a forelimb and to roll onto her back.

"What I struggle to understand," Quinn said, "is how a slight girl of seventeen could disembowel a seasoned thug."

"Maybe he was dropover drunk." Kila flopped back into her pillows, now feeling restless and irritable. "I doubt you get into Viller's Killers by leading a sober, pious life."

"Perhaps. But she eluded the Watch, too."

It was all very strange. But then cats bonding to anyone was strange.

"I wish I could sleep," Kila said shoving her covers aside and getting to her feet. "But I can't. I feel the city out there, beckoning."

Quinn grinned.

Wriggling her bare toes, Kila lamented the softening of her feet. Running the roofway on a cold, slushy night would be pure misery. "What sort of shoes d'ya think'll be best, Lady Peline? Ya know, fer sneakin'?"

"I'm sure I have something in one of my closets. But may I ask where we're going?"

"Critt Sanglo's."

A nervous look flashed across Quinn's face. She hefted Black and waggled the belt straps. "Would you help me with this?"

Kila took the belt and began to fasten it around her friend's waist. The dagger was on Quinn's right hip, hilt angled forward, ready to draw. For a right-handed woman. "Uh, you'll have to reach across unless we thread the belt the other way through the scabbard."

"No. I want it there. I want to have to think before I draw."

A moment of quiet passed. "I'm sorry I dropped it in the Derslin Wheel," Kila said, cinching the buckle tight.

"Don't be. I was pitying myself and you put the lash to my bottom. I didn't like it, but it was needed. And this is the last time you help me with this."

No more words were needed.

Nax, are you coming to Cheapsgate?

Nax rolled onto her other side and squirmed beneath the blankets until she was just a small lump on the bed.

"Let's run!" Kila said to her raven-haired friend.

THE WEARINESS of the day's events was replaced by misery as Kila and Quinn slipped and shivered on the roofway. At one point Kila tried running without shoes and found her feet so soft and fragile she cursed herself for a Gristenside lily-toe. Quinn was not amused by this.

The snow had not melted on the roofs, making a strange white landscape that hid all manner of tripping hazards. It seemed that one of the young women was either in the process of falling or climbing back to her feet at all times.

"I should have roused the driver and made him put the blues in harness," Quinn said.

"Wen would never have let me hear the end of this. And Father . . ." It was shameful to be so inept. And the cold fingered into her borrowed cloak and found all the soft warm spots Kila had developed on sunny Garden Island.

By the time they made it to the Cheaps their pants were soaked and their whole bodies covered with soggy brown snowmelt. Kila decided to risk going through the gate rather than the thinnie tunnels. She doubted she'd be recognized now. For one thing, she had only a fuzz of hair and for another, she was dressed posh in her cloak and the Highest of Kil garments. Quinn's glare nearly froze the Watch guards where they stood once they deigned to emerge from their little wind-break shack.

And then Kila and Quinn were through.

The smell hit Kila like a particularly bad memory. "Ugh. It's gotten worse."

Quinn laughed. "No it hasn't."

A few thuggish men tried to corner them during their traverse of the Cheaspgate roofs to Critt Sanglo's. Kila wanted to remain masked, so she relied on her newly learned sideways talk to shoo the stupid grunts away. "Dox is waiting for me."

One simple phrase and hulking idiots slunk away to find easier prey.

They heard music and raucous laughter as they got closer to their destination. The chimney smoke and rotten fish stench had always been thinner near Critt's, but to Kila's nose it was nearly intolerable.

"You've been bathing for a few months," Quinn said. "I assure you, Cheapsgate smells the same as it ever did."

Making a disgusted face, Kila dropped to the alley to enter Critt's establishment. She was suddenly conscious of her clothing, her lack of hair. And of the two gold skillets she had tucked into a pocket before they'd left home. Two skillets could buy a night of absolute trezzed-up inanity. Not that she wanted to waste her coin making herself sick.

Two gold skillets. That was what had started her down this Kil-damned path. To collect the two-skillet bounty on Oly. Now here she was. Rich as a lord and some sort of prophesied doom-bringer. More powerful in the mercus than all the Donse Masters combined.

Yet she felt vulnerable here on the cusp of re-entering Critt's world. As if abandoning her Cheaps-speak and her filthy clothes and her skim of grime and stink had also stripped away the armor that had protected her all those years.

"What are you waiting for?" Quinn asked.

Kila pushed through the door. The throng was as sweaty and sweary as ever. The squeezebox and nickelharpa were drowned out by stomps of feet and gleeful shouts. A tavern in Cheapsgate always pulsed with dangerous energy. The joyful grins might flitter to leers if you looked at just the wrong moment. The mischievous eye-flutters of pleasure-ladies could be seen as batting away desperate tears.

Kila got many stares as she wended through the unwashed throng. Conversations were interrupted by sharp elbow jabs and a thrust of a tankard at Kila. "Lookie, mate. That lass be shorn like a sheep."

The diversion lasted only as long as she was in view. All manner of things were seen in Cheapsgate and the hubbub revived in her wake even as the stillness preceded her.

Critt was lording over the bar, a huge man with bulging shoulders and bull-shanks for forearms. He spotted Quinn first and gave her a grin and a welcoming nod. "The Garden spit ya out, lass?"

When she didn't respond his eyes flitted to Kila. They lingered, unrecognizing for a moment longer. He leaned forward, squinting. "Kil's teeth! Get in back!"

Kila trusted Critt more than she did anyone else in Cheapsgate, which was not saying much. But he had known her father, and he had been there to help her and Wen when they'd needed it. He'd even reset her arm into its socket once. So she obeyed his urgency.

His room in the back had little in it aside from a bed, a table, and a whale oil lantern. A book on the bedside table drew her attention. *Eye of Iops.* She thumbed through it, noting an interesting map of the great southern island. She did not recognize a single word of the writing. It wasn't Cigil-Tinian. Strange that it had an Ennish title. She shrugged and returned the book to the table as Critt swept in.

She didn't get a word out before he swept her into a bear hug that took her breath away. "Ah, my sweet lass. I canna lie, I missed yer wee elflish face, I did." He turned to Quinn. "And you, Shadline, well met. We embark in the mornin'."

And then he was turning back to Kila. "Ready to speak the Shadline oath? I didna think so. Ha ha. Ya better come, too. Though I 'spect the Dirth'll squeeze the words from yer lips, be you willing or no."

"What are you talking about?" Kila demanded. "I'm not going anywhere."

"What's a Dirth?" Quinn said.

Critt sighed and wiped a meaty hand across his face. "I forget yer both like little mushrooms growin' in a cellar. The Dirth be a council of Seven Shadline Knights. They called an Armory, a meetin' of all the Shadlines in the world."

"Well *we* can't go," Kila said. "We're headed north, to Ceronhel."

"And what be lurin' you t' those crumblin' ruins?"

"The Hargothe."

He pursed his lips and gave his beard a little tug. "I see. Canna stop ya, Kila Sigh. But Shadline Peline be hooked through the gills by her oath. And she don't have a—Kil's eyes, girl! Where'd yer fightin' hand go?"

Quinn held up the stump. "An accident. But I still have this one." She waggled her fingers. "I'm none too deadly with it yet."

Critt's throat rumbled. An approving hum. "A bit o' practice and you'll do fine. Mark me, lass. That left hand'll strike a mighty blow one day. I best be gettin' back to the bar. Shadline Peline, bring only one satchel, lightly packed. Kila, good fortune."

"Wait!" Kila said. "We came here to ask you something. About Binni Keel."

"Ah. Killer Keel. Saw her the night she gutted that nasty Targle fellow. Woulda given her a night's free drink fer that, had I known."

"She bonded a cat," Kila said.

A change came over him then. He grew quiet and serious. "She came in that night looking for yer brother. At first I mistook her fer you. Better fed, but a fair likeness. More hair."

Kila flashed him an impatient look. "I don't care what she looks like, I want to know where she is."

"That I canna answer except t' say she vanished."

He told a brief story of the girl coming in search of Wen and looking like she'd lost her true love when she discovered he'd died. She departed but returned in the wee hours, looking a bit plump in the middle, as if burgeoning with child. She asked Critt to hide her. Just for an hour. And he put her in this very room. He stood at his post behind the bar the entire time. He never saw her leave. But when the hour had passed, he returned to find her gone.

"An' a strange stink in th' air, to boot." He made a sniffing sneer. "Burnin' hair. Very faint."

Kila knew instantly. "Flaumishtak," she said to Quinn, who nodded in agreement. "What is that Kil-damned creature up to?"

"The cat," Quinn said.

Yes. Startle was the key to this puzzle. Cats loved Flaumishtak. He seemed to return the feeling. Perhaps he'd encouraged the pairing. And if he'd dymensed Binni and Startle away, they could be anywhere in the world.

But likely safe. "If the demayne is involved, then she didn't kill Targle. Not by herself."

Critt had one hand on the door. "I best be settin' this ship in order. Be ready Shadline Peline. *Pelican* at dawn."

He left them alone in his bedroom. "He didn't ask about the demayne," Kila said.

"He's a Shadline."

It was hard to remember that. Critt was such a jolly, simple man. A disguise, she supposed. She wondered where he'd hidden his weapon all these years.

"I suppose we learned what we came to learn," Kila said, now feeling sleepy. "Let's hire a hack and get back."

Once through the Cheaps it only took Quinn five minutes to turn up a driver willing to make the trek. For two gold skillets.

A horrific sum, but the man would not budge. "Folk are already startin' to fill the plaza. Want a good view for the Justice in the morning."

The Watch had dispatched several patrols to maintain a corridor through Dunne Medow Plaza due to the throngs already crowding through the Harridan Gate.

"I'd better return to the lower slopes tonight," Quinn said. "I'll never make it to the docks in time otherwise."

"What?" Kila said as they steered around the bend by the Baths. "You're not truly planning to go."

"I didn't plan to, but I am. I'm a Shadline. I spoke the oath. I don't want to leave you, but if I stay I wouldn't be worthy. You see that, don't you?" Quinn's eyes were shiny onyx in the dimness of the carriage.

Kila felt a sudden urge to embrace her friend, to hold on to this woman who had been the source of so much strength. But more than that, Quinn had taught Kila to be a woman, and to hear the truth inside the sideways words of powerful people.

"You have an excellent advisor in Henley," Quinn said.

"It's different with him than it is with you."

"Of course it is. He's a man."

The carriage pulled into the drive of the Peline Greathouse. Quinn knocked on the roof to have the man stop short of the house.

She paid him another gold to wait for her return.

Kila and Quinn slipped into the house, stealthy as shadows aided by the silence of Quinn's drawn blade. It seemed that if she held to Kila's arm while holding the blade, both of their movements were silenced.

Kila waited in her room while Quinn packed for her sea journey. When she returned, Kila swallowed the ache in her throat. "I wish I could dymense you where you need to go."

Quinn offered a slanted grin and waved her stump. "I'll wait till you've practiced a bit more." But she laughed, deeply, and hugged Kila hard. With a press of her lips to Kila's cheek, she backed away. "Chin up, Highest of Kil. Remember, always ask yourself: 'What do they want?" Because deep inside, they all want something."

"What do you want, Quinn Peline?"

"To be a Shadline. And what do you want, Kila Sigh?"

"What it I've always wanted. To recover what was stolen."

An uncharacteristic tear welled in Quinn's eye. She let it fall and hugged Kila again. "I love you, Kila. My dear, dear sister."

And then Kila could no longer hold back her own tears. "And I love you . . . sister."

Kila broke the embrace this time. "Kil's blessings upon you." She made a vague motion with her hand, garnet ring catching the mercus light near her bed.

Quinn made a mock curtsy, flourishing her stump. "Highest." She then drew her blade and slipped silently from Kila's room.

38

HER ENLIGHTEND'S KISS

The cell in the Westbunk was a five pace by five pace shell. There was a wooden bunk, no padding. A lidded bucket stood in the corner. Moldy rushes were strewn about the floor. They stank.

Tym Hamlickten paced back and forth, fists clenched in his effort to contain his growing panic. It wasn't execution he feared. That he welcomed. No. It was being locked up here. Trapped.

He'd rather they execute him immediately. The fearsome woman who had spoken his death sentence—which he saw as a reprieve—had broken the old man's hold on Tym's mind. For that gift alone he'd offer a lifetime of devotion.

But the release did not provide as much relief as he'd hoped. It had brought forth all the hateful things the old man had made him do. The murders along the journey from Ceronhel to Starside. The tortures. The other unspeakable abuses he had committed. He relived each one, as if witnessing the events as a spectator. What he saw horrified him. Not just the crimes themselves, but his own carnal delight in the moment.

He'd resisted each time. He knew he had. But now, in the clarity following his release from the Hargothe's control, he admitted that each time the resistance had been less.

He knew animals had viciousness inside them. A necessary quality in a wild world where survival required ruthlessness. He had not known such was inside himself. But perhaps every man hid animal violence deep in his heart. Perhaps it was only the regulation of good moral upbringing, or maybe just the expectations of his fellow man, that kept those unthinking lusts submerged.

Odd then that the most powerful man Tym had ever met —the Hargothe—had sought to release such impulses through Tym. The old man had spoken so much of Til, of "righteous order." Why then unleash animal chaos on the world?

The only conclusion Tym could reach was that the Hargothe was a hypocrite. That he was more consumed with carnal lusts than most, and that his ultimate aim was not to curb such things, but to unbridle them.

Already Starside was infected with fear. How much worse would it become when all of its citizens behaved like cornered badgers?

Fortunately for Tym, he would be dead.

A rattle and clatter came from the hall. Other prisoners moaned as their uneasy slumbers were disturbed by the racket. Heavy boots clomped closer, accompanied by the jangle of armor. They were coming for him. At last.

Tym smiled. There would be pain. More than he could bear, no doubt. But at the end of it, peace.

The guard was accompanied by the commander of the

Watch, Captain LiTishke. A rotund man in regal uniform, featuring many gold buttons and medals on his red jacket. An impressive array of whiskers thrust from his lip and lower face.

"I have recalled something important," Tym said. "A woman name Weese went to the baths. She is a danger to the merculyns there."

"Bring him," Captain LiTishke said.

Tym was taken to a room that looked like a spare officer's quarters. Bed, lantern, wash basin, and mirror.

"Wash. Put on those clothes." LiTishke pointed at a shirt and pants. Black.

The guard did not give Tym privacy as he stripped and scrubbed the prison grime from his skin. Tym avoided his own reflection. No need to see the face that would soon be slack in death.

The fabric of the clothes was good, sturdy. It was new-made, with creases from having been folded while still hot from drying by a fire.

He was not provided shoes.

A meal was brought. Coarse bread, meaty stew. Good food. Likely what the Watch ate. A cup of wine. He ate it all, taking delight in each swallow.

The air outside was cold and damp. A light drizzle added moisture to the slush. Tym was put into the back of a wagon, the sides and top made of iron bars. A cage on wheels. He was about to be paraded.

His shirt was none too thick. The chill clung to him.

As the wagon trundled from the gate of the Westbunk fortress, it joined a procession of men on horse. They were in their parade uniform, burnished breastplate, plumed helms, serious eyes. The horses clomped at a steady pace, the nostrils sending forth plumes as their heads swung side to side. Their decorative bridles and festoons of red cloth gave them a festive air.

The only words spoken were the sharp, brief orders of commanders as the horses fell in with the wagon.

They descended past Gristenside greathouses, where servants who had not been released to attend the execution were allowed out to watch him pass. A few called him "villain" and "murderer" and other, darker things. He accepted their disgust and hatred as his due.

The procession was joined by an ornate carriage, drawn by rare, white atlens. The birds' plumes hung limply from the damp, but their alert eyes and curved beaks seemed to challenge the skies. Their strong legs and huge talons drew the vehicle alongside Tym's wagon. A curtain drew back in the door facing him, and an elderly woman wearing a jeweled headpiece peered at him. He didn't recognize the woman but knew she had to be a high Sensual. Perhaps the Voluptuary herself.

And then they were through the Trialti arch and plowing through an enormous crowd of spectators. Faces jeered at him. Fists shook. Roars of hatred and curses crashed against him like indomitable waves of the sea.

The great bell of the Abbey tolled. *Clang!* A pause of fifteen seconds. *Clang!* Repeating the slow cadence of his march toward death.

Tym had never seen so many people in one place. There was not a bare patch of stone. And the surrounding rooftops were clogged with youngsters and rascals. They waved their caps at him, faces bright with the joy of hatred.

The wagon stopped before a huge wooden platform. The

guard unlocked his cage and he climbed down. It seemed odd that his hands and feet weren't chained. It would be just, he thought, to be restrained before this crowd.

But unnecessary. For where would he run? A line of sour-faced guards, whipaxes on their shoulders, lined a narrow walkway to the stairs of the platform. Even could he break through their ranks, the crowd would be more than pleased to rip him apart.

His legs betrayed him as he climbed the steps. The strength of muscles that had propelled him up mountains and through high passes and along his trap loop suddenly gave out.

His guard caught his elbow and jerked him upright. "None of that, now," the fellow said. He was Tym's age, weathered and scarred. "Walk yer last steps as a man."

The admonishment was a mercy to him. And it gave him strength. The guard knew he was a vile murderer, but he still saw the scared animal inside Tym. And in seeing it, decided not to add to his suffering.

He was guided to the post, a thick trunk of pine stripped of bark. Spine pressed to the post, he was commanded to spread his feet apart to where they were bound to iron rings mounted in the deck of the platform.

Two shorter posts thrust up a foot behind him, left and right. To these, each wrist was fastened. He was spread before the hating crowd, vulnerable to their calls, their spit, thrown bottles. Most of the last were deflected by guards before they struck Tym.

The spectators grew more excited as the old woman from the carriage ascended the steps. She was soon joined by a Donse Master descended from the Cathedral to his right. The man was flanked by nine more Donse Masters. He must be Highest Binel.

Finally, a thin, severe woman emerged from the crowd. She wore white and the medallion of the Way of Pol. The guards let her pass and she came onto the platform. The Coin.

Captain LiTishke spoke with each new arrival, kneeling once to accept blessings from Highest Binel. Finely dressed men—Radiants, Tym thought—came up to join the leaders of the Ways.

The crowd now chanted: "Justice! Justice!"

"Burn him! Burn him slow!" came another round.

Tarek PiTorro arrived. He kept his head down as he swept up to the platform. A guard tried to hold him back, but Highest Binel interceded on his behalf. The Radiants did not look best pleased to have a mere merchant joining them.

PiTorro looked pale and he flashed unreadable looks at Tym.

The crowd fell silent as a column of slow-marching soldiers emerged from the Trialti Arch. The Fell Guard. So tall, so regal. Each carried a spear, topped with the long steel point called Her Enlightened's Kiss.

Quiet murmurs of awe rose as they passed. Tym soon discovered why. Her Enlightened walked at the center of their protective column. By comparison she looked like a child. But with her shoulders back, face serene, and stride almost a perfect glide, she radiated supreme authority. She wore a black cloak of sable, the edges fringed with gray. Each stride fluttered the hem, exposing black boots and a flash of blue trousers. A stunning tiara of blue and white jewels rested atop her hair, a dark mane that spilled like ink over her shoulders.

Not one scoundrel offered a jeer or off-color remark.

Instead, all removed their caps, all bowed or dipped a knee. Many murmured her title, faces so rapt the Donse Masters must surely be enraged, for none looked so devoted during their Tilsday services.

Tym's eyes blurred as grateful tears rose. He was not a citizen of Starside, yet he loved her completely. She had saved him even as she had condemned him.

She topped the stairs and nodded to Highest Binel, the Voluptuary, and the Coin. A man emerged from among the Fell Guard, one nobody had noted because all attention had been on the monarch. Marlow. He scaled the steps and listened to her whispered command. He nodded.

Her Enlightened raised her hands slightly, like a choirmaster preparing his singers. The crowd took in a collective breath and seemed to hold it. Then she lowered her hands and they let it out. And with that gesture, the rage of the crowd drained away.

In its place was the solemnity of a funeral. A few folks dabbed at their eyes.

Tym's mercus spark was weak, but he felt the woman take hold of her power. It magnified her voice as she spoke.

"Flekk's son, Rathman, please come to me."

One of the men of the Watch broke from the ranks below and marched up the steps. His children's blood was on Tym's hands. His mother's. The man was trying to keep his face expressionless, but color rose in his cheeks. His eyes held the hollowness of grief.

The monarch greeted him at the top of the steps. Her voice did not carry, nor did his short responses. Despite his loss, he gave quick bows with every other word. Tym suspected he was grateful to Her Enlightened for the chance to wreak vengeance on Tym.

She drew a dirk from her belt, handed it to the man. He took it, eyed the slim silver blade. She placed a hand on his shoulder and encouraged him to approach Tym.

The woman's silence dropped. It had to have been mercusine. And then her voice rose all around the plaza.

"The City's Justice."

Rathman approached. In his hand, the dirk trembled.

39

THE CITY'S JUSTICE

On a rooftop across the plaza, perched among eager youngsters, side-street bullies, and a few aspiring thieves, Kila and Henley watched the proceedings. She knew many of the faces around her, but none seemed to recognize her. One boy had even knuckled his forehead in a sort of half-bow, half-salute. It was something lower slope boys did when they meant to mock someone of supposedly better blood.

Already she'd fended off three attempts on her coinpurse. Finally she opened it and handed out the skillets. After showing the young villains it was empty, she patted Cayne. "Try fer this and you'll get it in yer gut."

She and Henley had come as spectators, but also as backup. Highest Quiv and Dunne Yples were going to the Library of Dunne Francis LiMillar in the abbey. Quiv was inexpertly masked, which would register to passing merculyns as a weak spark. The *vaz'on* muted Dunne Yples's spark somewhat, too. He would keep his hood up.

Kila knew they could alert the whole city to her presence here. And she was loosing a man of enormous power—wearing a relic that gave any merculyn access to that power—into the heart of the Way that sought her death.

Kila had warded the *vaz'on*, but she was not confident in such feats. If one could see the bolts, one could negate them. She'd put a little surprise into her ward, just in case.

But now all attention was on the execution platform. On the man carrying Her Enlightened's blade toward the murderer.

He came to a stop before the bound man, said something. Kila wished she could release her mask. She wanted to hear the words. So did the rest of the crowd. People began to shout, demanding to know what was being said.

"Oh!" Henley gasped. "They are coming!"

"What?" Kila said. "Who?"

"Merculyns. Lots of them. From the cathedral."

The doors to the cathedral swung open. But nobody was looking. Rathman had raised the blade, pressed it to the murderer's cheek. A roar rose from the spectators, urging him on. The calm the monarch had laid over them had faded. Faces were red, fists raised.

"She's masked. She doesn't know!" Henley said.

"Who?"

"Her Enlightened. They have circled to form source-taps. Look near the Harridan gate." A passel of Spinsters, all in white, pushed through. The crowd parted as if thrust aside by the prow of a great ship. On the platform Her Enlightened watch the guard slowly draw the tip of the blade down the murderer's cheek, parting the skin until it wept crimson.

But not deep. Not particularly disfiguring. It would heal a

faint scar, Kila thought. Except the man was not going to get a chance to heal.

"Kila," Henley said. "They are coming for her."

The guard pulled his hand back. His body trembled. He wanted to draw more than a scratch. He wanted to thrust the blade into the man's throat. Again and again.

But this was the City's Justice. He would have to wait. As if pulled by a puppeteer's strings he stumbled back to the monarch and returned the blade. She again patted his shoulder before approaching the murderer.

"They are preparing a feat," Henley said. "I don't know what."

The Donse Masters had formed into squads of four. They stood arrayed on the steps of the cathedral. Outwardly there was no indication they were wielding the mercus.

Same for the Spinsters. There were thirty of them, also split into squads. They moved into the crowd, drawing irritated looks and raised fists, which dropped once the man or house-mistress saw who they were. One did not strike a servant of Luck.

Her Enlightened was radiant in her sable and crown. A goddess. She spoke to the prisoner, raised the dirk to his other cheek and striped it with a quick stroke. The man flinched but didn't cry out, though his fists were clenched so tightly they had turned white.

The monarch returned to her post and handed the dagger to Highest Binel. He took it with a polite nod, eyes flashing toward the Donse Masters on the cathedral steps.

"What's happening?" Kila demanded.

"I—I don't know. They are holding the mercus. I don't sense anyone taking the source-tap from the squads."

Binel took his turn with the prisoner. Even with her senses dulled from her mask, Kila could see the Highest's hand shake as he cut through the man's sleeve, rent it wide, then drew a slash across his forearm. This produced a low cry from the man, which was answered by cheers from the crowd.

Her Enlightened stood imperiously at the edge of the platform, hands folded before her. Binel returned and handed the dirk to the Coin. The woman snatched it and marched to the prisoner. She did the same as Binel with the man's other arm. Business-like, the way one would split open a fish.

The prisoner was weeping now, lips moving. "What's he saying?" Kila asked.

Henley didn't answer. He was looking at the Donse Masters, eyebrows knit with concentration. "Light and heat, but negated. They are not as good at the negation as you are. Each of the squads has formed it. But who is controlling—I see now. They are not circled. They are independent. One or two forms the senses the other negates."

A disturbance in the crowed drew Kila's eyes to the Trialti Arch. "Look, Hen. Sensuals."

"I felt them earlier."

They moved into the plaza, displacing spectators with ease. But it was like adding dry wood to a fire. The crowd was already mashed together. The new arrivals forced man to press against man against woman against child. People cried out in indignation and anger.

"She needs to calm them," Henley said. "Whatever she did before."

"Why is she masked?" Kila asked. "So foolish!"

The Voluptuary took the dirk from the Coin and proceeded to the prisoner. Her own jeweled headpiece sent dazzling flashes into Kila's eyes. The boys near to Kila speculated about how many gold skillets it would fetch. One hazarded as much as a hundred. His friend punched his arm and told him that was way too high.

Kila didn't dare drop her mask. It was a wonder none of the merculyns were looking to her rooftop perch already. Henley outshone all of them now. But since they were holding the power, perhaps they had their hands full.

The Voluptuary stood before the prisoner.

"She's put up a silence sphere," Kila said. Her Enlightened was watching. Her features were small from Kila's vantage, but there seemed to be a dip in her brow. She took a step toward the Voluptuary.

The Coin caught her sleeve and whispered something. She pointed into the crowd. Surely the monarch had seen the encroaching merculyns by now.

By why would that raise her suspicion? Surely they had as much cause to witness the City's Justice as anyone.

Marlow slipped along the back of the platform. He didn't seem to care about the Voluptuary's silence either. Kila gasped. Marlow wore her old queller ring. He didn't know about the mercus being held by the squads throughout the plaza.

But Binel and the Coin certainly did. And all the Donse Masters who stood with Binel.

The Voluptuary raised the dirk. And she raised her other hand, too. She put the flat of her freehand on the prisoner's cheek.

The crowd cried out. The Voluptuary was still holding the man's face, but his eyes had rolled up into his skull.

"She's healing him!" Henley said.

Sure enough, the red stripes had closed, leaving only the trailing streaks of blood to mar his skin and clothes.

Marlow spun from where he'd been conferring with the Captain of the Fell Guard. Her Enlightened pulled away from the Coin and rushed to the Voluptuary.

Kila knew the Voluptuary. And some instinct thrilled in her now. The woman's posture was wrong, the scowl she turned on the monarch was wrong. With two quick slashes the Voluptuary severed the ropes securing the prisoner's arms. Suddenly the bonds at his ankles smoked and dissolved.

Her Enlightened stopped.

"Her mask is down," Henley said.

The Voluptuary turned her back on the monarch and slipped the dirk into the rope binding the man to the post. He stumbled free, face contorted with glorious rage.

"Why isn't she doing anything?"

"Oh no!" Henley said. "We have to—"

The Voluptuary turned, stepped close the monarch and drove the dirk into the woman's belly.

"No!" Kila screamed. Her cry was lost the crowd's roar.

Her Enlightened's face contorted, mouth opening as if trying to voice Kila's own cries.

"The Hargothe," Henley shouted. "I feel him there. Right there!" he was pointing to the platform. Right at the murderer.

Kila dropped her mask.

40

———

GODDESS OF FURY

In Ceronhel the blind seer shuddered where he stood, his knuckles white from gripping his staff so firmly. Fifty dead nosg littered the hall, dropped one by one to feed the Staff of Nihil in preparation for this feat.

But the Hargothe was not present, not aware of the cold hall, nor of the pounding of a rebellious band of nosg-kin at the door. He need not worry, for Yiothizandra stood guard, wings folded away in demaynic insubstantiality beneath her armor. She was in woman-form now, full fed, and unconcerned with the hundred or so nosg who wished to kill the Hargothe in vengeance of their fallen.

This uprising would soon be quelled or quashed. Millions more of their kind—and worse—lurked in the Haelshok mountains. All would serve her when she swept south.

Yioth wandered the hall, listening to the fibers of the straining man's muscles. His heart rammed out a cantering beat. She did not feel the mercus as he did, for she had chosen different sensitivities, more attuned to hungers and lusts than to baser instincts like hate and fear. But there was plenty of hunger in the man now. That had been her doing.

The ramming increased at the door. She found it tiresome so she thrust aside the great wooden bar and let the nosg flow in.

The first three dozen burned. Those behind fled, screaming.

THE HARGOTHE OCCUPIED the trapper fully now. The excess of mercus flowing from his staff could not be wielded through the man, but it did give him the power to shirk off his host's fatigue.

The crowd leered at him, screaming and throwing things. Some began to surge forward. There was very little time. The old Voluptuary had been slow; she'd fought the commands he'd planted in her through Weese. In the end he'd temporarily taken over her mind and restored his force-bond to the trapper. Even now she was carrying out his last command, driving the blade into the whore's belly.

He cast an eye to Highest Binel. The man had not been force-bonded yet. But those around him were the Hargothe's, all having succumbed to his clever force-bond, spread like the thinnie plague from merculyn to merculyn over the past day. Even now he could feel them as tendrils extending from his mind.

The trapper's execution had been such a glorious opportunity, proof that the force of destiny guided the Hargothe toward righteous domination of this world. The Enlightened bitch had strode right into the midst of his hive of merculyn wasps, masked, as he'd known she'd be.

Two men squirmed through the ranks of the Watch. One held a dagger, the other a sword. Spittle flew from their lips. They meant to have vengeance upon the trapper.

The Hargothe laughed at them. "Fools!" The trapper's spark was pathetic, but his channel was wide. He waved to the cathedral steps and a source-tap was offered. He accepted and power flooded through him. Forking his bolts, he struck into the encroaching men's minds. No need for a bond here, just a twist and snap and . . .

They fell like boneless dolls.

He turned to the tableau on the platform. The Voluptuary still twisted the blade in the monarch's gut. The woman's serenity had vanished. In its place, agony. Ah, what a delicious sight.

The Voluptuary's face mirrored the monarch's, as if she drove the blade into her own bowels. That, too, was delicious.

The Coin watched, her face hard and frank. If there was an interior war for control going on there, her face did not betray it.

And look at Highest Binel, the fool, backpedaling and calling for help. His band of Donse Masters moved in to grip his arms.

Where was Marlow? The Hargothe spun, loving the lithe strength of the trapper's body. Brilliant of him to have the woman heal the wounds before she'd released him. Marlow had dropped behind the platform and was fleeing. The Hargothe had to credit his brother for an unerring instinct for self-preservation. He would deal with Marlow later. At his leisure.

He turned back to the gutted monarch. He stalked to the Voluptuary's side, full of his source-tap's power. "Bar all exits from the plaza," he ordered the old woman. He took the dirk from her hands and pulled it from the monarch's abdomen.

She still hadn't fallen, though her face was pale, eyes glassy. Such strength! He could not deny the truth of her fortitude. But now he knew what she was. He'd always suspected.

"Greetings, dragnithan," he said through clenched teeth.

"Why did you kill them?" she asked. Her voice was clear, strong though her face was contorted with pain.

"Those men were going to kill me."

"Not them. Flekk and the children."

"Til collected them to his bosom, for theirs was a sacrifice for power, to strengthen this man's feeble spark. Now drop your mask!"

He pulled the dirk free and plunged the blade into her flank, tearing a new wound even as blood spilled from her belly.

She still hadn't raised a hand to fight or defend herself. Odd.

The Fell Guard was trying to come forward, but the closest men were frozen by circles of Donse Masters and Spinsters. The Sensuals were following the Voluptuary's orders to bar exit from the Plaza.

The hair on the back of his neck prickled. The dying monarch was staring over his shoulder, a blood-stained smile on her lips. He followed her gaze, across the plaza, to the rooftops.

To a blaze of mercusine flaring like the sun. In his passion of triumph he'd ignored it, had thought it a swell of power coming from a Spinster squad or some such.

Back in Ceronhel the Hargothe staggered and fell to one knee as his hold on the trapper's mind frayed. "No."

It was the girl. That infernal girl!

With a cry he pulled himself to his feet and reasserted his hold on the trapper. His vision wavered then came into sharp focus. The monarch still stood. The trapper's hand still gripped the dirk driven into her flank. She was laughing with the deep-throated and lascivious rasp of a tavern harlot.

And then she fell forward and thunked onto her face. He held her dirk up. Blood soaked into the steel and vanished. A Shadline blade. What other secrets had she been hiding?

"More!" he cried, signaling to his other source-taps, calling to the Spinsters and Sensuals to offer up their mercus to him.

The Voluptuary had gone rigid, her jaw bulging, eyes squinting as she fought with all her will to resist commands he had lain into her mind at the first instant of Weese's touch. He laughed to think of the horror of it. It would have been wondrous to occupy her as fully as he did the trapper. She was powerful, her spark bright, but her channel too narrow for his needs. No, the trapper was perfect as long as he had source-taps to draw from.

The crowd seethed, pressing against the Watch, faces torn with fury as they sought to reach him, kill him. Fools.

"Captain LiTishke!" he cried. "Suppress the crowd."

Ah, the glory of forcing the Watch commander to take orders from the very mouth of the man set to be executed. But LiTishke could not resist the bolts of allure the Hargothe added to the command.

LiTishke shouted: "Hold them back, men! Do your duty!"

A Watch man's whipaxe fell. And another. A woman's face

split apart under the curved axe blade. An old man took a blow to the shoulder that nearly cleaved his arm off.

Panic bubbled from the crowd, adding to the brew of hate. Starside was rank with it, like a ferneater's potion. At the Harridan and Trialti, people began to discover their way blocked by Sensuals and Spinsters. A few were desperate enough to push. They were blown back with lashes of mercusine whips or blasts of air. The faces of the merculyns were hideous in their failing battle to disobey his commands. They were his now, their unwilling cooperation punishment for their past sins.

"Come girl!" he shouted to Kila Sigh, who stood brazenly at the edge of the far roof. A companion star stood next to her. Ah, the boy, Henley Mast. Such power the lad had cultivated. The Hargothe would drain him to the last drop of mercus then have his body thrown into the Sourwater. But the girl was a danger. He had not expected her.

He sought her mind, sending forth his mercusine strike like lightning even as similar strands flew up from select merculyns in the crowd. Theirs were weak compared to his, but they were needed to distract her.

The girl deflected them all with a casual feat. It had been so fast, so short-lived he hadn't been able to see what senses comprised the bolts.

Her feet lifted from the rooftop. The boy brought a flare of golden light into existence, a haze that backed Kila as she rose, illuminating her with a goddess's aura.

And the steaming crowd saw her. Their hate and terror transmuted to awe. They screamed and pointed. Faces of rage turned away from the Hargothe to bask in the golden light of the girl who could fly. Wind buffeted them, drawn from close to the ground and sucking among thousands of feet, bringing with it the debris of the mad city.

Bits of paper, and ash, and skims of snow rose beneath her. The Hargothe saw she was held aloft upon a thick upward thrust of air. Women's skirts lifted; cloaks fluttered up. A child on her father's shoulders raised her arms, head back in ecstatic joy as her blond curls fluttered all about her.

And above all, the goddess of fury approached. Her hair was cut short, barely a fuzz atop her elfin head. But her brows were flat, eyes fierce, and her arms spread wide as she descended toward the platform.

She wore black trousers and a coat of fine weave embroidered on each sleeve in glossy black. Ravens.

Her feet touched the wood and she stalked toward him. Not a tall girl, and no more than seventeen, but ageless nonetheless. Her eyes sparkled with hatred. "Hargothe."

A blast of blue came from a squad of Spinsters, sending up an attack to protect the Hargothe. It dissipated into smoke before striking the girl. The Hargothe noted her technique but was startled by the casual effort.

Squaring off to face her, he struck again with his mental probes. As powerful as she was, she possessed not a tenth of his skill at such feats.

She sliced the tendrils of his attack with the same reflex as she had killed the Spinsters' blue sphere. More merculyns attacked, thrusting flame, spikes of air, and mental jabs. These were like the blows of a small child against an armored warrior. Many lacked the focus or strength to carry all the way to her.

Kila seemed shielded from them without effort. The Hargothe backed away, furious to be denied his victory here.

He had been so close to taking the city without having to move a mile from his Ceronhel holdfast. The so-called Enlightened was dead, every merculyn of power was bound to obey and protect him, the city was rank with fear. All that was needed to bring righteous order to Starside was a leader of true merit.

Oh, he would reign here. That much was certain. But perhaps he would have to accept a delay.

He spun toward Tarek PiTorro, who cowered at the rear of the platform. The man flinched away, but the trapper's hands gripped his mind with mercusine bolts. *Obey our agreement.* And with the command he placed the slightest twist and knot. The Hargothe would not be able to possess the man, for he had no spark. But he would bring his caravan. Of that there would be no doubt.

That settled, he turned to the girl. Still backed by the god-glow of the boy's light. He saw now it was more than glow, the boy had offered himself as a source-tap.

Til's tears! The girl held such power. And yet she had not immolated him on the spot. Why had she stayed her hand?

"Release these merculyns, old man," she demanded.

Ah. That was why. He glanced at the dead monarch. She'd had the skill to unwind his knot on the trapper. But she was dead. Kila surely had enough power, but did she have the knowledge? He doubted it. She was no better than a hedge-merc, untrained. A toddler with a giant's strength.

Perhaps . . . a gambit rose to mind.

With a growl he cried. "I shall have thee, girl. Mark me. And when I have Kil chained at my feet, your power will be a mere flickering candle in the gale. I shall possess thee utterly and use thee for whatever purpose I wish."

He relinquished his draw on the source-taps so only the trapper's meager spark remained. He forced his face to go slack, dropped the dirk, and staggered. Bringing his hands to his head, he moaned. "What happened?"

He gaped at the blood on the platform, casting his eyes all about as if seeing the plaza and the awe-quietened crowd for the first time. "Who are you?" he said to Kila.

A desperate gambit.

He went to a knee and cried out. "Ah me, he's gone."

Behind him the Voluptuary collapsed as her will-battle reached its inevitable conclusion: absolute exhaustion. Her hands were sticky with the monarch's blood.

In Ceronhel the Hargothe slumped, grasping his staff with both hands, using it to keep himself upright. He hadn't been controlling all his force-bonds directly, but he'd spared power to battle their will-struggles.

With that release came great relief.

But he was not present in Ceronhel. His mind still occupied the trapper's.

The girl moved toward him slowly, still full of awesome power. She could ash him in a heartbeat. The Hargothe doubted his mind would survive such. He *had* to retreat before she killed his host. But not yet. Not yet.

"Please!" he begged. "Help me be rid of him!"

The only sound now was the creak of the planks beneath her feet and the distant cry of gulls drifting upon currents above the plaza. He was vaguely aware of the smell of blood. Binel had collected himself even as his Donse Masters were swaying in the aftermath of his press of will against them.

He flicked a glance to see the Coin flat on her back. Good. Perhaps she was dead, too. The gambling crones were a vein of gangrene. Once he was victorious, those Spinsters he did not drain would be put to the torch right here in Dunne Medow Plaza.

Kila drew nearer. She was almost within arm's reach.

"Stand, murderer," she said.

It was not natural to the Hargothe to offer anyone deferential respect. But he forced himself not to look at her face. He thought he'd fooled her thus far, but he could not always master his face. She was suspicious already. If he revealed the wrong expression, she would blast him from existence.

There was a dagger on her thigh. Her hands were slim, small. Strong. And on one pinky a gold ring with an exquisitely cut garnet. It caught in the light, sending flecks of jewel-spark onto the planks of the execution platform.

The ring drew his focus for it resonated in him. It did not appear to be a heller. He breathed in through his nose, seeking the scent. Having lived so long in the crypt beneath the cathedral the Hargothe could catch smells unnoticed even by hounds.

The scent of the ring was like the monarch's blood. Not the same, but cousin to it. He couldn't place it. An eerie, prickly sound came from the gem. Not entirely pleasant. He was both repulsed and drawn to it.

She took another, shorter step closer. "Stand."

He rose. The crowd murmured, a bit of their hatred for the murdering trapper reigniting.

He lifted his hands. "Please. I beg mercy. Please!"

A keening cry drifted down from on high. A boy atop the roofs spotted the source. He screamed, shrill and girlish. "Dragon!"

A trickle of power seeped from the Hargothe, a gossamer

spider-strand. His fast strikes had not worked, so he lifted a slow one. Lofting it upward.

More cries of "dragon!" arose from already scream-torn throats of the spectators. Awestruck faces collapsed into terror. The Hargothe spared them no notice. These fools were too overwrought. They'd spotted a frigate bird or tern and their minds had made it a dragon. Bah. There hadn't been such a beast in Starside in a dozen years.

But that shriek!

It came again. Closer. Doubt made his hair-thin mercus probe waver, but he regathered it as gently as cupping a butterfly.

Kila Sigh looked past him now, to the monarch. She tilted her head, as if listening. And so the Hargothe flitted his tendril closer.

41

ARE YOU SO WEAK?

She lives! came the voice into Kila's mind again. Not Nax's, not the Hargothe's.

This was deep, commanding, ancient. This was Harnzyne, the dragon who had allowed her to collect scales in the eerie behind the Citadel. The deep basso rattled her skull.

The piteous trapper stood before her, hands raised in a plea. She shouldered him aside and knelt by Her Enlightened. Already Kila's hand was cupped, swirling the mercus into the crimson brew she'd learned from Flaumishtak.

Peripherally she was aware of Highest Binel stooping to help the Voluptuary to her feet. She was stammering, trying to say something, but the words never formed into anything intelligible.

Henley's source-tap was not needed, but Kila appreciated it. He had offered it without word and she had accepted it without acknowledgement. Somehow he'd split his power, reserving some for himself. She'd felt the shielding power of his mercus aura, allowing her to focus all her attention on the murderer. The Hargothe. She'd recognized him in the man's contorted face. She had not recognized the spark. The flavor was off, as Henley would say. But the feats. Dropping those men. Compelling Captain LiTishke with hard allure. Bold and nuanced and crafty. Masterwork of mercusine, and all of it the Hargothe's specialty. Had she not been forewarned, his strikes against her would have penetrated. Only reflex had saved her from them.

The man was a coward when it came to face-to-face confrontation. Now he'd released his force-bonded murderer and retreated back to Ceronhel without more than token strikes at her. She could only assume the distance sapped his power.

The Fell Guard had been frozen before. Now released, they stomped forward to surround the monarch. Two others lowered their spears and were about to hoist the murderer on them.

"Fell Guard, hold!" Marlow cried. He scrambled between them. "We must question this man. He has been possessed by an enemy of Her Enlightened."

They stopped, spears poised.

Most had surrounded Kila and the monarch. One was barking at Kila to stand aside.

"I may be able to heal her," she snapped. Giving them no further attention, she plunged her awareness into Her Enlightened's body, seeking the wounds, seeking the heart.

With so much blood spilled, Kila held no hope. Only the insistence of the dragon drove her on.

It is not her time, Harnzyne sent.

The spectators were screaming now. Kila was vaguely aware

of a shadow over her. Down-gusts from great wings made Her Enlightened's hair flutter.

Kila disentangled the lovely crown. Setting it aside, she rolled the woman onto her back. Grievous wounds in her abdomen gaped red and raw.

Kila tipped her hand and poured mercus healing over the rents even as she felt for the woman's heart. It did not beat. There was little remaining blood for it to move. Her chest did not rise.

I cannot save her, Kila sent. *I'm sorry, Harnzyne.*

Look past the blood, girl! She is dragnithan!

As if that explained anything. But Kila searched deeper. What could be beyond the blood?

An odd itch plagued Kila's mind. Like a buzzing fly around her face. She swiped her hand around her head to chase it off.

Save her!

A high-pitched shriek tore across the plaza, ending in a deep grumble. The crowd broke, trampling man and child alike to clear a space near the platform.

The ground shook as the beast landed. Men of the Watch cried out and scrambled to hide under the platform.

Marlow shouted at the Fell Guard.

The trapper laughed.

From across the plaza, Henley shouted Kila's name. A warning. But Kila was gone, submerged in the strangeness of Her Enlightened's body.

Kila knew the general anatomy of a person well enough, having done this sort of thing before. She didn't know what all the guts and bits were called, nor what they did. But nobody she'd healed before had ever had a web of mercusine flowing through their flesh.

It was similar to the mesh of blood vessels, but this was a blue-glowing web of power. And the deeper Kila looked, the more she discovered. She had to brace herself with her hands to keep from tipping forward into the woman's gore-covered body.

"Dragnithan," Harzyne had called the woman. Meaningless to Kila, but now she saw why the woman had such incredible mercusine power. She was seemingly made of mercus. But there was something else—

The buzzing in her head intensified.

Henley's voice carried through her focus. "Kila!"

Listen! Nax sent, full of urgency. She had thought the cat still at the greathouse. But she felt close by.

"There you are," the murderer crooned. "Easily done." Kila's scalp tingled with horror.

A strange hissing grew from behind her. Armored men jumped from the platform, spears clattering, armor clanking.

Heat washed across Kila. A shrill cry, then silence. The smoke of burning flesh. Kila pulled her awareness from the monarch and turned back to see a black scorch on the platform where the trapper had been. Henley's source-tap was gone, too.

Have you given up? Harnzyne sent. *Are you so weak?*

No!

Henley had ashed the trapper. The Hargothe. She knew it with a certainty.

At least that annoying buzzing was gone from her mind. She dove again into the monarch's body, driven more by curiosity now than the dragon's insistence. She was vaguely aware of the Fell guardsmen circling her, enclosing her with the monarch. Anyone who came within reach of their spears would die.

One of the men was asking her a sharply worded question. The dragon cuffed him on the helm with the tip of its wing.

"Let me through," Marlow said. "I may be able to assist."

Marlow appeared at Kila's side. He plucked off his queller and gasped. "By Kil's throbbing handle, girl. What—? Oh dear."

Kila found the woman's pulse. Not in the heart, but in the mind. A slow ebb and flow of mercusine. Already Kila had sealed her wounds and knitted the damaged organs. But she didn't know how to manifest blood from nothing. Intuition guided her to compress the heart with mercus touch while coaxing the woman's own mercusine to take up the blood's work. And it *was* just coaxing, like cooing enticements to a pup or chick until it came to her hand.

The blue-glow flowed to the woman's heart then coursed through her veins. The heart convulsed. Once. Twice. Then began to throb on its own as the mercus flowed in.

Thank you, Kila Sigh, Her Enlightened sent. *Now get out.*

Kila was ejected with a force so great that she was flung backward, her spine cracking into a Fell Guard's armored calf. Marlow grabbed her and pulled her to him.

"Astonishing! I saw. I saw all you did."

Her Enlightened rolled onto her hands and knees, pausing long enough to pluck up her crown and affix it to her head. Then she stood.

Kila thought she looked none too steady on her feet. "Come to the Citadel, girl. We have much to discuss." Kila climbed to her feet as the Fell Guard moved aside.

Highest Binel and the Voluptuary called to the woman, both faces white as snow. With a jerk of mercus, the monarch drew her dirk from the platform and returned it to her belt. She moved to the charred circle that had once been the trapper. She swiped her toe through the smear of ash. "Pity."

And then she strode onto Harnzyne's proffered wing and took position on his neck, right at the base of his skull. With ponderous flaps that sent an ash-swirling gust across the platform, the dragon launched skyward.

The Fell Guard were already trotting in formation for the Trialti Arch, boots and armor clanking in a drumbeat of urgency as they raced to take their posts at the Citadel. They left two behind guarding the Voluptuary, the woman who had stabbed the monarch.

Are you well? Nax sent. The cat was near, though wisely not in view. Somewhere on the roofs.

I'm fine.

Are you sure?

Yes.

The Voluptuary tottered forward, smiling coldly though there were tense wrinkles around her eyes. She removed her jeweled headpiece and dropped it to the decking. She turned to the two Fell Guards still poised to strike her down, their great spears pointed at her chest. The woman had stabbed Her Enlightened. But she was also head of the Way of Ori. Her Enlightened's chief counselor had told them to hold. They were paralyzed with indecision, and the monarch had given them no guidance.

The Voluptuary's face went red and her lips pulled back. Fists clenched, she let out a horrific groan. It appeared to take all her will to utter the words: "Do it. Free me."

"No!" Marlow said. "Her Enlightened banished the Hargothe from the trapper's mind. She would not have the Voluptuary killed before such an attempt was made."

Kila reached the woman in three strides. The Fell guard didn't stop her as she gripped the woman's temples and plunged. But seek as she might, she did not find the Hargothe there. She was about to withdraw when she saw the faint wrongness. A twisted tangle of mercusine overlaid so cleverly Kila saw no way to disentangle it.

"Do it, girl," the woman hissed. "Whatever. You. Must." Blood trickled from the Voluptuary's mouth. She had bitten her tongue.

Kila ripped the entanglement free.

The woman gave two violent jerks and went limp. Kila caught her and guided her inert body to the planks. Something fell from her hands and rolled across the platform to stop at Kila's feet.

Four Donse Masters lunged for it, knocking Highest Binel aside in their eagerness. They were like Cheapsgate boys scampering after a dropped coin.

Kila drew the object to her hands with mercus touch. It was a lovely gem, crystalline and faceted on all sides. She recognized it. The Voluptuary had wielded it against Flaumishtak once. A Bane Eye.

"That is a mercusine relic," Highest Binel said, now recovered from his shoves. "By right of the Synod of the New Pantheon, all such must be remitted to the Way of Til." He held out his hand.

Henley trotted onto the platform to join Kila.

"The Triumvirate is dead, Highest Binel," Kila said. "The covenant of the Synod is broken. I would no sooner hand this to you than I would my cat." She turned her back on him. "Why did you ash the murderer?"

Henley put his hands on her face, drew her nose close to his. For a moment she thought he meant to kiss her. The idea froze her in startlement.

"Hold still," he said. "The Hargothe touched you."

"No he didn't, he—"

"Mercus. A strand so thin and faint I almost missed it. But I didn't. I think I got him before he completed it. You need to let me in."

Had it been anyone else, any other merculyn in the entire world, Kila would have refused. But she trusted Henley. Completely.

"Go on, then."

"It may hurt."

"Do it."

The spectators had pressed back to the platform now that the dragon was gone. The two remaining Fell Guard positioned themselves to defend Kila. She had only a moment to note it before Henley struck.

Kila heard nothing more, for Henley drove mercus probes into her mind more deeply than the Hargothe had ever done.

42

THE PEAK OF HER GLORY

Something fluttered on one of the cross beams that spanned the ceiling of the great hall of Ceronhel. A snow hawk.

The Hargothe was dimly aware that his body was numb from the cold. That was because he'd fallen onto his back on the stone floor. He must have been here for a while.

His last moments in Starside had not been pleasant, all his focus on laying in his bond on Kila Sigh. His warning of the attack had been brief. But it had been enough.

"Yiothizandra?" He lifted his head. The hall was lit by gray light coming through the uncurtained windows. His tongue was sticky and foul with the taste of burned flesh.

She didn't answer.

He wrinkled his nose at the stench of dead nosg lying about. For a moment he feared that the boy's attack had burned his own flesh, for the air was filled with the stink of charred meat. With a groan he got to his feet.

He reached out with his senses and felt the contours of the

dead. A concentrated smear near the hall's great entry doors showed where Yioth had burned a slew of nosg. The doors stood open letting in a blessing of fresh air.

He picked his way through the bodies, slippers splashing through what remained of the puddle in the center of the hall.

The air outside was still and crisp. He was too weak to resist the cold, so he pulled his robes about himself and searched for his demaynic lover. "Yioth!"

His voice carried back to him on three long echoes. No wind stirred. The absolute stillness was eerie. There should at least be the clang and grunt of nosg work crews laboring away at bolstering walls or carrying away debris.

"Yioth!" he called again.

"I'm here." The voice came from behind him.

He reached to her with mercus touch, running his aware-ness across her. She had shed her armor and was clothed only in a robe. It parted to expose her bare thighs as she strode down the crumbling steps to join him. Her hair tumbled down her back in a regal wave. His senses formed an image in his mind, aided by what he remembered from seeing her through the nosg's eyes. She was terrifyingly beautiful, but his newly awakened lust did not respond. He felt as weak and unsteady as a day-old colt.

"I killed your little cousin," he said. "I felt that trollop's blood pulse over my hand as I twisted her own blade into her guts."

Instead of looking pleased, Yioth merely scoffed. "Killed a dragnithan with a dagger, did you? Next you'll be telling me you slew a dragnithor with a tailor's needle."

"I saw her. Face down in a pool of her own blood."

"And how many blows did your trapper suffer in the battle? What mercus feats did she hurl at him?"

"None." And that troubled him. Why had she not defended herself? Surely the Voluptuary's initial strike should have provoked some response. "But how can one live without blood?"

"How do you see without eyes?" She snaked her arms around him. "Your gambit failed, my love. It had little chance anyway. But you still hold Ceronhel, and after you bring the shamans to heel, the nosg will return to serve you. Besides, Starside ought not distract you. It is not necessary to claim it before Kil comes."

Not necessary? That showed Yioth knew nothing about him. Starside was the *key*, for it was practically unassailable except by sea.

First Starside, then the world. Unless Kil's power would grant him the world without conquest, the war had to proceed logically.

"Kila Sigh was there," he said. "I tied a little knot into her mind before I was forced to withdraw."

"Excellent. Bring her here."

He had already planned to do so. And now he wanted nothing more than to meditate in the subtle realm of the mercusine and feel her. But the bond was incomplete. He was sure of that now because he could barely sense her. He would not be able to place any compulsion on her. Not from afar. But at least he would always know where she was. And if he sacrificed a dozen or so more nosg, he'd have enough power in the Staff to see through her eyes.

If he'd only had more time. "You say your cousin is a dragnithan? But I did not see her fly and spew fire."

"She prefers her woman form. I sometimes think she wishes she were not dragnithan at all. She chose the path of the mercusine." Yioth's husky laugh told what she thought of that choice. "What do you know of the dragnithor demayne?"

"I don't care about dragnithor. I ask of dragnithan."

She went on as if he'd not spoken. "A dragnithor is what your kind calls a dragon. Kil favored them with powerful forms, breath of flame, and keen intelligence."

"Beasts," the Hargothe said. "Feeding upon the bodies of cattle and men alike."

"Meat is meat, darklove. But until you have conversed with a dragnithor, do not think to know their nature. Those whose first flight was beneath the sun are weak, for they resign themselves to living in this world forever. They see peace with man as a high aim, and they do not recognize Kil as their Lord. Those whose first flight was beneath stars seek freedom, and any man they see might be ignored or devoured as suits the needs of the moment."

Yioth grasped the Hargothe's hand and led him back toward the hall. "Dragnithan too have first flights beneath the sun or stars. She who reigns in Starside forsook her wings and flame to stride under the sun, upon her feet. You should have seen the mothers and fathers of Day. They prostrated themselves before the child and spoke of prophecy. The mothers and fathers of Night recoiled in horror and disgust. And when the eldest of Day bade her to fly, she sprouted raven's wings. Ah, her agony was a joy to behold, for I hated her instinctively. Every night flyer is of serpent-kin, you'll find no feathers upon our wings or crowns." She made a spitting noise as they passed back into the fetid hall.

"Her flight was brief, and when she returned to ground,

she was taken away and not seen again until she claimed The Raven Throne."

The Hargothe said, "The throne has been held by the LiMinluit family since men claimed Starside over one thousand years ago. The current occupant is a woman of thirty, born and raised in the Citadel her entire life."

"No. She is a dragnithan, still young to me, but ancient to you. Name any Enlightened of history. Loyann LiMinluit? Duri the Harridan? Ashel? And now Ell. All of them a single dragnithan, appearing to age, appearing to be murdered, and then appearing to be born."

"If the Radiancies knew this, they would revolt!" The Hargothe had enough strength to bring fire into the great hearth. He stood near to it now, Yioth holding his arm and bearing up some of his weight. "But what could they do? They are all so intent on positioning for the throne themselves they could not cooperate long enough to bring down a tree."

"They are ants," Yioth said. "Without an army of merculyns they stand no chance of deposing her. She has never feared them. I doubt she spares them any more thought that she does you."

"You are a dragnithan. She is a dragnithan. And yet she is also a merculyn. You are not."

"That is the path she chose. She is *of* the mercusine, as am I. It is our essence, flowing into us and through us. It builds in me and I fly, I feed, I fornicate. It builds in her and she . . . does whatever she does." Yioth's fingers stroked his arm, provoking tingles of arousal. "You thrust a dagger into her guts and drained her blood away and yet she lives." There was a ringing of metal, a dagger pulled from a hidden sheath. The chill flat of the blade pressed to the skin of his throat. She removed it and put the hilt into his hand. Parting her robe, she placed the tip to her own belly. With impossible strength she guided his hand to press the blade into her flesh.

But it did not go in.

"Nothing can penetrate me," she said. With smooth, expert movements she disarmed him, tossed the dagger away to clatter onto the stones. "Nothing save what I allow."

Her hands continued with more expert moves, disrobing him, throwing him to the floor. And then she attacked with womanly wiles, and the Hargothe was subsumed by her insatiable lust.

At the peak of her glory he tested her with a spidery strand of mercus. He slithered it into her mind and discovered a raging storm of mercusine inside. Chaos. Disorganized charges of light and sensation, roiling and boiling like a fellstorm of the mind.

But Yioth didn't notice this particular intrusion. Perhaps her haughty dismissal of all things human was her one vulnerability.

The Hargothe's practice of spreading his force-bond through the trapper had given him a subtlety he had never needed when living within his crypt beneath the cathedral. When the fly came to the spider, the bite was quick and full of venom. But when the spider crawled beneath a dragon, it must needs be quiet and careful, and stay beneath notice.

Yiothizandra's mind was *deep*. But the chaos of the storm was pure noise. All of that was atmosphere concealing solid ground beneath. How else could she reason or speak if not for an organized mind at her core?

He probed deeper and deeper with his mercusine tendrils

even as she writhed and scraped his skin and scalded him with her physical heat.

And just as he was about to lose all hope of finding what he sought, the clouds of chaos parted and the strange realm of her demaynic mind was revealed.

His brief time bonded to the Beloved One had given him opportunity to explore similar terrain. Similar but different. A cat's mind existed in other dimensions, its concerns having little to do with men. But Yioth's mind overlapped with the realm of man, whether she would admit it or not.

And so he tied his little knot, so delicately, so complicated that neither tailor nor sailor would comprehend its intricacies. The last twist and tug slid into place as she finally collapsed in delighted exhaustion.

But the Hargothe was not spent. Not in the least, for what he discovered within her was greater than he could have imagined.

When she said a dragnithan was *of* the mercusine, he had not understood. But now he did. And if all demayne were of the same source, they were all like her. No wonder humans bonded to Beloved Ones grew in power, for they were bonded to a being manifested entirely from the mercus.

And now he was, too. It was like force-tapping a merculyn, save the inflow was not so limited. With a casual flick of his hand he gripped the Staff of Nihil with mercus touch and drew it clattering over the stones and into his palm.

Yioth was lost in somnolent contentment, still unaware of how she fed power to him. He extricated himself from her and dressed. By the time he again strode from the great hall the chill no longer touched him. The Staff was overstuffed with mercus power, not that he needed it. If he had eyes, he imaged they would have been aglow with mercusine fire.

It was nothing now to raise his fist and form the bolts. Mercus green haze rose from the ground and caressed his shins.

And then he dymensed.

43

HIS BLADE AFLAME

The lost city of Cigil-Tine was not empty.

This awareness came over Fallo as a hair-prickling sense of dread. And that was on top of the skin-crawling trepidation caused by the path from the vergent pass to the city. That had been strange, indeed.

Paved in smooth stone, the way had been easy, following a gentle slope toward a bridge that spanned a ravine where a fork of the waterfall lake drained.

But the Cloak had soon called a halt, drawing their attention to the path behind. Or the lack thereof.

With every step they took, the path vanished behind them, leaving a rocky slope in its place. Of the arch they'd passed through, there was no sign. Neither did Fallo's attempt to backtrack reveal the path.

"A vergent pass goes in only one direction," Zirhine said, as if this were the simplest and most widely-known bit of vergent lore.

"Might have mentioned that before we came through," Fallo said.

But it wouldn't have mattered. The pull forward was insistent in Fallo's growing Shadline instincts. And as they crossed the arched bridge with its moss-covered balusters and the spiky unlit mercus lamps at each end, a rightness settled over him. Whatever had pulled him from the Kovi-Mest beach to the tomb, and thence to this place, was close at hand.

As was abject danger. The city was not empty.

He drew his dagger, now wishing it was a whipaxe and that his body was encased in armor. Behind him, Zirhine and Cloak followed his lead. The sing of Tosuin pulling from the scabbard gave Fallo a bit of comfort. The Cloak would protect him. Set fire to whoever, or whatever, was lurking behind the dark windows that gaped over the street.

And what a street!

Had his skin not been thrilling with gooseflesh, Fallo would have marveled at it.

Leading from the bridge, a narrow street sided by half-crumbled palaces, opened into a boulevard so wide that twenty atlen-drawn carriages could have raced along it with room to maneuver.

It was paved with huge slabs of gold-flecked granite fitted so tightly together only a scattering of weeds had managed to take root among them. Only at building corners, where ancient leaves and windblown dust collected, had trees sprung up where they didn't belong.

Cigil-Tine was an unkempt garden, for between the street and the rows of palaces stood a wide band of greenery. Even after all these untold ages, the intent of the city planners was clear. And the trees and flowers they had chosen long ago still thrived where they'd been planted.

Fallo did not know the names of the flowers, aside from roses and lilies. But even he would have enjoyed the profusion of pink and white and orange blooms that hung heavily from the elegant trees bordering the boulevard. Would have. Except for the heavy presence of doom that filled the air.

The veil falls kept up a continuous rumble to the east, and a cloud of mist hung over the lake there.

The colossus of the maiden towered to the east, straddling the boulevard, her feet lost behind some lesser palaces. Her spear returned to the ground at a park kept clear for that purpose. It was as big around as an ancient oak.

She had to be at least as tall as the Divide, he thought. And she was seamlessly made, no sign of brick or block at all.

A half mile west was a fountain, still shooting spouts skyward.

"Someone is watching us," Fallo said.

"I feel it, too," the Cloak said. "It is . . . an ill feeling. They do not want us here."

"On the contrary," Zirhine said. "They do not want us to leave. Ever."

No words could have been calculated to send more thrills of horror over Fallo's skin than Zirhine's. "What—what are they?"

"Can't say for sure until I see them. Smells strange. Beneath the floral scent, there's something rotten."

"Why haven't they attacked?" the Cloak asked her. "They want to. I can feel it."

"Someone holds them back. They want us to go deeper

into the city. They know we came by the vergent pass. Perhaps they fear we have vergent powers."

Fallo sniffed the air, seeking the rotten scent she had mentioned. He picked up something musky, sour. An animal stink. He checked the wind, coming out of the west. That meant the smell was coming from the direction of the fountain.

"Every impulse is telling me to flee," he said. "But the pull that brought us here is telling me to go toward the fountain. Is there a way to amend my Shadline oath? Maybe we can find another fool to carry Ol' Rusty until we get to a cozy tavern with some plump serving girls to dance with."

Lop, where did you go?

Inside.

Get out. There are terrors lurking in those palaces.

Not where I am.

Come out. The Cloak and Zirhine think we're going to be attacked at any moment.

That is an argument against coming out.

Fallo couldn't counter that reasoning.

"The quiet is hiding something," Zirhine said softly. Her voice was tense. She had Reft in one hand and a handful of dried leaves in the other. She popped a few into her mouth and chewed them.

Her pupils went narrow. Spitting out the weeds, she whispered over them. "Come to me, men."

The Cloak obeyed instantly. He bent and she marked his forehead with a smudge. A circle bisected top to bottom and side to side with lines. "Come, Fallo," she insisted.

Fallo had always tried to keep himself clean and tidy. He

wasn't eager to have Zirhine's spit smear wiped on his forehead.

"It will offer protection," she said. "For a while."

"In some lands this would be the honor of an entire lifetime, boy," the Cloak said. "Do not insult her by refusing."

Fallo complied and allowed the woman to smudge his forehead. His skin felt cold where she marked it. But a surge of energy went through him a moment later. His focus sharpened and his limbs fairly hummed with newly awakened strength.

Fortified by Zirhine's ferneater magic, he led the way toward the fountain. He did not move quickly. In fact, he found himself crouched, dagger up. Not very sneaky to be skulking about in the center of a boulevard in full daylight, but he wasn't about to go inside one of the buildings.

Trying to keep his eyes on all the windows was making him a bit dizzy. "I'll watch the north windows," he said.

"And I the south," Zirhine said.

The Cloak said nothing, but Fallo had no doubt the man was keeping an eye to the rear. And that was a comfort. He could trust the Cloak.

Funny that he should only realize that now. But he trusted the man absolutely. He had never met anyone so committed to his purpose—even though he apparently didn't know what his purpose was most of the time. But he was committed to the Shadline way. He cared nothing for gold or palaces or women. Only listening and obeying.

"Are either of you, uh, *hearing* anything?"

They knew what he meant. It was wearing to be the only Shadline among them who was receiving the call. It gave him doubts, but it also put too much burden on his shoulders.

"I hear that we are hated," the Cloak said calmly.

"I hear that we are desired," Zirhine said. There was no note of contradiction in her words. In fact, she and the Cloak seemed to think those two facts quite compatible.

The windows to the north were dark. Not just shadowy. But black. If there was such thing as mercus dark, Fallo thought it would create that lightless effect. Daylight should have skimmed in and shown hints of the rooms beyond. Perhaps a haze of a rear wall. But there was only inky nothingness.

Another great dome loomed just ahead, a quarter of it broken away. Light did penetrate there, showing faded frescoes painted on the inside of the dome. Columns held up a covered gallery that fronted the palace. It was difficult to discern what color the walls and columns had once been, for they were dusted over with dirt and lichen. Huge tangles of vines embraced the walls, thick sections probing into the dark windows.

The fountain hissed ahead. The mist from its spouts drifted toward Fallo, chilling his skin. Most of the water plunged into the circular fountain pool, contained in a shin-high wall covered in bas relief.

The feeling of being watched intensified. And it wasn't just a set of eyes here and there. It was as if every window was crowded with leering spectators.

The trio of Shadlines reached the fountain, moving around it to get out of the direct chill of the breeze-blown mist. The water was clear, though the basin's floor was skimmed with green growth. Zirhine dipped a finger, whispered ferneater words over a drop, then put it to her tongue.

"Safe to drink."

Fallo's throat was certainly dry. But turning his back to the windows made quivers crawl up his back. Lop appeared and hopped onto the pool wall. She reached with dainty paw to bring droplets to her tongue.

Did you see anything? Fallo sent.

I saw all manner of things.

Any squirtles or bogdins?

No. But the claw-tooth-beak spirits are crowded in the buildings.

The what-tooth-what?

Rather than explain herself, Lop sent a range of feelings through the bond. Hunger, frenzy, the feel of a mouse body in its death throes, warm blood on the tongue, exhilaration, fear, hate, the scruff rising, fur standing out, the charge of confrontation.

Are they going to attack us?

Of course.

Why didn't you warn me?

I just did.

Fallo clenched his free fist to keep from shoving the cat into the fountain pool.

You don't seem too concerned about it.

They're hunting you, not me. I expect you'll escape. You always do.

Escape? How? I can't even see them.

You have the dagger. Fight! Lop was wearying of the conversations. Her tone was quite impatient now.

At least show me what they look like.

How?

"The catsight, you fuzzy lump of flab!" he shouted.

His words bounced back as a quick echo. The Shadlines looked at him and then the cat.

The catsight! he sent. *Can't you send me a vision of what you saw?*

Lops tail-tip flicked irritably as she stalked along the rim of the pool. She let out a meow and flashed an image into Fallo's mind so forcibly he fell onto his backside. His vision filled with a looming figure, all hulking shadow. Round shoulders and thick, bare arms covered with a sparse forest of wiry hairs. Deep-set eye sockets sparked with pinpricks of reflected light, and stark shadows of a face relieved by a round blob of a nose.

It wore sturdy, if crudely fashioned, bits of armor, a breast-piece of hide, fur loincloth, forearm bracers and shin guards. Hide boots with tufts of fur sprouting at the tops which rose to knobby knees.

But in the dimness of the vision, what stood out most were the creature's thighs, for they were massive, sculpted by muscle and lined with veins. The impression was of vast strength. And this creature was not alone, but stood crowded among many others.

Before Fallo could scramble to his feet, Lop smashed him with another vision. This was a similar creature, dressed in a crude gown that fell to its shins, the sides laced with sinew, leaving just enough room for skinny arms to poke through. These limbs were encumbered with innumerable bracelets that appeared to be fashioned from animal ribs. A necklace of rat skulls—hundreds of them—hung around the withered neck. In one hand, the creature held a staff topped with another sort of skull, clearly of its own kind. The eyes were inset with uncut gems, one red, one orange.

"Nosg," Fallo said. "Lop saw nosg in the buildings."

"They let her pass?" the Cloak asked.

They did not see me.

Fallo noted with absolutely no satisfaction that Lop had answered the Cloak's spoken question.

"She says they did not see her."

The Cloak sneered and clicked his tongue. "I don't see how nosg could have come here. There would be refuse everywhere, smoke from fires, and surely hear them."

"Nor would they have waited this long to attack," Zirhine said.

They are dead, Lop sent. *Long dead. But they are coming.*

"She says they are dead."

Zirhine gasped. *"Zol-Hidir!* Unrelinquished souls."

"Lop says they're coming."

The Cloak went one way, Zirhine another, blades in fists, eyes scanning. Fallo did the best he could to look for a threat, but there was nothing to see. "Lop showed me one. A warrior. Thick legs, hide armor. There was another, older, skinny in a gown. Staff topped with a skull."

The Cloak cursed. The first obscenity Fallo had ever heard from the man. He followed it with a simple explanation: "Shaman."

"That explains the darkness," Zirhine said. "There must be one in every building."

"Merculyn nosg?"

"No more a merculyn than I am," Zirhine said. "They have a—" Something fluttered in the air overhead. A moment later a clank and clatter behind them. The unmistakable sound of an arrow striking a building and falling to the street.

"How can dead nosg loose arrows?" Fallo said, voice rising in pitch. "How can they do your ferneater tricks?"

Zirhine furrowed her brow but didn't answer.

They are coming, Lop sent. She hopped from the pool and crowded between Fallo's feet.

I don't see anything.

Another arrow struck behind them.

"At least their aim isn't good," he said, not at all comforted by the observation.

"They cannot see us clearly yet," Zirhine said. "We must keep moving."

"Yes. Let's get out of this place."

"No," the Cloak said. "Forward. Fallo, lead on."

"I'm pitch-covered and Kil-damned," Fallo mumbled. But he was already moving, continuing along the boulevard in the direction they'd been going.

He hated leaving the fountain behind for some reason. Maybe because he was still thirsty.

Lop decided she was done walking. With no words she demanded he stuff her in his satchel. He complied, if just to keep from stepping on her. He was starting to think her casual disinterest in the nosg was a put on.

More arrows smacked the pavement behind them.

"Their sight will improve as the sunlight fails," Zirhine said. "Get us to the fate's-piece, Shadline PiTorro."

He hadn't thought of the inexorable pull forward as leading toward a fate's-piece, but now that she'd said it, it was obvious. And the pull was strong. It didn't require pausing and listening.

The smattering of arrows had stopped falling behind them now, but the oppressive feeling of watchers increased with every step. And no wonder, there were ever more windows overlooking the boulevard the farther they went.

A massive palace lined the southern border, the ground

floor obscured by tangles of flowering trees, vines, and weeds. But four more stories rose up, each punctuated by window after window after window. The glass remained in a few. These reflected the golden warmth of the failing day. But the others gaped like black mouths, the jagged remnants of glass now glimmering like golden tooth-shards.

They are coming! Lop sent.

The first scuffle of footfalls came from the north. More answered from the south. It was disordered, not the cadence of a battalion on the march, but the shuffle of a throng eager to be first.

Through the still air carried a cry, guttural and full of bloodlust. It was joined by more, then more, until the boulevard was a riot of noise. Arrows again clattered onto the stones behind the three Shadlines as they continued to move, always toward the setting sun.

The pull of the fate's-piece had been strong, but now Fallo could point to it, straight ahead. The broad street was interrupted at its end by a final grand palace. An enormous dome rose dead center of their path, and a dozen more towers and spires stood to either side. Several were broken, their forms rising to end in jagged ruin. Others leaned precariously, on the brink of toppling. It was to one of these, just to the left of the massive central dome, that Fallo was pulled.

An arrow skittered ahead of him, the iron tip sending sparks from the stones. The shaft was black, the fletching of mismatched feathers.

The cries were closer. The nosg should be in view by now.

"The ire-smudge protects us," Zirhine said. She was breathing hard now. "But the ball of the sun has descended, the last rays fade."

Even as she spoke, the forms of the onrushing nosg resolved into view. Not entirely, for they were shadowy shapes, through which Fallo could see the palace and trees beyond. Every step that brought them closer, made them more substantial.

"Four gr'hil's behind," the Cloak said.

"Seven to the south," Zirhine reported.

Fallo assumed that "gr'hil" was the name of a nosg throng. Five such formations converged on the Shadlines from the north, and so Fallo called out.

Each gr'hil contained between ten and thirty nosg. They carried spears, axes, swords, bows, and hide-over-plank shields. Crude blood marks indicating clan or rank were emblazoned on their fronts.

The gr'hil were on the run, coming generally at Fallo, but a few on a course to miss them entirely. He assumed they would discover their error the moment the sun failed completely.

"Faster!" Fallo called, leaning forward and putting his head down to sprint. The grand dome of Cigil-Tine still lay a thousand paces ahead. A long way to run with full out effort, but Fallo discovered being chased by a ghostly nosg army gave his legs extraordinary strength.

Zirhine's ire-smudge must have added considerable measure to his power, too. His satchel banged on his hip as he ran. Lop sent annoyance through the bond. Fallo returned it with, *Get out and run if you don't like how I carry your mangey hide.*

Sweat beaded on Fallo's brow, made his shirt stick to his back. His legs throbbed with his efforts. His breath came in ragged gulps.

The sound of the charging nosg shades drowned out the

bootfalls of the Cloak and Zirhine. The dome ahead was a black silhouette against the fading blaze of daylight. The sky was orange and violet ahead and dark blue behind, the first sprinkling of stars already peering down at the chase transpiring on Cigil-Tine's main thoroughfare.

The boulevard widened into a vast plaza. Perhaps on market days the expanse had been filled with stands and pavilions. Now it was windswept.

The Cloak grunted. Metal clanked against something very hard. That something gave beneath the Shadline blade. Was it a shield, a skull, a shin? Fallo cared not. All he knew was that the first blow of the battle had fallen. In answer, a great shriek of agony went up. Like throwing whale oil on an open fire, a whoosh of orange cast Fallo's own shadow ahead of him. Tosuin had chosen to set fire to that first victim.

That blow was followed soon after by a second. Whatever the Cloak had struck perished in anguish.

Scores of arrows clattered around Fallo. They hissed through the air to his left and right, raising his hackles and sending gooseflesh across his body.

Wide stairs climbed ahead, ascending to a covered gallery fronting the grandest palace of the city. The spire that drew Fallo's Shadline instincts was farther left now, but it was clear they had to go through the rotunda beneath the dome to get there.

His foot gained the first step. A spear shaft glanced from his shoulder, its flight just enough off that the wicked iron point missed his flesh. An arrow jerked into his satchel, ripping a jagged hole in the side.

Lop!

No answer, but Lop was unharmed. The matter of an inch.

A new sound came past his head, a whirling, pulsating in the air. Zirhine's curved blade, Reft, arced into a black opening at the top of the stairs. A cry rose from within, hollow and echoey. A moment later the blade flew out from the darkness. Fallo ducked as he ran, the blade skimming just over his head.

"That way is blocked," Zirhine called.

Fallo looked left and right. Five more gr'hils pounded toward him, pouring from doorways in the grand palace. The Shadlines were tidily hemmed in. It was the arched main entry, or turn and fight, surrounded.

He reached the top of the steps and stumbled forward. Arrows, thrown axes, and slung stones pelted the ground to his left and right.

Their aim is terrible, Lop!

Like a quickly drawn window shade, the last light of day failed. Flame lit the way now, the victims of Tosuin's rage consumed by mercusine fire.

The pull of the fate's-piece strengthened, but it was momentarily outshined by Fallo's own unthinking reflex. Ol' Rusty came up to deflect an arrow. The impact of iron tip on dragon tooth steel sent up a musical ping and a white spark.

Kil's eyes! Did you see that, Lop?

I'm in a bag.

Again the Shadline instinct drew up his hand, another arrow spun away. The gr'hil was upon him. No longer were the nosg black shades. Now they had become substantial, real, and full of animal fury.

A mace made of a somewhat spherical granite ball bound to a thick wooden shaft came swinging down. Fallo ducked, Ol' Rusty thrusting as he squeezed past the attack. The tip bit into a shoulder, and the thick-legged creature screamed as if

Fallo had hewn off its arm. Its mouth stretched wide, slaver spraying in thick globules as it screamed. The cut left a deep black scratch and yet the nosg fell backward, flailing and shrieking as if mortally wounded.

No time to observe, for three slobbery beasts lunged toward him, a spear thrust, a sword swipe, a sweep of pike toward his head.

The Cloak had trained Fallo in the basics of dagger fighting during those first weeks in the wild. Even Fallo had not considered himself a particularly apt student, though he had made a good faith effort to learn. But those hours of drill had entrained reflex and the ability to put the force of his hips into each blow.

Yet that did not explain how he survived even the first few seconds of the assault.

It was Ol' Rusty, he realized, thrusting the blade into an eye, even has he began to drop his weight low to dodge a sword thrust that would have severed his spine. The blow carried forth on the nosg's momentum until the blade impaled one of his comrades, loosing pulsating squirts of black blood onto the stairs.

Fallo was peripherally aware of Zirhine, a swirling blur of death. She chanted as she fought, gutting one nosg, taking off a quarter of another one's skull, and spinning to hamstring another in one continuous dance.

Beyond her the Cloak had become death. His black garment—his very namesake—billowed as he moved from blow to blow, his blade aflame. The gr'hil were no longer pressing to attack him for the front ranks were struck with such terror they backpedaled to escape.

Fallo marveled as he danced through his own parries and

attacks, for he sensed all that happened around him. He could not see behind him, and yet if the moment were frozen, he could have told with exacting detail how a nosg drew back its arrow, gnarled fingers pressed to grizzled cheek as beady eye squinted to find aim on his neck. He could have told of the spear-wielder shuffling forward, two hands gripping the shaft and ready to lunge. And of the thin shaman, holding up a short skull-headed rod, summoning unnatural forces that set the jewel-chips in the skull's eye sockets aglow.

It was that last that Fallo knew he must address first. He finished one nosg with a parting of its throat, already spinning. His blade twirled in the air, he caught it underhanded and flung it, end over end, to strike the shaman in the eye. The creature shrieked and flew back. Its unexpended power ignited the skull, which exploded in red flame, ripping the entire remainder of the gr'hil apart.

Fallo was already tumbling, ripping Ol' Rusty from the dead shaman's scorched face.

The arched opening lay before him. He powered forward, feeling what lay within. First was the dead nosg Zirhine had killed with her exploratory throw. A gr'hil waited inside, held back by a shaman already on the verge of releasing his bolt of power. This registered in Fallo's body as a rise of every hair on his body. His Shadline instinct shouted an imperative to flee.

But his companions had crowded in behind him, now pressed by a convergence of gr'hils all driven relentlessly by their shaman chiefs.

"On the ground," Zirhine said, shoving Fallo hard. He hugged his satchel to his belly and folded in on himself. The Cloak fought a rear guard engagement, his flaming sword hewing off heads and limbs like a farmer taking a sickle to a weedpatch.

But Zirhine now stood still. Reft rested on the floor, tip to stone, the hilt leaning against her shin. In both hands she held something Fallo could not see. Her words were unintelligible, but a bluish green glow illuminated her face, at once lovely and terrifying.

The shaman shouted in his own lurkmire tongue. His skull rod glowed red. The build was too much. Fallo's fighting instinct brought no defense or attack to his limbs. Only desperate cowering remained.

Lop, it was an honor feeding you.

It was.

Zirhine's voice battled with the shaman's. Abruptly she spread her hands and flung a flutter of leaves into the air. Each glowed the same blue green as they spun. And then stopped in midair, held aloft by forces unseen.

The light merged each to each, forming a curving wall separating the three Shadlines from their foes. The Cloak stepped back and took a knee. He breathed hard yet was otherwise still.

The shaman released his attack. Rays of narrow red light flared from the gem-chip eyes, struck Zirhine's leafwall, and rebounded to strike the shaman's chest. He looked down in shock, then tumbled forward like a felled tree. When his skull rod struck, it released its remaining power and destroyed the gr'hil and blew apart a door that stood behind them.

Zirhine lowered her hands and the leaves fell, the glow failed. The Cloak leapt to his feet already swinging, carving back through the press of nosg to the rear. He battled toward a shaman, lopped off his head, then began to seek out the next. Fallo understood immediately.

He was on his feet and flinging Ol' Rusty before the thought was complete. It took a shaman in the throat. And then Zirhine's Reft was taking off the final shaman's head.

The nosg began to break, running and screaming to escape Tosuin's rage.

The Cloak pursued, striking down a half dozen more before giving up the chase. He returned to the arched passage, nodded to Fallo, and simply said, "Proceed, Shadline."

Fallo retrieved his blade and guided his companions into the rotunda.

44

DROWNING OR FLAME?

Upon an execution platform in the city of Starside, a fiery-haired young man pressed his hands to the temples of the Highest of Kil. He scoured her mind with mercusine blades and pincers, calling upon demaynic senses as strong as anger and deep as love.

An advisor to Her Enlightened Majesty stood by, face tight with worry. Two Fell Guardsmen stood at tense attention now, for the crowd that remained after the dragon had flown were still a danger to the girl who had saved Her Enlightened's life.

The girl, the Highest, hair cropped to a blond fuzz, stood rigid, eyes rolled up into her skull. In one hand she gripped the Bane Eye, the Voluptuary's prized mercusine relic. Her other was clenched in a white-knuckled fist. A garnet ring glimmered there, spraying sparkles onto the charred and blood-stained decking.

Two cats huddled on a rooftop of the abbey, shoulder to shoulder, peering down with curious interest. Their tails flicked in synchrony.

The Highest of Til, Binel, conferred with his aides, all of whom still reeled in the aftermath of will-struggles against the Hargothe.

Deep in the abbey, two men wove through an empty library. The hooded figure found a section of chained tomes. "All these are Wrong. Take what you will." He immediately found the volume he sought, heavy, large. Priceless. "Choose quickly Highest Quiv, a war rages outside."

A merchant who had been present on the platform earlier was heading toward the entry of the Moriterren Pass, for the Hargothe had made clear what the penalty of lateness would be.

Rumors about the disastrous execution were just reaching the few Radiants who had chosen not to attend. Her Enlightened had been healed by a girl who could fly. The murderer had been burned to ashes by a dragon. No. It had been by a Sensual hidden among the crowd. No. It had been Her Enlightened herself who had done it.

South of Starside, a single-masted ship hugged the coast, triangular sail billowing on a hard northerly wind. It would approach the Archipelago of Scin soon, a dangerous pass to make in the winter.

Critt Sanglo stood at the prow, blunt face spread in a grin. His one-handed companion was sicking-up her supper over the rail. They had a thousand leagues to go. But the ship was theirs for the duration due to the enormous sum Sanglo had paid to the captain. The Shadline's coffers were bottomless.

To the west flashed a message light, pulsing irregularly just at the horizon. It was the relay of Sea Bastion One. The flashes were codes, which would be received at the spire of the

Citadel, and then handed to Her Enlightened. Perhaps it was word from the Colony, forty days' sail to the east.

In the Eerie above and behind the Citadel, Harnzyne rested, wings folded, seeking to return to his much-needed slumber. Ell's call had startled him awake, disturbing a particularly interesting dream.

Kila Sigh had listened, though Harnzyne thought the girl a bit thick-headed for one so powerful. And now Ell had dymensed back to her tower, where she could clean herself and think about the silliness of attending the execution in the flesh.

Her Enlightened Majesty, Ell LiMinluit, soaked in a copper tub filled with nearly boiling water. It would have raised blisters on human skin, but she was dragnithan.

Kila Sigh's wondrous healing had left scars, just the palest lines across her abdomen. The pain, gone.

The fear. Very much present.

Ell leaned back and closed her eyes. How long had she reigned? A thousand years. No, it had been more. She'd claimed the throne long before the ridiculous Synod of the New Pantheon had destroyed everything she'd built. She should never have tolerated it.

But she had listened and obeyed. And it had nearly gotten her killed today.

Her thoughts ranged to the Hargothe. He had been here in her quarters not long ago, seeking to have his brother installed on her small council. Marlow had turned out to be invaluable, and loyal. But how she wished she had killed the old man when she'd had the chance.

Kila Sigh has come into her power, she sent to Harnzyne.

The dragon was on the verge of sleep again. *Yes. It was interesting. She flew without wings.*

She's Kil's daughter. Semüin changed everything, capricious child that she is.

He takes form in his hall. Perhaps the Sigh girl is the necessary answer to him.

And what of our night flying brethren? Do they whisper taunts at you still?

This made Harnzyne uncomfortable, she knew. He had first flown at sunset, on the verge of light and dark. That had left a golden tinge on his wings and claws, his scales aswirl with nightsky reflections. It had earned him the mistrust of both wings of the dragnithor. Just as she had disappointed the lords of Day by choosing a human life.

Harnzyne sent, *I would tell you if such whispers continued. But I have been napping for most of the past one hundred years. Except when the Sigh girl came for my scales. What did Yoznithan Flaumishtak need with so many anyway?*

A good question. She had been putting off asking him directly since she suspected he wished to kill her. But she was well warded here.

She rose from her bath and donned a thick robe. A flash of power steamed the water from her hair. It felt good to exercise her mercusine. Keeping it hidden for so long had begun to bottle it up inside her. Her back ached to release her wings all of the time now. Deep hungers had rekindled of late. To fly, to devour, to mate.

Listen and obey. Perhaps it was time.

She padded from her bath chamber to a warm study where the walls were lined with tall shelves packed with books. Many of the volumes would fetch a stack of gold Ravens. Some were priceless. Unique. Most would have been declared Wrong by the Way of Til.

It was a powerful place for Ell LiMinluit. She shoved aside the great oak desk near the fire until the inlaid circle was revealed. The Citadel was a First Race structure, so the circle had already been here when she'd taken the throne. The inlaid metal had likely been poured into the carved groove while molten.

For a dragnithan, calling a yoznithan took no special power. There was no beseeching nor cajoling. No repetitious phrases or cutting chicken throats. The circle would keep him contained. She did not fancy a battle just now.

"Yoznithan Flaumishtak, I know you're listening. Come. I would speak with you."

He delayed answering, of course. Petulant beast! She repeated her summons adding Force to her words with a bit of concentration.

He dymensed into the circle, tall, imposing, outwardly calm. He held a felnithel in his arms. One of the Beloved Ones recently come to the city to bond ragamuffins from the lower slopes.

She offered the cat a small curtsy of greeting and respect. Clearly this one had stalked under the stars, for he squinted at her in disdainful disinterest before offering a meow.

Flaumishtak scratched behind its ear with a black claw. Yoznithan and felnithel were perfectly suited to each other, just as man was to hound. "Dragnithan," he said in his low rumbling voice. His sulfur scent drifted across the barrier that held his physical person inside the spirit circle. If he was annoyed by her precaution he didn't show it. If anything, he appeared amused. "Did you know the Hargothe granted me your life?"

"I'm not surprised. Why have you delayed in claiming it?"

"Because it doesn't serve my purposes."

"That's not why." She began a slow walk around the perimeter of the circle. Flaumishtak did not turn to face her. "You fear me. And that is wise."

"You fear me, too, obviously."

"Again, wisdom. You first walked beneath the stars, no?"

He snorted. "You don't know? But of course you wouldn't. I've lived for ages and ages. Your birth was hailed as a Fate and I watched you walk and then fly. By then I had already been raised to Arch."

"You first walked by night," she said, ignoring his lording of his age over her. As if it mattered at all in this realm.

"I walked in the twilight before dawn."

"In darkness."

Do you need me to drop him into the sea? Harnzyne sent.

Apparently the dragon allowed Flaumishtak to hear this comment, for the demayne did turn then. "Ah, your pet dragnithor has not improved his manners, I see."

Go to sleep, Ell sent to Harnzyne.

She studied Flaumishtak's fiery eyes. This yoznithan was pure affectation in her opinion. The hooves, the green mist, the claws, the hair that swept back into smoke. All a glamour to intimidate humans.

"I want to thank you for ridding my city of some of the larger rats."

He barked a laugh, startling the cat. He cooed softly to it, accepting its annoyed hiss as his due punishment. "The

Hargothe granted me a dozen lives per day. Did you know he also granted me Henley Mast's life?"

"And yet the boy lives."

"My prerogative. The Hargothe would not grant me Kila Sigh, alas. Such a delicious morsel she would be."

"You'd choke on her. But I supposed she doesn't know that."

"She and I have an understanding of sorts. In fact, I offered to teach her to master her powers. The first lesson went quite well. Unfortunately she left the Garden in significant disarray. But of course, you knew that would happen when you sent her. Voluptuary Minn and Coin Inlina tried to promise-bind the girl."

He was taunting her with knowledge she had no way of knowing. "What promise?"

"As I understand it, Kila would be bound to use her power only for healing. Can you imagine?"

A noble idea, if a terrible one. "Dem-Kisk is upon us. The Kil-notion seeks to come into this world. Why?"

"He's bored. Or maybe he's weary of infinite ecstasy in the great pleasure halls of Ractin-Pliy. Perhaps he fancies a game of armies. He does not yet have voice enough to tell me anything. He is . . . inchoate. He is, as you said, a notion."

"And since when did he choose the name Kil? Last I saw him, *she* was Victi of the seven arms. Or did the Synod nonsense penetrate into demaynic minds so much that she recognized herself as the piece excluded from the Triumvirate?"

Flaumishtak's flat lips pursed as he considered all these speculations. Finally he shrugged, a very human gesture. "Names aggregate power over time, no? Perhaps an accumulation of men using the name Kil in their favorite curses has clumped together enough power that Kil has become interesting."

"So Kila Sigh truly is of his mercus-line," she said.

"Surely. He is thinking of himself as Kil. Millions of people over thousands of years have manifested him as power-fully as an intentionally formed bolt of mercus power." He sniffed the air. "Speaking of which . . . you have been recently healed. I recognized the blend. It still clings to you. That is *my* feat."

"The girl used it to seal a dagger wound."

"Remarkable. She has no idea what she does most of the time."

"She is a Shadline."

"She bears Fate-Breaker. But I do not see how *that* blade could grant her such exceptional ability."

"It isn't the blade, fool. She has been guided by Shadline instincts since she came out of Semūin's vale. She listens and obeys, yet has never once been taught the doctrine of the Shadline. Now *that* is remarkable."

"She'll need more skill than that if she is to survive bringing Kil into this world."

So there it was. She continued walking the circle, stopping when she'd returned to her starting point. The daylight was dim here, for the windows were frosted over. The light illumi-nated Flaumishtak, though he did not cast a shadow. She could see his expression clearly.

"And she has refused to accept your help. Can you honestly tell me you are surprised?"

"She didn't refuse. She has merely been distracted from her

training. But time is running low, the day fails. Your cousin Yiothizandra counsels the Hargothe even now."

Ell spat an uncharacteristic curse. *Harnzyne, did you know Yioth was back?*

No. That is . . . ill news. The dragnithor sent a stretching feeling to her. *I must fly!*

"Yioth means to bring Kil here," Ell said, putting the pieces together. "And the boon she expects from him?"

"What else?"

"Freedom." Suspicion narrowed her gaze. "Why do you aid the Sigh girl, then? I would think you more desirous of freedom than anyone else."

"Think you I wish to destroy this realm? Or that I wish to drain the blood from a million, million men and women?"

"Yes. I do think that."

"Then you are mistaken. There is about to be a void in the demaynic realms, one that will need filling."

Ell laughed, a true and hearty laugh. "You? Take the Kil-notion's place? Yoznithan or no, I doubt the Hel Lords will look kindly upon such base striving from you."

Flaumishtak glowered at her, eyes flaring so brightly the cat's creamy fur turned orange for a moment. "I did not seek your opinion, *girl*. And if we are to be allies, you would do well to attend to events in this realm. Leave the demaynic ones to your elders."

"Very well, Flaumishtak. But how can we be allies if you wish Kil to come here and I do not?"

"Because you are wise. Is that not what you said earlier? The force of destiny is bringing us all to a culmination. Do you believe such pressure will keep Kil away from this realm? It will not. If

Kila Sigh does not bear him forth, the Hargothe—and Yiothizandra—will. I have seen that much. Which Kil would you prefer? One born of the loyal-hearted girl, or of the hateful man?"

It was like the tavern philosophizer's question. Which death would you choose if you must choose one: Drowning or flame? Yioth would bring flame, no doubt. But which would Kila Sigh bring?

As one she and Flaumishtak jerked their heads toward the window. East. Toward the sea. No. Not that far. The middle slopes. Dunne Medow Plaza.

A new merculyn had appeared. Not suddenly unquelled, but through dymension.

"He's here," she said.

"So is she," Flaumishtak answered.

"If I release you will you aid her?"

"Not against him. My bargain with him is inviolable. I cannot harm him through direct attack."

"Then begone!" She voiced the command with so much Force the effect was instant. Yoznithan and felnithel were gone, leaving a faint green haze to dissipate.

Ell LiMinluit, the Enlightened monarch of Starside and all its realms, hurried to her armory.

45

TRUTH OUT OF LIES

"I—I think I got it all," Henley said, releasing Kila. Suddenly free of both his mercus intrusion and his grasp, her knees buckled. She would have fallen right onto her face if Henley hadn't caught her up in his arms.

"I need to sit," she said.

"Yes. Sit," came a familiar voice. She had trouble focusing on the figure who stood across the platform. He held a staff in one hand. His thick gray robes draped onto the planks, eyeless face aimed squarely at her.

Henley groaned and his mercus flared.

The Hargothe had come. Kila tried to climb to her feet, but the world was spinning. Her head felt raw, as if Henley had used a curved knife to scrape the inside of her skull.

She was aware of Henley throwing up a mercusine ward to keep the Hargothe's attacks at bay. But no attack came from him, though his spark had been magnified a hundred fold, perhaps a thousand fold since she'd last been near to him.

"I am done with this little game," he said.

Highest Binel and his crew of Donse Masters threw themselves into prostration before the old man. The two Fell Guardsmen lowered their spears and moved to interpose themselves between the intruder and Kila.

Henley hugged her close, and she sensed his hate and terror through more than his trembling arms. His work in her mind had left something. A bond.

"Did you—? Did you force-bond me?"

"I had to. It's temporary. It was the only way I could block him entirely."

Kila had never felt so tired. And that was strange, for she had been full of power so recently. Healing the monarch should not have drained her this much. Not even her flying stunt should have done so.

"Get up, girl," one of the Fell guardsmen said. "We'll escort you to the Citadel. Her Enlightened wants an audience."

"She'll go nowhere with you," the old man said. He motioned with his free hand and the two men went rigid under a heavy willshift. They turned to face each other, jaws clenching, helms shaking from their efforts to resist. But they failed. Their spear tips swung around, each pressing a tip to the other's throat. And then they thrust.

The men crumpled forward, bleeding, limbs jerking. The Hargothe came toward Kila, his robe hem dragging through the ash of the murderer he had so recently possessed.

Wincing against the pain in her head, Kila fumbled for Cayne. There was no question of her using mercus touch to bring it forth. It was all she could do to use the strength of her arm. She held the blade up, warning the old man to stay back.

The remainder of the execution spectators stood quietly in

the plaza, spellbound. The splash of the great fountain in the center of the plaza was the only sound remaining.

Henley's mercus ward stood strong. The Hargothe had not dashed it to pieces. He had not even tried.

Kila sought her own power. It was there. It always was. But wielding it now took all her will. Too much pain, she realized. She recalled her lesson with Flaumishtak. Fear could sap one's ability to form bolts with the mercus because it broke one's concentration. It was true of pain as well.

"Let me go. I can stand," she said to Henley.

Henley released her. The Hargothe still hadn't attacked. In fact he was looking to the Citadel, a thoughtful expression on his brow.

"He has grown in power," Henley whispered. "That staff might be a heller."

"It is no heller," the old man said. He clunked the pointed staff on the planks. "In fact, I don't need it at all anymore. But I shall keep it nonetheless. I see you have learned to craft a ward, boy. Cleverly done. You learned well from my teaching."

"If you call torture teaching," Henley spat. "Then yes, I learned quickly." The young man struck, sending forth the Hargothe's own bolts of mind-probing terror.

He was met with the same in return. The ward absorbed the Hargothe's strike. Henley's did not penetrate either, for the seer swept them aside like stray bits of straw on a gust of wind.

The Donse Masters had gotten to their feet and were again forming a circle. Highest Binel was edging away from his brethren and looked like he wanted to run.

Marlow had replaced his ring, quelling himself to protect against his brother's mind intrusions.

Kila held up her blade, squinting to see her hated enemy

more clearly. Whatever Henley had done to clear the Hargothe's force-bond, the effects were like the morning after one too many cups of trezz.

"I'm glad you came back," she said to the old man. "Saves me a long journey to root you out of Ceronhel."

The Hargothe's bolt formed and flew in the space between heart beats, his hand outthrust and sending forth jagged fractures of light. All Kila saw was white streaks, like the patterns of broken window glass webbing toward her.

Her response was an automatic counter. The blue sphere Dunne Yples had hurled at her, and which Flaumishtak had taught her to spike with fear, burst into existence just as the Hargothe's attack flashed out.

Her instinct to pepper her feat with persistence—learned from the Bone Chill blade's power—paid well, for the Hargothe's bolt was heavy with despair and weakness.

He struck again, targeting Henley this time. Kila's counter was too late. Henley shuddered and fell to his knees, face contorted with imposed misery.

"No!" Kila shouted at her friend. "Rise!" She added a bolt of exuberance, which jerked his head up. Henley threw out a blast of flame, not to engulf the Hargothe directly, but to ignite the planks under his feet.

A brilliant move, forcing the seer to sweep backward and form heat negations to douse his flaming robes.

The Coin, unnoticed until this moment, came forward and took hold of Kila's arm. The light in her eyes was full of wrongness. Already the woman's medallion was coming up to press against Kila's forehead. On reflex, Kila sent heat into it until smoke issued between the woman's fingers. Face crumpling with agony, the woman squeezed her medallion tighter and thrust it at Kila.

And then she folded forward as Kila drove Cayne into her belly. The wrongness vanished as the Hargothe's occupation of the woman instantly vanished. She gaped. "Not possible. I *saw* you die. A dozen smiles that you would die. Here."

A phrase frequently heard at the Garden came to Kila's lips. "Pol is not merciful." She rent her dagger from the woman's body and blew her from the platform on a gust of wind.

The exertion burned the inside of Kila's head. But it also eased the pressure that had made her skull feel stretched to bursting.

The Hargothe had used the Coin to distract Kila long enough to pull Henley across the platform and subject him to a hard press of willshift. The boy was kissing the old man's feet, weeping, and shaking as he struggled to resist.

The seer had brought his staff up, showing Kila how the base was sharpened to a spear-like point.

She wheeled as the source-tap circle of Donse Masters attacked. The man wielding their power, portly Nare Fillus, had little skill, but with their power joined the feat came with enormous force.

She negated his fire, but not before stumbling backward to escape the searing heat of it. Never one to take a blow without returning the favor, she reflexively slammed them all with fear as she shouted, "Run or die!"

Several fell flat in their haste to jump from the platform, others landed on aged legs that gave under the impact. Their cries were echoed by the crowd. But something had infected the onlookers, and they too ran for the Harridan and Trialti, desperate to get away from the mercus battle.

It had been Kila's own command that had struck terror in them, she realized. Even Marlow was quivering.

The Hargothe had driven her to this, to use the very skills she hated.

"It would be a pity to sacrifice such a bright spark," the Hargothe said. He brought the tip of his staff to press into Henley's back. The boy jerked slightly, but the willshift kept him in place.

Kila! Nax sent. *Henley says the Hated One is sending a whisker toward you.*

A whisker?

A . . . tendril.

Kila cocked her head and closed her eyes. Where was it? Where . . . ?

There. Like a stray strand of spiderweb fluttering in a disused doorway, invisible unless the sunlight caught it just so. And it was near her left ear. Tentative, but coming closer, reaching once again to penetrate her mind.

Henley's force-bond was there already. Kila could feel his presence, not ill-fitting, but unusual. It reminded her very much of the bond she'd placed on Gian.

Henley? she sent, stepping to her right. The tendril followed. The Hargothe pressed the staff harder, now drawing blood. Henley trembled on all fours, but he did not scream. He wasn't allowed to vent his agony.

Henley! Can you hear me?

"You are weak because you will not sacrifice him," the Hargothe said. "I hold him firmly in my control, therefore I hold you. You see that, do you not?"

She marveled at the old man's newfound patience. In their previous encounters he had assumed such superiority in power that he had not bothered to toy with her. But this was all meant to be a distraction from the approaching tendril. If he lodged it once again in her she would have no last minute blast of fire to send him back to Ceronhel. This time he would own her.

Henley!

He answered, weakly. *Kill. Him. Please!*

She could severe the man's subtle attack easily. But she wanted to lull him as much as he was trying to distract her. Again she sidestepped.

In her right hand, Cayne. In her left, the Voluptuary's stone. The Bane Eye. She probed it with her senses, asked it to tell her what it was for. She had only seen it once before, when the Voluptuary had used it to chase Flaumishtak away. It had been aglow with white light then.

She gave power to the Bane Eye. It accepted, latching hard to her as it came to life. Kila screamed as the relic instantly— and ravenously— took hold of her power. Its inner light flared.

The Hargothe began to laugh, a dry, raspy sound. She could barely spare enough attention to recognize his hateful mirth, let alone mark the progress of his tendril attack.

The Bane Eye burned! She flung her hand out, releasing it, but the sphere did not leave her palm. It had attached like a burr. And it burned as it sucked her power.

Go, Kila! Henley sent, his voice another agony in her head. She could no longer see him, for her eyes were squeezed shut against the searing pain of her own mercusine flooding from her and into the Bane Eye.

The Hargothe must have leaned his weight onto his staff, for Henley's agony came through the bond. Somewhere far away a cat shrieked. Kila's own throat burned from her scalding cries.

Nax! I can't—I can't—

There was nothing to hold to as her power flooded into the Bane Eye. The relic had interposed its own thirst between her and her mercus spark. Just as the Hargothe had done in the crypt. A force-tap.

She recalled the mercus lantern she'd recovered on the ash-barrens. The poor acolyte who had powered it had died, completely drained of mercus and life by the relic.

The agony demanded an answer. Death would be preferable. It would be sweet mercy. But she had to save Henley. Had to end the Hargothe. And to those ends, she would sacrifice anything.

She swung Cayne around, brought the blade to her own wrist. Pressed the razor edge into her flesh. But will alone would not make Cayne bite. A new power interceded, preventing even this desperate recourse. This power seemed to come from Cayne itself.

My love. I'm sorry, Henley sent. *I couldn't protect you. I—*

The Hargothe drove his staff deeper into Henley's back even as his tendril probed into Kila's ear and wove into her brain. She could not sense it at all, for her mind was a raging storm of pain coming through Henley's bond.

"Drop the blade!" someone shouted into her ear.

Marlow. His face was close to hers. His lips moved, but his words came seconds later, as if traveling through a realm of syrupy time to reach her.

Cayne had not parted a hair on her arm, much less

scratched her skin. The Bane Eye shone a brilliant, starlight white.

Marlow took her wrist and pulled Cayne up, away from her skin. With a hard yank, he pried the weapon from her fingers. She had no more strength left to fight.

His hands were warm as he fumbled with her fingers again. And then Bane Eye went out. Her mercus cut off, and the pain drained in an instant.

The Hargothe grunted and stumbled backward as if slapped. And the shouts of the remaining stragglers in the plaza rose.

Marlow had slipped his queller onto her finger. Gathering up Cayne, Kila bounded to her feet.

Though her legs trembled and her knees threatened to give, she stalked toward the Hargothe.

He had Henley pinned to the planks, the staff driven all the way through the boy's body. Henley was still under the willshift, unable to express his agony through jerks of his arms and legs.

"Ah, perhaps now you will cooperate," the Hargothe said. His papery lips spread revealing a black smile. "Perhaps I'll allow you to heal him if you surrender to me. I could make good use of him in the days ahead."

Cayne left her hand, flicking end over end. It struck tip-first, sinking an inch into the Hargothe's chest.

Damn him. She had forgotten he knew Marlow's trick. But the pain the blade inflicted was real. The old man stumbled back, hands releasing his staff and reaching to pull Cayne free.

She threw the Bane Eye next, but it missed. It sailed off the platform to clank onto the stones. The folk there backed away from it in horror.

She ran now, straight for the old man. She would throttle him. She would seek with greedy fingers into those eye sockets and find that brain of his. He dared send sneaky tendrils into her? He dared tie knots onto her mind? He *dared* to impale Henley like a hog?

Now free of the Bane Eye, she plucked off the queller, tossed it over her shoulder, and guided it to Marlow on mercus touch. Power flooded into her and she formed a bolt of fear-fueled fire in one hand and a mind-strike with the other.

The searing headache returned, but it was nothing compared to her fury.

The Hargothe now held Cayne, his other hand pressed to the bleeding wound on his chest. Her fire blasted around him, but did not touch. A ward, craftily made.

Her mind-strike met a wall of granite-like impermeability. She did not relent, sending ice daggers, lulling allures, spheres of spasming plasma, and her own willshifts at the man. Each was met by a counter that destroyed her attack before it touched.

But the Hargothe was on his heels now. His power was great, but his skills were no better than Kila's. Perhaps less so when it came to physical attacks. The man had relied too long on his mind probes.

She looked down on him now, from a height ten feet above. She had risen from the platform upon gusts of supporting wind. The effort was a natural as running.

"SUBMIT!" she screamed, putting golden tones upon her own voice. These sent the Hargothe reeling. Two hundred citizens of Starside fell to their bellies and offered up their palms. The Hargothe snarled, raised his fist, and began to dymense.

"NO!" Kila hurled a jagged arc of white energy at him. The platform where he stood exploded, sending splinters and smoke skyward. Bits and pieces began to rain onto the crowd, their jagged ends spearing into flesh. People shrieked in horror and agony.

Kila hung above the fountain, turning slowly, seeking. There. She felt the Hargothe in the cathedral. She swooped toward the huge carved entry doors. With a thought she burst them off their hinges, sending fragments of wood skittering into the nave beyond.

He wasn't there. No. He had dymensed to his instinctive shelter, his place of comfort. His crypt.

Kila had been there. Oh, she'd never forget that horrid place. The bed, the channels carved into the floor where heated water ran, the whale-oil sconce, and the low vaulted ceiling.

Ice chill coursed down her back as the world vanished in mercus green. She appeared in the crypt.

The Hargothe struck like a snake. Not with the mercus, but with Cayne. The point hit right where Highest Fley had jabbed Bone Chill into Kila's flank. But it did not penetrate, the blade itself unwilling to pierce her.

Kila's hand swept under the Hargothe's, her other hand clamping onto his wrist. Levering his forearm up, she reversed the blade and drove it at his throat. The blade scratched along his flesh, tearing a shallow gash.

His brief retreat had given him enough time to bolster his mercusine armor. Kila could not understand where all his power had come from.

She lashed with mindstrike after mindstrike, barely aware that her feet were not touching the stone floor; not seeing how the light radiated from her to glare upon the walls; not noting how the Hargothe attempted the same penetrations and she fended them off with fast clips of her own mercusine shears.

And then he was gone and Kila was choking on the mercus green haze he'd left behind.

She dymensed back to the plaza and resumed her seeking.

Another bright mercusine spark was approaching from the west. Not the Hargothe. This one was airborne.

Kila rose higher, clearing the spires of the Cathedral so she could see along the Starside Wall. The Divide still loomed a hundred spans above her. A glint of silver and sparkle of blue caught her eye. And there, skimming on air currents unseen, came a vision.

Borne upon glorious raven's wings, Her Enlightened Majesty flew. She wore a silver breastplate, and a bejeweled helm, the mother to the crown she'd worn to the execution. Sapphires and starstones caught the sun, as did the dirk in her hand. The same one recently driven into her own gut.

Finally, the monarch had come to defend her city. Kila spun away from her, seeking the Hargothe, knowing he had not gone far. Not yet. He desired her too much.

She had felt his unbridled hunger—a lust deeper than what burned in any man's loins—a desire for total possession, down to her soul. He craved her with more appetite than did Flaumishtak, more than a trezz-fiend longed for one more cup.

"COME FACE ME!" she cried, again putting gold upon her voice. The prostrated crowd below jumped to their feet and obeyed, heads tilting back, faces beaming, arms raised, beseeching her to shed more of her glory upon them.

That was not what she wanted! No. No. No.

Seeing them, her eyes shifted to Henley. Bleeding. Still impaled.

She dymensed to the platform, knelt by him. Her hand closed upon the staff. She pulled it free and tossed it aside. She was vaguely aware of Marlow scurrying to pick it up.

The healing cup of her hand already swirled with crimson. This was simple to her, especially when the need was so great. She healed his wound. She delved into his body and found his heart. She traced along the force-bond he'd placed upon her mind and found his mind and she screamed into him: *AWAKEN!*

And he did. Eyes fluttering open, he searched to focus. "I'm dead," he said softly. "I'm dead and Til's maid has come to lift me to the heavens."

"Yer not dead. And I can hardly be Til's maid if I be Highest of Kil. Now stand." The golden force was on those last words, unintentionally. But he obeyed. He fairly scrambled to obey.

"Raised from death," cried a man. "She done it twice in an hour!"

Kila saw the bodies then. They were everywhere. The Fell Guardsmen who had tried to protect her. The Coin, an inert white lump on the paving stones, several Donse Masters with their legs twisted at unnatural angles, the Voluptuary still unmoving since Kila had rent the Hargothe's knot from her mind. And then there were the men the Hargothe had killed while still in the trapper's body. And citizens of every quarter lying face down with shards of wood through their backs, or face up and open-mouthed in their final fire-charred agony. The rich in their embroidered coats lay sprawled and bleeding over raggedly dressed boys fallen from rooftops when the byblow of mercusine feats had swept them to their deaths.

Henley held to her for strength now, trembling from fright, from disorientation, from the strength her healing had sapped from his body.

The Hargothe came alight in her mind, his spark now revealed. He had retreated to the Blasted Quarter.

"Marlow, take Henley and the cats to the Derslin Wheel. I'll meet you there when I'm done."

She did not stay long enough to hear their arguments. Fist raised, she dymensed.

She reappeared three miles north, at the edge of the Blasted Quarter, a realm she knew well from her thieving days.

The Hargothe was not standing there waiting. No, he was hiding. He had masked his mercus. She did the same and sped across the street and into the first of the crumbled buildings.

She kept moving, calling upon her old climbing skills. Her favorite lookout perch still stood. At last, Pol was with her in something. A building in the Blasted Quarter might stand for centuries with no more foundation remaining than two walls and a corner section. Another that appeared whole and hardy might crumble into a cloud of bricks and dust tomorrow.

It was a quiet place, dry. Even now, in the middle of winter, the air was warmer here. Not in a pleasant way, but as a midden pile might steam on a cold morning, producing a foul heat all its own.

She gained her perch, the top of a mostly whole building. Only the wall facing south had crumbled away, revealing all the rooms inside like a gigantic dollhouse.

She had come here with the boys on many occasions.

Some of them sad, some of them joyous. She had never hunted here. Until now.

She crouched behind a thrust of wall and peered over the rest of the quarter. Mostly she listened. Not only with her ears, but with her instincts. She felt an immense aliveness now, like the zing that had presaged the rise of her mercus vision back in the days before her life had become a tavern tale.

A crack and tumble of stone did not mean someone had jarred them loose. That was just the quarter speaking its own language of decay. There were always bits falling from buildings here.

Far off came the gong of a bell. From the Baths of Ori, she thought. Tolling the loss of the Voluptuary perhaps.

The Hargothe had placed a bond on that woman. That was obvious from her attack on the monarch. Same for the Coin.

Which meant the trapper—the murderer—had spread the bond somehow. The implications made Kila curse under her breath. She hadn't had time to consider just how much control the Hargothe had over the merculyns of the city. If he had claimed both those women, how could any of the Sensuals or Spinsters have escaped his subtle bonding?

Marlow was free of it, she was certain. Else the Hargothe would have used him to attack her. But Marlow had been in the Citadel, away from the growing sickness of mind in the city. Highest Binel hadn't behaved like the others either. Kila snorted. The man had probably been too busy cuddling with one of his favorite girls the past few days.

Her Enlightened had not been taken either. And where was she now? By the time Kila had climbed to her perch, the winged monarch had alighted somewhere else. Probably looking for Kila. But with her mask up, Kila would not be easy to find.

Kila had Cayne back. That was good. She would have loved to have Quinn at her side, though she was glad her friend was safely away from this danger.

Cayne had not been able to kill the man. As long as he had use of his mercus powers, the dagger was not going to end him.

So far she felt she had overmatched him. But his ability to dymense while under attack infuriated her. If she could keep him in one spot for long enough, she'd break through his defenses. And once she did, she would not stop until he was a pile of ash at her feet.

A flutter sounded behind her. She spun, already throwing Cayne. The blade rang off steel. Her Enlightened landed, wings folding in and vanishing. Cayne spun off to clatter in the corner, deflected by the woman's dirk.

"Where did you come from?" Kila demanded.

"When you mask your power, you blind yourself. I dymensed to the north and came in over the sea." She removed her helm and tucked it under an arm. "You do not know where the Hargothe is?"

"No. Do you?"

"I would be killing him right now if I did. You must listen to me, Kila. I know of your training with Flaumishtak and I know what he's told you."

"This isn't the time, Your Majesty."

"LISTEN!" She put golden force upon the command, and it struck Kila dumb.

The woman crouched in front of Kila, coming eye to eye. Her presence drew all of Kila's senses away from the Blasted

Quarter to focus on the vision of elegant, fierce beauty before her: the dark hair tumbling over silvery shoulder pauldrons, the metal etched with the Raven-in-Flight insignia of her high office.

"I have spoken to Flaumishtak. I know what—" Her Enlightened's eyes fell to Kila's garnet ring. A second of shocked recognition crossed the woman's face, giving way to a smile of disbelief. "Highest of Kil. Annisforl is dead, then?"

"He turned to ash."

Nax's presence suddenly moved far away. That was good. She and the others must have passed into the cavern of the Derslin Wheel, just as Kila had ordered. That was the safest place to be in Starside.

"Your ascension to Highest goes to prove what Flaumishtak told me. If the Hargothe was already dead, I might kill you myself, right here. But fear not; I will soon know if Flaumishtak spoke true. And if he did, then you must bring Kil into the world. For if you do not, the force of destiny will move someone else to do it. Though in truth I see nothing but ill weather either way if a true god comes into this world."

"What do you mean a true god? You're the Enlightened. Your grand-grand-grand-grand-mother sealed the Synod and said it was true."

The woman tapped the tip of her dirk against her palm. "Compromise can make truth out of lies. My position then was weak, the peace was fragile, and my instincts told me to agree to it. You are a Shadline, too, and you will soon learn how powerful our creed is. Listen and obey. And that is what I wish you to do now. Listen and obey."

"I'll do as I wish, beggin' yer pardon. The Hargothe is out there, and I mean to put an end to him. And then we can put this nonsense about Kil out the window and never think about it again."

"You think you have a choice?"

The Hargothe's spark flared into existence. Both the women turned to face it. Three buildings over and near the top.

Kila leapt, unmasking her power, and took to the air. Her Enlightened was a moment behind, raven wings sprouting. "Wait, girl!"

Kila unleashed a blue sphere, loaded so heavily with fear that oily black swirls oozed across its surface. It smashed into the wall concealing the Hargothe. Stone blew apart and drifts of rubble and dust cascaded away. Kila's power forced the sphere through the floor and the wall beyond. It continued, striking the next building and the next, each erupting in beige dust and crumbling debris. The ground shook as walls impacted the street.

The first structure wobbled side to side, then paused at a sickening angle. It fell, crushing a neighboring building, and beginning a chain of topples. The world thundered. Dust billowed skyward.

At street level, a roiling wave of debris blasted through alleys and side streets. Stray dogs sprinted for clear air; roosting birds took to the sky.

And then the people began to emerge, thin and frail. Dozens of them, outcasts. Hated for their rattled minds or odd faces, they had taken refuge in the only place left to them. These were folk even Cheapsgaters wouldn't tolerate to live among them.

They coughed and wept, holding bits of rag to their faces to keep from breathing the killing dust of Kila's rage.

The destruction continued to shake the ground, making other structures outside of the collapse lose sections of their walls. Kila's favorite perch gave way, setting off a new round of collapses.

Screams came from the inner quarters and folk rushed from their homes and shops to watch the cloud of dust rise ever higher.

The Hargothe's spark appeared across the city. Dunne Medow Plaza.

The monarch cried: "Wait, you petulant—"

But Her Enlightened's words were lost to Kila as she once again dymensed.

46

THE PATH IS CLOSED

The Palace of Thizrūil held darkness in its halls as if flooded with ink. It was the same thick lightlessness that had filled the entry to the tomb back on the Kovi-Mest coast. Zirhine had once again chewed up blobs of glowing blue weed, and again a clump was stuck to the point of Ol' Rusty.

The nosg-shades had bled. A lot. But the Shadline blades had absorbed it all. This was not a revelation to Fallo. He knew of that strange property of the magical weapons. But to see it happen, to witness the *drinking* of the blood, had given him both a new fear and a new respect for his blade.

Perhaps he shouldn't refer to it as Ol' Rusty, he thought. It was, after all, a legendary blade made from a dragon's tooth. But it felt a bit ostentatious to call it Telt. A bit "reachy," as his mother used to say.

He held the blade up to shed a faint blue oval of light on another of the thousands of frescos adorning the walls of the palace. "Thizrūil, you say?" He moved aside so Zirhine could inspect the image more closely. She'd been the one to declare the name of the place.

Father had sometimes hired balladeers to perform in the great hall of the PiTorro greathouse, though Tarek often said that, to him, music sounded like the jangle of broken glass in a jar, and that singing was less pleasant than the howls of a broken-legged hound.

Naturally, Fallo loved the songs, jokes, and the recitations of epic tales. He'd also noted the glimmery, gimlet-eyed attention balladeers got from the ladies, young and old.

One rather long song was "Saedi of Cigil-Tine." It was more of a chant than a tune. And as it progressed, a skilled performer varied the intensity of his words from whispers to shouts, the pitch rising and falling, but not forming into melody. The effect was magical. And for Fallo, who was a rather skilled mimic of others' voices, such things helped him remember bits and pieces of performances he'd heard only once. As the son of a wealthy man, he'd also been privileged to own books of the texts, which he'd imbibed like a trezz-fiend.

So now he recited:

"In the tower of lost souls she weeps,
The lady of Thizrūil, locks of red.
The mourning witness never sleeps;
Dire Illizshian rules the dead."

Zirhine nodded as she traced the scene on the wall. It was a depiction of Cigil-Tine as if viewed from a tower in this palace. The boulevard they had just traversed shrank in the distance, lined on both sides with lesser palaces, lush and tidy gardens everywhere. The central fountain sprayed sparkling droplets skyward. Beyond it, the colossal maiden was backed by the great falls, which appeared as a haze of white framed by majestic cliffs.

On the streets, tiny figures moved about their lives. Those farthest away were mere shapes, suggestions of a living being's form. They could be humans or nosg. But nearer to the palace, more detail showed. And most striking of all was the lovely grace, the square shouldered bearing, the high brows, ears delicate and pinned back in a manner unlike any human's.

"They were like us," Zirhine said, "but also not like us. Cigil-Tine was built at the height of their age. Illizshian reigned here for three hundred years. But a sickness came over them and they declined. By the time men came to Stermūin, their entire realm was empty. The Divide stood, Moonside was sequestered, and the great Citadel lay hollow as a seashell."

"The fate's-piece is this way," Fallo said, pulling himself away from the fresco. It would take a lifetime of work to catalog and study all the art in this place. He could only imagine how much more there was throughout the city.

The art was all that remained. With the exception of a few mundane items, like stools, buckets, and doorstops, all the artifacts of the lost race had been removed. "Did the nosg take everything?"

"Perhaps. Perhaps those who fled took some of it. But I think they never required much in the way of furnishings. Have you noticed that most of the rooms we've been through have been galleries? This palace was built to display this art."

"Surely they had beds and dinnerware."

"Yes. But scholars believe there were at most ten thousand residents in Cigil-Tine. Half that in Stermūin."

He pressed into the darkness, allowing his instincts to tell him when to turn from a corridor or when to continue.

The sense of being watched had gone now. The defeat of the nosg-shades had relieved the city of tension it had held for an age. He doubted the ones that had escaped the Cloak would attack them again. That doubt arose to a total certainty as soon as he considered it.

"I just felt a certainty come over me," he said.

"Speak of it," the Cloak commanded.

"The nosg ghouls have returned to their posts. They are watching, but not for us. We have passed the test."

Zirhine drew in a sharp breath. Fallo turned to see if she'd stepped on a nail or been bitten by a snake. But she was merely looking at him in astonishment. "A test? They were guarding the city as a test? Keep speaking. No." She shook her hand violently, which made strange shadows waver behind her from the blue glow on her fingertip. "No. Do not think. Just speak. Speak. Speak."

"I don't know what to say, I think—"

"No!" the Cloak barked. "Speak. Every thought. Speak it."

"The test . . . the test is a trial. A thing you have to do to show worthiness. A test of skill. A test of merit. A test of heart. A test that the pull of the fate's-piece is greater than fear. No one can come this far without the power of our Shadline blades. Our instincts. Or mercus power. Or timing as we did, to come with sunlight. But the path is closed. It is closed. One can only come at sunset. The vergent path is closed."

And then he had nothing else to say. It all came out in a rush, so quickly it bypassed his own understanding. He stood dumbly in the glow of his spitblob, watching the reaction of his companions as they understood what he'd said before he did. It took time for him to reflect on his own words, to bring them into his thinking mind.

He shouldered past his friends to return the fresco of the city. It was covered with dust. He swiped his hand across it, then showed his companions the black on his palm. When they stared blankly back at him, he swiped again, as high up as he could reach. Above the waterfall. Back and forth he stroked, dislodging the accumulated dirt of a thousand years.

More had been painted there, the cliffs framing the water fall rose to severe peaks. "The sunset is behind the palace," he said to himself. "We know that because we saw it while we were running and dodging spears and arrows. The waterfall is to the east."

He continued to swipe at the wall, but he could not reach high enough. "Boost me."

He was so intent on his task, he barely noticed when the Cloak dropped onto all fours and Zirhine helped him to stand on the man's back.

This is stupid behavior, even for you, Lop sent.

Maybe I'll dunk you and use your hide as a sponge to clean this picture.

That put a quick end to Lop's commentary.

"There," Fallo said, after a final brush with his sleeve. He stepped off the Cloak and admired his discovery. A rightness settled over him. "Zirhine, your fate's-piece?"

She already had it out, the scrap of paper unrolled.

On the fresco, the constellation of the goblet stood directly above the falls. The peak to the right formed the inverted V, the notch in its side now revealed as a cut-out on the side of the mountain. A sliver of moon shone to the right. Where the sketch looked like the scribble of a child, this portion of the fresco had been created by a master. "That is the place, but it is not yet the time. The fate's-piece beckons."

The Cloak hadn't finished brushing off his knees before Fallo continued to obey the pull deeper into the palace.

47

MERCUS GREEN RISING

Kila Sigh appeared once again high over the fountain of Dunne Medow Plaza.

Before the chill of dymension had faded she was assaulted by mindstrikes. Flailing with reflexive feats, she severed them. A blast of chill followed, which she barely negated. But not before her eyelashes froze together.

Half blinded, she lashed out, throwing hate-bolts, arcs of jagged black learned from Dunne Yples, along the trajectory of the incoming feats.

The Hargothe dymensed before they struck. Now he was inside the cathedral. Kila threw sphere after sphere, obliterating the front of the cathedral, sending Donse Masters scattering in the plaza. Slabs fell forward, dashing onto the wide entry steps, sending shards and dust tumbling. A spire toppled and smashed the execution platform to splinters.

Kila was already descending toward the opening she'd blasted, sending gusts of wind ahead to clear the air. The old man was in the nave, working up a mercus feat of his own. Kila listened with all her senses. There was nothing of the basic five in what he was conjuring. Wholly demaynic, then. But why hadn't he released it?

She threw a sphere. It dissipated in sparks, undone by his prepared counter.

"You prove yourself to be what I thought you'd be." He spoke near her ear it seemed. Not sent into her mind, but his voice made close through a new mercus trick. *"Gloriously powerful. Reckless. A wild animal in need of taming."*

She caught the gist of his speech bolts. She replied, using the same technique. *"You prove yourself to be what I thought you were. A spiteful, corrupt man hiding behind Til's name."*

For the first time she wished she'd learned more from Flaumishtak. Her methods of attack were limited because she had not trained in such things. She was just a scrappy Cheapsgate girl, winning fights through sheer viciousness. The Hargothe, too, had a limited repertoire. And so they had come to this, neither able to defeat the other. She saw now what he had prepared. Not an attack. He was poised on the brink of dymensing again.

He stood in the exact center of a clean patch of the floor. The rest was covered with dust and debris. He must have created a shield of some sort to keep from being crushed. He was looking up at her, eyeless sockets fixed on her. His chest bled from Cayne's shallow bite, a tear-shaped blood stain marring the front of his robe.

He sensed her attacks as easily as she sensed his. She descended through the gaping hole she'd made in the cathedral ceiling and alighted on the floor, just beyond where the doors had been.

A swooping of air behind her announced the arrival of the monarch.

"*And you have taught me much, Kila Sigh,*" the Hargothe said, a whisper in her left ear. "*For that, I thank you.*"

She was wary of the spidersilk tendrils he'd tried before. They relied on bolts of boredom and inattention, a very difficult demaynic sense to manifest, she realized. The man must have studied and practiced such things for thousands of hours to reach with them so skillfully now.

She produced a negating shield of alert focus around herself and the monarch.

"I'll admit that you have taught me as well," she said, reaching with simple mercus touch for a stone shard next to him. A jagged cornice broken from the ceiling. He could sense her effort, surely. But would he understand its purpose?

She went on: "You taught me that Til has no power in this realm. Had he, you would have been quashed long ago. Everything you have done has been in the service of evil. Til is a mask you wear to conceal your true nature. And that is why you seek to bring Kil into this world."

"Kil will be my footman when this culmination peaks. And judge not the indifference of Til, for he granted to us the liberty of our choices. That freedom is his test of our moral rectitude. He watches. Oh, he watches and notices all. And when Kil sits at my feet, and the world has been brought into the light of righteousness, Til *will* smile upon me. And you . . ."

He was stepping closer now, leaving the chunk of cornice behind. Kila moved her touch to another shard, larger, half buried in a crater of its own making.

". . . you he will cast into the scalding ice fires of the lowest demaynic hell. Submit to me, girl, and I shall cleanse you of your wickedness and turn your great power to the service of Til."

"Make Kil your footman?" she said, incredulous at his arrogance. "How will you do that? Isn't he a god?"

"He is but a lord of the demayne, child. Subject to the same constraints as any of such blood. Is that not true, *Dragnithan* LiMinluit?"

Her Enlightened Majesty laughed and stalked forward, wings extended. Her dirk began to glow, white hot. "You betray your dangerous ignorance, Hargothe. But you will die now, and we can be done with your ridiculous war before it begins."

A shrill cry echoed in the vast nave as something thumped from the shadows behind the old man. A body. It bounced and jerked over the floor.

It was Henley. His face was black and blue, his body covered with dust. His shirt was bloodstained, a gaping hole in the center where the Hargothe's staff had penetrated. Kila had healed that wound, but he had since suffered others.

His right leg was bent at a weird angle, and Kila realized that his knee had been crushed, making the lower portion of his leg twist to face nearly backward.

And yet he crawled and thrust with both legs. The Hargothe's willshift overpowered all agony.

"You think me the hare and you the hound?" the Hargothe said. If he feared the monarch's threat, he didn't show it. "Such hubris from someone so young. Like this boy, who thought he could burn my host and suffer no consequences."

He flashed out with flame. Kila negated it before it reached Henley.

"Look at her, boy," the Hargothe said, forcing Henley's head to twist toward Kila. He was on all fours now, leaning against the Hargothe's leg like a devoted dog.

Henley! she sent along his force-bond. *Fight him. Willshift can be broken.*

The monarch was circling, moving to position herself on the Hargothe's flank. Kila didn't understand why she hadn't attacked already. Why hadn't she brought down lightnings from the heavens to smite him?

A glance showed the woman scowling, furious as she looked above and beyond the blind seer. She was distracted. Of all the times to lose attention!

Henley, listen to me. We have both endured this before. Cling to Huff. There is strength in the bond. Get your footing and fight!

Huff. . . gone. Taken.

Fury flashed through Kila. The Hargothe had once stolen Nax's bond from her. Unforgivable. And now he'd taken Huff? Fire leapt from her outstretched hand, but she killed it before it reached her enemy. Henley was too close. She felt for the stone shard again. But it was so big that Henley would be struck if she used mercus touch to hurl it at the Hargothe.

The monarch was muttering to herself now. Her wings fluttered in agitation. The dirk was raised before her, not poised to attack but like a lantern lighting the way.

"Why?" the woman asked through clenched teeth. "Why do you make me stay my hand and merely watch?"

For a moment Kila feared the Hargothe had willshifted her. But then the woman turned to offer a sad, half-apologetic look to Kila. "I must listen and obey." With a jump, she took to the air and swept from the cathedral.

The Hargothe chuckled. "The dragnithan are powerful, but constrained in this realm." He began to walk, forcing Henley to keep up..

Kill him, Henley sent. *Kill me if you must. But kill him. Now, Kila.*

A merculyn circle was forming on the plaza just outside. Surely another of the Hargothe's attempts to distract her.

Henley moaned and tried to stand. The Hargothe tsked and Henley flopped to the ground, forcing his cheek to tiles.

"Ah!" the Hargothe exclaimed. "I see now."

He knows! Henley screamed into Kila's mind. *Kill him. He knows!*

Knows what?

Our bond. Run!

But it was too late. The tingling fingers of the Hargothe's attack appeared from within Kila's mind, scrabbling, scratching, digging with hook-like claws.

The willshift began to stiffen Kila's limbs. The Hargothe had discovered Henley's force-bond in Kila and now used it as a passage straight to Kila's mind. No sneaky tendrils needed.

And no way to stop it.

Cayne clattered to the tiles as the Hargothe forced her fingers to spread. He moved more swiftly toward her, Henley shuffling and groaning to keep up.

His lips were parted in a foul smile, teeth brown and black.

"The harlot monarch has abandoned you, girl. This lad is my hound. And now I possess you. The more you resist, the more agony you will endure before I relent."

He placed a hand on her head and petted the fuzz of growth there. His thumb traced along her brow, down the ridge of her nose, fingers running along her cheek.

"So delicate," he marveled.

Her revulsion had no outlet, for Kila was willshifted into immobility. Or nearly so. She could still move her fingers a bit. Her eyes were free, though she kept them on the skin-wrapped skull before her.

She had healed him once to save Nax. And in so doing, had strengthened him. But it had not erased all the years of living in darkness. He was pale as a grub. He smelled of chimney smoke and burned flesh. And blood. The wound on his chest still seeped, the stain slowly spreading as it wicked through the fibers of his robe.

His jaw was clenched. She realized he was straining hard to maintain the willshift over two powerful merculyns. Those circled outside into source-taps were now sending him even more power.

And then she knew. He intended to dymense with them. The concentration required to wield so many different bolts was too much for him. He was failing.

She stopped struggling with her limbs and instead put all her will into curling her lips into a smile.

The mercusine was vibrant and alive to her and her senses were thrilling with the awareness of every sound and smell and color in the broken cathedral.

The Hargothe had used Henley's force-bond to infiltrate her mind. That meant he was relying on Henley's mercus power. He was at war with Henley right at that moment.

Henley! she sent, a strange instinctive inspiration rising, a feeling she knew well: Desperate hope.

The Hargothe's lips clamped tighter, brow pulling down.

He brought his other hand to her head. This should have brought a hard intrusion of pain as he burrowed into her mind, but there was no such strike.

Henley was trembling, head hanging low as he cowered on hands and knees.

He could hear her, but he had no strength to respond. All his concentration was on resisting the Hargothe.

But the bond was there. The mercusine connection was there. Established and tied off as surely as a sailing ship's lines were secured at each end to sail and yardarm.

Join with me, she sent. *Surrender.*

There was no additional feat of mercus needed. This was a skill Henley had learned from Huff, and he had used it to save Kila on the ash barrens.

Surrender, she sent, trying to keep her voice calm and welcoming. It was not a command, but an invitation. She sent welcoming through the bond, the sense of open arms, of love.

The Hargothe's hands squeezed Kila's skull with amazing strength just as Henley's essence filled her.

Kila, run! he called inside her. And it wasn't the same as sending through the bond, for this arose as her own thought. The joining was complete.

With Henley vacated from his physical body and now held within her own mind, the Hargothe's grip on the boy failed. And with it, his willshift on Kila slipped for a fraction of a moment. Mercus erupted into Kila's control, her hands came up, blazing with blue flame. They struck away the Hargothe's arms, and she followed with two palms to his chest. She did not release a sphere of power or flare of fire, but pressed her awareness into his body.

She found his heart easily. With a feat of mercus touch she squeezed, seeking to still the pulse and—

A counter blow took her in the side of the head. The Hargothe had struck her with his fist.

Kila! Get away from him, Henley cried.

I'm going to kill him. Now.

You can't. He's connected to another source. It's too powerful to—

The old man's mouth opened as the agony of his squeezed heart took his breath away.

Bolts formed from the plaza. It would be fire, Kila knew. That was the most these Starside merculyns could muster. But such would kill her if not negated.

She spared enough attention to meet the loosely formed bolts as they arced into the cathedral at her. She negated them from existence.

And still she squeezed. "Your crimes are too many to list," she said, now pushing the man back. Henley's body had collapsed. He looked like a battered Cheapsgate tough, sleeping off a bad beating in an alley. The sight of his ravaged body drove her fury hotter.

"Die, ya sick ol' bastard!"

He was trying for his own mercus feat. His lips pulled back into a sickly grimace of agony. She smelled the tinge of mercus green rising.

"No! No! I will not allow it."

She squeezed harder. For Henley, for Nax, for the untold numbers of boys he'd drained of mercus. For the Voluptuary who he'd corrupted, for the Coin. For merculyns of every Way whose will he had subverted through his force-bonds.

His body was shimmering now as dymension built. His

claw-like hand reached again for her, sliding down her face. He meant to take just her with him now. She could feel his intention.

Kila Siiiigh. You are miiiine.

Her grip on his heart slipped.

"No!" She bent all her will to keeping him here. She negated bolt after bolt as he attempted to complete his dymension. His strength was bottomless, as was hers. Again she gripped his heart in mercus touch.

Old man! Tenn. You are MINE!

With a scream she clenched her fist. In response her mercus touch compressed, making his heart stop pulsating. And then she destroyed it utterly, squeezing it to pulp.

His eye sockets raised to the sky, papery face stretching in agony.

But Kila was not done. She dove into that festering mind, her strikes now unopposed. She ripped through the intricacies of his twisted brain. The nodes of his force-bonds were aglow, like beacons. These she ripped free, not with care, but with the vicious efficiency.

His body shuddered. He fell to his knees.

Kila backed away and watched him fall. A plume of dust kicked from beneath him as his body thudded onto the floor.

Kila's body heaved as she sought her breath. Her arms and shoulders were knotted with fury, like Yples's unending exertions when gripped by his madness. She looked down, shocked to discover her left hand soaked with blood.

She uncurled her fingers and spilled out a handful of ash.

Is he gone? Henley called. *Is he gone?*

He's—he's dead.

Kneeling, she turned Henley's body over. His face looked

so young, so wounded. She bent over him and pressed her lips to his forehead, tears falling from her eyes and dripping on to his face.

I killed him.

Truly?

Truly.

The circling source-taps on the plaza dissolved. Their unspent power dissipating to nothing. Flakes of white drifted through the huge hole in the ceiling. They fell all around like ash-spirits. Snow.

Someone coughed in the shadows deeper in the nave. Kila remembered where she was, in the midst of a hive of enemies. She did not want to fight them, did not want more blood on her conscience.

She rose into the air, pulling Henley's body upward with her. He floated into her arms, heavy and inert.

The plaza was a chaos of bodies and debris. Donse Masters and Sensuals and Spinsters stood gaping at her. The snow fell soft and silent, salting their robes and hair, laying down a skim of white to mask the dead. Those still conscious looked utterly confused, as if slowly coming to awareness of where they were and not remembering how they had come to be there.

Putting the gold light of command on her voice she said: "Return to your rooms and await instruction."

They scattered. She wasn't sure they'd obey for long. She didn't think the Hargothe's mind knots would remain with him dead. But she couldn't be sure until she began looking into skulls, and that would have to wait. Henley needed her now.

She dymensed, reappearing in the Derslin Wheel beneath Starside. Marlow and Nax were there. And to her astonishment, so was Huff. Henley had said Huff had been taken. But apparently not by the Hargothe. By Marlow, just as she'd ordered. Seeing Henley's orange cat brought her so much relief her vision blurred.

She slumped and put Henley on the floor. Marlow jumped up and joined her. "If you're not Dem-Kisk, then I don't want to be alive when it comes."

"It's over, Marlow. It's never coming now."

Huff sprang into her arms to nuzzle her face and was soon joined by Nax. She welcomed the armful of furry love but was puzzled by Huff's choice. Until she remembered that she held Henley in her mind still.

We are safe, she said to Henley.

Put him back, please, Huff sent. The cat's voice startled her.

I don't want to go back, Henley said. *My body is broken.*

I'll see to that, Kila said. She put the cats down and began to inspect Henley's injuries. What she saw horrified her. Not just because of his mangled leg and horrific bruises, but because she knew his body did not have the strength for the sort of healing she could perform. She had already used up most of his strength healing his impalement. Just mending his knee could kill him.

But the longer his mind remained out of his body, the weaker it would become. And then he would die.

I'm sorry to do this, she said, steeling herself for the cruelty her love demanded. With gentle firmness, she thrust him out.

Henley's eyes shot wide and then immediately squeezed shut as he screamed. Marlow held him down. His ring removed, he offered a bit of soothing to Henley's mind, but the vaguest touch of an outsider made Henley panic. Only Kila and Huff could reach him. She lay next to him, holding him. Huff pressed to one flank, Nax to the other. She stroked his hair from his brow and pressed her nose to his cheek. She spoke in soft whispers and promised him all would be well. In time his screams gave way to sobs, which surrendered to soft moans, until he was asleep.

Kila lay with him a while longer, now fully aware of her own exhaustion. Shaking it off, she began to swirl her healing draught, crimson streaked with black. She saw now components of it she had not noticed before. Bitter tastes of strange weeds only Finta Sahng could identify.

That gave her an idea. She applied her healing sparingly, not repairing his shattered knee, but simply easing the pain. She dared not do more.

"He needs a bed, food, and warmth," she said.

"The Citadel," Marlow said. His robes were covered with dust, the hem soaked with blood, none of it his apparently. He looked like he'd aged a decade in the past hour. He had the Hargothe's staff in one hand, the Voluptuary's Bane Eye in the other.

"I can only safely dymense to somewhere I've been," she said. "Do you want to walk or go with us?"

"With you, Kila Sigh. If you please."

The cats knew to climb onto her shoulders. Marlow lifted Henley, though he could barely stand under the weight. Kila put an arm around Marlow and rested one on Henley.

She did not need to raise her fist. That was merely a cue, a mental trick. She did not need such things anymore.

They vanished in mercus green.

48

A WILLFUL BLADE

"Do you hear that?" Fallo said. "Water."

They emerged from the inky black of the corridor into twilight. A clear sky, full of stars, stood overhead, framed by the jagged edges of a collapsed dome.

The rotunda was enormous, easily the size of the nave of the Cathedral of Til back in Starside. A fountain stood in the center of the debris-strewn floor. It did not spray high into the air like the one on the boulevard. This burbled from a huge marble flower, spilling in clear sheets over the petals to splash on bits of crumbled roof that had fallen into the pool. That water overflowed the fountain wall and streamed away in a shallow channel that bisected the room. A huge oak tree sprouted from the broken tile to one side of the fountain. Its thick trunk rose to a glorious crown. The leaf edges caught the starlight, making them luminous with silver.

A man stood at the base of the tree, two-handed sword tip-down on the tile. His armor was stained with the patina of age, dust, and even a bit of moss on his shin guards. His head was bowed, and for a moment Fallo thought him a very life-like statue.

But then he raised his head. His skin was dark, irises black, hair bluish-black. He leaned forward as he raised his weapon into a guard position. With sharp jerks of his knees he broke his boots free from the tile, where time had apparently cemented them.

"He has not moved for a thousand years," Zirhine said.

A rush of Cigil-Tinian came from his lips. Fallo didn't understand it, but the meaning was clear.

"This is another test," he said.

"A First Race warden," Zirhine said. "My mentor would have paid any price to meet him."

"The price may be our lives," the Cloak said. He stepped forward, Tosuin in hand, but not raised. "Fallo, listen."

But Fallo already had his eyes closed, seeking guidance from the strange force that had guided them this far. Lop squeezed free of his satchel and went to the water flowing from the fountain. She daintily lapped at the spillage. She hadn't spared the warden the slightest glance.

The man stood on the opposite side of the canal, poised between two thick, gnarled roots of the tree. The starlight was too dim to make out the true color of his armor. But the blue glow of Zirhine's spitblobs reflected in azure sparks from his teeth and blade, which was unsullied by the accumulation of time.

The Cloak swept the cape of his black cloak back from his right shoulder, freeing his sword arm. At his most effusive, the Cloak was a stolid man, but the warden made him look agitated by comparison. The warden stepped one foot back and pulled the hilt to his cheek, sword point forward. A more aggressive stance. An invitation to battle.

The Cloak raised Tosuin, flames flickering along its length. The light cast his own shadow behind him, the orange catching fire in his eyes. "I do not wish to spar with you, honored warden. We have been drawn here by the Shadline pull to find a fate's-piece. If what we discover must be removed from the city, I vow to return it if such be practicable. If not, I vow it shall be used in service of goodness, not evil. For honor, not depravity. And when its service be done, it shall be given a place of honor, if any such place remains in this world."

Fallo had heard men speak of vows before. Merchants made them all day every day. "Vow" was a sideways word when such men used it, a promise they hoped to break at the soonest possible moment. But when the Cloak used it, Fallo felt the oath seal about the man, and just for an instant he thought a hazy glow appeared around the man's head, an aura of eldritch light.

The warden spoke again, this time enunciating each word very slowly. The way one might speak to a child. *"Allis uandish, vennis kassh."* The accent was very different from Fallo's Donse Master tutor, but the words slowly sank in.

"Did he just tell the Cloak he was going to, er, castrate him?"

"More or less," Zirhine said. "Actually, more." She spoke louder, so the Cloak could hear. "He's taunting you, seeking to provoke you into attacking."

There were four exits from this chamber. One they'd entered, two blocked with rubble, the last stood open beyond the tree. To get there would mean crossing the channel. An easy leap of five feet. Fallo knew that setting foot on that side would prompt the warden to attack.

Lop leapt over.

What is wrong with you? Fallo sent.

That tree is interest—

The warden sprang into the air, sword drawn back, arcing straight toward the cat.

Lop!

Though she'd put on a bit of cushioning during the boat trip down the Sagmarsh Wash, Lop was still half her old Starside weight. The warden had too far to fly to catch her by surprise. She scurried directly toward him, so that he carried over her head. A swipe of his blade severed a tuft of fur from her tail.

In three bounds she made the tree trunk and was clambering up and onto the lowest limb. She spat at the warden, fur up, tail floofed out.

The warden landed with a crunch then calmly stalked back to the tree. He tilted his head up, studying the cat just out of reach.

Climb higher, you idiot! He can jump high enough to swing at you.

For a wonder, Lop obeyed and was soon lost among the leaves, her passage betrayed only by the shaking of limbs ever higher.

The warden looked up, then looked at the Cloak, then proceeded to begin hacking his sword into the trunk.

Even with a proper ax, such a task would take hours, maybe even days for one man. The trunk was at least five feet across.

"I'm hearing nothing," the Cloak said. "Except that I must

not fight him. Zirhine?"

"Nothing. Fallo?"

He raised his face to the stars and closed his eyes. Not to listen, but to beg the heavens to know why it always fell to him to decide what they must do. The unfortunate truth was that he didn't hear anything either. Except the steady crunch and whack of the warden's two-handed sword biting into the ancient tree trunk. And Fallo's instincts only pulled him to go through the door behind the tree. They had no opinion about the warden.

And then he had it. "You have to stay here, Cloak Einlin. The warden will let me pass."

"And me?" Zirhine asked.

"You'd better not test it."

The ferneater Shadline did not look best pleased. Fallo eyed the jump, then leapt. His feet struck the opposite side. The warden stopped his chopping and turned to face him.

Fallo waggled Ol' Rusty, blue glow on the tip tracing a wobbly line in the air. "Just going through, sir warden. Proceed with your chopping." He made little swings with his blade.

The warden stared at him a second longer then turned back to his task.

Zirhine landed beside Fallo.

The warden stopped. And this time he did not turn to look, but sprang, spinning in midair, sword coming down at Zirhine.

She threw Reft toward his head, his killing blow diverted to strike the curved blade aside. Zirhine rolled under the next blow as Fallo backpedalled and nearly toppled into the fountain.

The woman popped up, hand out to receive Reft as it returned. Just in time to bring it up and catch the warden's blade as it swung for decapitating strike. The force of it knocked her onto her side.

The Cloak stood his ground, watching, but not joining the fight. Such restraint must have cost him dearly, but he was a true Shadline. He listened and obeyed.

Fallo did not need such subtle guidance, survival imposing its own imperatives on his body. He dodged in a wide circle to stay out of the arc of the warden's blade, making for the doorway. Zirhine, desperate to escape, rolled along the floor. She deflected another blow, catching the warden's blade in Reft's curve, then threw a spray of dust into the warden's face. *"Alish!"* she cried.

The powder whooshed alight a sickly green. The warden grunted and fell back, covering his eyes. Zirhine jumped across the canal.

The warden coughed and sneezed and blinked furiously. When his hand came away, half his face was blistered from her fiery attack.

He stooped to splash fountain water on his wounds, then returned to the tree and began to hack.

But Fallo he let pass.

Not because I'm special, Fallo thought. It's Ol' Rusty. Has to be.

"Don't let him kill Lop," he called as he plunged through the exit.

Don't let him kill you, Beloved One, he sent.

Don't let her *kill you,* Lop sent back.

Fallo didn't bother asking what Lop meant. He knew. He'd known since he'd seen the fresco.

The passage continued on, presumably to more gardens and domes and towers and galleries. But Fallo stopped by a closed wooden door. It was finely made, hung upon lovely hinges carved to look like vines around flower stalks.

It opened without making so much as a whisper of sound, revealing a stairwell. Up he went, feeling the pull ever more strongly. Soon he was running, taking the steps two at a time.

When he reached the top his brow was damp and his shirt clung to his back. Another door, just like the one below.

He knocked.

The chamber within was sparsely furnished. A cot on one wall, a writing table with ink pots and quills. A bookshelf held perhaps two dozen volumes.

The woman stood in the center of the room, barefoot upon a thick rug. Just like the warden, she was perfectly still. Fallo thought her rather underdressed. A loose blouse, laces undone, hem falling to mid-thigh. Loose pants that cinched around her shins with knotted laces.

A dagger lay on the rug near her feet. The skeleton of a small animal was sprawled behind her.

Recalling a bit of etiquette from his childhood, Fallo made a leg. "Queen Illizshian. You are looking well, considering your, uh, age."

The dagger drew up from the ground. It shot straight at him. Reflex brought Ol' Rusty to bear, but the incoming blade stopped just out of reach. It hung in the air, spotless as the day the smith had finished crafting it.

It was a twin to Ol' Rusty. The same length, the same angles, the same hilt. But this one was clean and bright. Not a scratch or nick in the steel.

But it wasn't the fate's-piece Fallo had come for.

"Illis alt anwal ish etel!" she said.

Fallo realized he still had Zirhine's spitblob on his blade. Torn between alarm at being nearly skewered by a flying dagger and his embarrassment at using a Shadline relic as a sort of stick, he failed to translate the woman's words.

She hadn't moved anything but her lips, and that had been very slight. The way puppet-talkers did to make it look like their hand creatures were truly speaking.

"You can't move, can you?" he said, lowering Ol' Rusty and wiping the blob onto his sleeve. The threatening dagger did not move. That had to signify something good, he thought. He guessed it was Ol' Rusty that had kept the death-stroke at bay. He held it up, hilt between thumb and forefinger to show it to the Queen.

"Didn't come here to get into a scrap with you, your Majesty. Just following the ol' Shadline call." He didn't know if the First Race thought of their weapons as relics or if they were as mundane as buckets and chairs.

"Illis alt anwal ish etel!" She spat the words out more slowly this time. Fallo repeated them back, puzzled. Donse Masters put separation between words in the Cigil-Tine tongue, but this woman was blending them all together and putting emphasis on the wrong syllables.

He hazarded a step sideways. The blade followed, the point aimed at his forehead. He had no doubt it could puncture his ugly skull and make a quick hash of his brain.

No matter how often he repeated her phrase, he wasn't able to parse the words. So he gave up. The fate's-piece was here. Behind the woman, he thought. He continued to circle, keeping a close eye on the hovering blade. Illizshian did not turn to face him.

She had access to her mercus power and enough control to move her lips. But she was trapped in that stance. A thrill of horror swept through him as he thought of the torture of being imprisoned in such a manner for a thousand years. More than that, likely.

The floating blade allowed him to walk a wide perimeter around her until he could see that the fate's-piece was not behind her. It must be on her person. He waggled his lips side-to-side as he considered the prospect of searching her for it. He wouldn't mind a bit of a snuggle-up with her—a thousand years old or no, she didn't look much past thirty—but he didn't like the idea of groping her while she was frozen. It was one thing to be a scoundrel, quite another to be a villain.

He finished his circle. Speaking Cigil-Tinian hadn't been of particular interest to him as a pupil. He could read it, rather slowly. He could understand his tutors, usually. Now he wished he'd been a more diligent student.

"Might as well wish for a delicate brow and a fine jaw while I'm at it." He scratched his scraggle of whiskers and pieced together what he could of a question. *"Glinee, ril-ne bou?"* He hoped that was "Why don't you move", but he worried it might be "Don't you shoe?"

Her eyes moved fractionally. *"Etel!"*

Etel. Etel. Etel . . . "You've got my wagon wheel in a mud-gom, Majesty. I don't know that word. I think—"

But maybe he did know it. Ee-tell? Emphasis on the first syllable. Now that was a word he knew. "Ink?" he said.

The Cloak would trust the guess, he decided. He edged to the desk and inspected the ink pots. He uncorked one, the stopper crumbled in his hands. The ink had long ago dried up. He sniffed it and noted a bit of oak gall.

He returned to Illizshian's line of sight and held up the pot. It flew from his hand as she took it with her mercus power. It floated close to her eyes.

"*Hact!*" There was a mournful tone in her exclamation. Enough so that Fallo was sure her word mean "dry."

He held out his hand. "*Joulne.* Please." He motioned for her to float it back to him.

She did. His skin tingled for a moment and he was sure she'd searched him with some mercusine trick or other.

He thought he knew what she wanted him to do, so he set about reconstituting the ink with a rather arduous round of spitting. The dry ink dust inside the pot soaked it up like desert soil. He quickly saw he was never going to get it done this way.

"Begging your pardon, Majesty. But I'm going to have to, er, excuse myself a moment." He put Ol' Rusty in its scabbard and backed from the room. Closing the door, he was left in darkness save for the fading blue of the spit blob smear on his sleeve.

He considered going all the way down to the fountain chamber for water, but decided upon a more expedient measure.

He unfastened his trousers and did what was needed to get more liquid into the ink pot. The excess went onto a wall. He hoped the Queen would forgive him for that.

He returned to her chamber and retrieved a quill. He brought them to the Queen's vision. "*Etel?*"

He was relieved to see her dagger had retreated to hover near her head. This allowed him to approach, which he did very slowly.

The inkpot and quill tore from his hands.

It seemed she could not move anything she could not see.

He scrounged around her desk until he found a blank sheet of parchment. It was beyond brittle and fell into flakes the moment he touched it.

He went for the books. These seemed in better shape. He didn't bother scanning titles. All he wanted was a blank page. So he was mightily pleased when he found a book with mostly blank pages in it. The first few were used up with a crudely drawn map, the following with dozens of symbols.

He brought it round and presented a spread of blank pages to her Majesty's attention.

The quill dipped and came forward to scribble. It did not take long, which Fallo was grateful for. The inkpot gave off a rather unpleasant stench.

When the quill retreated he turned the book to see what she'd written. He was delighted to discover that she had forgone using words and instead had drawn two images.

They were simple, barely sketches, but they contained all he needed to know. The first showed a spray of fountain and a man holding a two-handed sword. The warden.

The second showed the same fountain, but the warden now lay on the floor, his head parted from his body.

She wanted him to kill the warden.

This seemed like an exceedingly bad idea. "I came for a fate's-piece, not to *meet* my fate. I don't want to seem a fox-handed tavern-lout, but if you'll just let me check your pockets, I can get what I came for and leave you alone."

A quick bit of inspection showed she did not have pockets. Nor was she wearing any jewelry. A new certainty came over him, and it made him utter a good long string of obscenities. *"Ollis?* How? "

The dagger again came forth, but this time it rotated, presenting the hilt. Fallo reached for it, not seeing how two daggers were going to help him defeat an armored expert warrior with a two-handed sword.

The moment his palm contacted the hilt, his back arched and a great heave of breath shot from his lungs. "Sweet Kil in a crib!"

His vision blurred as shudders of ecstatic ache flowed from the base of his spine through the top of his skull. It felt like rays of pure light were shooting from the crown of his head.

A single word came into his mind.

Skeye!

And then the Queen's blade, the dragon-tooth sister to Ol' Rusty, settled its bond onto him. The ecstatic bonding finally relaxed and he fell to the floor, panting. He raised his eyes and discovered the Queen's face had gone slack. Her shoulders rose and sank on deep breaths, then she swayed and fell forward. Fallo had to drop Skeye to keep from stabbing the woman as she collapsed directly onto him.

He gathered her up and carried her to the bed. He flopped her rather unceremoniously onto it. The legs of the bed gave under her and crashed to the floor. A great gout of dust rose from the linens, making Fallo cough. He went to a window and inadvertently ripped the latch completely off. Everything in this room was in lousy shape despite outward appearances.

He put an elbow through the pane and fresh air tumbled in.

He retrieved Skeye and held it next to Ol' Rusty. "Been a while, hasn't it?" he said to them. He was relieved when neither of them spoke. But it wasn't much relief, because the fate's-piece he'd come for was not the Shadline blade. It was the woman herself, it seemed. And he knew that to leave this place without her would be to endure the pull of her on his mind for the rest of his life.

But to take her with him would require defeating the warden.

"A quick death is better than a life of torture," he said, quoting his father. He realized his father might have been foreshadowing his attempt to have Fallo killed.

No sense in carrying the Queen down the stairs if he was going to die. He went to her and shifted her limbs to make sure she was reasonably comfortable. "Pardon the gropes, Majesty. Just making sure you don't have to spend eternity with a bad cramp."

He pulled away, but her hand lashed out to grab his wrist. There wasn't much strength in her grasp, but she pulled on him. He bent forward to listen to whatever unintelligible thing she might have to say. But instead of speaking she grasped his head with her hands and blazed his mind with mercusine power.

When she released him he felt rested, stronger. "Thank you," he said. He'd have to ask Kila why she'd never bolstered her friends in dire situations.

The new strength gave him a spark of confidence, so he bounded down the steps and into the chamber of the fountain.

The warden was still hacking away at the tree. Lop peered down from a high branch.

I'm going to die, Lop, Fallo sent cheerfully. He held a dagger in each hand. He rolled his shoulders and made some sweeps and jabs to loosen up.

The Cloak and Zirhine watched from across the canal.

Fallo didn't look at them and he didn't answer their calls. He strode to the warden.

"Warden! Stop choppin' and let's have at it."

The man surely didn't understand Fallo's words, but he understood Fallo's tone. He turned, sword resting on his shoulder. His stare dropped to Skeye, then raised.

There was resignation in his eyes as he bowed slightly, then moved into a guard pose. Perfect equanimity.

Fallo didn't know a pose for fighting with two blades, so he mirrored his foe. Right leg back, side on, Skeye forward, Ol' Rusty near his ear.

The warden swung. The air sang with the ferocity of the effort.

Not much time to consider his choices, which were parry, duck, jump, retreat, or attack.

Against all rationality, he chose a duck and parry, with both daggers overhead and angled to divert the oncoming blade's power rather than to stop it.

Steel scraped on steel as the daggers deflected the blow, and the warden's momentum twisted his torso around. Fallo lunged, both blades piercing the man's breastplate as it if were made of cloth.

It would be a killing blow for any man. Something charged through Fallo, like an echo of Skeye's bonding. The double strike sent strength from the warden into his own body.

Fallo's vision shuddered and a tremulous moan escaped his lips. Zings of energy enlivened his arms and legs, a hundred times stronger than what Illizshian had just given him.

With a roar, Fallo stood, heaving upward, hoisting warden

—armor, sword, and flesh—upon his blades. The man groaned and released his sword.

The body struck ground. Fallo pulled blades free and stabbed again. "Leave my cat alone!" This time the blades refused to come out, and again the warden's power flowed into him. The energy jolted into Fallo, making his arms jerk and his vision go red. It was too much. He tried to release the blades, but they would not release him. Even his teeth tingled and his eyes buzzed.

"Don't touch him, Einlin," Zirhine warned. She was close by.

"What are they doing to him?" the Cloak demanded.

"I don't know."

Finally the surge faded. Fallo pulled his blades free. The warden's blood absorbed into the weapons. Skeye looked as it had before. But Ol' Rusty was rusty no more. It was now pristine. Not a flaw on the blade. Even the leather wrap on the hilt was restored.

But Fallo felt something else had changed. Something in him. He staggered a bit as he turned to face his companions. "Do I look different?"

For the first time ever the Cloak's eyes went wide with amazement. Zirhine's, too.

"Is my face worse?" he said, panicking now. He was accustomed to frightening small children and making women whisper to each other whenever he passed. "Have I grown horns or some such?"

"No. No. Not worse," Zirhine said. "You look much the same."

Much? He pushed past them and knelt at the edge of the canal. But there wasn't enough light on his face to show him a reflection. Zirhine whispered *"rahsh!"* as she produced a fresh blob of glowing spitweed. This time it shone with a pure white light.

"My last fillshader leaf," she said. "True as sunlight."

I can't get down, Lop sent. *Get that sword and keep chopping.*

Fallo paid the cat no attention. His reflection had not changed. Not much. His single eyebrow was still a thick black caterpillar over both eyes. His lips were still too thin, his cheeks and jaw weirdly shaped, chin too pointy.

But his eyes, so dark brown everyone said they were black, had turned a light, bluish gray. "I can't decide if makes me look like a ghoul or if it's rather dashing."

"That'll depend on your manner, lad," Zirhine said. "But I can tell you that it means you have the blood of the First Race in you."

"You haven't met my mother or father. If you had you'd not have suggested such a preposterous thing."

"You did not get it from them. You got it from him." She pointed at the fallen warden. "Through them," she nodded at the blades in Fallo's hands. "Did you not feel a surge of power when you struck him? It looked rather painful."

"Oh, I felt it."

The Cloak knelt next to him, eyes flinty in the bright white of Zirhine's spitlight. "Skeye and Telt," he said. "It is no wonder you felt the pull so strongly. Clearly the blades sought to be reunited."

"Perhaps that was part of it," Fallo said, offering Skeye for the man to inspect. He did not take it. "But this isn't the fate's-piece that pulled me here. That is still in the tower. Come."

They did not balk at his tone of command, but merely followed.

Wait. Get me down! Lop sent.

You have claws. Use them.

Lop sent the equivalent of a cat curse through the bond, a feeling of wet fur and a yanked tail. Fallo shrugged it off. He'd experience far more disturbing sensations in the past quarter hour.

They found Illizshian right where Fallo had left her. But she was not at all the same.

"She was alive!" Fallo was too repulsed by the withered, dry-skinned corpse to touch her hands. The youthful skin, the fierce eyes, looked sucked dry now.

"Such a pity. I would have loved to speak with her," Zirhine said. The Cloak had spared only a moment's glance at the husk of a woman before beginning a patrol of the room. He seemed as agitated as Lop.

Fallo explained what had happened. "She only spoke Cigil-Tinian, and nothing like I was taught. It's actually a beautiful tongue, believe it or not."

"Oh, I believe it," Zirhine said wistfully. She placed a gentle hand on the shriveled brow. "Who was she?"

"Illizshian," Fallo said. "I assumed you knew."

"What? Not possible. She died—"

"It was her. Same woman in a fresco I saw in Misen-Tine. And I think those bones on the rug are her cat. Sad, really. I don't think Lop would wait around more than a quarter hour if I were frozen like that."

The Cloak was standing just off the rug, looking at the cat bones.

"How are we going to move her?" Fallo asked.

"Why would we?" Zirhine said. "It is ill to move the bones of the dead save to the place of their final rest. This room is well suited for that purpose."

"But *she* is the fate's-piece."

"That can't be."

"Why not? I was his." Fallo jabbed Skeye in the Cloak's direction. The man had knelt next to the cat bones and was picking through them. Suddenly he sucked in a breath. He held the small skull in his fingers. He turned it upside down. Something gleamed inside.

Lop stomped into the room, fur soaked through. She meowed discontentedly and made a point to ignore Fallo. Instead she stalked to the Cloak and rubbed along his knees before nosing at the skull.

"Why is there a gem in that skull?" Fallo asked, since neither of the others had deigned to voice the obvious question.

The Cloak tolerated Lop's intrusion, then set the skull down so the cat could sniff it. Suddenly she cried out in utter grief and curled her body over the skull.

Do you know that cat? Fallo sent.

"Shadline," Zirhine said. "Illizshian is not the fate's-piece. Look."

She held her hand over the dead queen's face. A soft white glow illuminated her palm. It came from the corpse's eyes.

Fallo knew she was right. The certainty clunked into place the way a well-notched roof beam slotted into wall timbers. "Ah me," he said. "I think it's a curse to be a Shadline." But the pull was too great to deny.

Lop's grief over her departed ancestor flooded through the bond. Fallo accepted it and sent what comfort he could. Skeye wanted to do the butcher's work, and it truly was not so bad as skinning a hare. There was no blood in the woman. Her skull parted and the gem shone brightly. It was larger than the cat's, but still no bigger than a chicken egg.

He plucked it out, amazed and slightly revolted by the warmth of it. It was the fate's-piece. That was certain.

"The journal there on the floor," he said. "We must take that, too."

Zirhine collected it. The Cloak stood. "Move this cat. I need to see under the rug. The call has been fierce since I entered the room."

Fallo scooped up Lop, who allowed herself to be stuffed in his satchel. He collected the cat-skull gem. It glowed a lovely emerald green, while Illizshian's shone a pure white. He bundled them together so that cat and queen could be together, then added this to the satchel where Lop could be close to them.

The Cloak flipped up the rug, sending cat bones tumbling. Zirhine scrambled to collect them, shooting the man an irritated glare.

Beneath the rug was nothing but a relatively clean circle of the tile floor. But on the reverse of the rug, embroidered in miraculous detail, a map.

"Zirhine?" the Cloak said. "You have a steady hand with the quill. I most certainly do not."

"Do you take me for a scribe?" she asked, still agitated by his disrespect for the cat bones. Fallo noted she was tucking them into her own satchel, probably to use in a ferneater ritual.

The Cloak merely looked at her. "Would you rely on any map drawn in my hand?"

"I can try it," Fallo said. In truth, scribbling had never been a great skill. He tended to press to hard and leave huge blobs of ink to obliterate half his words.

"No. I must listen and obey," Zirhine said, gathering up the ink pot and quill. She sat before the rug, tongue clamped in her teeth, and began a meticulous copy in Illizshian's blank journal. Her skill was extraordinary.

"I shall fetch the sword," the Cloak said. He patted Fallo's shoulder fondly as he passed. "It looks like we'll make the Armory after all, if that map be true. The Dirth will be satisfied."

"We will? How? Where?"

But the Cloak was gone, footsteps fading as he descended from the tower.

Fallo moved back to study the map. It was obviously of Cigil-Tine, including a large circle of the surrounding mountains. The context made clear that the city was sheltered in a bowl hidden in a vast range. But twisty paths led away from the city here and there. All ending in the same symbol. A viny arch.

"A map of the vergent passes," he said. "Remarkable." Each had two symbols above it. They showed the destination or origin of the path. But since they only went one way, the second symbol told that, too.

"Where will the Armory be held?" he asked.

"Jallisea." Zirhine tapped an arch she'd already sketched in.

"But that's where we were headed. To go to the observatory to inquire about your sketch."

She kept drawing, not seeming bothered in the slightest by the pungent odor of the ink she used. Fallo decided it best not to tell her how it had been reconstituted.

He noted that Lop had gone to sleep. Fallo's own burst of energy had quickly faded and he felt as if he could sleep for a ten-day.

Zirhine was soon satisfied with her copy of the map. She hastily collected as many of Illizshian's books as she could carry.

The Cloak returned. He had fashioned a sort of scabbard for the warden's sword across his back using a belt pulled from the dead man.

"Another undiscovered Shadline blade?" Fallo asked.

The Cloak nodded, but he didn't offer more.

"What's going to happen at this confab of Shadlines in Jallisea?" Fallo asked as they emerged from the palace of Thizrūil. There were no nosg ghosts about, but they were certainly watching.

Zirhine led now, guiding them beyond the palace toward the south boundary of the city. A winding stair hewn into the slopes showed the way. A very long climb.

"I dare say the Dirth will be astonished," the Cloak said after a while. "I shall enjoy seeing the looks on their faces when they see your dragon tooth blades."

"They will not be best pleased," Zirhine said.

"Why not?" Fallo sensed an odd sort of humor in their words, as if she and the Cloak shared a joke.

"We all know a culmination comes," the Cloak said. "But the appearance of your blades presage the coming of *the* culmination. The Shadline have their own prophecies. The dragon blades are central to them. Alas. But by Kil and his eighteen wives, it will be a glorious time to die."

Zirhine did not seem so taken with the notion of glorious death. "Illizshian gave you that blade?" she asked.

"Yes. She saw I had Ol' Rusty. I guess that made me worthy."

"Until the Dirth can advise you, do not use Skeye. Best put it in your boot or in that satchel."

"I concur," the Cloak said. "I sense it is a willful blade."

They had reached the stair. A wind had picked up, seeping down from the northern peaks, bringing with it a crisp chill.

A thick wall of cloud came quickly after, shrouding the stars and leaving nothing but Zirhine's fading fillshader light to guide them. And then that, too, failed. They stopped for a quick repast. Zirhine complained that she was nearly out of the weeds necessary to make even her blue light.

Fallo suggested bringing out one of the skull gems they'd collected, but neither of the other Shadlines wanted to do that. Lop didn't either.

The darkness didn't matter to Fallo, for he quickly discovered he could see quite clearly.

Thinking their faces hidden by the blackness, his companions' expressions betrayed concern whenever they looked at him.

Zirhine produced enough spit blobs to light the steps before them. Their brief rest finished, they pressed upward.

Kill them, whispered a subtle voice.

Lop hissed. *Who's talking?*

I think it's the new blade, Fallo sent.

Again came the voice. *Kill them.*

No. They are my friends.

Taste them.

Behave yourself! Fallo snapped. He felt Lop send a bit of ire toward the blade, the way she might at a littermate trying to snitch part of her chicken dinner.

Ol' Rusty had never said anything. Fallo thought blades shouldn't be talking at all. Bad enough to have an insolent cat volunteering opinions all the time. Still, he couldn't fault the blade for wanting to do what it was made to do.

Fallo's resistance seemed to irritate the blade, and it became sulky. In a way it was lot like Lop.

I won't let a dagger boss me around, he sent to Lop. *That's ridiculous.*

I like Skeye, Lop sent. *She's a bit whispery, so keep your ears perked. She might suggest something so softly you don't notice you're obeying.*

That sounded very much like a trick that Lop would use on Fallo. Especially in her fat and happy days in Starside.

"You can rest easy, friends," Fallo said. "I am in command of Skeye. She wanted me to kill you, but I said no. I think Illizshian commanded her, too. Lop's bond gives me the upper hand."

He tucked Skeye into his boot. No sense in letting it be too close to hand.

Ol' Rusty? Telt? Can you talk, too?

No answer. That was good. He trusted Ol' Rusty.

They climbed and climbed. It rained. They climbed.

"When was the last Armory?" he asked, more for the distraction than from curiosity. It annoyed him that neither had seemed surprised that Skeye wanted them dead. He supposed their own instincts would warn them anyway if the force of destiny thought it necessary.

"Four hundred years at least," Zirhine said. "The culmination comes."

"At last," the Cloak said. "The Shadline rises."

49

THIRTEEN GIRLS

Yiothizandra felt the Hargothe's knot slip free from her mind. She knew instantly what it meant, for the man would never have willingly relinquished such power. "You thought I did not feel your mercus knot within my brain, Tenn? You should have marked me when I told you *nothing* penetrates me but that which I allow."

She was standing outside, upon a rampart overlooking the vale. A sluggish river wended through the snow swept lowlands. "I'll admit, I did not foresee *this* eventuality. How could I have hoped for such good fortune? The force of destiny is with me." She patted her belly. "Kil quickens within me, darklove. I have no need of you now."

She stretched, cat like, then shivered delightedly as icy winds pressed back her hair. There would be no more fires in Ceronhel, save for what came from her.

She considered the abandoned fortress to be hers already. For one of her kind, even ancient memories stayed very fresh. She had been here at the time of Ceronhel's height of power and could still see the Elnisian folk striding about with their haughty faces and fine clothes. Ah, the Elnisian had been beautiful.

She returned to the great hall, mind already sinking deep into planning. The Hargothe had seen quite clearly what needed to be done. An army—a vast army—would of course be required.

The nosg were not the greatest warriors. They fought recklessly and they had no mind for strategy. But they were an older race than even the Elnisian, far older. Their shamans had access to deep powers. They need only be reminded how deep.

A sniffling sounded from the hallway outside the chamber. "Come in, nosg. Tell me your name."

It shuffled in, bowing with every step. It skirted the dead when it could, stepped on them when it had no other choice. It looked all around, searching for its blind master. "I am Noi-Ick-Noi. Is he gone?"

"He is dead. I am your master now, Noi-Ick-Noi. Do you accept that?"

The creature looked at the bodies of the soul-drained and the charred. He prostrated himself and mumbled his devotion to her in his lurkmire tongue. She knew the language well, for it was derived from the speech of dragnithans an epoch past.

"Send for the shamans. I would issue them my commands directly." She turned away from the creature and considered her needs. With Tenn dead she was blind to what transpired in Starside. That would not do. And she required information from many other places.

That meant she needed spies and a way to communicate with them. Fortunately, she was a demayne. She may be trapped in the realm of man, but she could summon those who traveled between realms. And she knew just who to call upon first.

With an effort of Will she manifested her wings, feeling the great heat already festering in her heart. She cleansed the dead with fire, finding the smell to be rather enticing. Soon all that remained were smudges of black on the floor. In one of these she scraped a rough circle using the tip of her sword.

"Yoznithan Flaumishtak. You know I'm beckoning. Do not insult me with delay."

The demayne appeared, holding a creamy white felnithel in his arms. Yioth bowed slightly to it and was rewarded with a small chirp.

Flaumishtak grumbled when he realized he had been restrained in a circle. "You dragnithan are not very trusting. Surely you do not fear me."

"I do not fear you, but I do not trust you. I require your services."

"Speak your bargain."

She arched an eyebrow, a very human expression she rather enjoyed. "Bargain? We are natural allies, you and I. Perform for me and you will be rewarded merely by my success. Why need you anything in addition?"

"You look different. Have your wings gone translucent? I thought you still quite young."

"What does she call herself these days?"

"You know very well she is called Ell LiMinluit. And *she* is still young. Not a feather out of place." The yoznithan clomped around the perimeter of his confines, making a good effort not to appear to care. He stroked the felnithel fondly. "Ceronhel has gone to ruin, I see. Pity."

"I want spies. In every Elnisian city where men now live.

What do you require?" She felt something stir in her belly. How long of a term would it be? She did not know. A decade? A century? Not likely so long as that. A year at most.

"The Hargothe will not like it," Flaumishtak said. "Or do you intend to kill him so soon?"

"He's already dead. Killed in Starside."

A remarkable change came over the beast. Yoznithan were known to be emotional, given to great humor and great rage. But not usually surprise. And that is what showed now. His ridiculous smoke-hair sent up twisted tendrils as his head bobbed with new understanding.

"That explains the ease I feel now. The bargain we struck has been released. Dead? I wonder . . . I believe I know who killed him. Interesting."

His eyes narrowed and he now studied Yioth with greater care. And suspicion. "I see *all* more clearly now. You needed the Hargothe to bring Kil into the world, but he's done his part already, eh? Such ambition, Yiothizandra. I'm quite impressed. Night fliers tend to be greedy, but also cowardly when true danger arises. Tell me, how did you know *he* could provide what other men could not?"

"Do you know how he gained his foresight, such as it was? It was not bestowed by divinity as he claimed."

Flaumishtak scratched his chin, considering. "A demaynic binding? I understand that to be rather excruciating for humans. But there must a thousand or more in the southern isles who've endured it."

"Yes, but Tenn took a rather large risk, for he sought heavier spirits. He sacrificed thirteen girls. A significant number under any circumstances. That would attract any qiznithan. But Tenn did not buy these children at market. He schemed for months to abduct children from high families, the sort of children that would be missed, the sort that people loved. Delightful, really."

Flaumishtak glowered at her. "A man feeding qiznithani is no cause for joy. Am I to understand this sacrifice drew the attention of an Arch?"

"Several. But it was a Lord who answered."

Flaumishtak's hairsmoke again billowed, and his flaming eyes turned a deeper red. "I doubt the Hargothe even knew he had been so blessed. But of course his oracular powers must have been a great source of mirth to the qiznithani."

"So you see, dear Yoznithan Flaumishtak. He was uniquely powered to help me achieve the end I seek. Kil will come into this world through me. Those who flew under the stars will shatter this realm and be free. Those who flew under the sun will perish. The inevitable evernight comes."

"Natural allies, you said. I did not believe you, but you have convinced me. You shall have your spies. But it is not the work of an instant. I am bound by other bargains."

"I could summon another yoznithan. Or perhaps a qiznithan would enjoy taking form in this realm. That would be something to see."

"No no. Confer one too much power here and you put seventeen demaynic realms at risk. That does not serve *your* ends."

"Once Kil is manifested, my ends will be his ends. What care I for demaynic realms when the heavens will be open to me?"

"Because when you bring Kil into this world, you will bring the others."

Yioth's wings flapped so hard her feet lifted from the floor.

Ash blew into the air from the sudden downdraft. "No. They have nothing to do with this. The Til-notion is asleep, Ori barely remains distinct as an idea. Only Pol is half-aware of herself as concept. They are so distant from this realm that Kil's awakening will pass like an anxious thought and then fade."

"Then you have naught to worry about," Flaumishtak said, making a mocking bow. "Release me and I will recruit your spies."

Something in his manner bothered Yioth, but she decided it was merely him in his entirety that bothered her. Yoznithan were such annoying souls to begin with, and Flaumishtak had taken on so many human affectations that he was unbearable. "Begone!"

He vanished in mercus green.

Yioth moved to a window and rested her hands on her belly. Had it grown already? Perhaps that was her hopeful imagination. Instinct told her the term would be short. The birth would be horrific. But pain was always the price of freedom. Soon this world and the races that lived within it would be forgotten, its very essence dispersed and absorbed by greater realms.

But for now this world was the arena in which she had to fight. And fight she would.

50

THIEF GIRL

Henley slept in a room fit for a Radiant. He had been plied with draughts made by Finta Sahng, whom Kila had fetched as soon as she'd delivered Marlow and Henley to Her Enlightened's private quarters atop the Citadel.

The old woman had not been difficult to find, for she sat at the bedside of her sister, the Voluptuary. That woman had not awakened from her sleep since Kila had ripped out the Hargothe's mental knot.

Kila now sat across from the monarch in her audience chamber. The fire burned pleasantly in the hearth, though as usual here, the window was open.

The monarch wore her blue gown, silver belt slanting across her slim waist. Her hair was pulled back and spiked into a loose bun. She held the jade fish in her hands, fingers turning it and turning it as she regarded Kila.

Marlow stood, hands clasped in front of him. Highest Quiv had a chair, which befitted his station. His face was drawn, a great bruise marring one side, apparently received when attempting to leave the abbey. Kila's destruction of the cathedral had nearly crushed him and Yples under flying rubble.

Pennie sat on the floor with Nax in her lap. She stroked the cat's body, head to tail, in long sweeps of her hand. Her sightless eyes looked at nothing.

A service of tea had gone untouched on a sidetable.

Marlow cleared his throat. "I have his staff in my quarters. The Voluptuary's Bane Eye as well."

His queller was back on his finger. Kila didn't know what to make of him. He was a scoundrel deep inside, but she trusted him.

Her Enlightened, on the other hand . . . Kila wasn't sure she trusted that woman at all. "Why did you leave me with the Hargothe? Together we could have killed him easily."

A voice came from across the room. Jil, a rather cool-eyed woman, with the unmistakable swagger of an experienced Shadline. "She listened and obeyed. Something you often do by instinct. And it seems you just as frequently ignore it, to everyone's detriment."

Kila didn't want a lecture from anyone, much less from a woman she'd just met.

"You will learn," the monarch said softly. "I do not blame you for your ignorance. That is my fault. I thought sending you to the Garden was the right course. Perhaps I misheard the whisperings. But now we are in the irreversible present. Dunne Medow Cathedral has been half-destroyed, the citizens watched you resurrect two people, saw you fly, felt your golden voice compel their obedience. You usurp me in my own city."

"I didn't mean to—"

"What *did* you mean to do?"

"To kill him. Nothing more."

"At the cost of hundreds of lives? Captain LiTishke reports at least two hundred and thirty dead, not including those lost in the blasted quarter. I have reports that two thinnie encampments were crushed during that calamity, killing more than seventy women and children. Highest Quiv, what was the toll in the Cathedral?"

"We were fortunate. Only thirty acolytes and Donse Masters killed. The damage was mostly confined to the cathedral." He didn't meet Kila's gaze.

"One of her stray balls of blue fire destroyed a row of houses in Terriside just outside of the plaza," Jil said. "Not the behavior one expects of a Shadline. Personal grudges are a severe weakness of character."

"You call it a personal grudge?" Kila said, sullen and irritable. "How was it different than the City's Justice? Let your mind be raped and then tell me of grudges."

"I don't need to test my oath any more than it is being tested by sitting in this room with you, girl."

"Jil, please," Her Enlightened said. "Antagonizing the Highest of Kil is not wise."

"Are you mocking me, Majesty?" Kila said.

"Not at all. I owe a personal debt to you, for you saved my life. Perhaps your actions also saved the city. But I'm not certain of that. I *am* certain that the City's Justice you mentioned was not done today. I had hoped to cool the building rage and fear by giving it a focus and release in the execution of the murderer Tym Hamlickten. Alas."

Marlow cleared his throat. "I do have good news. Based on

a few exploratory efforts of my own it appears the Hargothe's force-bonds unraveled with his death."

"That is good news, indeed," the monarch said. "But we must study the technique and learn to ward ourselves in the future. I watched the Voluptuary restore the bond on the trapper on the execution platform. I saw exactly what she did. I had hoped she would attempt the same on me, for that would have given me a chance to reach through to the Hargothe himself."

"Is that why you let her stab you?" Kila said, feeling a tiny sprout of respect emerge.

"Partially. But I mostly I listen and obey. My instinct told me to wait. My eyes were pulled to a rooftop, and then you came alight. A glory to behold, you descending from on high, an aura of golden light around you. Jil, do you have the paper?"

The woman jangled across the room and put a roll of paper into the monarch's hand, who in turn offered it to Kila.

It was hastily scrawled message: "SB 2 reports: Leaflet from Garden Isle. Image of bald girl in Kil's crown. Animal behind. BEHOLD! HIGHEST OF KIL! KILA SIGH! THE MERCULYN WHO FLIES!"

"How did this get here so quickly?" Kila demanded. Any ship leaving Garden Island with one of those leaflets would still be two months from Starside.

"A ship stopped at Sea Bastion Two bearing a stack of leaflets. The Sea Bastion commander immediately relayed this message here, as was her duty."

"You don't need to worry," Kila said. "There is no Way of Kil and there never will be. I'm not summoning Kil. With the Hargothe dead, Dem-Kisk is over."

Marlow shook his head, face sad. Her Enlightened's eyes gleamed with unshed tears. Jil scoffed and jangled back to slump in her corner seat. But it was Pennie who spoke. "Dem-Kisk has always been born, from seed to blade to seed again. Red are the blades of the dying age. I see them waving beneath the sun. This is prophecy to the gods, not from them: Words cannot contain nor the mind apprehend the unconscious will of time. The force of destiny has meter, but, alas, no rhyme."

In one swift motion Her Enlightened moved to grasp the child's cheeks. Pennie's face had flushed bright red as she spoke, her voice raspy with the effort.

"Who speaks?" the monarch demanded. "What is your name?"

Pennie opened her eyes, which had gone pure black all the way across. She sucked in a shaking breath. "I am Roya Reth."

Highest Quiv was crouching near her now. Jil had her blade out, ready in case any heads needed lopping.

"Roya Reth!" Quiv said. "Clarify your prophecy. Highest Fley is dead. You need not obfuscate the truth."

Pennie began to shake. Nax meowed and slipped off her lap, tail flicking.

She is gone, Nax sent.

Where?

I don't know.

"Speak, Reth," the monarch urged.

Pennie's mouth opened wide, as if to gag. But out came words, not in her voice, but of a different sort of child, dreamy and at peace.

"Beware allies,
Embrace spies,
Trust in lies,

Dem-Kisk rise!"

Pennie shuddered then wilted into Her Enlightened's arms. The monarch pressed her forehead to the child's and whispered softly. She eased the girl onto her back and arranged her arms across her chest.

"She sleeps. I fear it will be a long night for her. The spirit of this Roya Reth called from very far. It would take a toll on anyone."

"But what does it mean?" Highest Quiv said angrily. "Why can't she speak plainly?"

Marlow manifested a blanket from somewhere. He tenderly covered Pennie with it. "It claimed to be Roya Reth, but we have no proof of that."

"It was her," the monarch said. "Marlow, please write down her words for me. I believe they are a fate's-piece. Especially that last bit." She shared a glance with Jil, who stood over them all still holding her blade.

Kila and Nax went to Pennie. The girl was breathing softly. The flush had gone out of her cheeks. "Whoever Roya Reth is, she's wrong. Dem-Kisk is over. The Hargothe is dead."

"You are ignorant," Jil said.

Kila didn't have the chance to voice a rebuke because Flaumishtak chose that moment to arrive. She noted that he kept his mercus green haze in check.

Oly immediately leapt down from his arms to go cuddle with Nax next to Pennie.

Her Enlightened stood, flaring with mercus.

The beast towered over the woman, but held out placating —if clawed—hands. "Peace, dragnithan! Peace. I come bearing ill tidings for you and me."

"Speak and begone."

Jil had her sword up as she circled to get behind the beast. Flaumishtak paid her no notice.

"The demaynic realms are ringing with a summons. A court of Night forms in Ceronhel."

"But the Hargothe is dead," Kila said.

Flaumishtak flicked an angry glare are her. "He was allied with Dragnithan Yiothizandra. She already holds Kil within her. The Hargothe may be dead, but a worse hand shall now guide Kil into this world. The righteous order the Hargothe sought to impose would be a paradise compared to Yioth's aims."

"Who is Yioth?" Kila demanded.

"A demayne, like me," the monarch said. "A dragnithan. She flew beneath the stars, and her heart is as black as moonless midnight. All of Night will come to her call."

"They will," Flaumishtak said. "And Day is weak. Such dragons are few enough, and the heart of man already sinks into twilight."

"I would think you delighted," Marlow said. "Has your time among men infected you with a conscience?"

"Bah! Speak not such silly things. My interests do not lie with Night any more than they do with Day. I would have them in contention for eternity if I could, for the shadows are where I play."

"Shadows sound like Night to me," Highest Quiv said.

"Have you ever seen a shadow where there is no light?" Flaumishtak rejoined. "No."

The monarch clicked her tongue and returned to her seat, face recomposing to equanimity. She locked eyes with Kila. "It falls to you, Highest of Kil. Dem-Kisk is here."

"I don't know what you two woolheads are yammerin'

about. Just banish this Yiothiziffra back to hell and be done with it."

"Yiothiz*andra*, girl," the monarch corrected. "Highest Quiv, have you read of Yioth in your studies?"

He must have, for his face had gone white. He raised a trembling hand to his brow. "I have indeed, Majesty. I have. I had thought her a creation of imaginative historians. If what this demayne says is true, does any hope remain? If she bears Kil within her, then all is already lost."

Her Enlightened looked to Jil. "Flaumishtak bears dire tidings. But I think the Shadline would hear nothing but silence if *all* hope were lost. Jil says an Armory has been called. I shall attend. And you should too, Kila. How long do we have, Jil?"

"A ten-day perhaps. The Armory will of course begin when the Dirth feels it's time. No sooner. No later."

A knock came at the door. Two Fell Guardsmen entered after a brief delay. They bore Kila's backpack.

She leapt up, furious. "That's mine. You better not have—"

"They didn't open it, I assure you," the monarch said. "I merely asked them to collect your things from the Peline greathouse. You will not return there."

"I'll go where I—"

"You will not return there!" The gold on the woman's voice dropped Kila back into her seat. The striking thing about it was that she did not use any mercus power. It wasn't a feat, but something else entirely. And Kila had done the same recently. Shock undercut her outrage.

"There is a Shadline blade in that sack," Jil said. "I can smell it."

"That'd be Shinane," Kila said. "A keepsake from Garden Island."

Her Enlightened closed her eyes and let out a sad laugh. Jil merely tilted her head and glared at Kila for using such an off-handed tone. Flaumishtak laughed.

"It's a shifty blade," Kila said, standing again. She took the pack from the guardsman, peripherally noting that neither man left. Perhaps it was the fact that Jil had bare steel in the presence of Her Enlightened. The Shadline seemed to realize this and quickly sheathed her blade.

Kila pulled out the history of Illizshian she'd taken from Kil's library back at the Garden Tower. She moved to flop it onto the seat she'd vacated, but Quiv snatched it from her hand. Next came the blank journal. Marlow snatched this as she tried to toss it to the floor.

Her bag of coin came next. She held it up in a sort of toast motion to the monarch. "Thank you again for this. Wish I had more chance to spend it." Finally she retrieved Shinane. "It's been called Bone Chill for a while. Highest Fley had it."

"It's been in the Tower reliquary since the Synod," Highest Quiv said. "We did not know its true identity."

"I don't recommend letting yourself be stabbed with it," Kila said, handing the sheathed blade to the monarch. "Feels terrible."

Jil's eyes widened. "And you survived it?"

"With help from Henley Mast. You understand now why I feel indebted to him. The blade has a rather simple perpetual mercus bolt infused into it that freezes the body. It's slow enough that a skilled merculyn can reverse it with the proper negation."

Her Enlightened studied the blade then handed it to Jil.

The Shadline held it reverently. Her face changed momentarily, shading to greed. The woman mastered it then quickly returned the blade to Kila. "Dangerous to one of weak will. I recommend you not bear it."

"Why would I? I already have a Shadline blade."

"It seeks its mates," the monarch said. "You are as good a bearer as any, I suspect. We'll discuss all that during your training. Flaumishtak, Kila Sigh needs instruction."

The beast said, "I will happily continue our lessons. But—"

"Then you will come when she summons you." There was no question in the statement. "You are excused."

Flaumishtak held out a hand and Oly returned to his arms.

"Wait!" Kila called. "What did you do to Binni Keel and Startle?"

"Who?"

Kila was tempted to blast the feigned innocence off his face. Instead she said, "Startle is Oly's littermate. He recently bonded to Binni Keel after she murdered a man in Cheapsgate."

"Oh, her. She looks a bit like you. Plumper. More hair. I removed her from the board. Call it a contingency."

"What does *that* mean?" Kila said, she took a step toward the towering demayne, no longer intimidated by his fearsome face. "Tell me where Startle is."

"Another realm. One as far from this one as I could take him."

Her Enlightened was fuming, too. "What have you done, yoznithan? What sort of contingency are you talking about?"

"The felnithel must be preserved, no? No matter what

happens here, they must endure. I have ensured it. Even should Kila destroy this world and all of the seventeen demaynic realms, the felnithel will endure."

It was the most ingenuous thing the beast had ever said in Kila's presence.

Nax?

He speaks true.

But what does he mean?

Just what he says.

Oly meowed impatiently. Flaumishtak bowed to Nax, then up went his fist, and he vanished.

"What do you make of that?" Kila said to no one in particular. But nobody had any answers. And apparently Her Enlightened wasn't capable or willing to compel the demayne to talk.

The monarch waved a hand in dismissal. "Jil, you will train Kila in the use of her blade. Yiothizandra has not won. She is close. But she has not secured dominion over this world. Highest Quiv, you must return to the Cathedral and make an inspection of the minds there. Be absolutely sure the Hargothe's knots have been unraveled. I will see to Pol and Ori. Marlow, the city is in chaos. Summon Captain LiTishke and Radiant Gilok. We must clear the debris immediately. I also require an inventory of the city's stores of grain, cheese, wine, preserved meats, potatoes, and the like."

Marlow nodded and dry washed his hands. "Majesty, may I ask—"

"War, Dunne Marlow. Starside must be prepared to send supplies—and men—north. The Hargothe was surely recruiting the nosg. Yioth will use them."

"But if Yioth brings forth Kil, what use with she have for armies?" he asked. Kila thought it an excellent question.

"What do you imagine Kil will be on that first day? Born into this world he must needs be a babe. Yioth will seek to gift him the world when he comes of age and fully ascends to godhood. His feeding alone will require millions of lives. And he will suckle upon the bloodshed of war."

Kila gave vent to her building frustration. "Then what purpose was I ever to serve in bringing him here? How was I to get with a demaynic child? That was what you wished me to do, wasn't it? Were you going to mate me to a demayne the way you might a prized pig?"

Her Enlightened didn't answer at all except to stare at Kila.

"You were! I s'pose I shouldn't be surprised. By Kil's throbbin' handle, that's a mighty low thing ta do to a girl. To anyone!"

Kila repacked her backpack with vicious grabs and stuffs of her coin bag, her tome—snatched from Quiv's greedy grip— and Shinane. On the way out she spotted her blank journal in Marlow's hands, the one Yples had been sketching his map in. She reached for it. "Since you surely have proper maps, I'll be having that back."

The man didn't let go of it. Kila yanked and it slipped to the floor where it struck spine first. The covers flopped open. The pages slowly slid to one side, stopping at Yples's map.

Kila bent to retrieve it but Marlow was there first, not merely grabbing, but on his knees hands pressing it down. "Wait, lass," he said, voice full of wonder. "Did you see?" He carefully turned past the main map and past Yples's Derslin Wheel symbol sketches. Finally he stopped. On the left page was a simple drawing, sketchy but elegant. A man with a two-handed sword, tip down. Next to him was the same man, prone, head a little distance from his body.

"That's not Yples's hand," Quiv said, peering over Marlow's shoulder.

The others in the room moved to surround them where they knelt, looking at the image. Even the monarch was bending over to see.

Marlow turned the page. And there, spread across two leaves was another sketched map.

"That is not Yples's work either. See how the ink is poor, brown and thin. The symbols . . ." Marlow raised his eyes first to Quiv's, then moved to Kila's. "This is a map of Cigil-Tine. And these . . ." He traced a finger along paths leading from the city to end in arch symbols. "Vergent passes."

"Every page of this journal was blank when I found it," Kila said. "If Yples's didn't put this in here, who did?"

He didn't have an answer. Nobody did.

"It is a fate's-piece," Jil said. "Of that there can be no doubt. The force of destiny still moves us upon the board. Hope is fading like the last rays of the day, but the light has not yet gone out of the world."

Kila moved away from the circled group, then left the room, Nax pacing alongside her.

She found Henley awake, if a bit bleary-eyed from one of Finta Sahng's concoctions. The old woman had returned to the baths to tend to her sister.

Kila sat on the edge of Henley's bed. He'd been washed up and lay contentedly amidst the finest bedlinens a monarch could demand. Huff slept in a ball beneath the covers.

Kila smiled at Henley and took his hand. He squeezed

Kila could leave now, dymense to Cheapsgate, buy passage on a ship. She could dymense to the Derslin Wheel and choose any column at random. They'd never find her.

But she wouldn't leave Henley.

She wouldn't abandon Pennie.

She wouldn't abandon Dunne Yples or Marlow or Quiv.

Nor would she abandon Starside, the city that had raised her, formed her into what she was.

And that meant she would stay.

And staying meant she would fight.

ABOVE THE CITADEL A RAVEN CIRCLED. Snow steamed from its wings as it soared. It called its dire warnings, a sound that carried over the wind, through windows, into bedchambers.

Those who heard it tapped their ears three times and said, "Die, raven, die." Those who did not shivered and checked to make sure the windows were fastened tightly. Perhaps they added another stick to the fire to ward off the chill.

The raven did not call for them, but for one.

Rise, Kila Sigh, Rise!

The End of *The Shadline Rises*